"Arlen pens a dynamite beginning to a new series, filled with wartime suspense, skillfully wrought emotions, and a liberal dash of romance. Readers will fall in love with clever and quirky Poppy Redfern and the colorful villagers of Little Buffenden, as well as their dashing new neighbors—the American Airmen."

—Anna Lee Huber, bestselling author of the Lady Darby Mysteries

"This engaging mystery introduces an intrepid new sleuth in Poppy Redfern and draws us into the lives of a small English village, upturned by war and the unexplained murders of two young women. I was enamored by the story and the residents of Little Buffenden from first page to last."

—Shelley Noble, *New York Times* bestselling author of *Ask Me No Questions*, a Lady Dunbridge Mystery

"*Poppy Redfern and the Midnight Murders* is a WWII gem of a novel with such a strong sense of time and place, you feel like you're there. Filled with characters you'll want to meet again, it's a compelling mystery that grabs the reader from the very beginning! A must-read for fans of historical fiction."

—Emily Brightwell, *New York Times* bestselling author of the Victorian Mysteries

"A dash of romance, moments of action, and twists worthy of Hollywood thrillers. For a relatively light, speedy read, it still has plenty of meat and rich prose; Arlen has once again crafted a winner. It'll be great fun seeing what Poppy Redfern faces next."　　—Criminal Element

"This is a well-crafted historical mystery with elements of romance. Highly recommended."　　—Historical Novel Society

BERKLEY PRIME CRIME TITLES BY TESSA ARLEN

POPPY REDFERN

— AND THE —

FATAL FLYERS

TESSA ARLEN

BERKLEY PRIME CRIME

New York

BERKLEY PRIME CRIME
Published by Berkley
An imprint of Penguin Random House LLC
penguinrandomhouse.com

(Penguin logo)

Copyright © 2020 by Tessa Arlen

BERKLEY and the BERKLEY & B colophon are registered trademarks and
BERKLEY PRIME CRIME is a trademark of Penguin Random House LLC.

Author photo owned by the author

Library of Congress Cataloging-in-Publication Data

Names: Arlen, Tessa, author.
Title: Poppy Redfern and the fatal flyers / Tessa Arlen.
Description: First Edition. | New York: Berkley Prime Crime, 2020. |
Series: A woman of World War II mystery; 2
Identifiers: LCCN 2020031994 (print) | LCCN 2020031995 (ebook) |
ISBN 9781984805829 (trade paperback) | ISBN 9781984805836 (ebook)
Subjects: GSAFD: Mystery fiction. | Historical fiction.
Classification: LCC PS3601.R5445 P664 2020 (print) | LCC PS3601.R5445
(ebook) | DDC 813/.6—dc23
LC record available at https://lccn.loc.gov/2020031994
LC ebook record available at https://lccn.loc.gov/2020031995

First Edition: December 2020

Printed in the United States of America
1 3 5 7 9 10 8 6 4 2

Cover art by Robert Rodriguez
Book design by Alison Cnockaert

To Nancy

ONE

"ISS REDFERN? FOR HEAVEN'S SAKE, WHERE IS SHE?" A TALL gray-haired woman was standing in the doorway to the Script Department of the Crown Film Unit. She lifted her voice over the clatter of a room full of typewriters. "Miss Redfern? Oh, there you are. Yes, well, will you join us for a meeting, please? Room four." She lifted an impatient hand and waved me to her.

I picked up my notepad and leapt to my feet. A desk away in the tightly packed room my new friend, Clary, fed four sheets of foolscap, layered with carbon paper, into the platen of her typewriter. Her face was set with concentration. "Only production meetings are held in room four—you're on your way, Poppy." She didn't lift her head as I squeezed past her desk. "I bet Fanny has an assignment for you!"

"Do you really think so?" I had waited for this moment for weeks, and now that it was here a feeling of dread had started in my stomach and was working its way upward, making it hard to breathe. I fumbled my notepad and dropped my pencil on the floor, breaking its magnificently sharp point. "Where's room four?"

Clary carefully typed as she said the words, "Fifth Octo-ber nine-teen-for-ty-two," and looked up at me. "Turn right out of here and go along the corridor to the back stairs all the way down to the basement. It's on the left." She waved her hand in dismissal of first-project nerves. "You'll be fine—isn't this what you've been waiting for? You're going to have a film with your name on it in tiny print at the end." I set off for the door. "And don't be intimidated by Fanny—he's always tetchy after lunch," she shouted after me.

I was intimidated by *everyone* in this shabby rambling brick building that housed the Crown Film Unit—even if our task is to keep British morale high. My mouth was chalk dry as I made my way along the cracked linoleum of the long basement corridor to a closed door with a crooked four painted on it. I wiped the palm of my hand down the side of my skirt and tapped so lightly on its dull gray wood that no one could have possibly heard me.

How long I stood there, uncertain and unsure, could only have been a matter of seconds, but I was simply paralyzed with anxiety at the thought of attending a production meeting.

I was rescued by the patrician voice of the main character of the book I had written: the heroine of my love story and murder mystery, who had helped me to win this wonderful new job as a scriptwriter. Her calm tones floated into my consciousness like a cooling breeze. The voice belonged to Ilona Linthwaite, girl-reporter extraordinaire and everything I was not: confident, worldly, and, sometimes, wise. *Come on, ducky, pull yourself together. Remember that you have a lot to offer these wretched people.*

I took a deep breath as I opened the door and peeked round it. The room was packed with the people I had seen racing past me, in corridors and hallways, all week. They looked up for the briefest moment and then carried on lighting up cigarettes and arguing. One of them waved a large pink hand.

"Yes, yes, come on in and find somewhere to sit." The hand belonged to a big man with a round bald head sitting at the head of the table. He looked like an overgrown baby in a pin-striped suit. There appeared to be no empty chair, so I edged into the room and stood with my back against the wall.

"This week in postproduction," the large pink man continued. "Nigel and Brian are working on a ten-minute short about the woman who trains dogs to search for unexploded bombs—for release next Tuesday. Who will edit this piece now that Cliff's been transferred?" This had to be Mr. Fanshaw, the Crown Film Unit's head of production. I tried not to catch his eye as he looked around the table at the faces of writers whose names I did not know; production managers I had heard terrifying stories about; unit directors who thought they were God; and a crew of round-shouldered film editors gathered at the far end of the cheap pine table.

Room four was large enough to hold ten at a pinch, and there were at least twenty puffing clouds of cigarette smoke at one another. My breath caught in my throat and I swallowed hard.

"Come on, come on, I need an editor. What about you, Roy?"

A groan from under a mop of fair hair.

"Good, now we're getting somewhere."

"But I've already got . . ." said the overworked Roy.

Fanny waved a dismissive hand and sat forward in his chair. "Right then, what's on the books for new and exciting projects?" His laugh was high-pitched as he looked around the table at lifted faces. "Ah yes, we all love something new." His fixed his eye at the far end of the table. "Jim and Derek, I want you to go to Eastbourne to do a piece about the teenage girl who rescued three sailors from drowning using a boat she made herself. Shades of Grace Darling, what?" There was a ripple of obliging laughter. "That leaves Annabelle to write up a quick five minutes about the old-age pensioner who knitted a hundred and twenty pairs of socks in one month for soldiers. She runs a grocery shop in Cardiff when she's not up to her eyes in yarn."

An attractive girl in a yellow beret put out her cigarette and shrugged her shoulders.

"Sorry about that, Annabelle, but we are stretching staff as it is." However fat and pink he was, Mr. Fanshaw's voice was quiet and there was enough finality in his tone to silence any dissenters in his group.

"Which leaves us with—" He looked at his agenda and smiled. "Ah yes, the Air Transport Auxiliary pilots. Huntley, I'm giving this one to you. I want a fifteen-minute short on these ATA women fly-ers. Take Keith; he's getting quite handy with a camera." He sat back in his chair. "Should be fun—they are a pretty glamorous bunch apparently. We'll send Miss Redmayne down ahead, so she can draft up a script for you—don't want any of you boys getting into trouble."

"Redmayne?" Huntley looked around the table. "Who's he?"

Fanny lifted his arm and waved across at me. "Miss er . . . Redmayne, isn't it?"

Somehow, I managed to get my tongue off the roof of my mouth. "Actually, it's Redfern, sir."

"So it is. Meet our new assistant scriptwriter, Miss Redfern, everyone. The ATA will be a good piece for her to cut her teeth on." I could feel the color in my cheeks building to a full-strength blush as heads turned to look at me. "Pop along to Miss Murgatroyd's office after the meeting and she'll give you your brief, Miss Red . . . and get down to Didcote Airfield as soon as possible."

I turned for the door.

"No need to run." Fanny's laugh was loud and inclusive, and I turned back to face him. His tongue was a startling raspberry pink. "Tomorrow morning will do."

Alone in the safety of the empty corridor, I exhaled in triumph as I leaned my hot forehead against its wall.

He seems nice enough, Ilona said. *Almost human, really, and he has a sense of humor. I think you are going to enjoy this job.*

I didn't care if Fanny ate assistant scriptwriters for breakfast. I was going on location—I was part of Crown Films' production team.

MISS MURGATROYD WAS round and deceptively maternal-looking with fluffy white hair. "Didcote ATA, did you say?" She picked up a wire basket and took out a sheaf of papers. "Your room has been paid for at the Fisherman's Lodge at Didcote for two nights, which includes a cooked breakfast. Don't forget to take your ration book. You will *not* be reimbursed for any meals on either of your travel days, so there is no need to save any receipts. Neither will you be reimbursed for any lost personal items, and if your portable typewriter is damaged, stolen, or mislaid you will be liable for the cost of its replacement: one pound, ten shillings, and sixpence. Please sign here . . . and here . . . and initial here." I obediently complied. "Rail passes—second class. Please don't travel in third and try to recoup the price difference." Three rapid applications with a smudgy blue rubber stamp and the passes were mine. "And *someone* rang this office at half past four. I did not take a message. This is not your personal telephone"—she tapped the instrument—"and I am not your secretary. Please remember that, Miss Redfern." I started to stumble out an apology, but she wasn't having it.

"He was an American." Disdain for our allies and their friendly invasion was not disguised.

"I'm so terribly sorry, it won't happen again," I managed to get out.

"It had better not." She sighed and pressed her lips together. A pause and another sigh. "He said he would pick you up outside your digs, I forget what time, and he mentioned someone called Bess."

THE LAST RAYS of the sun shone on a bright red Alvis drophead coupe parked outside 122 Elms Road. Leaning up against its long glossy bonnet was a man in American Army Air Force uniform. Sitting demurely at his feet was my little dog, Bess. Her bob of a tail stirred apologetically as she looked down her nose at me as if going for a walk on Clapham Common with Lieutenant Griff O'Neal was the event of the year. Then, remembering who fed her every day, she got to her feet and danced between us, yodeling with delight as I crossed the road to join them.

I felt just as enthralled about seeing him as she obviously did, but I managed to greet him with the cool reserve we English practice at the best, and worst, of times. Unlike my prancing little dog, I kept my feet firmly planted on the ground.

"What on earth are you doing here—are you on leave?" No one could tell from my polite welcome that my heart was thumping like mad, and to my immense relief the old awkward schoolgirl shyness that always threatened when we first met only revealed itself in a slight blush.

He leaned down to spank dog hair off his immaculate trousers. "We've been a bit busy lately." It was his term for flying missions. When he lifted his head, I saw that his face was thinner, the skin more tightly drawn around the eyes. I saw something else as well. There were two silver flashes on his shoulder.

"Captain? Oh, Griff, congratulations!"

"Yes, I told you we'd been busy." He shrugged off his promotion from lieutenant to captain as if it might be more of a burden than an acknowledgment of skill and experience. "Our commanding officer has packed me off for seven days of what he describes as long-overdue rest and recreation. He sends his regards to you, by the way." Like Griff, Colonel Duchovny had become a good friend of my family when the American Army Air Force had arrived to take possession of their new airfield earlier this year. It had been built for them on my grandfather's farmland outside the village of Little Buffenden: a village our family have lived in for generations. "And your grandparents send their love too, of course. I had dinner with them yesterday evening."

"Did you cook?" I laughed. "Or did Granny?" I could see Griff in our tiny kitchen contentedly sautéing mushrooms in half a pound of American military-issue butter. My grandmother is an authority on toast and jam. Griff is . . . well, let's just say he is a man who takes pains with the things he likes to eat.

"They were our guests at the mess. Or I should say, they were *our* guests in *their* old dining room." When the War Office had requisitioned our farmland for the airfield, our lovely old farmhouse had been turned into the headquarters and officers' mess for the AAAF. My grandparents now lived in the lodge at the bottom of the drive to what was now known as Reaches Airfield.

"Your grandparents told me you had managed a visit, to pick up Bess. They miss you—but wouldn't dream of saying so, of course. Your grandad talked about your new job, nonstop—you could have only topped it by joining the navy. But your grandmother is quite sure that after a couple of months of life in London, you will be desperate for the peace of the country."

I laughed. My visit to my grandparents had been heaven: there is nothing like spending a weekend with those you love and allowing yourself to settle back into comfortable old habits, especially in these uncertain times, but the quiet village streets of Little Buffenden and the repetitive gossip of its inmates had palled after a day. I had adjusted to a faster pace of life since my arrival in London four weeks ago. The city with its bustling, crowded streets was gloriously anonymous; no one cared what you said or did or discussed it avidly with their next-door neighbor. I didn't say that the one person I missed most from life in Little Buffenden was now standing in front of me.

Bess, fed up with being ignored, stood up on her hind legs and put her paws on my knees.

"Yes, I know, Bessie, I'm with you: I'm famished." Griff folded his arms in a cloud of dog hair. "Why don't you go and put on your hat, Poppy? I have reservations for dinner at the Savoy."

"But I can't! I'm leaving town tomorrow morning, early. I have to pack, and I have heaps to read." The excitement of writing my first script was momentarily eclipsed at the thought of Griff here in London and me . . . where? On an airfield in Hampshire.

"I hope it's somewhere exciting."

I stopped behaving like my spinster aunt. "Oh, it is, Griff, it really is. It's my first assignment—a fifteen-minute film about the Didcote Air Transport Auxiliary."

The sun slipped below the horizon and he became a dark shadow by his car.

"Blimey!" It was clear that Griff's infatuation with cockney slang was still with us. "That's what I call good news. Now we have something to really celebrate!" The slightest pause. "Did you say the *Didcote* Attagirls?"

I nodded. How on earth had Griff heard about these astonishing women when I had only discovered them this afternoon? "The Attagirls? Is that what they are called?"

"Not sure if that's what your guys in the Royal Air Force call them, but we do. They've delivered a couple of aircraft to us at Reaches."

I might have known that American pilots would have a catchy name for a group of Englishwomen who thought nothing of taking off in a fighter plane and flying it to an airfield in far-flung Yorkshire or Scotland.

"Can I invite myself along? I'll pick you both up after breakfast and we can have lunch on the way down to Didcote."

I bent down to ruffle Bess's ears as I considered what was turning out to be a splendid end to a perfect day. "You can come on one condition," I said as I stood up. "That I drive to Didcote."

He laughed. "Then we had better plan on having dinner on the road too."

TWO

HALF A DOZEN WOMEN STANDING BY A MAKESHIFT BAR IN Didcote's Air Transport Auxiliary's mess turned appraising faces toward us. For one panicky moment I felt I was back at boarding school on the first day of term.

"Good morning, Miss Redfern. I'm Vera Abercrombie, Didcote's commanding officer." A compact-looking woman with a direct, no-nonsense gaze introduced herself. I suppose, like everyone else who first met her, I was surprised that the Didcote ATA commanding officer wasn't the standard-issue senior male RAF officer with a waxed mustache. Vera Abercrombie was probably in her mid-thirties, but her fair northern skin was deeply lined, either from years of flying or from the burdensome responsibility of her wartime job.

She carried a clipboard with a sheaf of papers pinned to it and her glance strayed to it often, as if she might have inadvertently overlooked some small but important detail. There are not many women who have shot to the heights of command that Vera Abercrombie had achieved without being conscious of their seniority every hour of their long working day, but there was no arrogance in her greeting and no feeling that this was her "show" and that Crown Films was lucky to be allowed to interrupt her demanding schedule.

"This is a friend of mine, Captain O'Neal."

Abercrombie glanced at the insignia on Griff's arm. "American Army Air Force." She extended her hand to Griff and then bent down to pat Bess's head.

"What a sweetheart," she said.

"Yes, ma'am. Eighty-Fourth Wing. I hope you don't mind my butting in here. We've had planes delivered by the ATA and I couldn't pass up the opportunity to meet you all." I've always envied Griff his relaxed and easy manner. It's something I've noticed that most Americans possess. We English tend to stand around in stiff, awkward silence as introductions are made, but Griff just sails right in, as if he's known everyone in the room forever.

Commander Abercrombie was clearly impressed. "Welcome to Didcote, both of you." She looked down at Bess again and smiled. "All of you! Now, let me introduce you to the first-officer pilots taking part in the film tomorrow."

She turned to the silent, watchful group of women at the bar. "From left to right: Officer Trenchard." A tall, athletic brunette with a serious face nodded and said, "Welcome to Didcote." I nodded back and smiled, but her face remained grave, as if introductions were not the time for friendly chitchat.

"Officer Evesham." A broad smile from a young woman with the bright, healthy complexion that comes from being active outdoors in all weather. She lifted a hand in greeting. "Please call me June." I caught the trace of an accent and wondered if she came from South Africa. June bent down and swung Bess up into her arms. Strongly aware of her independence and dignity, my little dog usually treats this sort of familiarity with a groan and struggles to be put back on the ground, but June's laugh of delight was so unaffectedly buoyant that Bess turned her head and gave her an affectionate face wash. More laughter as the rest of the group relaxed. June was the jolly sort: easygoing and unaffected. Her intelligent blue gaze carried only a natural curiosity and a willingness to get along.

Commander Abercrombie turned to the next pilot. "Officer Partridge is your . . ." She got no further. A petite and very young woman with immaculately waved ash-blond hair and a vivid red mouth walked toward us. She nodded briefly at me, ignored Bess's best pirouette in greeting, and put her hands on her hips to give Griff the once-over. "Fighter or bomber?"

Griff laughed and stuck out his hand. "Griff O'Neal—Mustang. Best plane out there." It was the sort of thing Griff always said, but the blonde took it as a challenge. She smiled, turned to her friends at the bar with her eyebrows raised, and drawled, "Well, we'll have to see about that. Clearly the captain hasn't come across a Spitfire yet! I'm Edwina Partridge. And this"—she waved her hand at a tall, stately girl with a thick mane of dark gold hair—"is Betty Asquith, but we call her Grable, of course." The tall girl smiled and opened her mouth to say hullo, but Edwina breezed on. "And next to her is Zofia Lukasiewicz. I should say Countess Lukasiewicz, but she wouldn't like that, would you, ducky?" She laughed at her familiarity.

The countess was a little taller than Edwina, but there all similarity ended. She was dark-haired and dark-eyed and greeted us with a gracious inclination of her head. No one would interrupt this woman, I decided. She was easily the most composed member of this group. "Hullo, what a handsome couple you both make, and such a pretty little dog!" Zofia's last name might be Polish, but her soft, clear voice gave only the slightest hint that she was.

Now that Edwina had paused for breath, Betty "Grable" Asquith had a chance to acknowledge us. "Hullo-how-are-you?" It was barely a question and neatly pinpointed exactly where Grable came from in our hierarchical British class system. The faint lengthening of aristocratic vowels, the level English appraisal from not unfriendly, but certainly not inviting, gray-blue eyes. It was clear that Grable came from the ruling class. Her smile was perfunctory, and she was certainly not going to offer something as familiar as a handshake. "Are you directing this shindig tomorrow?"

"No," I said. "That would be Huntley Masters, our unit director. I am here to write up a script. The rest of the crew will be here in the morning to start—"

But Edwina had not finished with her introductions. "All of us have licenses to fly *two*-engine planes, but Letty here . . ." She waved at a pretty girl with fine, straight fair hair that hung loose to her shoulders. Two extraordinarily round, very blue eyes fixed themselves on my face as she stepped forward. A friendly nod and a smile. "We are so excited about being in your film!"

She completely ignored Edwina, who lifted her voice to continue. "Letty is the only one of us who is licensed to fly the big chaps: four-engine Lancaster and Fortress bombers.

"All of them"—Edwina's hand waved at the lineup along the bar—"are taking part in my film." Having made her point, she looked up at Griff through heavily mascaraed lashes. "I can fly anything, but the Spit is the love of my life," she declared.

Commander Abercrombie cleared her throat, as if she was used to being sidelined by Edwina. "Will you join us for a glass of sherry before dinner?" she asked me, and turning to Griff: "We have beer . . . if you would prefer, but unfortunately no . . . um . . . Coca . . ." She fumbled for the word "Coca-Cola" as if that was what Americans lived on.

"Beer will be fine, thank you, Commander."

The door opened, and a tall man with gray hair walked into the mess. "Sir Basil, just in time to join us for a drink before we eat. I'd like you to meet Miss Redfern from the Crown Film Unit: she's here to write a script for tomorrow's film. And her American friend, Captain O'Neal." She turned to the older man, her right arm extended, with a particularly proud expression on her face. "Sir Basil Stowe, Ministry of Aircraft Production," she said with a smile that could have been interpreted as almost winsome.

Griff and I walked over to shake hands with Sir Basil. He was one of those men who become more attractive as they age. Sir Basil Stowe was probably in his early fifties: broad shouldered, still slim, and elegantly fit. He wore a flawlessly cut suit that whispered Savile Row as if it were comfortable old tweeds, and he had a look of burnished well-being, as if he had just returned from somewhere in the Mediterranean. He stood a hair taller than Griff, and the two of them immediately fell into conversation, leaving me stranded with Edwina.

I took a deep breath and decided that the best approach, as with all sizable egos, was to spread the butter nice and thick. "Since you are our star, I would love to have some background on you—I have only two lines from Crown Films. How long have you been flying? And when you say you love Spitfires, do you fly other planes too?"

Ilona, the protagonist of the mystery novel I wrote, often floats her observations into my head when I'm feeling tense or tongue-tied, and this little creature made me feel extraordinarily nervous. *Just let her do all the talking,* Ilona advised. *I don't think she's much of a girl's girl.*

Edwina ripped her gaze away from Griff and folded her arms. "Flying solo since I was eleven." Her voice was flat with ill-concealed boredom. "I've flown everything there is to fly, but I won't fly heavy fighters. I'm not sure why we have them in this flick—they look ugly on the ground, and they'll look even worse on film. I mean"—she laughed and shrugged her shoulders—"the Spitfire is the real star here. No one gives a damn about all the different planes we have to deliver." Her tone was sharp, and Bess got up and trotted back to the group of women by the bar, who were laughing at a story that Grable was recounting.

I hadn't a clue what a heavy fighter was, but I struggled on. "So, tomorrow you are going to give us a demonstration—an aerial performance in a Spitfire?"

There was no humor in her laugh. "I can't imagine a performance on the ground being much fun!"

This was the star of our picture? I felt the beginning of alarm. "I don't actually know very much about aeroplanes." I felt an awkward need to explain and perhaps to elicit some understanding of my ignorance. Let her be the expert if that's what she wanted.

She was only about five foot two, but her confident, immaculate presence made me feel like my hands and feet were too big and that I should do more than just brush through my hair in the morning.

"Why are you writing the script if you don't know anything about planes?" The question was so direct that I couldn't think of a thing to say. "I mean, it seems a bit ridiculous to send someone who doesn't *actually know anything about aircraft*. Oh, and by the way, we don't call them aeroplanes—we just say 'planes.'" She was still staring at Griff's back, her arms folded, her forefinger with its long scarlet lacquered nail tapping the pale blue of her uniform shirt.

I flashed her a bright smile. "Actually, I don't really need to know anything about aircraft at all," I replied. "Because I have all of you to tell me about them."

She laughed. It was a genuine laugh and I almost liked her for it. "Oh, touché!" she said. "Come with me." She steered me through the group, which had now left the bar in ones and twos, to stand me near the woman with the suntanned face. "June"—Edwina's voice was loud—"is a walking encyclopedia on aircraft. Aren't you, Junie?" A strong, firm handshake from June Evesham.

"I wouldn't put it that way." Now I recognized the Australian accent. June focused her smile on me as Edwina returned to Griff. "Most aircraft are similar depending on how many engines they have. Letty here is the only one of us who is licensed to fly four engines." They laughed at my confusion.

"Look, we have this crib sheet for you." Letty handed me a page with six different aircraft illustrated in two silhouettes: one from the side and the other as if seen flying overhead. "We've written our names next to the planes we're flying tomorrow. They were chosen because they are easy to identify both in the air and on the ground."

"Thank you, how thoughtful of you." I took the sheet of paper and read: "Annie Trenchard." I glanced at the tall brunette who had said nothing since she had been introduced by Commander Abercrombie. "Fairey Swordfish, is that the name of a plane? It sounds so dainty!" Nods and laughter, and Letty smiled at June as if to agree with her that I wasn't a stuck-up know-it-all from the films after all. "June Evesham: Mosquito; Letty Wills: Avro Lancaster bomber, gosh, that's a huge thing!" Annie, June, and Letty had raised their hands as I read their names. "You fly that monster?" I asked Letty, and June replied for her with pride, "Like a bird."

"Zofia Lukas-ie-wicz?" I stumbled over her name and blushed.

"Please, just Zofia." I looked down at the Polish countess, who was on the floor playing with Bess, oblivious to the dog hair all over her uniform.

I corrected myself. "*Zofia*: Hawker Hurricane, that's a fighter plane, isn't it?"

Zofia stood up and brushed ineffectually at her uniform jacket. "You see, you know more about aircraft than you think!"

I read the last name but one, "Betty Asquith: Anson air taxi."

Betty "Grable" levered herself forward from the top of the bar with her elbows and turned her mouth down. "Yes, that's me. I was a London cabbie in my last life." Good-natured laughter. And I felt my shoulders come down a notch as she said, "And Edwina, of course, will be flying a Spitfire."

My lesson over, I surveyed the group of women I had come to write about and felt as if I had known them for years.

"That's all you need to know! Just make sure you get lots of film of Edwina," said June to more laughter. "And don't let her scare you away."

Zofia lit a cigarette. "She is what you English call a character, but she knows everything there is to know about flying. Once she gets to know you, she is very generous and goes out of her way to help. To make you feel at home." She raised her eyebrows slightly as if waiting for someone to say otherwise. No one did. But Grable cleared her throat.

"What she's trying to say is that Edwina is a good sort—underneath," Annie Trenchard translated with a slight frown at Grable.

"Underneath the reinforced concrete and the barbed wire?" June said to roars of laughter.

I hadn't known what to expect of women volunteers who flew military aircraft. I had imagined them all to be a bit daunting after I had read the ATA recruiting leaflet Miss Murgatroyd had handed over with my travel vouchers. Even the distraction of driving Griff's zippy Alvis along the winding lanes of Hampshire hadn't been enough to subdue my apprehension about meeting these impressive women. I had imagined they would be rather hearty in their manner, with the sort of swagger that pilots in the RAF had adopted, the sort of women who would be competitive at field sports. Edwina might look like a starlet, and Grable and Zofia exuded a self-assured worldliness that I was unused to, but Letty, June, and Annie were the sort of well-scrubbed wholesome girls who liked to swim and play tennis: the sort of girls I had grown up with at school.

"Can you really fly thirty different types of aircraft?" I asked them.

Zofia shook her head. "Don't be put off by that ridiculous number. Fighter planes are all very similar, and so are heavy fighters. Once you've flown one, you can fly the others. But 'thirty different types' does make us sound astonishing, doesn't it?" She looked around at her friends and then fixed dark, serious eyes on mine, and her full-lipped mouth made a puff of dismissal, as if flying different aircraft was a meaningless achievement.

She was the most arresting woman I had ever met. Not pretty by today's standards: Zofia's nose was too strong and her chin too firm for the popular taste of today. But her skin was as pale and as fine as an eggshell, without a scrap of makeup, and there was a grace and sensuality about her that any man would have found alluring.

"Edwina," June said to Miss Partridge's back, but Edwina did not turn around or acknowledge her name. She had cut in on Griff's conversation with Sir Basil, leaving the older man at a loose end.

Whatever Edwina was saying certainly had all my friend's attention. I hoped their conversation was confined to comparing Mustangs and Spitfires, but I could tell by the expression in Griff's eyes that, with her gesticulating hands and fluttering lashes, Edwina's subject was much more amusing than aircraft.

"Edwina." June obviously agreed with me, because she lifted her voice. "Why don't you tell Miss Redfern about your brush with the Luftwaffe?" It was an invitation for Edwina to take center stage and I would have thought she would leap at it. She turned her head, eyes shining, her expression still animated from the story she was actively recounting and frowned at us. "You tell it," she said to June in what I had quickly come to recognize as her aggressively dismissive voice. "You do it so much better than me."

June snorted and glanced at Letty. "Such a flirt," she said under her breath, and then perhaps hearing herself she said to me, "But she's one of the most skillful pilots here." There was no envy in her voice—simply a professional's acceptance of superior ability—but I happened to glance at Letty and saw her normally good-natured features harden into a mask of contempt as she folded her arms and stared at the floor.

"I'm more of a ground engineer," June explained.

"A first-rate ground engineer," said Letty with such understated but sincere loyalty that I decided that the scorn I thought I had seen on her face had been a trick of the light.

"And a second-rate pilot," June insisted.

Letty rolled her eyes. "Fishing?" she said to laughter. "Please, don't say that when you know it's far from true." She turned to me. "June's a first-rate pilot, and she can fix any engine: plane, car, or motorbike." Her admiration for her friend was vivid in contrast to the evident distaste she felt for the star of my film.

"Motorbike?" I must have looked surprised, because June explained.

"My father flew commercially in Queensland: he was a crop duster. We lived miles from anywhere, so I was taught to fix all engines: cars, tractors . . . motorbikes, you name it. I was a working pilot when I was fourteen. I never had the overwhelming desire to fly, to stop at nothing to become a pilot like everyone here, perhaps because it was expected of me. I am a competent pilot." She squinted her eyes and waggled her hand in a so-so gesture. "But I am a *really* good ground engineer and mechanic."

"How did you come to be recruited to the ATA?" I seized on the opportunity for more detail for my script.

"I was traveling in Europe when the war broke out, so I came to England. The ATA had just started their recruiting program: they had plenty of RAF servicemen to work on planes, but not enough pilots. Those young and fit enough were in the RAF. The ATA had finally accepted the painful fact that they needed to find women who knew how to fly." A slightly self-deprecating smile. June was what Griff would call a straight-ahead type. "So, here we all are. All of us knew how to fly small private aircraft before the war, and now we are civilians volunteering our services for the very people who believe women should not fly in combat."

"Our HQ at White Waltham ATA have a flying school, and the other volunteers in our ferry pool have been trained in the last year or so," said Letty.

June looked around the room. "You are in the rarefied company of firsts: Vera Abercrombie is the first woman commander appointed to the ATA; actually, she might be the first woman commander anywhere. Letty is the first woman pilot to ever be awarded a Class Five license to fly four-engine aircraft. Sir Basil was the first flying ace of his company in the last war and then went on to design some of the most advanced aircraft of his time. Recruiting women to the ATA was his idea in the first place." She had bowed her head to each as she acknowledged them. "And then of course there is our first star pilot: Edwina Partridge." I glanced at June to see if she was being snide, but her pleasant face expressed nothing but acknowledgment of Edwina's skill.

"What about you, Miss . . . Wills? Did you fly before you volunteered for the ATA?"

"We are all on first-name terms here; even our commanding officer prefers to be called by her Christian name. Please, call me Letty." She had the clear-pitched voice of a young girl, but I could see fine lines around her eyes and realized that she was about the same age as their commanding officer. "I have been flying since I was twelve."

After my snub from Edwina, I asked, "Do you mind if I jot this down?"

She waved away my request. "No, please go ahead. I was one of the original three women to join! My father was always keen on flying, he flew during the last war, and I was the only girl in a family of five boys. We were all taught to fly. I wanted to join the RAF, but they don't take women pilots, and the Women's Auxiliary Air Force is all about flying a desk." Letty shrugged off shorthand and typing. "So, I joined the ATA. I couldn't ask for a better job!" This was just the sort of information I wanted. I scribbled down notes as fast as I could.

"Have you ever flown?" Letty asked, and it took me a moment to realize that her round blue lollypop eyes were quite serious. "No, I would love to, but I have never had the opportunity!"

Letty looked at June, her eyebrows raised. "What do you think?"

June nodded her agreement. Edwina might be the star of the show, but after Commander Abercrombie, it was clear that June was their natural leader.

"If you don't mind getting up really early, I'll take you up tomorrow morning." I didn't know whether to be pleased or terrified at Letty's invitation.

I glanced at my cheat sheet to see what plane she was flying in the film. "In a Lancaster bomber?"

"No, in a little two-seater biplane, as a passenger. We can take the Fairey Swordfish up if you would enjoy it. Annie will be flying it tomorrow for the film, so we have to have it back by eight o'clock. Would that be all right with you, Annie?" A brief nod of acquiescence. Annie was clearly a woman of few words.

"I'd love to, I really would." I think she hadn't expected me to say yes quite so quickly.

"Good for you." She looked me over again as if she hadn't quite seen me the first time, with that direct, assessing gaze they all seemed to possess. But there was nothing tough or challenging about Letty. I could almost see her wearing a pair of her brother's jodhpurs and an old comfortable hacking jacket as she jumped her scrupulously groomed pony in our local gymkhana before the war.

A steward came in through a door to the left of the bar and announced that lunch was ready. Sir Basil made his way over to me. "I know it's old-fashioned, Miss Redfern, but may I?" He was smiling as he extended his arm. As I slipped my arm through his, it occurred to me that if my father had survived the war, he would probably be about Sir Basil's age.

"My dad was a fighter pilot in the last war," I said.

"Lieutenant Redfern?"

I felt the hairs on my arms prickle as he said my father's name. "You knew Clive Redfern?"

"I knew him well. He was a damn good pilot, and a courageous leader." His face grew serious for a moment. "So, you are Clive Redfern's daughter." A smile broke through. "Of course you are. There is something about him in you that I recognize: he was the quiet, thoughtful type, and I suspect you are too. But clearly you are your mother's daughter. I only met her once. She was very lovely."

I rarely refer to the fact that I was orphaned when I was two days old and brought up by my grandparents, but Sir Basil's informal courtesy invited confidences. "I'm afraid that my mother didn't survive the war either. She died in the influenza epidemic after I was born. Until very recently I lived with my grandparents in Little Buffenden—they have a farm there."

Why was it so easy to talk to this man? As an only child raised by my grandparents, I have always been more at ease with older people than those of my own age, and Sir Basil Stowe was comfortably at ease among the women he had encouraged to fly for their country. Vera Abercrombie might be the commanding officer here, but Sir Basil was the ATA's godfather.

I heard a shriek of laughter from Edwina as she and Griff joined us in the dining area at the front of the mess and saw her put a white hand with its long red nails on his arm. Griff pulled out her chair for her and sat down next to her, his eyes riveted on her face in a most unsettling way. If I was under the impression that the delights of driving down to Hampshire with Griff, along sun-dappled country lanes, meant that he would be dedicating his time to me at Didcote, I was clearly mistaken.

Simmer down, why don't you? You made it very clear to him how important your first assignment is to you, Ilona reminded me. *He's just giving you a little breathing room.*

THREE

R EADY TO LAND?"
Our early morning flight over pastoral England was so
beautiful it had taken my breath away. For more than half an hour
I had been spellbound by a miniature world laid out below us like a
meticulously arranged model world of fields, woodland, and the
river. Tiny buildings sat on the edges of roads that outlined the con-
tours of the land. The sky over us stretched to horizons farther than
I had ever traveled. Thirty minutes had gone by in as many seconds.

But would landing be as terrifying as taking off?

One moment we were above the country and then among it. We
skimmed over treetops and then dropped lower to hedgerows. The
vivid green of the airfield came up fast toward us. My heart was
beating frantically, but I kept my eyes wide open. A slight bump,
and another, and we were racing across the grass toward hangars
and the massive outline of a great Avro Lancaster bomber. The first
flight of my life had rushed by in an exhilarating flash of earth, sky,
and sea.

We came to a halt next to the Lancaster. There was something sinister about its massive size; the Fairey Swordfish was an insubstantial Christmas-cracker novelty next to it.

"Look at the size of its wheels," I said to Letty as soon as I had caught my breath.

"Go and stand next to one. You're quite tall, so you should just about come level with the top of its tire." Letty climbed out onto the Swordfish's wing and jumped down, pulling her leather helmet off her head and shaking out her straight hair. I clambered out of the cockpit, and as I landed on the short turf I realized my legs were shaking.

"Air legs!" Letty smiled.

"It was incredible; it was wonderful. I can't thank you enough for ... for ..."

"I'm really glad you enjoyed it."

"Would the ATA have me? Could I train to be a pilot?" I asked.

"Yes, they would." June was walking toward me with Zofia, who was holding Bess; they were both laughing. Zofia passed around cigarettes and they lit up, throwing back their heads as they blew smoke into the clear fresh air. How confident they were, the three of them standing in the morning sun, surrounded by their aircraft. "But you're a writer, aren't you? That's your war work," June said.

"Yes, I suppose it is," I said, as an idea for my next book floated into my head. Ilona Linthwaite, the intrepid protagonist of my first book, would take to the skies!

Are you quite sure about that, darling? I know you had fun up there, but I was in fear of my life, every blasted minute.

FOR SO FEW women, and considering the early hour, the mess was loud with voices that morning at breakfast, as I went from one

Attagirl to another, adding to the background notes I had worked on well into the night.

Annie Trenchard's usually stern expression softened as she talked about her family. "My mother is an angel, a saint, really. I think my job is easy in comparison to looking after my two girls." She took a sip from her cup.

Letty leaned toward us. "Tell Poppy about *your* Luftwaffe story," she said. "Go on, tell her." And to me: "It's quite a tale."

Annie shook her head, her lips pressed together, her eyes fixed down at her plate. Letty leaned across her, to me, her hand on Annie's forearm. "Sharpen your pencil, Poppy," she said. "Because this is a story worth hearing. Before the fall of France, Annie was delivering a plane to an airfield in Normandy. What were you flying?"

"I can't remember."

A sigh from Letty. "It was probably a Mosquito. Anyway, it was late afternoon—in August?"

I started to write.

"It was early winter," said Annie in a long-suffering voice.

"She dropped down to land in a heavy ground fog. Much thicker on the ground than she had first thought, right, Annie?"

"It was mist, a patchy mist."

"She could just about see the airstrip, and some large planes—they looked like bombers—off to the right."

Annie nodded; now there was a faint smile on her lips as Letty continued. "As she pulled back the throttle to make her landing, the mist cleared a little and Annie saw—" Letty started to giggle. "On the tail of one of the bombers, as she skimmed past it at ground level, she saw a swastika! Can you believe it? She was about to land in a German airfield!" Letty sat away from the table and jogged Annie in the ribs with her elbow. "Come on, *tell* her."

"Oh, thank you, my turn now, is it? What is there left to tell?" Despite her initial reluctance, Annie willingly took up the tale. "I had somehow lost my bearings and there was a strong wind coming from the west. I must have drifted northeast as I flew across the Channel and mistaken the coast of Belgium for France." She ducked her head and laughed at her mistake. "I had never left England in my life, and here I was ferrying a Tiger Moth to an airfield in north France!" She shrugged her shoulders. "Well, anyway, my wheels touched the airstrip once, and then I saw that swastika! I thought my heart was going to burst out of my chest! I opened up the throttle and took off again as fast as I dared to." She shook her head. "I must have cleared their tower by this much." She held her hands six inches apart.

June leaned across the table to me. "She hates it when we tell this story," she teased.

"She hates it when we tell anyone about her German boyfriends." Grable, on my right, imitated a German accent. "Oh, Annie, *mein Schatzi*. Why the rush? *Please* come back to us!"

"That's quite enough," said Annie, recovering her habitual sangfroid.

"What happened next?" I asked, flexing my fingers to ease writer's cramp.

"Well, I turned around, of course"—an impatient shake of her head—"and using my compass flew west to France. As soon as I was sure of where I was, I brought the plane down in a big flat field in Bayeux." She made it sound like she had taken the wrong turn off the Great North Road and ended up in Sheffield instead of Doncaster.

"That's an incredible story," I said.

"Thank you." A barely discernible smile as she glanced at Letty. "I hope you are happy now." And to me: "Getting lost is easy, especially if you are flying over the sea: no landmarks! But Letty loves to tease, so does Grable, and it's all grossly exaggerated."

June glanced over to the next table, where Edwina was sitting. She was reading a newspaper and drinking coffee with her habitual cigarette held upright between the fingertips of her left hand.

Get it over with, I told myself as I walked over to join her, with Bess, ears down, trailing after me.

"I would love to hear what happened with *you* and the Luftwaffe," I said as I pulled a chair up to her table.

"And so you shall, when you interview me on film." She had glanced up as I sat down, but now she was looking out the window toward the Spitfire parked first in line on the edge of the airstrip.

"But we don't actually interview on film," I explained, remembering my briefing from Huntley. "We have a commentator who will tell your story as we show film of you flying your plane."

Edwina clearly thought otherwise. "No, that wouldn't work at all. *I* want to tell my story. Not some half-baked old twit who can't even drive a car, droning on in the background about Britain's finest hour."

I didn't like to tell her that most amateurs make terrible actors: they either become self-conscious and stumble their words or simply can't stop talking. The commentator was trained to read from a script, and it was he who would provide understated drama to the visual of the film.

Edwina's face was set, her mouth tight. I hadn't noticed before, but her brows were heavy and dark, and they were drawn in a fierce scowl. I reached down and stroked Bess's head. I wasn't going to argue with this tough little woman—about anything. "Huntley Masters is the film's director. I think you should talk to him about your idea to tell your story." The little I had seen of Huntley told me that he was more than able to deal with this girl.

"Well, I will, then." She almost tossed her head.

"But, as your scriptwriter, I must record the story so that Huntley and the film editor can refer to it later."

She looked around the room. "Where's your friend the American? What's his name? Griff?"

Griff had driven us to the airfield from our hotel and joined Sir Basil and Commander Abercrombie for breakfast in her house next to the mess. He was avid for details of the different types of planes the ATA delivered.

"I think he's with your CO. Will you tell me about your Spitfire?"

A theatrical sigh as she shrugged me off with a shoulder. She reminded me so much of the girls in my village when their mothers asked them to help with the washing up that I had to bite the insides of my cheeks to stop myself from smiling.

"Huntley will need this information before he starts filming." I strove for firm: pleasant but firm.

Another sigh. "What do you want to know?" Not waiting for my question, she trotted out some facts for me. "To be accurate you should refer to it as the Supermarine Spitfire. It can reach an altitude of forty-one thousand feet, but we don't fly that high. Top speed is rated at three hundred and fifty miles an hour, but I can get more out of them than that."

"I heard that you can only fly planes at a thousand feet when you are delivering them. Why is that?" I had already been informed by Letty, but I wanted Edwina to get used to answering my questions.

"So we can see the ground. That's how we find our way." She was slowly unbending; Edwina liked attention. "Most of us are familiar by now with the route we must fly from factory to airfield, but if it is a first-time delivery we find our way with a compass, and we have to be able to see the landmarks below us that are marked on our maps: railways lines, rivers, bridges, church spires, that sort of thing. That's why we have to make our deliveries before it gets dark, and we don't fly when there is fog." She shrugged. "Though fog is an accepted hazard in autumn and winter."

"What are the greatest dangers for civilian pilots in wartime?"

Her earlier reluctance gone, she laughed. "Everything! I don't like barrage balloons—we have them marked in red on our maps, and the airfield will bring them down when they know we are arriving. But if there is an air raid"—she jerked her thumb—"up they come. You can fly below the balloons, but the cables that tether them to the ground are the real danger."

"What happens if you get into difficulties?"

She snorted and put out the half-smoked cigarette in her saucer. "We don't is the straight answer. There are no radios in the planes; we can't be chattering away and jam the airwaves. That would really mess things up for the RAF."

"What about weapons?" I was working my way carefully toward my target.

A derisive sneer. "What, and get into a scrap with a Heinkel or a Messerschmitt?"

"What did you do when you ran into enemy aircraft?"

"I flew my bloody plane—that's what I did. Evasive action, it's called."

"How many of them were there?"

A deep sigh, as if the effort to remember cost her dearly. "Two Messerschmitts. I was ten minutes' flying time from RAF Biggin Hill. The bastards ambushed me from behind a bank of cloud. They were that good, I didn't even spot them for a second or two." I didn't dare write all this down in case she stopped talking and demanded to speak to Huntley first. I was here to get this girl's story, and if it meant flattery I was quite willing.

"Terrifying," I ventured.

"No time to be bloody terrified. I couldn't deliver a bullet-ridden plane to Biggin Hill, and I certainly didn't want to go down in flames. So, we played hide-and-seek." She lit another cigarette and inhaled deeply. She looked up and caught the look of concentration on my face and laughed. "You going to write this down, or what?"

I picked up my pencil. "So, what did you do?"

She rattled her red fingernails on the tabletop and caught her bottom lip between her teeth. I suspected that underneath that studied nonchalance was a woman on the edge of her nerves. And something else occurred to me too: she didn't like talking about her attack. Had it scared her that much? And if it had, why wouldn't she admit it?

As if she was aware of what I was thinking, she sat back in her chair, threw one leg over the other, and blew a lazy plume of smoke. Her pose, because that's what it was, was almost defiant.

"One of the cheeky what's-his-names flew alongside and saluted me. I could see him as clearly as I can see you now. It took him a moment to realize I was a girl. You should have seen his jaw drop." She inhaled smoke with her eyes closed, then opened them to see my reaction. "That pause, that moment of surprise, gave me an edge. I peeled away sharpish, I can tell you. June Evesham wouldn't have lasted a minute up there. The only other pilot who could lead them in the dance as I did is Zofia. Now, there's a girl who can fly." It was interesting to hear her express admiration for another woman. Clearly, the pair of them were close. Not as close as Letty and June, who were amiably chattering away to each other as they finished their coffee, but I had picked up on the mutual respect and admiration the countess and Edwina felt for each other.

"What happened? Did they just go away?"

"No, dear." Her tone was flat, as if I bored her. "I did, quick as a flash. The next thing I knew I had overshot RAF Biggin Hill by twenty miles." I raised my eyebrows to demonstrate how impressed I was, because no matter how unattractive this woman's manner, her bravery made for great propaganda.

She smiled. "I know, it's quite a story."

"It certainly is. Huntley will love it and so will the public."

"All in the line of duty." She rolled her eyes at the credulous British public and I wondered for a tiny second if her story, like her makeup, was a bit overdone. Edwina's outlandish manners and overt displays of sex appeal were part of a cover-up, I decided. Underneath she was just as scared as the rest of us. She looked up. "Here's your boyfriend." She got up from her chair. "Now, if you don't mind, I want to talk shop. American shop."

I bet you do, I thought, and said out loud: "Oh, please go ahead. Just one more thing: where did you learn to fly, Miss Partridge?"

A flare of annoyance—no, it was stronger, it was anger—lit up her eyes for a fraction of a second. "The circus." I must have gaped. "A flying circus. It was my uncle's. I was an aerial acrobat when I was six." She looked down at me, both hands planted on her curvaceous hips. And then she said in a matter-of-fact voice, "Are you dating him?" I gaped some more. "If you are, you should watch him; he's a right charmer." She laughed.

In that moment I felt a wave of jealous anger so strong it took all my self-control to stay in my chair. Breathe deeply and stop making such a fuss, I told myself as I watched her saunter across the room, hands in pockets and an unlit cigarette dangling from her lips.

Now, that's what I call a fast mover, Ilona's voice observed. *I mean really, darling, talk about obvious.*

Griff turned and his smile faded a little as Edwina caught up with him and he signaled to me to join them, but I shook my head and held up my notes. I was a working girl. I looked down at my notepad and heard Ilona snigger rather unkindly. Griff might be a bit of a flirt, but he was quite a conservative chap: underneath the swashbuckler was the heart of a knight-errant. He certainly wouldn't approve of Edwina's chain-smoking and her dockworker's language. Griff's boyish charm had landed him in the consommé, and this time it wasn't chilled.

FOUR

R EADY TO ROLL?" HUNTLEY ASKED HIS CAMERAMAN, KEITH, A shortish and very young man from London's East End who wore his flat cap back to front. Griff would do well to tune in to Keith's cockney accent, fresh from the Mile End Road.

"Soon as this war's over I'm off to Hollywood," he told me as he set up his camera. "Westerns, that's what I'm going to make, with John Ford and Gary Cooper." He was thoroughly likable—I put his age at somewhere around seventeen and hoped the war would be over before he had to join up.

"Keith!" Huntley was all business. "You can tell Miss Redfern about your Hollywood contract this evening. Now, if you are ready?"

"Half a mo', guv." Keith fiddled with his camera. "Right, ready when you are!"

Huntley turned to the group and all chatter died down. "Okay, girls, gather round, please. Here's what I want you to do. Line up by the first plane, the big one, and run toward us. Keep in a straight line and at the same pace: not a full-out gallop, just a nice, con-trolled lope. What are in these packs?" He pointed to a heap of heavy, square bundles on the ground. "Parachutes? Good, sling one over your shoulder, just as if you are off on a mission. That's the way."

"They aren't part of our uniform, you know. My rigger puts mine in my plane for me," Edwina said as she lit a cigarette. "They weigh thirty pounds, so they're bloody heavy to run with."

As I suspected, Huntley knew a thing or two about getting and keeping control. "Then why are they lying there waiting to be picked up? You are only carrying them a few feet, and they make you look like serious pilots. Are you ready?"

When they were all kitted out, they stood in a line in front of Huntley, their Sidcot flying suits over their uniforms. With their heavy boots and now with their parachutes over their shoulders, they certainly looked the part. June, Zofia, and Annie pushed their flying goggles back onto the tops of their leather-helmeted heads. Edwina had refused to put hers on.

"None of us wears a helmet either, unless we're in an open cockpit," Edwina chimed in when Huntley tapped his head at her to put hers on. "No point in wearing a helmet anyway, because we don't have radios on board, and they mess up our hair."

I caught Keith's eye and he grinned at me. "Right little twist, in't she? Needs to grow up," he said under his breath as he adjusted the camera lens.

"Twist?" I could see I was going to need a dictionary to understand this chap.

"Twist and twirl—little girl."

I turned back to the altercation going on between Huntley and Edwina. His jaw was set, but he kept his temper. Edwina had been correcting him ever since he had arrived; if she wasn't resisting all his ideas, she was heavily flirtatious. He had gone from embarrassment to confusion, and now he was just determined to get his film wrapped up, so he said nothing when she dropped her helmet on the ground behind a campstool.

He turned back to his directing. "Okay, off you go and line up. Start to come forward at a steady pace when I call out 'Go!' What d'you think, Poppy, about the parachutes, I mean?"

"It's what people expect pilots to carry."

"But the ATA girls can't use them effectively at the height they fly at. Most chutes deploy between a thousand and eight hundred feet at the very least," Griff added.

"What's wrong with that?" Huntley asked.

"The ATA have to fly at under a thousand feet, so they can find their way by landmarks," I said, keen to show off my newly acquired aviation knowledge.

Griff nodded in agreement. "The average airmen need at least seven hundred feet to jump without injury . . . none of us are given the time to practice that kind of skill."

Huntley hesitated and thought it over. He looked up at the sky. "If my plane caught fire lower than a thousand, I would climb higher and then I would use my chute," he said, as if that settled things.

Griff looked away, but I could see that he was smiling. "If you had an engine to climb with," he said.

"You ever had to jump?" Huntley asked, his face serious and his manner a little more respectful.

"Yes, once."

"I hate heights. I don't think I could do it," Keith put in.

"You could if your pants were about to catch light," said Griff.

The three of them laughed and, in the strange way that men have, became friends in that moment. Ever since Huntley and

Keith had arrived, Griff had stuck close to them, clearly intimidated by Edwina's zealous pursuit. I was polite enough to him, but too busy and completely engrossed with learning the ropes to spend any time with him, and I was still smarting at how foolish I had felt when we had walked into the mess together on our arrival and he had immediately showered attention on Edwina.

The Attagirls had reached the plane and were standing in a ragged line in front of it. "Can we have the tallest in the middle?" Huntley shouted, and they shuffled about until Annie and Grable were in the center of the line, flanked by Letty and Zofia, with June and Edwina at each end. He turned to Keith. "Focus on the one that looks like Betty Grable, the one with the legs." He called out to Grable. "You in the middle, would you take your helmet off, please?" I could hear Letty and Annie giggling as Grable took off her helmet and tossed her hair back. "Struth," said Keith.

"Like ripe barley," Huntley replied. "It's got to be natural: women like her don't dye their hair. We'll shoot them with parachutes first and again without. Just two takes, Keith. Are you ready?" he shouted to the lineup; Grable gave a thumbs-up. "Go!"

It took four takes to satisfy him. June, the shortest of the group, on the end of the line, fell over once. Edwina insisted on fixing her hair before each take, and I realized that filming was rather boring: more waiting around than anything else. In the third take Bess got so excited that she raced out to join them, jumping around them like a little porpoise.

The Attagirls ran toward us one last time.

"Cut!" shouted Huntley. "Very nice," he said to Grable as she dropped her chute on the ground and plonked herself down on the grass. "Lovely, in fact. Now"—he rubbed his hands together— "let's get these planes in the air."

Grable tilted her head back to look up at the sky. "Perfect day for flying," she said.

"Perfect day for filming," said Keith as he gazed worshipfully at her golden tresses blowing in the breeze.

I HAD ARRANGED our morning so that we filmed each of the Attagirls taking off in their assigned planes, with Edwina going last to show us what could be done with a Spitfire.

"Actually, it doesn't matter what order we film them in," Huntley explained. "The editor will cut the film in the sequence we want it. That's the beauty of film: you can splice together all sorts of random pieces and make it all look as if it happened in one smooth piece of action. Of course, the weather and the light have to be the same."

He paused to finish reading the script I had written up. "You've done a really good job here. I like the stories you've included for each of them. Homey bits like Annie Trenchard being the mother of two girls who want to be pilots too, and that June Evesham was brought up on an airfield in the outback and learned to fly when she was a kid but only wanted to travel. It has appeal and that's what we want, just as much as the adventurous bits. They are quite a tough bunch, aren't they?"

I wouldn't have described them that way. "I think they *appear* to be tough because they have to be so self-disciplined. There isn't much room for error in their job. But when they are in the mess they are just girls together—good friends."

"Even her?" Huntley jerked his head over to Edwina.

"Well . . . she is not exactly the chummy type, but they really respect her."

Huntley acknowledged "chummy" as if I was joking.

———

VERA ABERCROMBIE AND Sir Basil strolled out to join us for a sandwich lunch at one o'clock. "Working lunch," Huntley insisted. "We'll lose the light at four."

We stood around Keith and his camera to eat our sandwiches in the clear air of a brilliant autumn day. After a while Keith started to film the Attagirls as they ate their sandwiches and chattered among themselves. They were a lighthearted, relaxed group and it was evident that they were enjoying their day. Edwina for once didn't bark instructions at us.

"How's filming going?" Sir Basil offered me a cup of coffee from a thermos.

I shook my head; too much Camp coffee had a way of creeping up on you. "Really well. It's fascinating to see different planes in flight," I said as we watched June's Mosquito come in to land. "How many pilots operate out of Didcote?"

"About thirty. They are all working out of White Waltham Airfield while we make this film. They will be back tomorrow evening. If you are not in too much of a hurry to leave, you might meet them; they are a great bunch of girls."

His eyes rested briefly on Edwina, who was eating a sandwich and alternating bites with sips of coffee. "My God that girl can eat," he said under his breath as he smiled at her. She frowned at him and turned her back. "I don't think I could eat that much Spam, even with Branston pickle on it," he called out good-naturedly, but she continued to ignore him.

Vera Abercrombie permitted herself a good-natured little chuckle as she joined us. "Can't wait to see the film when it's finished. When is Edwina going to do her demonstration?

"Zofia is next, then Grable, and then it's Edwina."

Vera smiled. "Look at her," she said with affection as Zofia got up from the grass and strolled over to Edwina. "Head's always in the clouds. I bet she has completely forgotten she's even flying today." Abercrombie relaxed her vigilance and lifted her face up to the sun for two brief seconds, and then she was the commander again. "Zofia, you don't have time . . . for coffee." She bustled over. She reminded me of the troop leader of our Girl Guide group at school: always vigilant, never off duty, and sometimes a bit too bossy.

Huntley sipped his coffee. "What plane is she flying?"

"Hurricane," I answered and pointed down the line to the last plane.

"Is it fast?"

"Yes, it's a single-engine, single-seater fighter plane similar to a Spitfire. Zofia says she prefers flying Hurricanes to Spitfires."

"Listen to you! Most people can't tell the difference between them." Griff's delighted smile would ordinarily have me glowing. "Next thing you'll be telling me is that you are joining the ATA."

Huntley emptied his coffee cup. "No poaching. I think she's a writer before she's a pilot!" And lifting his megaphone, he broke up the laughter and the chatter. "Okay, Zofia, off you go. Just like the others. Take off, fly around the airfield a couple of times, and then land." He turned to Grable, who was sitting with her face turned up to the sun. "If you could be ready to take off as Zofia comes back?" He squinted briefly up at the sun as well. "We should just about catch the light if you are ready to go after Betty," he called out to Edwina. She didn't turn her head or acknowledge him.

"Miss Partridge!" And then under his breath: "Oh, for God's sake."

She half turned her head and said, "Don't wait for me." Her face wore a withdrawn expression: shut off and remote as she returned her gaze to the horizon. Her defiant determination to impose her will on the way the film was directed had gone, and she had been quiet since the end of lunch. There was a brooding quality to her as she stood on the edge of things and smoked a cigarette halfway through before grinding it out and lighting another.

"Okay, Miss Partridge, off you go," Huntley called out as Grable circled the airfield and came in to land. "Bang on time," he said to me, and I looked at my watch; it was half past three. Edwina was already strolling toward her Spitfire.

"This will be something to watch," said June to me. "She may be a bit tiresome sometimes, but she knows how to put on a good show." She lifted her hand to shade her eyes, but there was no need to cover them; the sun, which had blazed all afternoon, went behind a cloud and a shadow fell over us. The hairs on my arms lifted in its chill.

"I hope she does put on a good show," said Huntley. "She needs to compensate for being such a pain in the neck all morning."

"What did you say?" Annie's voice held a strong note of reprimand—her brows were down and her chin out. I had taken her for the quietest and most unassuming member of group, and so had Keith and Huntley. Keith looked up from his camera and Huntley's head whipped round, his mouth open.

"Edwina is the best pilot we have." Annie took a step forward. "And, yes, sometimes she loads it on a bit, but you need to be more respectful. She knows what she's talking about and she wants us to look like professionals and not just a bunch of amateur movie stars."

Huntley looked like he had been stung by a wasp. He stared at Annie for a moment until he found his voice. "You're right," he said. "I apologize. I know what a demanding job this is and how hard you work. I didn't mean to sound . . . critical in any way." As he turned away he caught Keith's sympathetic glance and rolled his eyes.

We waited as Edwina climbed into her plane. We waited another five minutes, maybe longer. Keith was crouched over his camera as Huntley's thumb clicked his stopwatch on and then off. "Why the wait?"

"She is doing a flight check," Annie said between clenched teeth as we watched the two groundmen pull away the chocks under the Spitfire's wheels.

"Any longer and we'll need floodlights," Huntley muttered under his breath to Keith. Annie couldn't have heard his words, but she had caught his tone. She turned as if to say something and Grable reached out to take her friend by the arm. She gave it a little shake.

"He's said he's sorry," she murmured. "Let it go."

"I'm sick of being treated like fools because we are women." Annie's dark eyes flashed. "He would never talk about a male pilot that way."

The Spitfire started to move forward, and Griff folded his arms. "I was wondering," he said half to himself, "if I could fly that plane before we leave." He turned to Huntley. "See the elliptical wing? That's what makes her so incredibly fast."

"A lady in the air," said Grable lifting a pair of binoculars to her eyes, "but a perfect bitch on the ground." All pilots called their planes "she." But I wasn't too sure if Grable was referring to Edwina or her plane. I caught June's eye and we giggled.

"And she's up," said Huntley. "Got her in your sights, Keith? Don't track her—just get the big picture for a moment."

The Spitfire climbed and leveled off, banked, and did a circuit of the airfield. Then back around straight at us, quite low. As she passed overhead, Edwina waggled her plane's wings.

"Saucy," said Huntley, glancing at Annie to make sure he hadn't crossed the line. "I like it. This is going to be good."

Around again until she was perfectly trim in the sky above us; then the plane simply revolved in the air. It was a lazy, almost sensual movement.

"Victory roll. Oh God, two of them." June threw back her head and laughed. "Trust Edwina!"

And then as Keith cranked, and Huntley and Griff swore under their breath in admiration, the Spitfire started to climb. "I bet she's going to do the Immelmann turn," said Griff. And to me: "That's an ascending half loop followed by a half roll, resulting in level flight in the exact opposite direction at a higher altitude. It is a dogfight maneuver and beautiful to watch if it's done right." As soon as he uttered the last words, he looked doubtful as the Spitfire, having completed its half loop, started to roll and then, instead of maintaining its height, went into a deep dive.

"Oh, sorry, she's doing something else. But why . . . ?" Griff's confusion disappeared in concern. "Jeez, looks like she might have stalled it." We watched the Spitfire continue to drop. "C'mon, c'mon, get her nose up and level her. Level her, for God's sake."

But, contrary as always, Edwina did nothing of the kind. The Spitfire fell through the sunlit air like a stone. "What's she doing?" Griff turned to Vera and June, but they had no answer for him. They were both staring openmouthed up at the sky and the falling plane.

Huntley put his hand on Keith's shoulder. "I think she's pulling some sort of stunt. Keep filming, Keith, whatever you do, keep filming."

I looked around me. Annie was staring intently at the plane. Sir Basil, Letty, and Grable were standing together, their gazes fixed upward. Only Zofia articulated what was happening. "She's losing control . . ." she cried, and I noticed how strong her accent was. "Pull up," she yelled. "Get that damned nose up."

And as if Edwina had heard her, the plane started to level out.

"Thank God, she's got it back again," someone said. The Spitfire was hardly flying level, but it had stopped its terrifying plummet. Now it was coming toward us, flying just above the treetops.

Sir Basil's voice, harsh with disbelief, lifted above the cries of distress. "What the hell are you playing at?" he cried out as the plane careered overhead. Neither a lady nor a bitch, and certainly no longer a creature of power and grace, the Spitfire was simply a metal tube with wings as it veered sharply to the right.

"It's too late. She's going to crash. I'm calling an ambulance," Vera Abercrombie answered, and she started to run toward the office.

With our heads thrown back, we watched in horror as Edwina's plane plowed through the top of a tall elm tree and, unbalanced by its heavy boughs, plunged sideways and downward.

It was the percussion of her headlong impact with the ground that propelled us forward toward the gate in the hedge that separated airfield from farmland.

"No fire yet," Griff shouted as he lengthened his stride. "We've got to get her out . . . before . . . the gas tank . . ." He sprinted ahead of us and was the first to the gate. As he vaulted over it, Keith pulled up its hasp and threw the gate wide.

"Prop it open," Sir Basil shouted as he passed Keith, running surprisingly swiftly for a man of his age.

Spurred on by adrenaline and sick with apprehension, I was way ahead of the Attagirls in their bulky flying suits as I raced into the field with Bess bounding along at my side. Debris from the sheared-off tree littered the stubble of its surface ahead of us. I dodged through a thicket of saplings and came out the other side completely unprepared for the sight of the broken body of the plane.

It lay before us, its remaining wing sticking helplessly up into the air and its long nose tilted into the earth of the field, surrounded by the shards of broken propeller shafts. The tail, titled at a madcap angle, was still vibrating from the impact.

Griff was already up on the sound wing, head and shoulders into the cockpit to unbuckle Edwina's harness. She's alive, I thought as her head turned toward him before lolling sideways on her rag-doll neck. Unconscious but alive! It seemed to take Keith forever as he levered himself up beside Griff to help haul the limp body out of the wreck. I caught up with Sir Basil, his face scarlet, sides heaving, "Ambulance . . . on its way," he called out to Griff. "Is she . . . ?"

Griff and Keith braced their legs. I heard Griff count to three as they lifted her up out of the cockpit. Her body looked tiny in their arms. The bright sheen of platinum hair caught in the rays of the sun as it shone through the wreck of the tree the Spitfire had ripped through moments ago.

As Edwina was lowered to the ground, Sir Basil knelt and lifted her wrist. It almost looked to me like she said something. Or at least tried to, because Griff dropped his head to hers.

Seconds passed; then Sir Basil looked up. "There is no pulse. I'm afraid she's gone."

"Get away from the plane." June was the first of the Attagirls to arrive. "Come on back, all of you." She took Huntley by the arm as he tripped over a fallen tree branch. Keith was sleepwalking, mesmerized by the wreckage.

We obediently retreated back from the hot, ticking metal of the plane, carrying the lifeless body of one of the ATA's most talented flyers as the ambulance came around the stand of trees and bumped across the tilled earth of the field, its bell ringing frantically, as if in some way it would bring Edwina Partridge back to life.

FIVE

THE AMBULANCE DROVE UP THE TRACK IT HAD CREATED ON its arrival. Behind it trailed a silently stricken group. It had taken minutes for us to race across the field's uneven stony surface; now we trudged back as if we were bringing up the rear of a defeated army.

Zofia, walking next to Grable, reached out an arm to her shoulder and half turned the taller woman toward her. They stopped, side by side. Zofia closed her eyes, and her lips moved as if attempting to articulate a question that eluded her. Grable shook her head in incomprehension and put both her arms around Zofia's shoulders and drew her toward her. Zofia rested her forehead briefly on Grable's shoulder and then lifted her face. "We need tea," she said as I came up to them. "A cup of hot sweet tea. Isn't that what you English do when things go terribly wrong?"

That wasn't what she was going to say, I thought. She was going to ask a question.

Grable's smile was a sad one. "I think I would rather raise a glass of brandy to Edwina," she said. "It's what she would have done if it had been one of us." She looked around at the quiet women who had gathered around them. "Come on, girls, drinks are on me. Sir Basil? Vera?"

"Yes, absolutely." Sir Basil's face was less ruddy from his run, but I could still see the thin network of capillaries that ran across his white cheeks. I wondered if he was reliving those many moments, long ago, when his close friends had been shot down in the first war.

"And she was flying a Spit." Letty put one arm around June's shoulders and the other around Annie's, not to comfort them, I thought, but to emphasize that they were comrades and friends, still in the world and still flying. She hugged them to her. June lowered her head and Letty lifted her hand and smoothed back her friend's ruffled hair.

We broke into three groups, the Attagirls walking silently ahead, followed by Vera Abercrombie and Sir Basil. Keith, Huntley, and I had slowed our pace. I felt like an interloper, and so evidently did Griff. I looked back to see him standing alone on the path, gazing at the topless elm tree.

"Brandy," Vera agreed as she turned from watching the ambulance round the corner of the drive and disappear in the direction of Southampton. "Come on." She glanced at Sir Basil and inclined her head toward the mess. "Then I'd better call Charlie Morse at White Waltham." She turned her mouth downward and raised her eyebrows in a God-help-me kind of way. "And I need to talk to the ground engineer who worked on the Spitfire."

Sir Basil reached out his hand, as if to slow down her self-imposed momentum. "Want me to talk to Mac? You are going to be busy with all the red tape; it's the least I can do." Vera stopped and pulled the hem of her tunic down and squared her shoulders. "Yes, Basil, thank you." She glanced at me out of the corner of her eye as if realizing that this had been a day about recording Edwina's skill as a pilot.

"I can't believe it," she said almost to herself. "Not Edwina!"

June, walking ahead with the others, stopped, turned, and came back to her commanding officer. "There can't have been something wrong with the plane," she said to Vera. "It sounded in top form: perfectly tuned and as sweet as a nut." Her voice was pitched low, for only Vera to hear. Vera lifted a hand to quiet her, and June nodded. "Yes, yes. I completely understand we have to find out what happened, and why." And they walked forward together, away from the group, their heads close together in discussion.

I found myself hanging back until Griff caught up with me. He looked shaken, but not unduly so. He glanced at me, shook his head, and gave a long whistle.

"Did she speak after you pulled her out of the cockpit?" I asked him.

"Mm-hm." He nodded.

"Did you understand what she said?"

He frowned down at the ground. "She said, 'I should never have asked why he . . .'"

"Why he what?"

"That was it. She was barely conscious, Poppy. She was dying."

"She said 'he,' not 'she'?"

"I suppose she could have said 'she'—" He stared at me, his mouth open. "You are not suggesting for a miserable second that this wasn't an accident?"

I felt ashamed of myself, truly ashamed. I hadn't liked Edwina: she was antagonistic, and she seemed to take a perverse enjoyment in making those around her feel uncomfortable. I had been jealous when she had monopolized Griff, and now I felt small: petty and childish. Griff was not my boyfriend in the serious sense of the word. I didn't own him. And he had enjoyed flirting with Edwina . . . at first. It was second nature to the man.

"No, of course not. It just seems a strange thing for her to say, that's all."

He stood with his hands in his pockets and then gave me a quick sideways look. "She could have said anything and it would have sounded incongruous."

"Yes, I suppose so," I said, but my uneasy stomach told me otherwise. I had seen dead bodies often in the last year, many of them pulled from the rubble of bombed-out buildings, but the one I would never forget had not been killed by a bomb; she had been murdered. I had waited in the dark for help to come with the same awful, sinking, nauseous feeling that I had now.

Trust your intuition; don't let anyone tell you different. Ilona's voice in my head righted me in a second. I had watched a young woman who was more at ease at the controls of a Spitfire than she was on the ground pulled out of the cockpit of her wrecked aircraft, which had been maintained by a respected ground engineer. What had happened to her up there in the remote blue of a world she was completely at home in?

"Come on, Poppy, you're in shock. There is something wholly terrifying about seeing someone die that way." Griff put his arm around my waist and walked me forward to the ATA mess, with Bess trotting at our heels, her long ears folded down her neck like a sad rabbit.

WE LIFTED OUR glasses. "To Edwina," we said and drank. The silence after our toast resonated around the room like a drumroll. Long after the first sip we looked straight ahead or down at the floor.

"At least . . ." June cleared her throat, her eyes down. "At least she went doing what she did best. God, that sounds so trite."

But if she was doing what she did best, I asked myself, why did her plane simply fall out of the sky?

I was thinking the same thing myself, darling, Ilona's cool voice replied. *Drink up, sweetie, it will do you good.*

I obediently lifted my glass to my lips. I am not rightfully keen on brandy; I have no idea why anyone would want to drink it unless they were suffering from frostbite on a glacier in the Arctic: the taste is quite foul. I swallowed a small mouthful quickly. The stuff burned down my throat and clouted my fragile stomach with such a wallop, I had to stifle a gasp. But the effect, after I had inhaled a quick draft of cool air, was undeniably resuscitating. I felt my chilled body warm, and two seconds later an easing of tension as my shoulders settled themselves back below my neck, where they usually sit. Here goes, I thought, and took another mouthful.

Griff gave me a gentle pat on the back as my eyes watered. "Try not to belt it," he whispered. My cough broke the silence: there was a babble of voices around me as the world that was Didcote tried to find normal.

Huntley put down his empty glass. It was the first time he had spoken since the crash. "I don't want to sound callous, but we have to leave you." He tilted his head toward Keith and me and looked at the door. "Got to do something about our film."

"You are not going to show Edwina's—?"

"Accident? No, of course not. The Crown Film Unit celebrate heroes, people to aspire to. We want young women to see all of you and say: 'That's for me, that's what I want to do.' Right?"

We made our way to the door. "Van's outside." Huntley opened the door for me.

I turned around to see Griff gazing wistfully after us. "I'll see you later, Griff, maybe for dinner at the inn?" It was the first time I had been the one to say when I would see him next. It was a good feeling. I should take the initiative more, I thought as I followed Huntley and Keith out into the last rays of the setting sun.

"I JUST TALKED to Fanny on the phone." Huntley had repeatedly run his fingers through his hair and now it was standing up in tufts. "He was all for scrapping the film completely. I convinced him to let us see what we could do to pull something interesting and compelling out of what we have, without using Edwina's story. He's given us twenty-four hours. Poppy, you are our scriptwriter, what do you think?"

We were sitting in the inn's lounge around a log fire, the boys were drinking beer, and our innkeeper, Mrs. Evans, had made me tea. I had to admit that I was grateful to be here in this snug parlor and not with the Attagirls in their barn of a mess.

"Edwina's story was dramatic, and she was glamorous," I said. "But she is not the only woman of the group who had adventures. In fact, all of our Attagirls have had their moments: incidents that might be just as fascinating to young girls who are ready to volunteer and think that nursing or working in a factory would just be one long round of slog. Edwina was a sensation, but the rest of them are more of the girl-next-door type; I think that is the perspective we might want to emphasize."

Keith nodded and Huntley put down his beer. "Give us a for instance," he said.

"All right, take June Evesham as an example. I had no idea until yesterday evening that she grew up as a working pilot and that she is a very talented aviation engineer. It was a lonely life growing up and working on an airfield in the Australian outback. Her dream wasn't to fly; it was to travel. When her father died, she sold the business, said good-bye to Australia, and set off to discover the world. She was in Europe and North Africa in 1939, supporting herself as a travel writer. Annie told me that some of her books are in the Didcote mess library. When war broke out, she never thought of volunteering as a pilot until the ATA was formed and she was recruited. See what I mean?"

Keith yawned and Huntley said, "Yes, interesting, but not fascinating. We need a stronger lead."

I was ready for him. "And then there is Annie Trenchard. I know she's down in our notes as a mother of two little girls who live with their grandmother, but there is far more to her than that. She had a brush with the Luftwaffe too. Before France fell to Germany she was delivering a plane to an airfield in France. It was about this time of the year and the light was failing. As she neared what she thought was her destination, a heavy ground mist came in off the river. She was touching down on the airstrip when out of the corner of her eye she saw a swastika on the tail of a large German bomber!"

"You're joking—what on earth did she do?" Keith leaned forward.

Got you! I thought and laughed. "Well, in the parlance of my American friend: 'she hightailed it out of there' and found her way back to France, but it is certainly an adventure worth telling, don't you think? Annie is still teased to this day about visiting her German boyfriends."

Huntley was so pleased with the image that he clapped his hands together. "I think her being a mother makes the story even more dramatic." He turned to Keith. "How much footage did you get of them all having lunch?"

Keith shrugged. "Plenty," he said, blushing, because there was probably more of Grable than anyone else. "I was shooting for fun, really."

"Exactly!" I pulled my notebook toward me. "They were all relaxed and at ease with each other: eating sandwiches and drinking coffee on the edge of an airfield full of planes! Their work is difficult and dangerous, but they also know how to have fun!"

"The cheerful takes-danger-in-her-stride woman of action," Huntley said. "A sisterhood of heroes." His voice imitated the even tones of the commentator as he mimed a cameraman shooting film. "'And as they wait for their next mission, the Attagirls enjoy a quick, lighthearted lunch together before they are off again, delivering planes to RAF airfields all over Britain!' Well done, Poppy. We show a group of attractive, youthful women taking the war in their stride, and if Edwina is in the shot, that's okay too."

"She wasn't with the group at lunch," I said. "She was really quiet after we had eaten. She was off by herself on the edge of things."

"What about the one that looks like Betty Grable?" Huntley wasn't interested in what Edwina had been doing.

Glamorous Grable, I said to myself and read from my notes: "Daughter of a peer of the realm, Lord something or other and related in some way to H. H. Asquith, our prime minister in the last war. She has been flying since she was tall enough to see out of a cockpit, but unlike Letty, whose father encouraged her to join the ATA, Betty's parents were actively against her flying in wartime. She tried to join the WAAF as a pilot, but since the RAF doesn't believe that women should fly in combat she had to join the ATA instead."

Huntley sighed. "Let's try not to pioneer for women's rights, Poppy. What about Letty?"

"Letty Wills is one of the few women pilots who can fly one of those massive Avro Lancaster bombers. I think that's pretty sensational in itself. They are all working tomorrow morning, but I can have breakfast at the mess and ask Letty a bit more about her experiences."

"What about the Polish girl?" Keith asked. "She's a looker too."

"She is a countess, actually." I wondered if Zofia would mind her title being referred to. "Hers is a story of pure romance. She was married to a handsome Pole: Count Lukasiewicz . . ."

"Easy for you to say." Huntley was smiling. "I love where all this is going, by the way."

I looked up and caught the admiration in his face. When Huntley's thick, dark brown hair flopped forward and his eyes lit up behind his round-rimmed glasses, he looked like a youthfully myopic Oxford don, an attractive one. I turned pages in my notebook. "When Poland fell to the Nazis, the countess and her husband managed to escape and find their way to England. Count Lukasiewicz joined the RAF and was tragically killed in the Battle of Britain, so Zofia joined the ATA. You see? All their stories are fascinating, even if they didn't get nearly shot down by the Luftwaffe." I looked up from my notes. "I am sure that all of them would love to share their experiences on film!"

Keith made a triumphant whooping sound. "I think we should get something on them tomorrow morning as they take off for work!"

"Good idea, Keith, and well done, Poppy. No, really, very well done. I'm going to telephone Fanny and give him an outline of what we want to do. We'll run through the film Keith shot right now, draft up a framework; then you can stay on for a couple of days to get more stories and write up the commentator's script." He got up from his chair. "Right, who wants another beer?" He looked at his watch. "Oh God, look at the time. Did you get a darkroom set up?"

Keith nodded. "Bathroom across the hall from us. Take me minutes to process the film."

"Okay, you get the next round, Keith, and I'll see if I can get hold of Fanny. And ask them if they have anything hot to give us for dinner, would you? I am sick of sandwiches. The one I ate at lunchtime is still repeating on me."

I DIDN'T SEE Griff come into the inn's parlor; I was too busy writing.

"Hullo there!"

I nodded as I marked a passage in Annie's story before I looked up. Bess, sleeping on her back with folded paws, was so exhausted from her day of filming that she merely opened one eye by way of a greeting. Griff hesitated in the doorway. "Hope I'm not interrupting anything." I decided that I quite liked a bit of uncertainty in this abundantly self-assured man.

"No, we're taking a break for dinner—want to join us? I think Keith is trying to rustle up something for us."

"I'm always hungry and then when dinner arrives I suddenly lose my appetite. Can I get you a drink?"

"Keith is getting me one."

"Oh, I see."

He sat down in a chair close to me. "Are you still going ahead with the movie?"

"Yes. Edwina was a perfect heroine, but in their own quiet ways so are the other girls. Anyway, we can tell their stories in more detail now there is no . . . no star, so to speak. There will be some group shots with her, but that's all to the good, because it will be a sort of homage to her bravery."

He nodded. "She was quite a character," he said after a moment. "Not as likable as the other girls." He glanced at me out of the corner of his eye.

"But a heck of a lot more inneresting," I said in a terrible imitation of an American accent. His smile was sheepish, and he was about to say something when Keith arrived carrying two tankards of beer and half a lemonade shandy for me.

"Howdy, mate." It was an eccentric greeting, but Griff seemed to appreciate it.

"Keith is a huge fan of American movies," I whispered. I could tell that the thought of spending an evening with a real live American was a tantalizing one to our young cameraman. He set down a tankard in front of Griff. "Saw you come in; hope you like English bitter . . ."

They lifted their beer. "Here's how," said Keith. His eyes swiveled over to me to check that I didn't think he was a complete idiot.

"Mud in your eye," said Griff, his face quite composed. He paused and looked at me.

"Here's to Edwina," I said as I raised my glass of shandy, and we drank in silence.

The formalities dispensed with, Keith reported on the inn's menu. "Not sure if turnip soup is your idea of dinner or not, pal. I saw some and it looks a bit gray."

Griff clearly loved being called "pal"—he ducked his head and looked up at me, his eyes alight with laughter. "It's a no to the soup. The ATA's Spam sandwiches are still with me. But there is a fish-and-chip shop in Didcote, and if the innkeeper doesn't mind our bringing food in here—I'd be happy to drive down."

Mr. Evans said he didn't mind. And so Griff redeemed himself—thoroughly, in my esteem—by treating us to fresh local-caught fish and lovely thick chips, and a gloriously delicious dinner it was too.

SIX

I WOKE EARLY TO CATCH THE REMAINING FIVE ATA PILOTS AT breakfast before they all went to work and was unprepared to find Griff waiting for me outside the inn in his Alvis.

"Thank you for dinner last night," I said as I lifted Bess into the jump seat behind us, where she immediately crouched forward so her head was between us. "And how nice of you to drive me to Didcote Airfield."

"It's a pleasure," he said. "Then, after you have talked to the Attas, we can drive back to London after breakfast."

And here was that moment again. An opportunity to emphasize my independence, without being mean-spirited or scoring points. "Actually, I'm not leaving this morning after all. Huntley has the green light from our boss to go ahead with the film. I am to stay behind for a couple of days and get a little more background on the Attagirls."

"Then I'll stay too," he immediately offered.

"Very sweet of you, Griff, really it is, but I am going to be busy. I need to start my rewrites and Keith and Huntley will only stay a few minutes this morning to get some film of the Attagirls leaving Didcote in their air taxi, but thanks for the offer."

"Okay, I get the picture. How will you get back to London?"

"By train."

"And what about Bessie?"

"If they won't let me have her in with me in the railway compartment, we can travel in the guard's van. But since she's such a little girl I'm sure it won't be a problem, will it, Bess?"

A resigned nod as he started the car. "Okay, I'll drop you at the ATA mess and be on my way. Any thoughts on Edwina's accident?"

Any thoughts on Edwina? I'd had a million of them. I turned in my seat to face him. Last night he had been quite determined that her crash was an accident—surely, so far as he was concerned, there were no more thoughts. "What do you mean?"

"Well, I didn't like to bring this up at dinner last night, but Sir Basil talked to Mac Wilson, the ground engineer who worked on Edwina's plane. And Sir Basil reported to Vera Abercrombie that the Spitfire was in tip-top working order. All the planes flying for the film were gone over that morning. There was no reason Mac could give for the engine stalling that way. But . . . I heard Sir Basil ask Vera Abercrombie if Edwina had been drinking."

"Drinking?"

"My reaction too. No one in their right mind drinks when they fly. But apparently Edwina was given a dressing-down by Abercrombie because she had a skinful a couple of times last week with a hangover so bad that she couldn't go to work."

I couldn't believe my ears. Competent Edwina, with her bossy know-it-all swagger, tended to overdo the gin and tonic?

"She wasn't drunk yesterday afternoon," I said. "She was alert and completely sober. I should know. I spent most of the day around her."

"Not one little tipple out of a hip flask?"

"Not that I could see. She ate enough sandwiches for ten men. Drank a couple of cups of coffee. She spent more time with her lipstick and her comb than she did with anything else."

He nodded with his eyebrows raised, as if he suspected I couldn't tell the difference between drunk and sober. "I didn't think you saw her stumbling around the grounds, taking swigs from a whiskey bottle, you know. People can get quite seriously drunk in a quiet way. Did she appear to concentrate a bit too hard on little things like, say, putting on her lipstick? Or maybe she dropped her comb a couple of times?"

"Not all. Did she seem drunk to you?"

He shrugged off the question. "I honestly wouldn't know. I was trying to avoid her. To be frank, she came on a bit strong the night before last."

"Not drunk, even then?"

He laughed and shook his head. "Girls don't usually have to have a couple of drinks so they can spend time with me." I realized I had hit a nerve: good-looking men do have a way of being easily disconcerted when things don't quite go according to plan. I realized I hadn't quite forgiven him for being so attentive to Edwina.

"I meant to say did she drink at all that evening?"

"No, she had a beer with her dinner, and that was all. After that she took me over to look at her Spitfire, and I was back at the inn by ten."

Dinner had ended at half past eight. That meant Griff and Edwina had spent a little over an hour together out on the airfield—alone.

It would be foolish not to admit, even to myself, that I hadn't thought about Edwina last night as I had worked on my script. Repeatedly, my tired mind had replayed the paralyzing sight of her plane hurtling toward the earth. And when I went up to bed, every time I was on the verge of dropping off I remembered her last words: "I should never have asked him how he . . ."

I repeated them to Griff, and he pressed his lips together in a tight line before he said, "Yeah, it was a strange thing for her to say. But people say the strangest things when they are dying. She was barely conscious, Poppy. Her last thoughts could have been about anyone, anything. Something that had happened years ago."

I left it there. The last thoughts of dying people were part of his world, not mine. Heaven only knew how many friends and comrades he had lost in this war.

But I had too many thoughts about *how* and *why* in my sleepless hours not to try to seek some answers today. "If the plane was in perfect working condition, and she was not drunk, then why did she muff a maneuver that was apparently a piece of cake for someone of her experience and expertise?"

He cleared his throat and reached his right hand over to stroke Bess's long ears down the back of her neck. "Yes, I thought about that too." He returned his attention to the road. "If she had been drinking, it would have had to have been a lot for her to make the kinds of mistakes she made up there. And surely one of us would have noticed that level of inebriation before she took off." He turned his head to me, his eyebrows raised in inquiry, as if he needed confirmation.

"I would say she wasn't drunk at all. But I haven't seen anyone *really* drunk, except for a sailor in London once, and he was passed out in the gutter."

"So, we both agree that she was not drunk yesterday before she flew. But apparently she was in the habit of drinking a lot, and more than just occasionally." He slowed down as we passed a cyclist wobbling along the side of the road. "And since we must accept that the plane was in good working order, then she was either ill or lost consciousness . . . but even that doesn't quite ring true, because she did regain control and then seemed to lose it again."

"Who says the plane was in good working order? I can't seem to let go of questions that point to an intentional accident."

"Such as?"

"All right, then, and please remember I'm just thinking out loud."

"Fire away, Sherlock."

"Just supposing someone benefited by her accident and wanted her out of the way? The Attagirls, including Sir Basil and Vera Abercrombie, are all such proficient aviators, so knowledgeable about the planes they fly. Surely any of them would know how to fix a plane to make it stall in the air. So instead of asking myself *how* Edwina crashed her plane, I find myself thinking *who* would want her dead?" I knew I had all his attention because our breakneck speed slowed considerably. "According to Letty, June was a gifted flight engineer."

I saw June's pretty, open-countenanced face. She was such a straightforward and unaffected woman. I couldn't imagine her doing anything as underhand and treacherous as sabotaging a plane, but that was not the question I was asking. I was looking for motive, something that would drive someone outside of their ordinary everyday self enough to kill Edwina. "Neither June nor Letty liked Edwina. In fact, Letty actively disliked her!"

He was genuinely surprised. He turned in his seat and stared at me as if I were mad. "What made you think that? I thought they all got on well together. They were certainly enjoying themselves yesterday. It was all laughter and sunshine."

Then you clearly don't understand women as well as you think you do, chimed in Ilona.

"I didn't mean yesterday when we were filming. It was something I observed about Letty in her manner to Edwina when we arrived."

I remembered the brief interlude between June and Edwina. "June attempted to draw Edwina in to relate her Luftwaffe adventure, and Edwina snubbed her. She told June to tell the story and then turned her back. It put Edwina in a bad light, it was ungracious behavior, and June had every right to be insulted. But if she was, she didn't show it. Her expression was impassive and then she attempted to laugh off Edwina's bad manners, but there was an almost gratified expression on June's face, as if Edwina's behavior was confirmation of a more widely held belief.

"On the other hand, Letty's reaction to Edwina's antisocial response was far more outward. Her expression was openly contemptuous. She made her disdain evident. She reminded me of an old aunt of mine who expressed disapproval so eloquently, without saying a single word, that you just wanted to shrivel up and disappear." I laughed at how accurately Letty had depicted the expression on my aunt Grace's face. I had been left in no doubt that she considered Edwina's manner odious.

"Are you saying that Letty hated Edwina?"

"No, that's too strong. I felt that Letty was contemptuous of Edwina, or at least her behavior."

His mouth turned down at the word. "Contemptuous? That sounds rather temperate, chilly even." He scratched the lobe of his ear. "Do people kill out of contempt?" We had slowed down to a crawl. The turning to the airfield was yards away and he evidently wanted to have this conversation before we arrived.

I knew he was alluding to what he called our great British reserve: our cultural dislike of emotional displays, our reticence about anything that suggests the airing of private feelings.

"Given enough provocation, contempt might easily escalate to hate," I pointed out. "I think people commit murder when they are in the grip of intense emotions: extreme jealousy, an overwhelming desire for revenge, or a desperate need to get someone out of the way because they pose a threat to you or someone you care about."

He nodded, his lips pursed, as he considered. "Yes, but to some extent everyone suffers from jealousy, envy, greed, and a desire for revenge, but they don't act on it, and if they do, it's usually in a petty way."

I nodded. "I wasn't talking about ill-wishing someone you dislike; I was talking about murdering someone you hate."

He stopped the car and folded his arms. "What about premeditated murders, when the killer plots away for months—years, even—to eliminate someone for some reason or other?"

It was my turn to consider. "Yes, of course, but 'some reason or other' is usually a human emotion taken to the extreme, isn't it? Cold, brooding hatred rather than an act of furious rage."

"Hah." He put his foot on the accelerator and we surged forward toward the gate into Didcote Airfield. "I can't imagine someone like Letty causing Edwina's death because she thought her manners were contemptible; she struck me as being a particularly pleasant, get-along type—they all did."

How little he knows the English! Ilona observed. *All those simmering emotions bubbling away under a veneer of frozen good manners.* It doesn't take much to scrape away that layer of civilization, I thought, and then you have entire countries murdering each other.

"Yes, they appear to get along really well! But supposing Edwina had done something so unforgivable that Letty's contempt escalated to hatred?" I waved my hand in an attempt to explain further. "This is all hypothetical, by the way."

"But you said you saw contempt, not hatred."

"That's right, but Letty might have discovered something more about Edwina that intensified her emotions. All I am saying is that two of Edwina's fellow pilots didn't appear to like her very much. They respected her skill as a pilot, but Letty demonstrated a dislike that bordered on contempt, and there has to be a reason for it, other than Edwina's bad manners."

"What you're saying is that Letty had absolutely no time at all for Edwina, and I'm saying that that is not a motive for murder."

I exhaled carefully, hoping that it didn't sound too much like a sigh of frustration. I completely understood what Oscar Wilde meant when he said, "Two countries divided by a common language." Even Bess barely suppressed a groan that, having stopped, we were still in the car.

I waited a few seconds so I didn't sound too impatient. "Yes, but it might be a reason to investigate this tight-knit group, who have lived and worked together for a little over two years."

"I think it's the writer in you—you can't resist looking for signs of malice and murder!"

I waved my hand to dismiss all possibilities of an overactive imagination. "I'm just naturally curious, that's all." I remembered Annie correcting Huntley's criticism of Edwina as a pain in the neck and telling him not to be disrespectful. "But it seems we have a divided camp where Edwina's popularity is concerned: Annie Trenchard and Grable didn't seem to actively dislike her."

"And the others? Have you had a chance to assess their attitude?"

"Zofia seemed to get on pretty well with her—at least Edwina was more relaxed around her. And Zofia expressed her admiration for Edwina"—I searched for the right word—"warmly. But Letty and June are in the opposite camp, and yesterday Edwina was downright rude to Sir Basil and he didn't like it at all, so not much camaraderie there either."

"So, we have three for Edwina and three against. What about Vera Abercrombie?"

Commander Abercrombie in my opinion was entirely wrapped up in being Commander Abercrombie. I suspected she was one of those matter-of-fact types who rarely show, let alone acknowledge, their feelings. "I don't think she can have approved of Edwina, especially if she was drinking heavily. As their commanding officer I expect she maintains a slight distance from all of them. I don't know if she actively *disliked* Edwina."

"And what about you?"

I laughed. "Funnily enough, even though she was brash and a bit uncouth . . ."

Bessie nuzzled my hand as a reminder to get out of the car—she could smell a good breakfast from miles away.

"Don't tell me you liked her?"

"Liking has nothing to do with how I felt. I—" I told myself to be honest, not syrupy in the way of girls who don't want to sound catty. *Go on,* demanded Ilona, impatient with my dithering. *Tell him what you think!*

"No, to be frank, I didn't like her. She just wasn't my type. I found her rude and rather intimidating. But underneath the armor coating I thought she was vulnerable, that her display of confidence was a cover-up. She was on the edge of things . . . she wasn't really part of their group, not even with Annie and Grable—I think she was ill at ease and tense with all of them. Except Zofia; they were friends."

He was gazing intently at me as I finished, and then he whistled, his long, low whistle that ascends, then descends in scale. Then he did a lot of nodding, as if he were making sense of the female consensus and what he had experienced.

"She was a mess," he finally came up with. "She was so . . . I don't quite know how to put it without sounding . . . judgmental. At first, I thought she was a pretty, outgoing, and vivacious girl, and then I found myself saying, 'Uh-oh, time to run . . . ,' and I'm afraid that's the size of it." He shook his head. Was it in embarrassment for showing an interest or because he had had a lucky escape? "But I can see what you mean about her armor coating, and she *was* pretty defensive."

There were a few perceptions of who Edwina was in what he had told me, and a lot about himself: "Oops, I've made a mistake about you—gotta nip this in the bud" summed up what Griff had probably thought.

"But do you see what I mean, about a camp divided, about possible enemies?" I asked.

He inhaled, closed his eyes, and exhaled in a gusty sigh. "I can't pretend to understand the subtleties of a group of women who live and work together. With men, it's entirely different, or maybe there are the same problems; we just deal with it differently. There are some guys on the base you get along with and some you avoid. And, yes, occasionally tempers run high, they are bound to, but we just kind of sort it out mostly by looking the other way. It can be claustrophobic living and working on an air force base. But we just have to rub along somehow."

"How do you 'sort it out'? Do you fight?"

"What? You've been watching too many Humphrey Bogart movies!" He chuckled. "It's against regulations to hit a brother officer. But one time, when we were in training at Lawson in Georgia, there was this particular guy, I think he was a gunner, or maybe he was a bombardier—anyway, there was something about him." He shrugged. "He was aggressive and so were his pals; they all had a bit of a chip. The weather in Georgia is heavy going: hot and really humid. He started a fight, and it got nasty. They had to call in the MPs."

He looked at me, his eyes shining with the memory. "That's my point," I said. "When you have a group of people who work long and dangerous hours and live together too, there is tension and some-times little things escalate into much bigger ones."

He beat a light tattoo on the steering wheel with the tips of his fingers as he thought. "Well, of course you are in the perfect posi-tion to find out what's going on here, because it's your job to ask them about themselves and the work they do. But seeing a plane crash with someone you knew on board is a disturbing experience, so go easy on yourself and them, okay?"

Hasn't he said something like this before when he encouraged you to investigate the Little Buffenden strangler? asked Ilona. *Are you sure there's no ulterior motive here?*

Bess and I got out of the car. She made a beeline for the mess, but I stood there for a while. "You're right. I am on edge; I haven't had enough sleep and I could probably do with some breakfast." I shivered and tried to shake off my mood.

"If your intuition keeps pinging you with what-ifs, I'll be back at Reaches in a couple of hours. Will you call me if . . . if you need anything at all? I've still got a few days of leave left, so I'm going to play chess with your grandad and use their kitchen to make dinner for us."

He gave me the laconic wave that Americans call a salute, let out the clutch, and roared up the lane to the gate. *Yes, go easy on them, but ask questions? That's a bit like saying be careful when you jump off that cliff.* Ilona had to throw her tuppence worth in, and I told her to keep her suspicions to herself, as Bess and I walked up the mess steps to have breakfast with the Attagirls.

SEVEN

I T WAS A FORLORN GROUP OF WOMEN WHO WERE GATHERED around the long trestle table by the mess windows looking out on the airfield.

"Morning, Poppy. Breakfast? We usually have a large one because it might be the only chance we have to eat today." June's face was very pale, her eyes were red-rimmed with fatigue, but she was lacing into a plate of eggs, mushrooms, and what looked like some sort of tinned corned beef. It was a deadly-looking array of overcooked and greasy food. I shuddered. Even before the war, when an English cooked breakfast was the envy of the world, I never understood how people manage to eat platefuls of protein first thing in the morning.

"I would love a couple of slices of toast and a cup of coffee," I said as Bess planted herself underneath June's chair and looked up at her with a particularly yearning expression. She was rewarded with a corner of toast with scrambled eggs that looked like pale yellow rubber.

"No more coffee for me; I'll take tea," Annie told the mess steward. "I want this war over soon, so we can have a good strong cup of real coffee with lots of sugar. What do they make this stuff with?" She had pushed away her coffee cup. "Parched acorns?"

Grable, after lifting her head briefly to say good morning, had gone back to staring bleakly out the window as she sipped coffee, and Annie became absorbed with making a toast sandwich with what looked like fried Spam, but her heart wasn't in it. The Spam slithered out from between the toast, and she pushed it aside with an impatient exclamation. None of them looked like they had slept well; their faces were wan, their eyes clouded with exhaustion. If there was someone sitting at this table who had caused Edwina's accident, her conscience had given her a rough going-over last night.

"I know this is not the time, but we have to do something about the film," I said.

Letty tucked a strand of hair behind her ear. June looked down at her plate, and Grable shook her head as if the last thing in the world she wanted to discuss was what had been the catastrophe of yesterday. I cleared my throat and waded in. "Huntley spoke to our boss at the Crown Film Unit," I said, aware that five pairs of eyes had fixed themselves on my face. "Of course, we will not include the footage of Edwina's last flight." June nodded as she chewed and swallowed and took a sip of coffee. "But we want to make this film about what you *all* do for us, and keep some of the parts where Edwina is with you when you were having lunch—Keith shot some film of that time, and it shows you as a group, together, having fun. So, the theme now is about a group of women who eat, sleep, and work together. Their job is a demanding one: they work long hours, often dangerous hours, but here they are enjoying a few minutes together in the sun before their next mission." I was careful to keep all mention of strong friendships and sisterhood out of it because I sensed that this might not hit the right note with them this morning. "Then, as the film shows each of you flying, the commentator will tell your story." I gulped down cold coffee. "Why you fly, what drew you to the ATA. If you have had some moments, some adventures, you would like to share with us, we can include them."

There was a long, thoughtful silence as I finished. I heard myself swallow again and waited.

I had expected Edwina's only real friend to be subdued today, but Zofia had been a statue since I had sat down at the table. She hadn't moved; she hadn't spoken. Her breakfast was put before her and she ignored it with effigy-like composure: the sculpted mask of Melpomene, the muse of tragedy, came into my mind.

"We will only share the stories if you want us to." I faltered. Zofia lit a cigarette, her eyes on my face. Why was I the one stuck with doing this regrouping speech? Where on earth was Huntley?

Letty pulled Zofia's plate toward her. "What a waste. How will you get through the day without breakfast, Zofia? Are you telling me you don't like fried bread?" she coaxed, and Zofia smiled. "Not this morning, I don't," Zofia said as Letty automatically forked down her plate of eggs and fried tomatoes as if it were a duty.

"I am not really newsworthy, and I am not sure Vera would want you to feature the German airfield incident," said Annie. "Most days all I do is wait for the Met Office to tell me the fog has lifted in the southwest so I can fly a Mosquito down to Devon, which, by the way, would be like driving a double-decker bus along a road. I spend my time knitting pullovers for my girls or writing them long letters telling them to behave themselves. I don't think that's heroic or adventurous." There was a ripple of laughter around the table and I relaxed.

"If you don't mind us sharing your German airfield experience, I am sure Crown Films will persuade Commander Abercrombie," I said with complete conviction. Mr. Fanshaw had clout with

Mr. Churchill, who loved a good propaganda moment, especially if he was the star or it involved dashing young women. Annie's brows came down and she pulled her mouth into tight-lipped disapproval.

"Are you up to my asking you some questions, like what made you want to fly?" They caught one another's eyes and the laughter increased in volume. It almost dispelled the air of despondency around the table.

"I don't think any of us knew what we were getting into." Grable lifted her hands in mock horror as she shook her tired head.

"Ice-cold feet; endless waiting to get back to Didcote after you've delivered a Tiger Moth; sudden ground fog, thunderstorms—where shall we start?" asked Letty with her mouth full.

"This film is really about recruiting young women into the ATA. As this war continues we need to redouble, even triple, your numbers. The ATA needs to deliver planes as quickly as they are manufactured. Your adventures and experiences are valuable even if they are not as dramatic as Edwina's Luftwaffe attack." I looked around the table. "If you are willing to share them, I think they will help make our film compelling and . . . real."

They all looked at one another. Zofia shrugged as if she didn't have the energy to tell me the time. "Our adventures," she said and shook her head from side to side. "It was Edwina who had the adventures. We just deliver planes."

"Not all of us nearly landed a plane on a German airfield, but there have been some pretty hair-raising moments: near misses, getting lost—that kind of thing," Grable said. Grateful for how quick she was on the uptake, I nodded my encouragement. "It doesn't have to be sensational."

"What about the time when Grable landed a plane at RAF Biggin Hill and a senior pilot gave her a right bollo—reprimand?" June put down her knife and fork.

I laughed as she corrected herself from using a vulgar expression used by the RAF. "What happened, Grable?"

Grable took up the tale. "I landed a Hurricane on a pretty crowded airstrip. It was a bitterly cold morning with a sharp wind, so I was bundled up: a Sidcot flying suit over my uniform, and a sheepskin leather jacket over that, and even though they don't have a radio earpiece, a leather helmet does keep your head a bit warmer. A group captain walked up to the plane and said, 'ATA? You chaps are up early this morning.'

"I nodded and jumped down. This was one of my first ATA deliveries of a fighter. I had been a wreck, worrying that I wouldn't pull off a tidy landing.

"He stuck out his hand and introduced himself. He was a really pompous little bloke. Big Biggles mustache, strutty walk." She smiled around the table. "They are always on the short side, the really unpleasant ones, aren't they?" There were smiles and nods around the table; the mood was lifting a little, and June said something like, "Too right."

"Well, of course I shook hands with him, and because it's hard to hear with a helmet, I took it off and—"

"Shook down that ladder of Rapunzel hair . . ." added Annie.

"And he completely lost his temper," Grable took back the story. " 'What the merry hell do you think you're playing at?' he bellowed. 'Who gave you permission to fly an RAF plane—is this some sort of joke?' He took me by the arm and tried to march me to their command post. There was quite a crowd by this time: ground crew, pilots, navigators, all standing there with their mouths open. You see, back then there were only five or six female ATA pilots. The rest were all men: war veterans, commercial airline pilots who were too old to join up—they called themselves the Ancient and Tattered Airmen. Anyway, old Biggles had me by the arm and marched me up in front of their winco—sorry, wing commander." Her friends had heard this story before, but they were all chuckling now, and Letty shook her head at the foolishness of pompous men.

"The wing commander let him continue to make a fool of himself: demanding my arrest for playing some sort of trick, or 'stunt,' as he called it. And then he extended his hand to me. 'Been waiting to meet one of you ladies,' he said. 'I saw you land that Hurricane, splendid bit of flying. Congratulations and thank you for the work you do.'"

Grable smiled. "I've never seen that silly little clot again, but I always look out for him when I ferry a plane to Biggin Hill—just in case he's feeling plucky."

However much I respected Grable for carrying off a straightforward example of misogynistic behavior, I suspected that it wasn't a story that Crown Films would feature, but her story had broken the tension. Zofia came out of her introspection. She clapped her hands together as she looked at me to emphasize her disdain for a world of men who unerringly jumped to the wrong assumption. Annie put her arm across Grable's shoulders. "I can just see you standing there, waiting for that idiot to catch on," she said.

Vera Abercrombie came into the mess carrying a cup of coffee. Her face wore its perennially alert, businesslike expression, but she had probably been up for hours toiling over her delivery schedule.

"Good morning, Poppy—your boss, Mr. Fanshaw, called and told me that you would be staying on for another day or two." She waved a hand to where we were sitting. "You are most welcome to work here if you would be more comfortable than at the inn." I thanked her and she turned to talk to her pilots. "Today's schedule is on: the Met Office says this fine weather will continue to hold, but please check again just before you leave, especially if you are going north. Here are the chits for today's deliveries." She passed out white cards to each of them. Zofia was given two or three, as were the other girls.

"Two Spits," said June as she read hers. "One to Andover and one to Yorkshire, nearly a perfect day." She almost smiled.

There were mild exclamations of pleasure as the rest of them received chits for what promised to be a day of flying fighter planes.

Wouldn't you think they would be reluctant to fly after yesterday? Ilona's voice brought the image of Edwina's plane crashing through the thick canopy of the elm tree. I looked around at the group at the table; it was hard to fathom their mood this morning. When I had first sat down they looked as if they had been put through a mental wringer, but after a hefty breakfast here they all were comparing routes and ready to start their day. Winston Churchill would have been proud of them; no wonder they were the ATA's poster girls.

Letty waved her chit across the table at June. "A Walrus, all the way to blasted Lossiemouth. What is that, a four-hour flight? I can never remember. It's ages since I've been that far north."

"More like five in that tub," said June. "Too bad."

"You up to it?" Grable looked closely into Letty's tired face. "Don't fly if you're not. Tell you what, I'll swap with you. I've got two short trips in the Anson after I drop you all off."

"No, no, I'm fine, but thanks all the same." Letty, who had taken on my aerial education, turned to me. "A Walrus is a heavy, cumbersome seaplane. It tends to wallow in the air and is even worse on takeoff. But I'm used to them; I have flown so many of them that it's almost second nature now, but there are planes I prefer more, especially flying to Scotland."

"You'll be just fine, Letty, just don't work too hard at it. You can always put down at Market Harborough if you run out of steam." I thought June's rather phlegmatic response a little callous considering that her two deliveries would be in planes that were easy to fly.

We sat around for another hour; trips were made to the map room and the Met Office on either side of Vera's command post. Letty came back with her map and looked out at a blue sky. "Autumn weather is capricious in Britain. Sun one moment, a downpour the next, and morning and evening fog are commonplace."

"What happens if the weather gets really bad?" I asked her.

She smiled. "Most of the time you can struggle through it, but if it gets rough you put down at the nearest airfield, and if it gets really wild, you just have to look around for a nice, big, flat field."

Vera Abercrombie came back into the mess. "Two Ansons are on their way in ten minutes. Please be ready by then." She gave me a brisk nod, as if I were holding up their departure. "I hope your crew are here in a minute or two, Poppy. We can't hold up the schedule for a piece of film; otherwise I'll never catch up." Her kindly demeanor of yesterday had evaporated to business as usual, and I wondered what her superiors had to say about Edwina's crash.

Annie was in the middle of reminiscing about their early ATA days. "This April, when they were delivering Spits to Malta, we had to sit in this mess for two days straight, all suited up and ready to go in an instant. Typical spring weather: low cloud and heavy rain. An hour went by like a day. And then it cleared, and it was go, go, go! Twenty of us delivered seventy Spits in the next fourteen hours to the aircraft carrier *Wasp* in Scotland."

"Annie must have knitted half a dozen scarves as we waited," said Grable. "We all still wear them, or what's left of them. They unravel at a fearsome rate." There was a lot of giggling as they struggled into their flying suits and organized themselves for departure. I felt immense respect for their pluck and resilience, their determination to make the best of things. We were interrupted by

Keith and Huntley, who had arrived in the van and set up their gear by the first air taxi that had landed on the airstrip.

"Any chance of a cup of coffee?" Huntley asked.

"I'm afraid not now." Vera was looking at her watch. "The mess kitchen will make you some before you leave."

"Are we all going to the Supermarine factory?" Grable asked as we filed out of the mess past the table where they collected a thermos of coffee or tea.

"No, Zofia and June are going to Armstrong. Now, listen, girls. Please remember to sign in for each plane you deliver and get your chits stamped, both when you pick up and again when you deliver. I want to balance my books this evening," she called after them as we walked on to the mess door.

Even after the enjoyment of recounting some of their adventures, they still looked tired and Zofia's earlier introspection had returned, but their working day demanded their concentration. I watched them check for compass and map, and stow their chits inside their Sidcot suits. Letty was still fumbling the zip of her flying suit. "Goodness, I'm all thumbs, and these Sidcots are made for men." She pulled her mouth down as she peered over her bosom to see the zip. "There it is, blasted nuisance." She zippered up and looked around her. "Where on earth did I put my helmet?" She laughed as Grable handed it to her. "It will be ice-cold up north."

"Come on, girls, get a move on, don't hold us up," Vera called to the stragglers. "Letty, *here's* your parachute; you left it by the door." She picked up Letty's forgotten chute. I suspected she would have been less lenient, but it was clear she was struggling for patience because of Edwina.

We walked out onto the airfield. There was a sharp wind blowing in from the sea. "A southwester," June shouted to Vera as she boarded. "We'll make up for lost time with a tailwind."

"I don't want to chivvy you, Letty, but would you just get in the plane?" The papers clipped to Vera's board were fluttering in the breeze, and Letty was trying to tuck her hair up into her helmet.

"I forgot my compass." She paused and then started to climb up the ladder into the aircraft. "Don't need one anyway. I could fly to Lossie in my sleep."

Keith had been filming as the Attagirls queued up by the aircraft; walking backward, he continued to film as they filed up into the two planes.

"Still be here when we get back?" Letty turned on the last-but-one rung of the ladder and looked down at me.

"Yes, I've loads of work to do. I'll still be here," I shouted back.

"Good, then, I'll buy you a drink." She gave Keith a dazzling smile over her shoulder and put one hand on her hip in a glamour-girl pose as he cranked away.

"Perfect, now pretend to blow us a kiss!" shouted out Huntley, and as she pouted her lips he said, "What an exit!"

Bent double, we turned and ran as the ground crew pulled away the chocks and the pilots ignited their engines. The first plane started forward to the head of the airstrip. "And the women pilots of the ATA leave on yet another day of ferrying planes from manufacturer to airfields all over Britain. What planes will they deliver today? Hurricanes and Spitfires? Tiger Moths and Fairey Swordfish? Or perhaps the great Avro Lancashire bomber with its four mighty engines! Whichever aircraft they are allotted to deliver, you can be sure of one thing: these young women will know how to fly them!" Huntley intoned in a creditable imitation of the commentator Bob Danvers-Walker. As the planes lifted into the sky, Keith trumpeted "Land of Hope and Glory" between closed lips.

"That last bit of film will make a good ending," he said. "But I'm worried about the Spit demonstration from yesterday; if we cut out the accident and we only have a few seconds of her taking off and flying overhead, that won't go down well with the great British public."

Huntley reached out and patted him on the shoulder. "We'll let Fanny make that decision," he said. He stopped, turned, and waited for me to catch up. "I don't think I'll ever forget making this one. I keep seeing that Spitfire barreling toward us. You know something?" He glanced over his shoulder at the shorn-off elm tree and lowered his voice. "I thought for one awful moment that she had gone off her rocker and was going to take us all out!" I could tell from his expression that he wasn't joking.

"Off her rocker?" I asked before he got distracted with packing up.

"Well . . ." He looked guilty. "Don't you think, deep down, that perhaps Edwina wasn't playing with a full bag of marbles?"

I half nodded and he shrugged and turned to Keith. "All right, Keith, let's pack up the van and get back to HQ."

We straggled up the drive, carrying the last can of film, tripods, cameras, and sound equipment, and put them in the back of the van next to the film shot the day before. There was a strong smell of the chemicals used to develop film and I was glad I wasn't driving back to London with them. Huntley polished his spectacles on his tie and settled them back on his nice straight nose. "You can drive, Keith," he said, tossing him the keys.

"Thanks, mate!" Keith got in behind the wheel.

"How are you doing, Poppy? Do you have some pages for me?" Huntley said as he walked around to the passenger door.

I must have had about three hours' sleep, but I was pleased with what I had written. "I'm fine," I said. "Here's my outline." I handed him an envelope of typed pages. "It's almost complete. I'll talk to

Zofia and Grable this evening for more detail on their background. So, what happens next?"

"Keith, the editor, and I will work on a rough cut this afternoon; then on Monday morning when you arrive, you can tailor your narrative to it and add any bits you need to. We get a thumbs-up from Fanny, iron out any wrinkles and that's it. The commentator, Bob, will add the narration. Now we've got to run. Thanks for all you've done, Poppy—you've been a brick." Just before he ducked his head to get into the van, he turned back to me, pushed his hair out of his eyes, and said, "I'd say this was a pretty significant start to your career with Crown Films." His eyes met mine, and I blushed.

THE TELEPHONE RANG again in Vera's office and I lifted my head briefly from my work. Sir Basil had joined her twenty minutes after I started typing up notes at the trestle table where we had eaten breakfast. Their quiet voices barely reached me through the open door as they talked together. Every so often the phone would ring and one of them would answer with a monosyllabic series of yeses or nos.

I lifted my head when I heard Vera's voice raised in dismay and was halfway out of my chair before I reminded myself that I was just a guest at Didcote.

"Dear God!" Sir Basil's deeper voice reached me at the table. "Where? Where did she land?"

"Land?" Vera's voice was tight with suppressed emotion. "Basil, she didn't land; she crashed."

Now I was on my feet, startling a slumbering Bess, who was stretched out on a sofa next to the heater. We both ran forward and stopped at Vera's office door. I knocked and pushed it further open.

The two of them were facing each other across her desk. Vera was still gripping the receiver of the telephone in a white-knuckled hand, her mouth opening and closing like a landed fish's. They turned as I walked into the room.

"Everything all right?" I asked, knowing that I would hear awful news.

I watched Vera struggle for composure: she inhaled and held her breath, looking at Sir Basil as if he had asked her a question. She shook her head. "Letty has just pranged her plane outside of a village called . . ." Her breath came out in a long, shaky exhalation. She went to a large ordnance survey map of the south coast on the wall. "Here," she said, more to herself than to us, as she traced a line from the coast inland. "At Elton. That was the Elton Home Guard on the phone."

"Anyone see what happened?" Sir Basil asked.

"Yes, a local farmer saw her trying to land. He thought she was having difficulty, and then he saw her crash. He got through to the Home Guard."

"How long ago did she come down?"

"About half an hour ago."

"Can you speak to her? Ask the Home Guard to get her on the phone. She is all right, isn't she? I take it she bailed."

Again, Vera shook her head, her brows down, her mouth a tight, straight line. I thought I saw, for one brief human moment, pain: grief for a fellow pilot whom she had worked with from the start of the war. She closed her eyes as she struggled for self-possession and said in a steady voice, "No, Basil, she's not all right." She leaned forward, her hands flat on the surface of her desk, as if to prevent her from falling over. She looked up at him. "Letty was killed outright when the Walrus crashed into a stone railway bridge."

EIGHT

FELT THE OLD SICK, SINKING FEELING IN MY STOMACH AS I walked out of Vera's office and sat down at the trestle table in front of my typewriter. A light rain was pattering against the window, the sky was low and heavy with dark cloud, and the cheerless empty room around me echoed the sound of rainfall. My hands were trembling so violently I had to hold on to them to keep them steady. Bess jumped up onto my lap. I wrapped my arms around her and bent my head to inhale the sweet dry-hay smell of her coat until the nausea passed.

The phone rang again, and I was on my feet, Bess clutched in my arms. The empty feeling crept back as I walked toward the office. I didn't care if it wasn't my business, if it was unmannerly to intrude. Letty, generous and good-hearted Letty, alive and eating her breakfast nearly three hours ago, was dead, and I could hear the words "pilot error" before they were uttered.

"Yes, just a minute, please. I'll hand you over to Commander Abercrombie." Sir Basil gave the phone to Vera as I came into her office and stood with his hands in his trouser pockets, head bent as he listened.

"Thank you for returning my call." Vera put her hand over the mouthpiece. "It's the farmer who saw her crash." And back into the telephone: "Mr. Mackenzie, yes, this is Commander Abercrombie." She listened in silence for a couple of minutes. "Did you actually go over to the plane, Mr. Mackenzie? Yes, of course, I understand. How high do you think she was flying? Oh really! And how did the plane look to you? No, when it was still in flight. Ah yes, I see." She listened for a minute longer. "Thank you so much for everything you have done, Mr. Mackenzie. Please call me if there is anything else you might remember. And by the way, someone from the ATA Accidents Committee will be in touch with you in a day or two. Just tell them what you told me. Good-bye and thank you for your help."

She put down the phone and folded her arms. The stress of Edwina's crash and now this news had layered years on Vera Abercrombie's already prematurely aged face: her skin looked dry and lined; her tired eyes moved restlessly around her office as if desperately seeking resolution to this appalling dilemma. Letty Wills, well liked by her peers and one of the most proficient and reliable of her pilots, was dead.

"Well?" Sir Basil smoothed his right hand over the top of his head. "What did the man have to say?"

Vera wandered over to the map and traced again with her finger. "Letty was flying north from Supermarine at Eastleigh. She must have been following the railway line that leads north-northeast up to Edinburgh." Her finger came to a halt, presumably where Elton was marked on the map. "Mr. Mackenzie, who witnessed the accident, was driving across his farmlands and heard the plane. He said it was flying low and in an erratic manner: one moment it banked to the left, then leveled out and immediately listed to the right. He calculated it was probably at about four or five hundred feet when he first saw it, but in sharp descent."

Sir Basil threw his hands up in the air. "What was she thinking?"

Vera shrugged. "I really can't imagine." Her face seemed to have crumpled in on itself. She stood in front of the map gazing at it; perhaps if she looked long enough it might give her some sort of an answer.

"Mackenzie followed the plane across a field. He said it looked as if as she was trying to land."

"On a railway line?"

Vera nodded, her eyes miserable and uncertain. "He said that's what it looked like. Just before it crashed, he said . . . he said that it looked as if the pilot was trying level the plane, and . . . he saw it dive straight into the stone railway bridge outside of the little town of Elton. He thinks Letty was killed immediately." The stress of keeping a cool head and a calm mind was taking its toll. Vera's mouth trembled, and she half raised her hand to her head. But Sir Basil wanted information and he wanted it now. "What did he mean by flying erratically? Did you ask him?"

She recovered her equanimity. "He said it was careering about, as if it was 'as drunk as a lord.'"

"She must have been ill." Sir Basil shook his head "Letty didn't drink."

"She ate a large breakfast and seemed quite as usual." Vera glanced at me as if she wished I weren't there.

"No one was quite as usual after yesterday, Vera. Perhaps they shouldn't have flown." It was the first time during this awful conversation that he had criticized her. I wondered how much flack Vera would catch at ATA White Waltham headquarters simply because she was a woman. Men will go out of their way to support a hardworking colleague if he makes a mistake; a woman simply shouldn't make them at all.

She picked up a pencil and tapped a rapid tattoo on the desk. "There is a war on, Basil. We can't give everyone a day off when there is an accident."

"Accident? Is that official, that Edwina's crash was an accident?" The sharpness of his tone was almost derisive.

A intake of breath and Vera looked across the desk at her friend. Her stare was steady and reproachful. "Yes, it is. Until we have the ATA Accident Committee's report, we must assume both were accidents."

He turned and walked to the window, jangling small change in his pocket. "I'm afraid I see a difference in the two incidents already." He shifted more change about and Vera closed her eyes. "Letty Wills was a conscientious and levelheaded woman: a responsible member of your team. Edwina was always a risk taker and a bit of a show-off . . . and a—" Vera cleared her throat and he glanced at me. "Letty Wills was the most rational and practical person at Didcote. There was something wrong with that ruddy plane: I hate those damned Walrus! What was it doing at Supermarine— in for repairs *again* is my bet!"

Vera's face was still set in a rigid mockery of composure. "Of course I haven't ruled out engine problems, Basil. But we won't know a thing until the ATA Accident Committee have done their job. And just for the record"—another glance at me, but I pretended not to see it—"Edwina might have been a bit reckless in her personal life, but I never saw her take a risk when she was flying. Ever. She was about to demonstrate an Immelmann turn, for God's sake, hardly what we would call risky." She lost her calm for a moment to frustration and despair. "So, please, will you not call her reckless? I find it . . . painful when you say things like that."

An exclamation from Sir Basil as he threw up his hand in disagreement. Good-looking, rich, and successful men, I realized, are far too adored and respected by the world. It is hard for them to deal with little things like disagreement, or failure. "Oh, come off it, Vera. She was a bloody fool, and she has been behaving badly and irresponsibly ever since the Luftwaffe attack. You should have grounded her. I told you so at the time."

They fell silent. Vera gave the man in front of her a long, hard look, and he glanced away, perhaps embarrassed for criticizing a young woman who was not there to stick up for herself.

"We don't usually have so many fatalities at Didcote," Vera explained to me as I stood there, still holding Bess in my arms.

"I had no idea that ferrying aircraft was so dangerous," I said.

"It's not . . . usually." She was instantly defensive.

"Yes, it is, of course it is! We lose one in ten," Sir Basil said, despite Vera's frown. "We calculate about one in ten pilots don't make it in the course of a year." He waved his right hand in a circular motion as if to summon all the reasons. "The weather can turn on you in a split bloody second. Airfields don't get their barrage balloons down in time for you to land." He snorted down his nose. "Even our own antiaircraft artillerymen aren't always sharp enough to tell the difference between a Spitfire and a Messerschmitt flying overhead." He looked at Vera as he said the last phrase with emphasis.

"What are *they* calling Edwina's incident?" I asked, wondering who the "they" were. Senior officers at HQ White Waltham? Commander Vera Abercrombie?

"Edwina's plane was in perfect order before she flew it. Until proved otherwise, she had an accident or it was pilot error." Vera quoted another authority. Clearly a decision had been reached. "Of course, we have to wait for the ATA Accident Committee to confirm their findings. And that is confidential information, Miss Redfern, not to be mentioned outside this office."

This morning it was "Poppy"; now it's "Miss Redfern." They're closing ranks, Ilona observed.

"And what about Letty?" I asked. "Was that pilot error too?"

"The Walrus was not a new plane. It had been damaged in combat and repaired at the factory. The single engine is above the cockpit, and Mackenzie said it was smashed to pieces on impact. We might never know why it crashed." She crossed to the map on the wall again and retraced Letty's last flight. "Letty was a seasoned pilot. She had a Class Five license—the only one here at Didcote," she said to the map. "She was thorough and careful."

Sir Basil stopped his pacing up and down Vera's office in front of the large window that looked out on the airstrip. "I don't like the farmer's description, that the plane's flight was erratic. I don't like that at all. What did he say? 'As drunk as a lord'? He saw the wrong accident; he should have been here yesterday!" His voice rose in derision. Vera barely threw him a glance. *She's much better at dealing with bad news than he is,* said Ilona. *He's behaving like a spoiled four-year-old.*

"That wasn't Letty's problem," she said under her breath. "Now, if you will both excuse me, I must contact Charlie at White Waltham, and I'm not looking forward to it."

I could only imagine that ATA headquarters would have a lot to say about a second dead pilot and two smashed-up planes. I glanced at Sir Basil as we left Vera to the privacy of her conversation. His cheeks were still red, and his usually immaculate silver hair was sticking up at the back. He looked like a disgruntled old man.

I WALKED OUT into the damp of a gloomy day. The wind had brought the rain inland and had then dropped. I dislike days when the sky is low and oppressive—it shuts in the air like a tin lid—but it was better than being in the pent-up atmosphere of the ATA mess.

I stood and watched Bessie sniffing around in a ditch. "There is something awfully wrong going on here," I said. At the sound of my voice she looked up at me, her long ears cocked to interpret my tone: was there food in the offing? A walk? When I sighed and scuffed my toe in the gravel of the path, she continued rooting about in the lank grass.

Ilona, however, didn't let me down. *You can say that again, darling. Two girls who knew their jobs inside out going down like that is too much of a coincidence.* I could almost see her standing beside me with her arms folded and her fine, pale forehead wrinkled in disbelief. I imagine that Ilona has a flawless complexion and fair hair: fine and glossy, arranged in a thick roll at the back of her head, because she's a fashionable girl. Unlike me, she is petite and always looks perfectly turned out in a beautifully cut suit that emphasizes her curves and her stunning legs. She has large, intelligent green eyes and a face that expresses every thought. She comes from a good family, without being posh or affected, and she is what we would call a thoroughly modern young woman. In her clear voice she shared her thoughts: *One pilot crashes doing a stunt she has done since she was a teenager, and the other wallops her plane into a bridge after months of flying Lancaster bombers all over the country.*

I calculated the time of this morning's events. Breakfast had started at seven. At eight the Attagirls were walking to their air taxis and somewhere between half past eight and eight forty-five they had been airborne. How long did it take to fly to the Supermarine factory, check in at the flight office, and walk to their assigned planes for takeoff to their destinations? And how long did it take to fly from Supermarine at Eastleigh to Elton, where Letty had crashed her plane? And what the hell was a Supermarine Walrus, anyway? Did it look like a fighter or a bomber?

I looked at my watch. It was eleven. Vera had been told twenty minutes ago that Letty had crashed the plane half an hour before that. Fifty minutes. I did the arithmetic on my fingers: Letty must have crashed her plane at ten minutes after ten. There were so many questions batting around in my head that I had no answer for because I hadn't a clue how long it took to fly a plane anywhere. How fast did planes go? Faster than trains? If she had been following the railway line, perhaps I could look up a train timetable and get some idea of airspeed and distance. "Damn," I said in my frustration, finally attracting Bess's attention.

I remembered Edwina's scornful observations about Crown Films sending a scriptwriter who didn't know anything about planes. Now would be my chance to learn. And if I was going to write my next novel with Ilona in the cockpit of a Spitfire, I had better start paying attention to the technicalities of flying. I needed the advice of an expert on why a pilot would or could crash her plane into a bridge. Had she run out of petrol? As this query came into my head I knew I needed help. Well done! I said to myself as I realized I had sent off the only person I trusted to help me.

I did more calculations, made easier because they involved the speed that Griff usually travels in his car. Surely he had arrived at Reaches by now? There was a telephone box a hundred yards down the road from the entrance to Didcote Airfield. "Come on, Bessie." I called her away from whatever awful thing she was sniffing at under a pile of dead leaves with such joy. "Walkies."

IF GRIFF WERE willing to return to Didcote, perhaps I could dream up a reason to stay here for the rest of the weekend? Would my need to rewrite the script be enough of an excuse? I would have to pay for my room at the inn. Miss Murgatroyd of Crown Films had made it quite clear when she had issued my travel vouchers for second-class train tickets that I was supremely fortunate not to be traveling in third and that I was responsible for footing the bill for all my meals during my visit to Hampshire.

As I strode up the drive and into the lane, Bess brought me a stick and I swung back my arm to pitch it ahead of us. She watched it sail through the air and land in a wet ditch. I had achieved perhaps twelve feet. She turned her head and looked at me in a pitying sort of way before she waded in and, picking it up delicately with her teeth, shredded it to pieces.

"You are supposed to bring it back!" I said to her. She wagged her little bob of a tail and brought me a twig, dropping it at my feet. "I'm not that delicate," I said. "He's much better at throwing, isn't he?" If she had nodded I wouldn't have been a bit surprised.

I stood outside the phone box with an open purse and quickly calculated the cost of two more nights at the inn and my meals for the next two days. I could just about do it if I cadged meals at the mess, which left me five bob for emergencies or for the expensive telephone call to Griff at Reaches. This is an emergency, I told myself.

The telephone box smelled of stale cigarette smoke and wet dog after Bess squeezed in with me. I emptied out the small change in my purse next to the half-full ashtray. Then, taking a deep breath, I picked up the telephone receiver, dialed the operator, and placed a trunk call to the officers' mess at Reaches American Army Air Force Base, Little Buffenden.

"Little Buffenden in Devonshire or Buckinghamshire?"

There were two? "The one in Bucks, thank you."

"That will be tew shillings and sixpence, please." A small fortune: there would be no sherry for me tonight. "When you hear the pips, please put the correct change in slot A."

Why, I wondered as I waited, did all telephone operators and train schedule announcers always have such terribly posh accents? The pips sounded and I counted change into the coin slot.

I prayed as I waited that Griff had driven back to Reaches and not stopped off somewhere for lunch with someone fascinating.

"Good morning, Reaches officers' mess."

I hastily pressed button A and heard the coins clatter into the box. "Hullo? Hullo, this is Miss Redfern, I want to speak to Captain O'Neal, please. Is he there?"

"Just one moment, ma'am, I'll go check." After what seemed like an eternity, Griff finally came to phone.

"Poppy?"

"Hullo, Griff, I'm in a phone box, so I don't have much time. I am afraid that something *is* terribly wrong here. Letty Wills crashed her plane this morning and was killed outright."

Silence.

"Hullo, hullo, are you still there?" I only had half a crown left!

"Yes. I was just thinking. Did she crash at Didcote?"

"No, she was ferrying a Walrus from the Supermarine factory in Eastleigh and crashed northeast of there at a place called Elton. She flew her plane into a railway bridge. The accident was seen by a farmer. He reported it to his local Home Guard, and they contacted Vera about an hour ago."

Another long silence. The operator's voice came on the line:

"Caller, thet will be tew shillings and sixpence, please, for anothah faive minutes." I dropped the rest of my silver into the coin box.

"Griff, I'm running out of change. Can you come back and spend the weekend here? I need help understanding how planes can be made to crash, or pilots made to err. And most of all how long it takes to fly from one place to another, depending on airspeed."

His response was immediate. "I thought you'd never ask. I'll be there by two o'clock and meet you at the inn. Can you reserve a room for me?"

"Yes, of course. Thank you so much, Griff!"

"Since you have time, why don't you wander over to that large hangar by the airstrip and have a chat with one of the maintenance guys there? I talked to our ground crew and they told me some pretty interesting stuff about early Spitfires. Try and find out a bit more about the one Edwina flew. It was an early mark, so they might have had to fit a Shilling orifice to it. If that's the case, then all anyone had to do was remove the orifice and the plane would stall when Edwina put the plane into a steep dive."

An orifice? What on earth was he talking about? "A what? What did you say it might have been fitted with?"

"An orifice." There was a second of silence and I could have sworn I heard him chuckle. "On second thought, perhaps don't go and talk to them; it might seem a bit odd your knowing about that."

The operator's voice came on the line again. "Thet will be anothah tew shillings and sixpence, caller."

"Griff, I have to go. I've no more change. I'll see you at two!" I said and was answered by a dial tone.

I put the phone down and breathed a sigh of relief. I could write up the rest of my script and be done with it by the time Griff arrived. Then we could spend a pleasant weekend of snooping and sleuthing, and *he* could talk to the ground engineer about an orifice.

NINE

I T WAS A RELIEF TO LEAVE THE FUG OF THE TELEPHONE BOX FOR
the sweet, tangy air, no matter how wet it was. Overhead a patch
of sky was clearing and then clouding over again, and the wind
came in salty and strong from the Solent. Early October is the best
time of the year in England if it stays dry.

I was humming as Bess and I set out up the lane toward the inn.
The cloud cleared and shafts of sunlight slanted through the rich
canopy of autumn leaves overhead. I walked quickly, swinging my
arms and breathing in lungfuls of air as if it would exorcise the ugli-
ness of the morning. I felt the tightness in my neck and shoulders
begin to ebb as Bess sprang ahead of me, delighted to be away from
human tension.

Surely, no one from ATA Didcote could possibly have sabotaged the Walrus's engine at the Supermarine factory? Perhaps
Letty's accident had been an awful coincidence. I hoped I hadn't
called Griff back on a silly whim, just because my fluttering stomach had told me that the details of Letty's crash sounded suspicious
to me.

"I don't know why I'm interfering in something I know nothing about!" I exclaimed one minute. And in the next: "But it is suspicious—isn't it, Bessie? Two pilots lose control of their planes in as many days—that can't be a fluke."

Bess gazed up at me in approval, her bobtail wagging as she trotted beside me, happy that we were on the move together.

We walked under the heavy branch of an apple tree that hung over the lane, and Bess stopped to pick up an overlooked windfall from the grass verge. She ran ahead of me with her neck bowed, shaking her head from side to side. When she was sure the apple was quite dead, she dropped it and started to chew it apart. A second later she cried out, and as I ran forward she was pawing her mouth and moaning in distress.

"Poor darling, you just got stung, didn't you?" I picked her up and examined her mouth. Her lip on the right side was swelling and I could see the black tip of a bee's stinger on its pink inside. "I'm going to pull it out, Bessie, so hold still." I laid her back in my arms with her short legs stuck up in the air and her eyes showing white around the edges in fear and pain. "I'll be quick, Bessie, don't be scared." I gently pulled out the little barb and kissed her nose. "You have to stop eating fallen apples, girlie." Her muzzle on the right side was still swelling. "When we get to the inn we'll put some baking soda on it. That will help."

I put her down, and she trudged along beside me with her ears down like a sad donkey, stopping every so often to balance on three legs and paw at her mouth with her right front. She would only make her lip worse if she carried on like this. I picked her up and, cradling her in my arms, walked on.

"You are such a dreadful little scavenger," I said to her as I kissed her nose again. "You have to stop stealing food and eating windfalls." I looked down into her trusting brown eyes staring up at me, and I couldn't help but laugh at her fat lip.

Bess may be a short-legged girl, but she has a burly body and I was gasping for breath as we arrived in the inn's kitchen. "My dog has been stung on her lip," I said, leaning up against the doorframe of the kitchen. "Do you have any baking . . . ?"

"Oh, dearie me. Now, what was it, did you see? A bee or a wasp? Different remedies for different insects. I always use . . ." The cook was the conversational type.

"I pulled out the stinger."

"Bee, then. Best thing for beestings is baking soda. Here." She handed me a box. "Mix a spoonful up into a thick paste."

As I mixed baking soda and water together, covered Bess's wound, and held her muzzle closed so she couldn't lick it off, the cook watched me closely, her hands on her hips and her head on one side.

"Lor', what a puffed-up lip." She threw back her head and laughed the smoky laugh of a nicotine addict. "By rights I shouldn't have a dog in my kitchen." She took a greasy gray dishcloth from the sink and wiped down the area I had used to mix up Bess's baking soda. "What's her name?" I told her as I put Bess down and she walked over to say hullo.

"Nice little mutt, in't she?" She bent over and made cooing noises as Bess snuffled around on the floor for dropped food. "How do you keep your dog going what with all this food rationing?" she asked. "Most people had their dogs put down at the beginning of the war. Sad, really, when you think that your little dog is getting on quite well with all the shortages."

I didn't want to talk about the horrors of that hideous month at the beginning of what we called the Phony War, when thousands of families all over England voluntarily stood in line at their local veterinarians to have their dogs put to sleep. That was how I had found

Bessie, a shivering and terrified puppy hiding in a ditch. How she got there I had no idea; I just knew that if she was found she would be euthanized. I had carried her home under my trench coat and persuaded my grandparents that she would be easy to keep.

"I share my rations with her," I explained. "She has practically become a vegetarian, except for the occasional elderly rabbit she manages to catch."

She laughed at that. "A vegetarian! Pull the other one, why don't you? You're talking about a *dog*, my girl. Ah well, I suppose they are natural scavengers, aren't they? And we all have to live." She tossed Bess a slice of raw potato to test her vegetarianism.

Bess snapped it down and looked up for more.

"Well, I'll be blowed, would you look at that?" She picked up another chip of potato.

"Perhaps if you have the end of a raw carrot?" I suggested. "She loves carrot."

"If she'll eat raw root vegetables, I am sure she wouldn't say no to a nice dead rat," the cook cautioned me. "My advice to you is better keep your eye on that nice little dog of yours. If she eats a dead rat it will be the end of her."

My heart stood quite still for a second before it started to thump in my chest.

"A dead rat . . . what could be the harm . . . ?" I could barely get the words out. In my mind I saw Bess dragging a large rat out from behind a dustbin.

She picked up an old kitchen knife and began to peel potatoes. "When did you last see a rat in daylight unless it was a goner? This is an old building, of course we have rats, and not just them either: mice, rats, squirrels. Lord, what a battle we have with them."

"How do you control them?"

"Mr. Evans baits traps with poison."

I pulled Bess out from under the sink. "Does it work quickly? I mean, how soon after the rat eats the bait does it die?"

She snorted in derision at the thought. "I don't have time to go out there and check the bodies of dead vermin. I just know they die." She looked at me as if I were a fool and then down at Bess.

"If I were you . . ." She put her knife down and gave me a straight look: the old and wise informing the young and stupid. But I had already clipped Bess's lead on her and was dragging her reluctant body out of the kitchen.

THE INNKEEPER'S WIFE, Mrs. Evans, met me in what she called Reception and what was in fact the area at the bottom of the stairs, where the telephone kiosk was situated.

"Oh, there you are, Miss Redfern. Two messages for you. Mr. Carrington from Crown Films has called twice in the last hour. He said it was an emergency." Puffed up with the importance of having a film unit staying at her inn, Mrs. Evans was almost out of breath to give me my most-urgent messages.

My preoccupied brain focused. "Keith?"

"That's right. He asks you to please telephone him right away. Said it was *most* urgent. Something about a lost can of film?"

I surrendered a pound note for change for my call, squeezed myself into the very narrow telephone kiosk, and put through a call to Crown Films. As I waited to be put through, I kept a careful eye on Bess through the glass of the box as she sniffed around the skirting boards and corners of the hall. Did they leave baited traps inside the inn too? I must ask Mrs. Evans.

The operator came back on the line. "Mr. Carrington is not in the editing room, Miss Redfern. He is in a meeting with Mr. Huntley."

Mrs. Evans was waiting for me when I came out of the kiosk. "Mr. Carrington was very perturbed when he rang," she told me. "He asked me to go and look in his room for him. Which I did. There was no can of film there, or any of his or Mr. Huntley's personal effects. The maid is scrupulous about checking."

She followed me up the stairs and unlocked the third door on the right, and we stood together on the threshold of Keith's room. "He shared with Mr. Huntley," Mrs. Evans explained. It didn't take a moment to see that Keith's can of film wasn't in this room. All surfaces were bare, all drawers empty. The wardrobe yielded some pink-satin-covered hangers swinging on their rail, and a mothball rolled across its wooden bottom when we pulled open the door.

"Bedside tables," I said as I pulled both drawers open. I got down and looked under the bed. No dust balls, no rattraps, and no cans of film. I turned to Mrs. Evans. "Where else could he have left it, do you think?"

She shook her head; her face crumpled in concern. "Perhaps the bathroom? They used the bathroom across the corridor for developing."

"That's probably where it is!"

But the large bathroom was empty, except for the smell of chemicals and the heavy blackout curtains still tightly sealing the windows.

We started toward the stairs and made a thorough search of the bar, the lounge, and the parlor. The dining room stood solemnly empty, its rows of cloth-covered tables set with cutlery and glasses.

"He probably left it in the van," I said, feeling dusty and disheveled.

"The trouble with most men"—Mrs. Evans spoke from decades of married life with Mr. Evans—"is they never look for anything properly. They just open a drawer and glance in it and then accuse you of losing their collar studs." Her lecture on the impracticalities of men was interrupted by a flash of gleaming red outside the window and the sound of a car pulling up into the gravel of the inn's drive. Griff had arrived.

"SO, YOU SEE, it might have been rat poison. Someone could have put it in their food." Aware that I was gabbling, I took a breath and slowed down. "The cook told me that they use it at the inn to keep down the vermin. Mr. Evans baits traps all the time." Griff nodded, his face solemn as he took a long swallow of beer. We had walked down to the pub on his arrival, because at least they had something other than soup or pie to offer us, and the image of the cook's greasy dishcloth was still fresh in my mind.

"But why rat poison?" He put down his fork and finished his beer. "That's better. You know for a country that makes such incredibly good beer, you would think they would be a bit more creative with their food . . . Sorry, I interrupted you. You were telling me about why someone would use rat poison."

"It's easy to get hold of, for one thing."

"Do you know what's in it?"

I shrugged. I had no idea.

"Arsenic, perhaps? Strychnine?" he pursued. "If Edwina had died from either of those it would have been evident when we pulled her from the plane."

"What do you mean?"

"I believe death from strychnine or arsenic is pretty . . . involved and painful. She would have been . . . a mess."

I shuddered. "Do you mean she would have vomited?"

"At the very least."

Edwina had looked like a rag doll when they lifted her out of the cockpit of her Spitfire. I saw her limp body as she lay in Griff's arms. Her face was composed; there were no signs of an excruciating death on her peaceful features. I thought of Flaubert's description of Madame Bovary dying in agony from taking arsenic. Edwina's hair was not dark and stringy with sweat, neither were her limbs curled up tightly in the death agony of my imagination. And since both strychnine and arsenic apparently racked the digestive organs, there was no bloody vomit all over her flying suit.

"To be frank, Poppy, I don't know a thing about strong poisons: how long they take to work, what they do to you, or how much it takes to kill a healthy woman. But I do know about aircraft. We could walk over to the airfield and talk to Mac Wilson, the mechanic in charge at Didcote. Let's rule out sabotage before we start to dabble in poison." He was already on his feet. "I need a nice brisk walk along the river."

After a lunch of beer and a shepherd's pie, Griff was, in his own parlance, full of beans. I glanced up at his bright hazel eyes, his laughing mouth, and that sweetness of expression he had when he was pleased with himself. All signs of his earlier fatigue had gone, and he was his usual chipper self. I caught his mood and I felt my earlier gloom beginning to lift. "Perfect day," he said, as if we had not discussed murders by poison over lunch and Letty Wills's body was not lying in a morgue somewhere near Elton. "Let's go and do some sleuthing."

TEN

W HAT I LOVE MOST ABOUT YOUR PICTURESQUE ENGLISH villages is how convenient they are. And they all follow a pattern, have you noticed? There is always a pub on the green so people can sit outside and watch cricket in the summer. And sure enough, there is the church on the green's further side, a respectable distance from the pub, with its comfortably dilapidated old vicarage close by. And then of course there is the village high street. Ever notice how well organized they are?" Griff stopped and waved an appreciative arm up and down Didcote's admittedly admirable main thoroughfare.

"Here is the butcher: no meat, of course, but that's not his fault; then right next to that . . . ah yes, here it is, the greengrocer's as you call them. He's certainly cornered the market on cabbage, carrots, and potatoes. A few apples . . ." We walked past both shops. "Next there will be a baker . . . and sure enough."

I laughed. "Really? This looks like an ironmonger to me."

"Ironmonger? Sometimes I think I am living in medieval England."

"What do you call this sort of shop in America?"

"A hardware store."

I didn't say how much the prosaic and practical name lacked imagination as we stood outside the open door of the shop. I sniffed the wonderful, oily metal smell that we English associate with iron-mongery. "What are you doing?" I asked as Griff walked up the steps.

"Got to get something to control the rats and mice in our mess kitchen."

We walked into the dark, narrow shop. A long, high wooden counter ran down one side of its long and narrow interior; dusty oak floorboards were covered in boxes and baskets full of useful things like washers, bolts, and hinges. From the ceiling hung an odd assortment of the necessary: galvanized tin washtubs, buckets, and watering cans predominated. I squinted up at a price tag and gasped. War had made anything made of metal outrageously expensive and notoriously difficult to find. This place was a handy-man's paradise. An assortment of cardboard boxes was stacked behind the counter, with labels proclaiming the length and diameter of the nails and screws they contained.

And before his horde of metal treasure stood a stooped elderly man wrapped in a heavy brown cloth apron. He put both hands on the counter and glared at us as Griff slowly turned the handle of an old iron clothes mangle.

"Sir?" he said and frowned at the mangle.

Griff reluctantly stopped watching the two wooden rollers spin tightly against each other. "Hullo there, do you sell rat poison?"

A nod.

"What's it made with?"

The man folded his arms and his brows came down. "Strych-nine," he said as if he was talking to the terminally stupid.

"How quickly does it work, d'you think?"

The shopkeeper evidently didn't like this question because he used more than one word in his answer. "What you want to know that for, ay?"

"I want to know how effective you think it is. Is it more effective than, say, arsenic?"

"Where are you from?"

"The States."

"We don't use arsenic in rat poison over here, not anymore." He looked us over, committing our features to memory, so that when he called the local police constable, he would know exactly how to describe our murderous faces. "We make it very difficult for the public to get its hands on arsenic in this country, my lad, or cyanide, before you ask."

If Griff objected to being called "my lad," he didn't show it. But it was clear that he intended to get an answer to his question. He put an elbow on the countertop and leaned in.

"That's interesting." He pushed back his cap with a forefinger and gazed into the sour face of the ironmonger. "You see, we use arsenic to kill rats on my dad's farm. Never heard of strychnine before. But here's my problem—perhaps you can help me—there are lots of old barns and run-down huts on our airfield here, simply teeming with vermin. I need something that acts fast and does the job properly."

Was he talking about my family's house—pristine, gracious, and beautiful Reaches before it had been turned into an officers' mess for the American airfield? I asked myself. What a blasted cheek!

The old man unbent a little and became almost garrulous. "Dangerous poison is arsenic. Illegal in this country. We use strychnine; it'll do the job all right, and fast. How much of it do you need?" He reached under the counter and produced a large round tin; it had a label with a black skull and crossbones on it. "That'll be five shilling."

"How fast does it kill them: five minutes, ten, longer?"

A glower. "They start dropping at about ten minutes, less if they are smaller. Takes a bit longer than that for 'em to die. Want this or not?"

I felt a nervous giggle begin in my throat as I waited for Griff to ask if you could fly a plane after you "dropped," and before you died would you have lost control of it?

"No, thank you, not now. I'll tell our sergeant to get some." He saluted the old man.

The cook at the inn's words came back to me. "If a dog was to eat a rat that had been poisoned by strychnine, would it kill the dog?" I asked the ironmonger.

He looked over at Bess, who was sitting by the door, patiently waiting for us to leave a place that held no interest for her, not even a polite hello or a pat on the head. "Wouldn't give much for its chances, and before you ask, I don't know how long it would take for it to die."

We thanked him profusely for his courtesy and stepped out into the street.

"I don't think they could have been poisoned with rat poison: Edwina was flying for only a few minutes before she lost control of her plane. She flew a good two hours or so after lunch, didn't she? If her Spam sandwich had been poisoned, she would have been dead, or at least showing serious symptoms, long before that. Did you see her eat or drink anything, say, minutes before she flew?"

I cast my mind back to that pleasant interlude when we had taken a break from filming for lunch. "She ate a lot of sandwiches, someone made a joke about it, and it was a good two hours later that she flew." I tried to remember what Edwina had been doing after she had finished her lunch. All I could recall was her sulky silence as she stood on the edge of things.

But I had questions of my own as we turned into the lane that led to Didcote Airfield, and they were about Letty's crash. "I know I asked you this already, but how long would it take to fly from Didcote to the Supermarine factory at Eastleigh?"

"What sort of plane?"

"I don't know the name of the plane; it's the one they call the air taxi. They took off at somewhere between half past eight and a quarter to nine."

"They use the Anson as their taxi. Let's see, now. An Anson from Didcote to Eastleigh. Short jaunt: about twenty minutes on a clear day from takeoff to landing." We were nearly at the airfield, so I stopped and let Bess off her lead. She bounded into the field and rolled in a patch of sunlit grass.

"Then she would have to check in at Supermarine, do her paperwork, and get to her Walrus. How long would that take?"

He squinted up at the sky. "Say thirty minutes to cover all the messing about that probably goes on with paperwork."

"Good. Then how long to fly from Eastleigh to Elton?"

"Where's Elton?"

I remembered the map. "Elton's about five miles south of Winchester. She might have been following the railway line from Eastleigh. About forty to fifty miles."

"The Walrus is heavy and slow, so say twenty minutes in the air."

"She crashed at about ten minutes after ten o'clock. So, calculate that back in hours and minutes."

He laughed. "Math is a problem for you, is it?"

I sighed.

"Okay. That would be eight thirty. Why?"

"If she was poisoned . . . if her breakfast was poisoned, it would have to be slow-acting. But she might have had to wait at Supermarine, and perhaps she was poisoned there, before she took off in the Walrus."

I saw the mess trestle table laden with empty plates, and Zofia pushing her full plate away. Had Zofia pushed her plate toward Letty, or just straight out in front of her? I closed my eyes and tried to recapture that moment, but all I saw was Letty picking up a fork and starting in on a second plate of food.

"Oh, good grief." I stopped him mid-stride. "Oh, for heaven's sake, Griff. Letty ate Zofia's breakfast."

He stood on the side of the road, his face serious as he considered.

"But the timing is off," he said. "I hate to say it but it's doubtful that it was rat poison, Poppy. It was hours before either of them crashed their planes after they had eaten something."

"But we don't know if they had a flask of coffee or tea with them. Sometimes they carry their own thermos." I racked my memory. Was Letty carrying a thermos when she boarded the Anson? She had certainly forgotten her compass. Had she forgotten her thermos too? And Edwina? Had she been drinking coffee before she sauntered over to her plane?

I wasn't prepared to give up on poison just yet.

"We can look at the film!" I shouted. "It will be on film. Edwina walking to her plane with her parachute over her shoulder yesterday. And this morning Letty stood and posed for us in the door to the Anson. Keith has all of it on film. If they were carrying a thermos of coffee, we would see it on the film." But my triumph was doomed. It slid, with the autumn sun, behind a heavy cloud, and a sharp, cold wind blew in from the river. "Blast and damn," I said as I remembered Mrs. Evans standing at the bottom of her stairs looking regretful about the missing film. "Damn and blast and damn."

Griff and Bess stood in front of me waiting to be of use. "There's a phone box just along here. How much change do you have? I must try and get hold of Keith."

He pulled some coins out of his trouser pocket. "Why is it that beautiful women only want to know how much money I have?" he asked as he offered me a pile of silver on the flat of his palm.

"Two, two shilling pieces; four sixpences; and a couple of half crowns," I counted. "Eleven bob. That's plenty—thank you!"

"Aha, I see your arithmetic is pretty sharp when it comes to money!" He tipped the coins into my palm. "No, no, you're most welcome! And here is our phone booth."

This time Keith was easy to find. "Did you check? It's a small can, ten inches in diameter, if that. It had a five written on the lid," were the first words out of his mouth.

"I checked everywhere: your room, the parlor, the lounge. It's not at the inn."

He used a word that well-brought-up boys don't use in front of nice girls. Then he groaned and asked me if I was quite sure.

"Yes, I am quite sure." I crossed my fingers. "What was on it?"

Another whimper of despair. "Oh Gawd, I'm really in the soup with Huntley now. It was the stuff I shot of the Attas, you know, when we were having lunch and relaxing? Well, it's gone, and don't ask me if it's in the van. I've searched it from one end to the other. It's gone."

"You mean the film you made of us all eating lunch?" I crossed my fingers, praying I had misheard.

"I was using up leftover film from an earlier shoot," he said. "I went out, earlier that morning, to set up the camera and shot the planes on the airstrip, just to get my eye in. When we broke for lunch I popped the last feet back into the camera and shot the girls relaxing and eating lunch. It was really good—they all looked so natural and at ease." His wretched tone told me that Huntley had already given him an earful.

If anyone had tinkered with Edwina's sandwiches or her coffee, it might have been captured on that piece of film. I swallowed down annoyance and frustration. Keith had already been given a going-over by Huntley; he didn't need me to add my irritation.

"Where are you now?" I asked.

"Editing room."

"Would you look at some other film for me? The bit with Edwina walking to her plane? Can you tell me what she is carrying, other than her chute?"

"I'm sitting here with the film editor now, Poppy, looking at footage of Edwina's crash. It's like watching a war movie. Hold on a mo'." And to the editor: "Rewind back to the beginning." A pause as I fed the coin box. "No, Edwina only had her chute; she was bare-headed, no helmet. No thermos, no bag, nuffink."

The afternoon darkened and a light rain pattered on the glass of the phone booth.

"Okay, thanks. Would you look at the film you shot this morning of the Attagirls leaving in their air taxis and tell me what Letty is carrying?"

"Have to find it. Why don't you ring me back in ten minutes?"

We waited outside the phone box, taking it in turn to throw sticks for Bess, and then I returned to the call box.

" 'Ello there, Poppy. Nah, nothing. Letty is standing at the top of the ladder with her chute, her map case, and that's all." I could tell he was smiling. "Ha-ha." He was evidently watching the film. "That's good, she's pretending to be a movie star." I realized that he had no idea that sweet-natured, kindhearted Letty had died. I swallowed down my anger at her death and told him about the crash. "She didn't make it," I ended, my throat aching with the effort of keeping the tears that had filled my eyes out of my voice.

"Struth, what are you saying? She's dead? Letty's dead?" Keith turned his head from the mouthpiece, and I heard him relaying the news to Huntley.

"Poppy!" Huntley came on the line. "Another accident? What the hell is going on there? Was it at the airfield?"

I gave him the few details I had. There was a stunned silence. "Oh God, poor woman. What a tragedy." I heard him give directions to Keith and the film editor. "Look, we have to come back. There's not enough footage of the Spit, just Edwina walking to the plane, a bit of taxiing, takeoff, she waggles her wings and does a victory roll." He lowered his voice. "And we can't even use that, Fanny's been told we have to turn it over to the ATA Accident Committee. He's going to get in touch with Commander Abercrombie and tell her that we have to completely reshoot the Spitfire sequence."

Vera wasn't going to like that much. "I hope Didcote cooperates," I said.

"Oh, they have to." Huntley was as crisp as lettuce. "Ministry of Information carries a lot of clout."

"Do you know when you'll be back?"

"I'll give you a ring at the inn when there's been a decision."

"When did Keith last see the missing can of film?" I asked.

The pips sounded. "It must have fallen out of the van." He muttered something rude about youthful neglect. "I saw him put it in the van when we set off to film the Attagirls going to work this morning. You might want to look around the drive, just in case."

"When you left the van in the drive, was it locked?" I asked, knowing the answer. Keith was an exemplary cameraman but slack about things like punctuality and other little acts of self-discipline.

"You would think so, wouldn't you, considering all our hard work was in there?" An expression of disgust. "I hope this damn film isn't doomed . . . Look, I've got to go. Ring you later." And he was gone.

I went outside to Griff and Bess. They were taking a break from stick work and admiring the view together, Griff with a cigarette in his hand and Bess with half a shredded branch in her mouth.

"Neither of them was carrying anything other than their parachutes. Letty had a map case. She paused at the top of the Anson's steps in a lighthearted movie-star moment." My eyes swam with tears again.

He nodded and ground out the half-finished cigarette under his heel.

"Let's go and talk to this mechanic fella," he said.

"But something really strange has happened." I told him about Keith's missing can of film. "You remember he shot film of us eating lunch? Everyone was having fun, relaxing. It was like a little holiday: a break from work, from war. Keith says that the can with that bit is missing. Huntley last saw it in the van this morning, when they came over to Didcote to get some footage of the Attagirls leaving for work in the Anson."

Griff shook his head. "Not at the inn?"

"Keith called Mrs. Evans earlier, and we both searched Huntley and Keith's room and downstairs. I am wondering if someone took it."

I had his complete attention. "Took it when the van was at the airfield this morning?"

I tried to remember the sequence of events that morning when Keith and Huntley had arrived and parked their van in the drive.

"There was a bit of to-ing and fro-ing." I closed my eyes. "Vera had already handed out the delivery assignments for the day. Keith and Huntley arrived and started to set up their equipment by the airstrip. They came in and asked about coffee, but Vera wanted to get everyone going. So, they went back to their setup to wait for us. The van was parked outside the mess on the edge of the airstrip. Keith admitted to Huntley that it wasn't locked."

Griff did his well-what-d'ya-know whistle.

I concentrated hard on this morning's scene, as if I were looking down the lens of a camera. "I think June and Annie were all suited up and ready to go. But Letty took ages to find her stuff. I can't re-member where Zofia was. Oh yes, she and Grable went to the Met Office to check on the weather in the southeast." I frowned with the effort of remembering each separate event in the right order. "Vera was getting annoyed that Letty was taking so long because the An-sons had just landed."

"In what way taking so long?"

"I think she was just tired. Anyway, Vera chivvied us out of the mess."

Griff folded his arms and stared at his shoes. "Did anyone go near the van, other than Keith or Huntley? Can you remember?" he asked, his eyes still down as he slowly tapped the toe of his shoe.

"No, I can't!" I screwed up my eyes tight, but I couldn't see the van at all.

"Don't try and make yourself recollect. If one of those women went near the van, it might come back to you. Memory is strange that way."

"But it's suspicious, isn't it? That the can with the piece of film of us *eating lunch* completely disappeared?" I was practically rub-bing my hands.

"Yes." He smiled at my enthusiasm. "I would say it's what you mystery writers call a significant clue!"

ELEVEN

────────

S IT WICKED, I WONDERED TO MYSELF, TO BE SO DAMNED pleased if what we first thought was an unfortunate accident might now have become a premeditated murder?

No, dear, said Ilona, *you are merely discovering the truth. And a horrid truth it is too.*

Someone had wanted Keith's piece of film badly enough, they had risked taking it from a truck parked in plain view. And the only reason that could be was that he had recorded something incriminating. My mind went back to poison; I simply couldn't help it.

"An autopsy would show poison in Edwina's system. I am quite sure about that," I said, determined to finish what I thought was a clever method to murder by aircraft.

Griff stared at me, rather like the way the ironmonger had gawped at him earlier. "An autopsy of a civilian volunteer pilot in wartime who had a bit of a drinking problem? I would love to hear how you'd word that request to Commander Abercrombie, who has just been given a big kick up the keister by her senior officer at White Waltham."

My face must have expressed the annoyance I felt, because he held up his hand. "No, no, I know you are onto something that points to murder, but I think a request for an autopsy should wait until we have discovered more—and you are in a perfect position to do so."

It was the old invitation for me to scout around for clues!

I hate to say this, ducky, but I think the blighter's right. It's still early days for things like autopsies: the ATA Accident Committee hasn't done their investigation yet. Ilona rarely gives poor advice on investigative procedure.

"Let's go and talk to Mac Wilson, and *you* can ask all the questions about Spitfires and their orifices to your heart's content. I'm not saying a word."

GRIFF COCKED HIS head in the direction we were walking: toward the airplane hangar where Mac Wilson, the ground engineer, and his crew worked on the planes used for training and taxi service at Didcote.

"Looks like we aren't the only ones interested in talking to Mac." We stopped in a gap in the hedge and watched Vera Abercrombie come out of the hangar with Mac and stand with him, their heads together in deep consultation. "Not sure this is the time we should barge in. What shall we do?"

I crouched down and pulled Bess into the constraint of my arms; it was not the time for corgis to barge in either.

"We could walk over to Edwina's Spitfire, and you can have a look at it before we talk to Mac Wilson. Can you tell if that thing you mentioned is in place?" He roared with laughter as we ducked through the hedge and walked on down the lane toward the field where Edwina's plane had crashed.

"You won't say it, will you?"

"I am not sure I heard you right in the first place."

"You did, which is why you are at your most reticent. When I tell you what it is, I want you to remember that this is not my name for a very useful piece of engineering, but the term used by the cruder members of your RAF."

We had come to the field where the Spitfire was still slumped at its ungainly angle. It looked ugly and forlorn lying there in a patch of trampled-down weeds.

"What happens to them, the wrecked planes?"

He stood with his arms folded and gazed across the tilled field. "If they can salvage the metal and other reusable parts, they turn them into other planes." I noticed that he didn't say, if there is anything left of them. I thought of all the planes, both theirs and ours, that came down in the English Channel and were now lying on its stony seafloor, and my arms prickled. Why did I think it would be more terrifying to plunge into the murk of those silent depths, than crash into a field?

We walked around the tilted body.

"Let me tell you all about the wonderful Miss Tilly Shilling and her clever invention that saved the Spitfire and the Hurricane from becoming death traps, even though they were invaluable in the RAF winning the Battle of Britain." He paused as if seeking the right words to his explanation. "The early versions of the Rolls-Royce Merlin engine, the engine used in the first Spitfires and Hurricanes, would stall when these planes performed a negative g-force maneuver, such as pitching the nose down hard in a dive or a roll, for instance." His mimicked the action with the flat of his hand, fingers pointed sharply downward. "In these earlier models, when the plane was in a steep nosedive, the fuel was forced to the top of the carburetor rather than into the engine, causing a decrease in power. If the negative g continued—that is, if the plane continued to dive—the fuel would collect at the top of the carburetor and then drop down into the engine and flood it. The engine would shut down. A serious drawback in combat, as you can imagine. With me so far?"

It seemed pretty straightforward to me. "Yes, I think I am. So, this Miss Shilling came up with something to prevent the problem."

"She most certainly did. She designed a simple device that could be fitted into the carburetor quite easily without taking the aircraft out of service. It was a thimble-shaped flow restrictor with precisely calculated dimensions to allow just enough fuel into the carburetor for the engine to develop maximum power without flooding or depriving it of fuel, causing it to stall."

"How clever of her!"

"Yes, very clever, and it worked perfectly until Rolls-Royce redesigned the Merlin engine. But there are plenty of Spitfires flying today with RAE restrictors."

Once again, I was enthralled by the sheer practical brilliance of women.

"Then why is it called Miss Shilling's orifice? If it was such a clever invention, why did they give it such a disrespectful and vulgar name?"

Because she is a woman, hissed Ilona. *If it had been invented by a man, "they" would have been bowing and scraping in their gratitude.*

Griff took inspiration from the far horizon. "Probably because of the device's shape and the fact that it was designed by a gifted engineer who happened to have the comic-opera name of Tilly Shilling: it is also referred to as Miss Tilly's diaphragm."

I frowned. I knew what an orifice was—I hadn't gone to boarding school just for Latin and Greek—but a diaphragm? I had an embarrassing suspicion that it was an even more common term than orifice, but I wasn't going to ask for clarification, just in case Griff was feeling more expansive than usual. He obviously didn't want to go into details either: he cleared this throat and hurried on. "I often think that pilots make fun of everything, especially danger, because it minimizes a dicey job," was all he said as we approached the Spitfire along the tire tracks made by the ambulance.

"Does that mean Edwina was given a faulty Spitfire to fly?"

"That is a possibility."

This was a much more practical method to murder than poison. "Or do you mean to say that someone could have removed Miss Shilling's device from this plane?" I said as we stood at what had been the propeller end of the wrecked Spitfire. "Can you check it now?"

"Not without taking the engine cowling off, and I'd make a huge mess, which would be spotted immediately by the accident committee inspectors. I just want to see if the engine is damaged, or if there is some sign of tampering with the cowling."

The nose of the Spitfire was resting on the earth of the plowed field in such a humble pose that I felt almost embarrassed that it had to be seen this way. It hadn't taken much for this powerful bird of prey to be reduced to a shorn-off wing and a twisted tail. I tried not to look at the cockpit.

Griff crouched down on the ground and inspected the area around its nose. He ran his hand underneath it. "Here is where the gasoline tank is, one of them, anyway." He patted the engine's tummy in the way you would pet a dog.

"How many rolls and dives did she do before the crash?" I asked.

"A double victory roll and then she started to do the Immelmann turn."

"Then if the RAE restrictor had been removed, why didn't the engine conk out before, when she did her victory rolls?"

He looked up at me. "But the engine did reignite; she pulled out of the dive and everything appeared to be fine. And then she was all over the place again, before she hit the top of that tree, there." He pointed to a lopsided uppermost branch of the elm and to the debris around the plane. "If she had hit the ground in a full dive, there wouldn't have been much left."

He climbed up on the sound wing and put his head into the cockpit.

"What are you looking for?"

"I'm not sure. Everything looks quite normal. Doesn't appear to be a gas leak. I remembered thinking at the time, when we were getting her out of the cockpit, that there wasn't an odor of gasoline or carbon monoxide." He jumped down.

"How do you know about Spitfires, anyway? Do your Mustangs have the same problem?"

"Yes, they did, but our P-51s were built after Merlin had redesigned." He folded his arms and stared at the machine. Then he lifted his right thumb and gently flicked its nail against his chin. "I'd give anything to fly one of these," he said, his admiring gaze traveling the length of the Spitfire's body. "What pilot wouldn't be fascinated by the Spitfire? It's an incredible machine: the design of the body is near genius." He turned to me. "And, like you, I am a naturally curious individual."

"If Edwina's and Letty's planes were sabotaged, could it have been done by an enemy agent?" I asked, hoping to spring a surprise question on him. His reaction was immediate: his head whipped round, and I could tell by his expression that he was trying not to laugh.

"An enemy agent?"

"Yes, so that the delivery of planes would be disrupted. It would be something the Germans would want to do wouldn't it? I mean, you know about things like that, don't you?" He didn't answer me immediately.

"You seem to forget, Poppy, that I am an American and you are referring to RAF planes."

"You mean the Americans wouldn't consider a bit of fraternization with the RAF on issues of national security?" I said. "I thought we were allies. Share and share alike!"

He was still smiling as he answered. "Not me, Poppy, I'm a simple old sky jockey. No fraternizing for me!"

"But you said that the ATA delivered Fortresses to Reaches air base. I heard you! So you do share and share alike when it suits you."

He walked around the plane whistling between his teeth. "And so they do. The ATA deliver all sorts of planes to all their allies in Britain. Did you know that there are American volunteer ATA pilots at White Waltham, and, yes, they are women." He did some more whistling as he looked the plane over. "This is a Spitfire Mark II. Probably saw service in the Battle of Britain." He stroked his hand down the long ellipse of the plane's undamaged wing. "What a lovely thing she is, to be sure. And after she had been fitted with an RAE restrictor she would be as reliable as they come. Fast and maneuverable: a joy to fly." He couldn't hide the wistfulness in his tone as he stood in front of the plane. "What a nose!" he said. "You British and your long, aristocratic noses."

I smiled, but my mind was too busy to join him in rhapsodic praise of perfect machinery. What had someone said yesterday? "A lady in the air and a bitch on the ground"?

"How can we find out if the restrictor was removed?"

He stood back from the plane with his hand caressing a line of rivets on the side of the engine's nose.

He dusted his hand along the line and then lifted his palm and looked at it. He did this a couple of times before he took me by the arm and walked me away from the Spitfire as if she might overhear our conversation. "I can't tell if the engine cover has been tampered with. I just don't know enough about these things. Let's stroll over to Mac Wilson and ask him what he thinks. Perhaps he has an opinion and can enlighten us on little things like cowling covers and restrictors."

"Wouldn't he have already checked the engine?"

"Possibly not, if he thought the crash was due to pilot error."

TWELVE

———

RIGHT OFF THE BAT I DIDN'T TAKE TO MAC WILSON, BUT I HAVE been brought up to believe that little things like looks and appearance should not count in our initial reaction to people.

Wilson watched both of us walk over to his hangar as he stood in its half-open doorway, his hands in his pockets and his head cocked to one side.

He had the pale, papery look of a man who avoids fresh air and sunlight if he can. I imagined that in his off-duty hours he spent most of his time at the Pig and Whistle in Didcote. He had a short snub nose and a pair of enormous light blue eyes. There was something vacant and empty in their expression: they reminded me of a doll I had been given as a birthday present when I was a little girl. A doll I had carefully hid in the back of the toy cupboard after my elderly spinster aunt had left.

"No dogs here," he said as Bess glued her nose to the ground and started to follow it. "You are both trespassing on government land." He had a cigarette stuck in the corner of his mouth and it jiggled up and down when he talked.

I made myself smile, a polite official affair.

"Sergeant Wilson?" I said without extending my hand. "I'm Miss Redfern with the Crown Film Unit, Ministry of Information." I flashed my travel vouchers endorsed with the impressive M of I stamp.

But not quite impressive enough. His disturbing eyes flickered for a moment and then returned to their vacant stare. "And him?" He jerked his head toward Griff. "That looks like a Yank uniform to me. Stand down, if you please, sir," he advised. "I only talk to people here on official British business."

Evidently Griff did please; he retired to a discreet five-foot distance with the offending beast and found a stick to throw for her.

"As you know, we were making a short film about the ATA. We have all the footage we need on our pilots, but as their ground engineer I wanted to ask you a few questions. If you have the time." He evidently did have time, because he was lolling against the corrugated iron wall of the hangar, his hands deep in his pockets, and one of those smarty-pants looks on his face. "Sir Basil had told me that the only planes they kept for training at Didcote were Tiger Moths and an Anson. The aircraft used yesterday were on loan from Hawker, Supermarine, and Avro, is that correct?"

" 'S'right."

"I see by your uniform that you are RAF. How long have you been with the ATA?"

"Since they been here."

"And how many and what type of planes do you typically look after? Of course, the star of our film is the Spitfire. Do you often work on those too?" He seemed to almost warm up to the idea of being interviewed.

"Beautiful plane, none to beat her."

"And when was the Spitfire first manufactured?"

He laughed, took his cigarette out of his mouth, and threw it down, grinding it into the dirt with his heel. "You're telling me you're making a film about planes and you don't know when the Spit took its first flight?" I kept my eyebrows raised in question and nodded enthusiastically.

"We are just film people, Sergeant, not aeronautical engineers. That is why we are asking you." Goodness, he was as uncooperative as Edwina Partridge.

"Government information." He said and snapped his mouth shut.

"Exactly, government information that it wishes to share with the British people. Our films are to inform the public, Sergeant. To give them something to be proud of. And the Spitfire has become an emblem of British ingenuity and engineering: the fastest, most maneuverable plane in the world, piloted by our courageous chaps in the RAF. You get the drift of it now. So, if you wouldn't mind just filling me in on some simple facts, we would be most grateful."

His mouth had dropped open a little. "'We'? The royal we, are you?" His lip curled in a sneer. "I take it that you have permission from Commander Abercrombie for these questions."

"Yes, of course we do."

He thought for a moment, and then to my surprise he said, "Here's an answer for you: the first Spit came out in 1938, before the war."

"How many marks are there now?"

"I dunno." He scratched his head. "Four? Yeah, four."

"And the one Miss Partridge flew yesterday was a what?"

"Ay, wait a minute. You could have asked these questions of Miss Partridge or Commander Abercrombie. So why didn't you? Are you trying to suggest . . . ? Yes, you bleedin' are . . . the ruddy cheek of it. That Spit was in perfect condition to fly. You want to know about the crash yesterday? There's only one person you can talk to, and that's Commander Abercrombie. Now, hop it with your snooty Crown Film Unit credentials." He took a step toward me and Griff did too.

"Sergeant, that's quite enough. You better calm down; otherwise I'll have you up on a charge."

"You don't have any authority here, mate. Now, take your lady friend, your little dog, and get out. Or I'll call the perlice."

Griff kicked at a late dandelion clock in a leisurely way as we left; he seemed to be counting under his breath. "Five," he said as he took my arm. "Why so many gasoline storage tanks, when they only have three or four training planes and a couple of Anson taxis?"

"WELL, WE HANDLED that just brilliantly," I said as we crossed the airstrip. "Do you think he rang Abercrombie?"

"I think we are going to find out when we get back to the mess. And when we do I'll ask her straight out about the RAE restrictor, so that we don't look as if we are sneaking around asking questions behind her back."

"I really didn't mean to put my foot in it quite so badly!"

"You didn't; you were polite and respectful. He was already on the defensive when we arrived."

Of course Ilona had to add her opinion too. *I think that little blighter is up to something shady. More investigation needed there.*

We walked up the steps and into the mess, and there was Vera Abercrombie waiting for us. "Just going to let you know that we will have quite a few of our pilots home tonight. I'm sure you would enjoy meeting all of the girls stationed here. You are welcome to stay to dinner." Her gaze, as usual, was steady as she treated us to her faint official smile, but there were dark circles under her eyes.

"Thank you, Commander Abercrombie." Griff was at his most open and frank. "We just bumped into Sergeant Wilson, and we might have upset him."

She nodded in understanding. "Not difficult to do, I'm afraid, Captain. Wilson is feeling very tender about Edwina's Spitfire."

"I noticed it was a Mark II. Was it fitted with a restrictor?"

Her gaze intensified as she looked from Griff to me and back to him. "Why would you ask that?" I noticed that she was clenching and unclenching her hands, the only sign of tension in this calm and controlled individual.

"Because for Miss Partridge to lose control of her plane while doing something as simple as an Immelmann turn seems kind of . . . well, kind of out of keeping with her level of experience, wouldn't you say?"

She hesitated, and in that moment I realized that the question made her uncomfortable, really uncomfortable. Then she pulled herself together. Not quite so straight-ahead now, I thought, and wondered if our invitation to dinner might be withdrawn.

"Funny you should say that." She tugged her tunic smooth at the hem and straightened her shoulders. "Sir Basil took Wilson out to the Spitfire early this morning. Made him open up the engine and check the carburetor—the restrictor was still in place."

"So the engine didn't stall because it was flooded."

A small tight smile. "Oh, no, Captain. If the engine had flooded, surely we would have all seen that telltale trail of black smoke along the fuselage." She shook her head and her voice took on an official tone: clipped and brisk. "I'm afraid it was pilot error. We were worried that there might have been a carbon monoxide leak from the engine into the cockpit, causing Edwina to black out, but according to Wilson apparently not."

According to Wilson! I wouldn't let that moron fix my bicycle, Ilona's voice cut in.

"As a matter of interest, what happens when a plane crashes like that?" I asked.

"The ATA Accident Committee will make their inspection in the morning, and then their report will be presented to our headquarters commander at White Waltham. After that the Spitfire will be repurposed."

"Mend and make do." I should imagine every woman in England has said this at one time or another during the last three years.

Her smile this time was genuine, and I realized that underneath the strain of her responsibilities, when Vera relaxed her commanding officer's vigil, she was an attractive woman. Her serious, formal manner had layered years on a woman far younger than I had first thought. "It must have been very distressing for you, Miss Redfern, to see such a terrible accident, especially as you had the opportunity to get to know Edwina. It's always a tremendous shock when someone we know is killed. However"—her face assumed her shutdown senior-officer expression again—"we are at war, and these things happen."

"Have you any more information about Letty?" I asked and saw her eyes half close, I thought, in pain.

The sound of aircraft engines filled the air, and she looked out of the window, shading her eyes from me. "Ah, look, here is the first Anson coming in to land." Visibly grateful at the arrival of her rescue party, she glanced at her clipboard. "You will be able to meet some of our other pilots, Miss Redfern. Some of them have only just earned their stripes: I am sure they would love to tell you about their adventures." The telephone rang in her office. "May I leave you to introduce yourselves? I expect that's White Waltham again." She bolted for her office and closed the door.

"What do you think?" I asked Griff as he stood there, cap in hand, staring at the door.

"She doesn't want to talk to us about what happened. I suppose I can hardly blame her. Her job is to keep morale up when one or two of her pilots go west, and she probably doesn't want outsiders asking questions she doesn't have the answer to." He hesitated. "But it's more than that. She's defensive, on guard. What do you think?"

"I think it's hard to be a commanding officer if you are a woman. And I really hope that is the reason why she is so self-protecting."

Even at a distance the arriving ATA pilots' voices filled the air as they climbed out of the Anson. There were only a handful of them in the first taxi, but their chatter almost drowned the sound of two more air taxis coming in to land.

"Do you really want to join them all for dinner, or shall we go back to the inn and eat there?" Griff asked as a dozen or so women strode across the top of the drive toward the mess. There was nothing svelte, well-groomed, or glamorous about this lot. They were any group of workingwomen after a long day.

"I rather think I'll have dinner with the 'ordinary' Attagirls. They look like a splendidly talkative group. I want to know more about Letty and Edwina. I want to find out what these girls, the rank and file, think about our six glamour girls."

He put his hand on my arm. "Don't forget that none of them know about Letty's death yet. I'll take Bessie back to the inn and she can share a pint with me." He put on his hat and made for the back door as the first group arrived: windblown, voluble, and ready for dinner.

———

"DID I KNOW Edwina Partridge? Only by sight—she never talked to *me*!" A woman who had introduced herself as Anthea Smalley lifted her head to glance at me briefly and then returned to inhaling her dinner off her plate. She looked as if she hadn't had a square meal in days, and her crumpled uniform made me wonder if she had slept in it more than once this week. "I am sorry that she crashed her plane, really I am. But these things happen." She lowered her voice as she scraped her plate. "On the QT, she was a bit of a show-off, and there was all sorts of gossip swirling around her—not nice gossip either."

The woman sitting next to her gave her a nudge in the ribs. "Gossip is rarely nice, Anth," she reminded her.

"Sorry, it's been a ghastly week." There was no remorse in Anthea's voice. "It's always a shock when someone goes for a Burton, even if you don't know them very well. I think it's best to talk things out, but you know, 'stiff upper lip' and all that nonsense." She put down her fork and leaned a little closer to me. "Earlier this year there was another accident. It was awful; set us all back, I can tell you. One of our girls smashed her plane into a hill near her parents' home. Maureen Crossley was very popular with everyone: thoughtful, considerate, and an all-round chum. Poor Vera had to go and view the crash site and stay with Maureen's body after the RAF had pulled her out of the wreck. It turns out that Maureen had flown into a solid wall of cloud and rain and wouldn't have been able to see the hill at all. Vera was devastated because it happened soon after Maureen transferred from White Waltham to Didcote. They had known each other, you see, from the start of the ATA. It was almost as bad as when Amy Johnson went down in the Thames Estuary. You remember her, don't you? She was famous."

"The long-distance solo pilot? Yes, it was in all the papers." I frowned because I honestly couldn't remember much about it.

"They never found Amy's body. But you won't hear anyone mention either of those girls' names around here." She lifted her finger and placed it lightly against her lips. "This can be a very dangerous job if you aren't on your toes the whole time you're flying. So, we honor our dead and then move on. Not good to dwell on death." She nodded as if she was giving me sage advice.

I stored this information away and changed the subject. "So, what are you all licensed to fly?" I asked. A gale of laughter welcomed this question.

"Don't laugh, she's spent the last two days in rarified company," said Anthea with her mouth full, as she dug into her pudding with the enthusiasm of a teenage boy.

"We fly everything that has wings," said a sturdy girl after she had doused her treacle tart with custard. "I have been away for almost a week ferrying Tiger Moths, Mosquitos, Hurricanes, biplanes, you name it. None of us"—she waved her spoon around the table—"are licensed to fly bombers . . . not yet! I did fly an air marshal from Southampton to Biggin Hill."

"Ooh, I bet that was a bumpy ride," called out an angular blonde with a strong East London accent.

"I flew *the* air marshal in *an Avro Anson*, for your information. You should have heard the language he used."

"Those senior rankers are the worst." A very young woman with a strawberry-blond victory-roll hairstyle closed her eyes in demure parody at the vulgarity of the RAF. "Most of them don't even notice we are women," she explained. "And some of them don't even care to tone down their language even if they do notice."

"Here is the drawback about being a female pilot," a woman of forty whose name was Cheryl piped up. "You spend the day flying and end up at some measly little airfield in some out-of-the-way place in Wales, and there is nowhere for you to sleep, let alone go to the you-know-what."

She was interrupted by my dinner partner, Anthea. "She's right, it's absolutely ridiculous: there are no facilities for women at most of the aerodromes. When I first arrived at Biggin Hill, I had to scramble out of my Sidcot flight suit and put on a uniform skirt, on the tarmac in the dark behind the plane, so I could report to their commanding officer in proper attire. He thanked me and sent me off into the night to try and find a place to stay. I bunked down on the sofa in the living room of a bed-and-breakfast and was only too grateful that they had a plane they needed to ferry back to East-leigh, so I could air taxi from there." She gave me a see-what-I-mean look.

By this time, I had long accepted that the stories I was being told tonight would not be suitable for our film, but they would be useful for my next novel. "What do you mean there was nowhere to stay at Biggin Hill?" Biggin Hill was one of the largest airfields on the south coast; surely they had accommodation for female pilots who had to stay overnight.

"Just that." Cheryl forked down the last of her treacle tart. "Sorry, I've been living on chocolate and stewed tea for two days. Yes, please," she said to the mess steward. "I'd love another piece." She turned back to me. "There are no women flying in the RAF, so there is no accommodation for them. At some RAF airfields women aren't allowed in the mess, not even to have a quick breakfast before we leave!"

The strawberry blonde lit a cigarette and blew a plume of smoke into the air. "The RAF is like a gentlemen's club—very exclusive. All pilots behave like stuck-up toffs unless they want something from you. The Women's Auxiliary Air Force, the WAAF, are only employed as clerks, typists, drivers, cooks, and cleaners, depending on their background and how rich their daddy is. But lord's daughter or commoner, they all play a very subordinate role. There are a few female mechanics, but not that many. The WAAF gals live locally and catch the bus to their airfield. There might be one WC in some airfields for women, but they are hidden away behind the bike shed or the kitchens." She rolled her eyes. "Anyone would think we had the plague!"

"You flew a late delivery into Biggin Hill, and they couldn't find accommodation for you in the town. What time did you arrive?" I asked Cheryl.

"Eight, nine. I honestly can't remember. Don't look so shocked, ducky; if they had women's quarters at the big airfields, you wouldn't want to stay there. Even if you were an old mum like me."

"I thought you had to be at your destination by dark!" I said as I shook my head to Cheryl's proffered cigarette.

The group around me rolled their eyes. "In the summer it's long, long days, with very little sleep." Anthea leaned toward me as if she were sharing a secret. "Are you telling me that Lady Betty Asquith didn't tell you about her exhausting flight schedule? And that she has to have every Friday to Monday off because of social commitments? Or that on Thursday she has her nails done, so no flying then?" She giggled. "Lady Betty has to have an ATA cadet with her to put the landing gear down for her."

"Landing gear?"

"Anson and Fairchild air taxis have manual landing gear; you have to crank them down by hand."

Cheryl waved for silence. "Or the famous writer June what's-her-name will only fly two-engine planes that she has flown before. She absolutely falls apart if someone suggests she fly something she is not familiar with. Complete life of Riley those girls lead, with their picturesque cottage in Didcote, entertaining Commander Abercrombie and Sir Basil to dinner." She looked at her friends and they laughed again, but there was no malice in them, just a lot of eye rolling as they cracked jokes at the expense of the elite members of their group.

"How do you get back to Didcote if there are no return planes to deliver?"

"By rail, which means sitting on your parachute in a guard's van of a crowded train. Last time I made a delivery to Scotland I slept in the luggage rack of the train compartment! There were two old maids sitting below me with their knitting. One of them said how unattractive women looked in uniform trousers. I leaned down and told them in the politest way that it was immodest to fly a Hurricane fighter in a skirt. Lord knows how many stitches they dropped." She pushed away her plate and drank some tea.

"But you all flew in just now in an Anson taxi!" I said, determined not to believe everything they chose to tell me.

"We delivered planes back to White Waltham so they can be ferried on to Supermarine tomorrow morning. The unlucky ones are probably sitting in a train siding in the dark right now, hunkered down on their parachutes, hungry, tired, and in a place they have never heard of."

I didn't dare ask a question that might be taboo among a group of women who were getting on with their well-earned dinner. One that would result in my being ticked off and sent to Coventry, the way Sergeant Wilson had ended my politely worded interview with him earlier that day.

"Where do you all sleep when you are here, at Didcote?" I asked.

"Up the drive, turn right toward the village, and go past your inn. Just before you get to the village there's a row of small cottages on the left and the Pig and Whistle," said strawberry-blonde victory roll. "There's a little lane off to the left and at the end is the old church hall. They converted it into a big dormitory for thirty with bunk beds. Problem is there are only two loos, but at least they rigged up a shower for us."

"I had no idea how tough your job really is," was my weak response.

"That's okay, how would you know what it's really like? After all, you spent a few idyllic days with the original pilots who joined the ATA and already knew how to fly—specially recruited, they were. The Great Eight, as they used to be. All of them learned to fly at age fourteen in one of their daddy's planes."

"We had only six pilots in our film, not eight," I said, "and Edwina grew up in a flying circus, as an aerial acrobat—she told me."

Cheryl snorted into her cup of tea. "Oh, pull the other one, ducks," she said, looking round the table to merry laughter. "Edwina's pop was a millionaire several times over before he went bankrupt and died. It was his brother who owned flying circuses, and flying schools. The brothers had a license to manufacture planes. There was some talk that both of them were diddled by their business partner. When Edwina flew it was only for pleasure, I can promise you that. Didn't you know that our CO has only ever asked her to fly Spitfires? She didn't dare suggest that Edwina might ferry an open-cockpit Tiger Moth, not even in the beginning when that was all they were allowed to deliver."

Anthea leaned in; she was holding up eight fingers. "Maureen, Amy Johnson, and Edwina." She put down three fingers. "The original eight are now five."

"Anthea!" A young woman who had been talking with her friends at the top of the table looked at our gossipy little group. It was a clear admonishment. There was an ashamed silence around the table. Embarrassed looks were exchanged. How long would it be, I wondered, before they found out about Letty's crash? How were these things handled when a pilot did not come back to the mess at the end of her working day? Did Commander Abercrombie make an announcement, or did she let the information leak out that another pilot had gone west?

THIRTEEN

——

I HAD EXPECTED MY NEW FRIENDS TO CRY UNCLE AND TURN IN for the night as soon as they had finished dinner, but they were made of sterner stuff. A few of them went off to have showers and wash their hair, calling out good night to the rest of us as they strolled up the darkened drive to their digs in the Didcote church hall.

Someone tuned the radio in to a Glenn Miller concert at the Bedford Corn Exchange. "Some lucky girl is dancing to 'Kalamazoo' right now, in the arms of her dreamy American GI," said the girl with the strawberry-blond hair, whose name, it turned out, was Mavis. She closed her eyes and swayed in time to the music, her left shoulder lifted as if she were in someone's arms. "Doesn't seem fair when most girls don't know how to jitterbug properly. Come on, Dolly, I'll show you the steps. My boyfriend taught me—he's from Boston." The music filled the air with the clout of excitement only an American dance band could produce to bring back life into the tired feet of working girls, and we turned our chairs around to watch the dancing.

"You play darts?" Anthea was still sitting next to me. "Never

played? Where on earth have you been? Come on, we'll teach you."
She jumped up and walked over to a dartboard in the far corner.
"Anyone for a game?" And with the energy of a woman who is determined to have a good time, Anthea put two teams together to
play darts.

I've never been much good at pub games, or games of any kind,
but as I waited my turn I treated my three teammates to half a bitter. It was the least I could do for them: with me on their side they
had no idea how severely trounced they were going to be this evening.

"Blimey, love, you've gotter do better than that." The lanky
cockney pulled my darts out of the wood surrounding the dartboard and gazed with horror at their points. "How much have you
had to drink?"

"Leave her alone; she's all right," called out Anthea. "She's one
of us."

"Doesn't sound like one of us. Sounds like that bloody stuck-up
Lady Betty Arskiss." The lanky one aimed and peppered the board
with high scores. "Bumped into her in Didcote the day before we
left for White Waltham—before your bunch came down here to
film. She was doing some shopping, and she pretended she didn't
know who I was." She lifted her beer to me. "Cheers, love," she said
by way of thanks.

The patrician Betty shopping in Didcote? What on earth would
she want to buy there? Shampoo? There wasn't even a decent chemist shop. I could hear Ilona stirring and beat her to the punch.

"Shopping for what?" I asked before I could stop myself.
"There's only a grocer and a butcher there, and the pub, of course."

"Oh, she wasn't in the pub, was she, love? Nah, she's just popped
in to buy herself a galvanized iron corset!" This produced a shriek
of derision among the girls from East London.

Anthea whispered, "Just ignore them," but I was too busy leaping out of my skin. *Bingo, sweetie. What did Grable buy in an ironmongery? Could it possibly be rat poison?* Ilona's voice purred in my head.

I WAS A ragged wreck the next morning. My head hurt and my mouth was as parched as a desert.

"Hangover?" Griff appeared looking as fresh as a meadow flower in spring as I finished off my breakfast in the inn's dining room: cardboard toast with margarine and dishwater tea. "I might have known if you hung out with that crowd, you'd feel like hell today. Come on, a quick spin in the country with the top down will blow away your morning blues."

"I don't have the time, I really don't."

He led me out into the bright morning sun. "Plenty of time, plenty of time. I'll drive you back to London early Monday morning. Come on, hop in. Look at Bess—she wants a spin in Uncle Griff's car, don't you, darlin'?"

Bess was already sitting front and center in her jump seat: ears up, eyes shining, and her little bob of a tail working away.

"Where are we off to?"

"Elton, to see a man about a plane. Or at least a plane crash. You thought I was just loafing about with a pint in my hand last night, didn't you? Well, I wasn't. I put in a call to Mr. Mackenzie of Elton Farm, and he has agreed to see us. We can ask him all the questions you like, and when we are done with him, there's a nice old senior citizen at Elton Home Guard who can't wait to make another report: official or otherwise."

Britain's Home Guard is made up of sprightly sixty- and seventy-year-old men who get together every morning and play at soldiers.

Up until just a few months ago they patrolled with cricket bats, shotguns if they had them, or a nice hefty golf club. Today they are armed with army-issue rifles and Sten guns. "I know everyone laughs at the Home Guard," I said a bit defensively. "But they were all we had if the Germans had invaded during 1940 and '41."

"I certainly don't laugh about them. I am completely in awe of your grandad. He commands a tight unit and is a ferocious tactician. I wouldn't want to bump into him on a dark night as I was walking away from my German parachute."

The sun poured down on us as the little car shot along narrow winding lanes in the sheer beauty of early autumn. And when we weren't going so fast that he couldn't hear me, I shouted out my conversation with the other Attagirls last night.

"Aha!" he said as I described their jitterbugging and darts matches. "Just as I expected. Of course, there are the greater Attas and the lesser variety; after all, this is England."

Griff loves to remind me of what he considers to be our extraordinarily rigid class system. Lesser and greater? Now he was classifying the Attagirls like birds.

"Oh, no, that's far too extreme: the girls I met last night came from a far wider cross section of the populace than that. And why do you think the British are the only ones with strong class divisions? You can't tell me that America doesn't have some sort of system of differentiating those who lead easier, richer lives and enjoy more privilege than others."

"There is the opportunity in America to make a better life, though. To dream big and know you can achieve."

I harrumphed. There were few things we disagreed on, but the disparity between the British workingman and the landowner was one of them. "And there is here too. Just look at all those English arms manufacturers' daughters marrying into the aristocracy after the last war. And all the black marketeers who made a fortune out of it too, and then became ultra-respectable afterward, while the poor old landowners scraped together money for death duties!"

"It's not the same. My grandfather could never have owned land in Ireland, but he owns thousands of acres in California."

I did not say that the American West was part of a well-organized land grab, but I did have to set him straight about the Attas.

"It's not just greater and lesser Attas, Griff. Take Anthea Smalley, for example. She is probably what we would call a middle Atta, if you want to be accurate about these things. Her father is a doctor, her mother a nurse. She told me that at the beginning of the war, the only Attas were the ones from the monied and upper classes, unlike now, where the ATA train their pilots."

He nodded at me, his eyes wide, as if he were making a salient point. "When you say 'monied,' does that include the aristocracy?"

"I suppose I might include the nouveau riche."

"And when you say 'upper,' are you referring to the landowning classes or the aristocracy?"

"Both. I think Anthea was referring to people who before the war had the time, the *leisure*, and the money to fly."

He slapped his knee as if he had caught me. "Right! Until there was a war the only people who owned small planes were those that could afford them. That's why the greater Attas keep to themselves, and the lesser ones all went to a government flying school and know their place. Wonder how things will be after we win this war? Do you think the lesser Attas will go back to scrubbing floors and being ladies' maids?"

"The pilots I talked to last night who trained at the Central Flying School come from *all* walks of life. Most of them are second officers, not as senior as our original Attas only because they have just joined."

We slowed down briefly for a rabbit that bolted across the road and I decided to change the subject before things got too heated.

"When I brought up Edwina's accident last night I didn't get the feeling her death was a terrible loss. They were polite about it, but they moved on pretty quickly. One of them said she was 'a bit of a show-off.' Even her story about being a performer in a flying circus is dubious: her father was a millionaire in aviation. Or at least he was in the early thirties; then he was cheated by his partner and lost everything."

We were back to our breakneck speed again and I held on to my hat.

"But here is the really interesting part: Grable was seen coming out of the ironmongers on the morning before we started filming." I paused to enjoy his distracted swerve. "Yes! The ironmongers! Imagine that."

He pulled up at the entrance to a tearoom. "Let me get this straight," he said, his eyes shining with delight. "Betty Asquith came out of the ironmongers carrying a huge green tin with 'poison' written all over it. I need a cup of coffee, c'mon."

We walked up the path to the door of an empty tearoom. It badly needed a coat of paint, and our footsteps echoed across a gritty floor to a long counter presided over by an elderly woman in a hairnet who was carefully dusting a display case with a solitary plate of biscuits set squarely in the middle.

"Good morning, and what a lovely one it is!" Despite her one plate of biscuits she was a cheerful old lady. "We only have tea or Camp coffee, will that do you?" She looked so apologetic that Griff said, "Love Camp," which made her smile.

"Where are *you* from, dear?" She almost bridled. "America? No rationing over there, I bet."

"Afraid not." He looked appropriately apologetic. "Have you by any chance got a tin of Carnation evaporated milk?"

A gentle smile. "Yes, we do. But it's terribly expensive: five shillings?"

My jaw dropped. "Five . . . ?"

"Great, we'll take it. Does wonders for Camp."

"Then it's all yours, and thank you, sir, for coming over and helping us out of a jam," she said, not quite able to look him in the eye, she was so in awe of his ability to splash five shillings on a tin of evaporated milk.

"Don't mention it, glad to be here." Griff, both gratified and embarrassed, cleared his throat. She shuffled off to get her tin of Carnation; it was probably her one and only tin judging by her canny price.

"There," she said as she came and punched two holes in the top of the tin. "If I open it for just two cups, there will be so much left over."

Griff took the hint. "Then offer it to your next customers." Griff lifted his cup and sipped. "Pure heaven." He sipped some more. I lifted my cup and tried not to shudder. It was what I imagine dandelion roots and alum would taste like if you burned them together for a couple of days.

Bess found a table that had some crumbs under it and settled herself in. "Go on," Griff whispered. "Put a bit of evaporated in it. You know you love it." He picked up the tin and poured a little into my cup. "More? Come on, you know it takes that bitter taste right out of it. Want me to tell you what I think Grable was buying in our friendly ironmongers?"

I nodded. "You actually know what she bought?"

"I'll tell you in the car."

We had another cup of coffee each and Griff polished off half the tin, being careful to leave some for other customers. Bess tore herself away from polishing the floor and we made a fond farewell to the lady in the hairnet.

"Let's take Bess for a quick walk in that meadow over there," I said, "and you can tell me about Grable's shopping spree in Didcote."

THERE WAS A chill in the air and the remains of an early-morning mist lifting up through the trees in the valley below. We strode out, full of warm, milky coffee, with Bess scooting ahead of us down the lane.

"What I enjoy about her most is her bossy little hind end," said Griff, smiling at Bess's retreating bottom. "She is such a force to be reckoned with; she is"—he beamed at me—"a true Brit." As if on cue, Bess turned around and gave us two short barks. "She's telling us to catch up." Bess barked again, picked up a stick, and ran toward us.

"Drop it, Bessie," I said, and we laughed as she let go of her stick and then picked it up again. Griff eased it out of her mouth, leaned back, and lobbed it over a gate and into the meadow. She slid under the gate as we climbed over it. She was in full form now; her paws barely touched the ground as she sped over tussocks of wet grass.

"She's always so sure we'll . . ." I turned as Griff came up behind me, and I found myself staring into his eyes. His expression was so serious my heart leapt up into my throat.

He lowered his head to mine, and I tilted my face up. I could hear my pulse throbbing in my head and feel the warmth of his hand as it cupped my cold cheek. The world dipped in a slow, dizzying waltz as he put an arm around my waist.

It was Bess who ruined it with her blasted stick obsession, turning bliss into agony as she rammed the broken-off end of her stick into the tender part just behind my knee. I performed a neat curtsy as Griff started to pull me toward him. Did he think I was turning away to avoid his kiss?

"That must be Elton down there." He pointed down the hill as he took a step away from me.

I turned my head and followed the line of his arm. "Ah yes, Elton!"

He squinted in the morning light. "And there is the wreck of the Walrus."

The wreck of the Walrus? The wreck of romance, more like. I could still feel his closeness, his breath on my cheek. I prayed he would take me in his arms again. I looked up at his averted profile and my throat ached. Blast and damn all dogs! Our moment had come and, with Bess's wretched stick work, had truly gone.

Should I move back into his arms so he could kiss me? I might really regret it when we got back to Didcote and he flirted with Grable or Zofia . . . I couldn't, I honestly couldn't be able to bear it.

So, sensible girl that I am, I stepped away from him and we both gazed down into the valley below us, together, as if it were the most fascinating sight in the world.

Coward, Ilona said to me. *I always have such hopes for you and then you ruin it all by being such a self-protecting coward.*

"You didn't tell me what Grable was shopping for," I said to shut Ilona out and break the silence between us.

He shrugged and picked up another stick for Bess. "She was telling everyone on our first night here that she had to buy a mousetrap. She's shares a cottage in Didcote with June, Annie, and Zofia. They have mice. That's probably why she went to the hardware store." He was still looking at the tiny plane off in the distance.

"Sorry to disappoint." He turned to me and smiled, his eyes not quite meeting mine. "Really, I am. Rat poison isn't our solution anyway; it works far too quickly for both their deaths . . ."

I reluctantly returned to business. "Do you know if Edwina shared the same cottage as June and the rest of them?" I asked.

He rubbed his chin in the way men do if they wonder if they should shave. "She said she lived in the village. But you know something, Poppy? I have absolutely no idea which house," he said. We walked back to the car and resumed our journey down into the valley in a silence strained with tension.

AFTER MAKING A few wrong turns, we found Elton Farm. It was a huge affair, bigger than my grandad's farm, Reaches, with one of those drives that go on forever through pastures of fat, sleek cows, and a huge redbrick Victorian house at its end.

Griff gazed around him in appreciation. "I always thought California was beautiful, but this . . ." He waved his arm at the deep lush grass, the wide canopy of oak and beech trees. Between them and set back at a distance, as if someone had decided they looked at their best there, stood a grove of birch with their silver trunks and filigree golden leaves waiting to be admired. "It's so peaceful in its beauty," Griff said as we meandered down the last yards of the drive.

"Worth fighting for?" I asked as I wistfully remembered the view of Elton from the meadow.

He turned and gazed into my face. "Infinitely worth fighting for, and worth waiting for," he said, and I felt the skin on my cheeks and neck warm in the sun-filled air.

I wanted to reach out and take his hand in mine, but Mr. Mackenzie opened his front door as we pulled up at the bottom of the drive in a circle of gravel, so I folded them in my lap instead.

"Quite a spread," said Griff under his breath as he helped Bess and me out of the Alvis. "Called it a farm on the phone; never said anything about an estate."

"One day, Griff, I'm going to take you somewhere spectacular like . . . like Blenheim Palace, where Winston Churchill was born, and you will understand what we mean by owning land and unlimited privilege."

"Can't wait," he said as I joined him on the gravel drive. "But so far as houses go, Reaches is far more beautiful than this one."

I nodded. "That is because Reaches is very old—Elizabethan," I said in what can only be called a prideful voice. "It's drafty and hard to heat in winter. This one was built around about 1890. It probably has central heating and really efficient plumbing!"

MR. MACKENZIE WAS A quiet countryman in his late sixties, with muddy leather brogues on his feet and a pair of glasses that didn't sit quite straight on his nose because someone had mended the right temple with adhesive tape. The sight of him standing in the entrance to his wood-paneled hall, with his two elderly springer spaniels waving their heavy tails in welcome, made me homesick for my grandparents.

Mackenzie led us into his lived-in drawing room and my yearning for home increased. There was a clutter of books and journals on side tables, a vase of late dahlias on a desk in the bowfront window, and a slightly disheveled air of comfort and welcome that made me feel I had stepped into our drawing room at Reaches before the war.

"Now then, a glass of sherry?"

Drinks in hand, and a toast to our king solemnly made, Mr. Mackenzie begged to know how he could be of use.

"It's about the plane crash," said Griff.

Mackenzie shook his head. "Terrible thing, terrible. I knew she was in trouble the moment I saw the damn thing meandering around the sky. You see, I flew in the last war, so I knew there was something wrong when I first heard it."

"Did you see or hear it first?"

The old man frowned down at the carpet with his hands on his hips as he considered.

"Yes, that's right." He nodded. "I heard it and calculated that it was coming from over by the lower field by the railway. I didn't know at the time if it was one of ours or theirs."

"Can you remember how it sounded, sir?"

Mackenzie cocked his head in concentration. "I could tell it was a single prop. The engine sounded smooth. No stalling, no putt-putt, but . . ." He fixed Griff with his eyes. "Awfully close, much closer than I usually hear them when they fly over from the factories. This time it sounded as if the plane was coming in to land."

"I take it that you couldn't see it from the house?"

He shook his head. "Too many trees, so I got in my old banger and drove down toward the railway lines." He waved his arm away from the house and up the drive. "As I came through the gate into the field, by the cutting, the plane came into view. Flying just above the treetops and following along the lines. I was shaken by how large it was and how low it was flying. Great big biplane with its engine suspended over a squarish cockpit between the upper and lower wing. I could tell by the landing gear that it was a seaplane. I drove alongside the railway lines for several hundred yards." He shook his head at the image he had conjured.

"What altitude?"

"Altitude?" He almost laughed and then wrinkled his nose in thought. "It was lumbering along at about a hundred feet. The pilot had obviously been trying to follow the railway line. There was no black smoke and the engine seemed to be working quite normally. It sounded smooth: no stalling or anything." He glanced at Griff and then at me. "I thought for one moment . . ." He frowned. "I thought for one moment a young boy was taking a joyride, because it looked to me as if the pilot had never flown before. You could have knocked me down with a feather when I found out that it was an ATA pilot with thousands of flying hours to her credit." He paused and looked away from us. "Then it simply piled into the bridge. Terrible waste. Awful thing to see."

Griff sipped his drink and nodded agreement. "How close were you when she crashed, sir? Do you have any idea what time that was?"

Mackenzie splashed some soda from a siphon into his whiskey glass. "First thing I did was look at my watch. It was ten minutes past ten." He shook his head as if to clear away the image. "You know, for one moment I looked right up into the cockpit, and I saw her. She half stood up and I thought it looked as if she was trying to do something."

"She was alone?" Griff asked.

"Oh yes, quite alone. I meant to say she was struggling—" He stopped in confusion. "Or . . . I don't know. Anyway, it was too late. The next thing I knew there was an almighty crash and the plane plunged nose first onto the bridge—three minutes or so after I first saw her."

My mouth felt dry, and the sherry had made my head ache. I put the glass down on the table next to my chair.

Mackenzie came out of his thoughts. "I jumped out of my car

and got up on the lower wing. The body of the plane was under the bridge, and the upper wing and the engine were behind it on the track. The door to the cockpit is in the roof and I couldn't get it open, but I could see her. I ran back to my car and found a wrench and levered the cockpit hatch open with that. She was lying on the floor. It turned out she was dead."

He dropped his head. "Funny thing is . . . it looked to me . . ." He passed his hand over his eyes. "This sounds strange, I know, but before she crashed—when I first saw her—it looked to me as if she might have been struggling to get into her parachute. I dismissed it at the time, but when I saw her on the floor she had one shoulder through its harness. If she was an experienced pilot, why was she putting on her chute at such a low altitude? Why wasn't she trying to get the damn thing's nose up? It doesn't make sense."

He drew in a long breath. "Elton is a few minutes up the line. I drove up to the Home Guard and called Elton Police. They took over from there. They had the line closed and called an ambulance. If she hadn't died on impact, I am sure she was gone minutes later. I helped them pull her from the plane."

"She was definitely dead?"

He nodded, "Oh yes, I am quite sure she was dead when I found her."

"I know this sounds unpleasant, but was there any evidence that she had been, say, drinking—heavily?"

Mackenzie looked at Griff as if trying to judge what he should say in front of me.

"Please be frank with us, Mr. Mackenzie," I said.

"From the way she had been flying that's exactly what I thought, and what I told the police and Commander Abercrombie. I said she looked like she had been drinking. Actually, what I said was that the plane looked as drunk as lord, but there was no smell of alcohol on her at all. She looked, you know, like she had fainted."

"No vomit?"

"No, nothing like that at all. It was easy to see that she was a nice-looking girl. It was such a terrible thing to see her lying in her plane like that."

"No smell of carbon monoxide in the cockpit, or maybe petrol?"

"Ah yes, I see. No, nothing at all. I was completely stumped and so were the police."

Griff got to his feet. "Thank you so much for your time, sir."

"Grateful to have helped. So, you work with RAF Intelligence, you say?"

I know my mouth dropped open like a landed codfish and I had to turn away. I had asked Griff on our way down how he had managed to get an interview with the farmer, and he had been his usual lighthearted and evasive self.

"That's right," he said, his voice offhand and noncommittal. "American Air Force and RAF have a unit that works together to try and solve incidents like these. I just happened to be at Didcote with Miss Redfern when this unfortunate accident occurred. No need for you to talk about this with anyone, Mr. Mackenzie?"

"Oh, absolutely not, Captain, absolutely not. Of course, my housekeeper knows, but she is not a gossip. I don't like these newspaper johnnies; they cause more trouble than they are worth." He walked us to the door and stood on his front step to say good-bye.

He nodded at Griff's car. "Now, that's a sporty little number. What is it?" He strolled out into the sunshine with us to admire the car.

"Alvis—drophead coupe."

"Splendid. I bet you can get some speed out of her." The old man's face lit up. "Ah, what it is to be young," he said. "Beautiful day, nippy little car, and a lovely young woman to keep you company." He reached down into the jump seat and ruffled Bess's ears. "Good day to you both. The King's Arms in Winchester is a decent-ish place for a spot of lunch, if you have the time. Just tell Ernie Walters that I sent you along." He smiled at us as if he knew that was where we would be off to. Then, turning, he walked up the steps to his front door, gave us a final wave, and disappeared.

"What a nice man. We should check out the King's Arms," Griff said as we chuntered slowly up the drive. "Now, what do you think about Letty's crash?"

"It sounds like she had been drinking something that didn't smell of alcohol."

"Aha, my thoughts exactly. Do you have any chemists in your family?"

"My family is very small. But I think I should call my uncle Ambrose because he knows absolutely everyone. And he's in intelligence, just like you, so I bet he has a chemist or two in his back pocket."

He laughed and did not acknowledge any dealings with military intelligence, counter or otherwise. "Now, we have a choice: either have a nice spot of lunch at the King's Arms, or we drive down to the railway bridge and check out the plane."

"I vote for the plane."

"I vote for both."

"IT'S AN UGLY-LOOKING thing," I said as we drove onto the part of the bridge that wasn't covered in debris from the crash.

"Yes, she's a tough old brute, all right, but if you're treading water in the drink and it's so damn cold you can't feel your legs, you would be only too grateful to see this old gal come in to land. Of course, the noise inside the cockpit would be pretty loud, and apparently they are as much fun in the air to fly as a bathtub." He climbed out of the car and slid down the muddy grass bank from the lane onto the railway track, then got up on the plane's lower wing, or what there was left of it. And down I slithered to be hauled up onto the wing that sat level with the cockpit.

Griff stepped down into the cockpit and turned to help me through, and to my surprise I found myself in quite a spacious area.

"Built for a rescue crew," Griff said as I looked around me.

"Good heavens," I said as I spotted an anchor and thick coils of rope lying on the floor.

"Yep, once she lands on water she becomes a boat, until she takes off again." He made a thorough check of the cockpit.

"From what Mackenzie said, Letty wasn't strapped into her seat when she crashed. Look, here's her chute." It was lying at the back of the plane behind the pilot seat. "Why on earth was she trying to put on her chute at a hundred feet?" He stood behind the pilot seat. "What the hell was going on?"

"Was she getting ready to jump out when it crashed?"

"Yes, you would think so. But at that height it would have been a liability, and Letty would know that if she was a Class Five. You know what I think? I think she was disoriented. Didn't know what she was doing." He sniffed. "Any gas in here would have long since dissipated out of that open door." He pointed upward.

"Carbon monoxide?"

"Yes, that's possible. Exhaust from the engine might have seeped into the cockpit from a leak. Too much of it will kill you; just enough will make you dizzy and disoriented; a good dose will knock you out. Mackenzie said he couldn't smell gas when he opened the cockpit door, and if there was enough carbon monoxide to make her disoriented, it would have made him pretty sick too."

We stood in the middle of the cockpit with its jumble of sea-rescue equipment. "What do you think?" he asked.

"Mackenzie said he couldn't understand why she was trying to put on her parachute instead of trying to get the plane's nose up. That sounds like she was confused and that she didn't know what was happening. How long would it take Mackenzie to get out of his car, down this bank, find the door jammed, and then go back for his wrench?"

Griff climbed up out of the cockpit. He jumped down off the wing and scrambled up the bank. When he got to the Alvis he looked at his watch. "He wouldn't do it as quickly as I did, so about four or five minutes at the most."

"So if there was a gas leak he would smell it?"

"Probably the first thing he would have noticed."

"Maybe she was disoriented from something else!"

He stood looking at me for a moment, and then he said, "Yes, I think you are right. She either ate, drank, or inhaled something that wasn't alcohol, carbon monoxide, or rat poison."

"And so did Edwina!" I said with more than a little conviction. "That is why the film of our picnic lunch is missing, and why Letty crashed her plane after eating Zofia's breakfast!"

"I don't think we have time to stop in Winchester for a decent-ish lunch after all," said Griff.

"No, but we do have to find a telephone box as fast as we can—I think Zofia might be in very real danger."

FOURTEEN

————

W OULD YOU BE PREPARED TO PAY A VISIT TO MY UNCLE
Ambrose in London?" I asked Griff as he started up the
car. "I have a feeling he might know of someone who could be helpful about poisons—or knockout drops. I know the government pay
a lot of attention to things like poison gas—you know the sort of
thing they used in the last war?" I turned my head to catch a long-
suffering look from the driver.

"Are you coming too?"

"No, I think I am going to drop in on the greater Attas if they
are at home—and see if I can get a sense of what was really going
on at that picnic on the airstrip."

"Perhaps I should come with you. I can be helpful about the
aviation side."

I had thought about this. Women tend to open up and relax
with other women, far more so if they are all girls together. The
presence of my dashing American friend would have the reverse
effect. "I think I would be better off on my own with the Attagirls,
but if Ambrose is free tonight would you please go and talk to him?
You know what questions to ask."

I could tell he didn't like the idea at all. "Whereas you would know what questions to ask of the Attagirls about flying?"

"Yes, something like that. I think I know what sort of questions to ask women who have lost two friends in as many days in flying accidents." To me the Walrus and the Spitfire had become murder weapons. The question that was pushing me forward was who had used them and was Zofia the next Attagirl to take a nosedive in her plane.

But Griff, who never lets small things stand in the way of the infinite possibilities, lifted his hands in surrender. "Sure, I'll go, if he knows someone who could help us. A man—"

"Or a woman." I was beginning to like the idea of us girls stepping out of line.

"Exactly, or a woman who has made a study of toxins: germ warfare, that sort of thing. And if he does, I would be happy to go up to London. I doubt very much if a poison expert would want to talk to me anyway, even if he was free this evening."

"Thank you so much, Griff." I looked at my watch. "Great heavens, it's almost two o'clock! We have to find a phone box quickly!"

There are three crossroads and two T junctions between Elton and Winchester, and not a single one of them had a telephone box perched conveniently by the side of the road.

"Damn," I said at the first empty intersection.

"Blast"—as we slowed down for the next.

"Damn and blast," I cried as we zoomed through the last one, well on our way to Winchester.

Griff slowed down as we came into town.

"The King's Arms—Mr. Mackenzie's recommendation for a decentish lunch," Griff said as he turned into the gravel in front of the inn.

"But we don't have time to eat," I wailed, wondering how anyone could think of food at a time like this.

"Hold on to your hat, Poppy. Good Lord, you're like a cat on hot bricks." He stopped the car. "There will be a phone here," he explained.

"Will you stay here with Bess while I go in and telephone?"

"Don't trust me, do you?"

I was already halfway to the inn.

"Hey, hold up," he called as I pushed open the door. "You got enough money?"

"MY DEAR GIRL!" Ambrose has what we English call a hearty voice, and I moved the receiver two inches from my ear.

"I have to be quick—this is a trunk call," I explained.

"Off you go, then, my dear, how I can be of help?"

What an obliging old darling my uncle is! Within minutes of the briefest of explanations he came up with immediate help, and he did so without a lot of prying questions. I like to think it's because he works at the Admiralty, where everything is studiedly hush-hush, but it is probably because my bachelor uncle is the soul of discretion and always respectful of what he describes as other people's privates.

"Where is young O'Neal now?" he boomed, causing the desk clerk to look in my direction and frown.

"We are in Winchester."

"Righto, just minutes away from Didcote. So, you can drive up and meet me and my old school friend Mathew Cadogan at my club. We'll be there early, at six. You are welcome to join us for drinks and then dinner."

"It will just be Griff; I have a dinner engagement." There was a long pause. We hadn't been cut off because I could hear him breathing like a horse.

"Splendid! Now, everything going well at the new job? Splendid, splendid. Tell O'Neal I'm looking forward to meeting him again." And he was gone.

I walked out to the car and found Griff staring through the windscreen with rather a bleak expression on his face. It lightened as he saw me.

"All set!" I said as he opened the car door. "Ambrose has a best friend from his old school days who knows everything about anything to do with poisons. He's in forensics, whatever that is. They will both meet you at Ambrose's club: the Travellers, 106 Pall Mall."

"Oh good." But he didn't seem to really think so.

"Thank you so much for doing this. I promise, Ambrose is one of those people who mellow on second meetings."

He pulled out into the road and turned the car back in the direction of Didcote. "That's reassuring. Last time I felt as if I had gone back to the days of the great British Raj. He was the viceroy and I was some sort of native bearer. I am sure everything would have been fine if I was an Old Etonian."

"An Old Wykehamist. He went to Winchester. It's just his manner. I know he is not quite so . . . well, as informal and pally as my grandfather." I thought about this for a moment. My grandfather is fascinated by young fighting men, and he reveres Griff, firstly because my father was a pilot in the last war, and secondly because he had never met a man who could go into a kitchen and come out an hour or two later with a perfectly roasted sirloin of beef. My uncle Ambrose can be a bit stuffy until he gets to know you.

"I know what you mean by Ambrose's interrogative style; it can be awfully heavy going. If he gets on to California again and starts asking endless questions—"

"Which he will."

"Then just tell him how many thousands of acres your father owns in Orange County. That'll shut him up."

"I seriously doubt it will."

THE SHADOWS WERE deepening to indigo as we drove back to Didcote. I took a long, appreciative sniff of the dank tang of autumn, underscored here and there with the sweet smell of woodsmoke as we passed darkened houses.

Griff glanced over his shoulder to Bess and nodded for me to observe that she had her long nose up in the air too.

"The violet hour," he said. "Do you think you'll take to flying?"

"It was enthralling." I remembered the tiny world below me and Letty's kindness. "I am not awfully sure I have that kind of physical courage, though. I think I'll keep it for Ilona. It's the sort of thing she would thrive on." He knew that Ilona was the protagonist of my first novel, but not that she popped in and out of my head with various observations, encouragement, and the occasional dressing-down.

"I'll take you up if you like," he said.

"Would you, Griff? I would love that." I thought of the meadow above Elton as I inhaled autumn air and gazed at a sky that was mauve and yellow on the horizon and a deep, darkening blue above us.

"Good, then we'll have to get our hands on a nice two-seater Tiger. Maybe the ATA would lend us theirs. The beginning and the end of day are miraculous from above. I don't think there is a flyer in the world who doesn't feel real peace in that moment of being airborne. It's the separation from all the worries of the world as you lift up and the earth drops away from you—I feel that way even if

I'm going on a mission." I turned my head to look at the darkening hedgerow whipping past me. I couldn't begin to imagine how that would feel, that moment of being airborne with him.

We drove on in silence down deepening lanes; the dimmed blackout headlights shone dully on the road's surface ahead of us. As night closed in and we drove through anonymous villages, I imagined that Griff and I were traveling together in time, skimming through the dark, entirely alone in the world. If I hadn't been anxious that poison was involved and that Zofia might be in serious danger, I would have wanted our drive from Winchester to Didcote to go on forever.

Just as we drew level with Didcote Airfield, I broke the silence.

"Thank you for driving up to London. I know my uncle can be a bit much."

I sensed his smile in the dark. "It's okay. I think it will be a useful meeting. Anything you want me to ask in particular?"

"If the poison was put in food it would have to be tasteless, wouldn't it?"

"Camp coffee would disguise something bitter, though. Are we looking at a couple of hours before it takes effect? What time did you break for lunch when you were filming?"

"One o'clock, but Edwina started in as soon as the food was brought out. She flew her Spitfire just after half past three."

"Two to three hours, then." He pulled up outside the heavy shadow of the cottage. "Hard to tell if anyone's in," he said as we peered into the dense shrubbery in front of the building. "There's a bicycle propped against the porch railing." The three of us sniffed the air. "And someone has a wood fire going."

He turned and leaned toward me, and on cue my heart rate picked up the pace. "And yesterday morning, breakfast was over at what time, eight?"

"What? Oh, breakfast! Probably a bit earlier: Letty was still eating. We got up from the table at half past seven and they were walking out to the air taxi at eight."

"Mm-hm. Plane crashed two hours after Letty ate Zofia's breakfast. We are looking for something that would knock them out or disorient them enough to lose control of the plane. Something that could be put in their food or drink without them tasting it. Pretty tall order for Ambrose's Mr. Cadogan. Wonder what he'll come up with." He got out and came around to open my door, and Bess leapt out and made a big thing of stretching on the path.

"How many of them live here?" I asked.

"June, Grable, Annie, and Zofia share this one. I have no idea where Letty put up. But I do know that when Sir Basil visits Didcote he stays at Vera's house at the airfield."

"They're married?" Nothing could have surprised me more.

I heard him chuckle in the dark. "What a sweet innocent you are. No, they are not married; they are just *good* friends. It's not a secret, but it isn't openly discussed either—so English."

Trust Griff to know about everyone's sleeping arrangements, I thought.

"Good hunting with the Attagirls. I'll just wait here until you find out if they're home." He was standing so close to me that I caught the faint cedar scent of his cologne.

"I hope you . . . don't think . . ." he said and ground to a halt.

"Think what?"

"Oh . . . that I am happy to drive up to London and leave you alone with four potential poisoners!" He got into his car, switched on the ignition, and waited as I lifted the iron-forged knocker.

That was not what you were going to say, I thought, as the cottage door opened and Griff pulled out into the road.

FIFTEEN

———

I T WAS GRABLE WHO ANSWERED MY KNOCK. SHE WAS IN HER
dressing gown, with her head wrapped in a towel.

"Come on in, Poppy, if you don't mind mounds of wet
towels—it's hair-washing night."

"Are dogs welcome?"

"We would be honored. Annie might even have a bone for her
somewhere." She crouched down and made the proper fuss that
Bess required.

It was warm and bright inside the long, low-ceilinged room that
served as both kitchen and living space. A scrubbed pine table with
an assortment of ill-matched wooden chairs clustered around it
separated the kitchen from the sitting room. It was furnished with
large, sagging sofas and chairs with loose covers of faded chintz.
The cottage's black-oak roof beams contrasted starkly with its
roughly plastered walls and ceiling. In a recess in the far right corner a flight of stairs that led up to the second floor was half-
concealed by a heavy curtain on iron rings. Logs burned in a deep
stone fireplace where Zofia was seated drying her hair. In the

kitchen in front of a heavy old-fashioned iron stove, Annie was frying something delicious in a pan.

"June not back yet?" I asked Grable as she straightened up from Bess and wrapped her head more tightly in its towel.

"Oh yes, she's back. Playing darts up at the mess with the others." By "the others" I assumed she meant the lesser Attas.

Annie looked up briefly from her frying pan and nodded a hullo, and Zofia waved a hand as she brushed through her hair. I had prepared myself for more shock and grief at the news of Letty's crash, but evidently they had only just returned from two days of ferrying planes, so perhaps they hadn't heard from Vera yet.

I had an excuse for the reason for my uninvited call ready, but now that I was standing in their relaxed, unpretentious home, I was saved from sounding awkward, or just plain insincere, by Grable.

"Have you come up with a solution for your film? Are we all going to be stars?"

A light knock on the cottage door announced the arrival of another caller.

Grable opened the door, and there, standing on the threshold with a bottle of red wine in his hand, was Sir Basil.

"I can't stop for long," he explained as he sauntered into the cottage, evidently quite at ease with three women in their dishabille, one of whom was brushing out gleaming hair that came down to her waist. If he was surprised to find me here, he covered it well. "Good evening, Miss Redfern." He half bowed in the courteous way of an older generation. "What an unexpected pleasure. I thought you might have already left for London."

I blushed as if I was guilty of overstaying my welcome. "Crown Films have decided to continue with the film, even though we lost its star." I felt my blush deepen. I made it sound as if Edwina had wandered off into the landscape and was still trying to find her way back. "So, we are continuing with featuring"—I turned to the three women—"Annie, Grable, Zofia, and . . . and . . . the others." He fixed me with a stern eye, his eyebrows raised, then slowly nodded, as if commending me on my wits by not including Letty as another lost star. Why on earth, I asked myself, haven't they announced her death?

That's not why he's here, Ilona said. *It's Vera's job to break the news, not her boyfriend's.*

He handed Grable the bottle of wine. "I'd pull the cork on that and let it breathe for a while." He inhaled with appreciation. "Should be quite good with pork sausages." Annie turned from the stove and started to lay another place at the table. "Not for me, Annie, thank you," he said.

Without hesitation she turned to me. "Will you join us, Poppy, or perhaps you are having dinner with Captain O'Neal?"

I sought for a reasonable excuse and couldn't come up with one. "Um . . . gosh, thanks! I'd . . . yes, thank you, I'd love to!" Drink and eat, in this house? I had spent the greater part of the afternoon convincing Griff to drive up to London on an errand he was reluctant to perform because I believed that the dead Attagirls might have been poisoned. And while Griff was speeding on his way to eat dinner with Uncle Ambrose and his pal at the Travellers, I had accepted an invitation to eat sausages with three potential poisoners.

"Dinner, Bess?" Annie said, and I nearly shrieked, No!

For heaven's sake, darling, pull yourself together. She's hardly going to poison a dog! Ilona's voice stopped me from snatching up Bess and making for the door.

"How kind of you!" I said as Annie produced a sizable chunk of what looked like mutton bone. There was no hesitation from a dog who had eaten porridge for breakfast. Bessie stepped smartly forward, took the bone delicately in her jaws, and crawled under the kitchen table with it. After a quiet moment, a rhythmic gnawing sound began, and we all giggled.

Sir Basil looked at his watch. "Good Lord, would you look at the time. I must be on my way to Vera; can't be late for dinner. Good night, ladies. Miss Redfern, when is it you're leaving?"

"Tomorrow night."

"If you have time I would be delighted to take you to lunch tomorrow. At the inn, say, one o'clock? Jolly good, well, good night." He threw open the cottage door and stood on its threshold; clearly Sir Basil didn't give a damn about blackout. I caught the gleam of his Bentley's silver hood in the light from the cottage door.

"What a sweetie," said Grable. "Always such a thoughtful old gent. How long 'til we eat, Annie? Is there time for a cocktail?" She was already shaking something up in a silver flask with ice. "Take a pew, Poppy, I'm making martinis. We've all had a very long couple of days."

"How lovely!" I said, my eyes fixed on the flask as I moved to get a better view of her.

"Where's Captain O'Neal off to? Didn't he drop you just now?"

"Yes, but it's been a long day for him too. He's driven back to . . . back to the inn."

Grable poured the contents of her flask into four glasses. We were all drinking from the same flask, so even if she was a dab hand with poisons I should be safe. "Olive?" She speared olives from a jar and put one in each glass.

"Annie?" she took a martini into the kitchen, which left me with a choice of three glasses. I handed a glass to Zofia and took one myself.

Bottom's up. Ilona was laughing. *Oops, perhaps I shouldn't have said that!*

"Cheers!" We raised our glasses. The martini was very dry and quite delicious, and I could feel the zing of alcohol singing through my veins.

Grable perched on the arm of the sofa. "We all want to know how you met the gorgeous captain!"

I took another sip of my cocktail. "I met him earlier this year. My family's house and some of our farmland were requisitioned by the War Office as an airfield for the American Air Force. That's when I met Griff. I was an ARP warden for the area, and we sort of bumped into each other in the blackout."

"Romantic." Zofia had braided her long hair and pinned it at the base of her neck. She sat back in her chair and took a sip of her drink. Half-lit by firelight, in her crimson-and-black silk kimono she looked like a heroine from a novel: exotic and enigmatic. "And now he is your boyfriend."

I felt my cheeks flush as I remembered our clumsy moment in the meadow above Elton and took another sip to buoy me. "Well, no, not really a boyfriend."

Zofia laughed. "Ah yes, I forget how deceptively modest some of you English girls can be." She glanced around the room. "Annie is the same way, aren't you, darling? She loves to go to parties to dance with handsome men in uniform, but that is all. Am I not right, *chérie*?"

Annie turned over something in her frying pan. "Strangely enough I think most of us are pretty 'modest,' as you call it. And please do not forget I am a married woman with two little girls at home. My nights of partying are rare and usually spent catching up on gossip with my cousins." I for one was glad to hear I wasn't the only unworldly woman in the room.

"Waiting for Mister—or should I say Lieutenant—right?" Zofia purred. "Even lovely Grable dresses up in a gorgeous gown cut down to there and up to here, and then says a polite 'good night' at the door. Don't you, *kochanie*?"

Grable laughed. "I'm not saying a word about my social life to you, Zofia. I am sure you were a modest little girl too, before you met the love of your life."

Zofia shook her head. "Me, modest? Of course I was—with all the other young men in the region I grew up in. But not with my Aleksy. I was sixteen years old when I met my beautiful husband, and we became lovers that very night."

I tried not to splutter into my martini. She had practically been a baby! I couldn't imagine anyone being interested in me at that age: puppy fat and pimples was how I remembered my sixteenth year.

Ilona became quite eloquent, as she often does when I have a cocktail. *Good Lord, would you listen to her? She sounds like an old crone reminiscing about her lost youth and she's all of what, twenty?*

Zofia picked up a poker and stirred the fire, gazing into its red embers. "You both escaped Poland when Germany invaded, didn't you?" I asked to keep her on track.

"Ah, Miss Redfern, you wish to know my story!"

Grable snorted. "She only wants the heroic bits, Zofia, not the bedroom scenes."

"My husband was the most perfect man I have ever met in my life," Zofia began, and paused to sip from her glass. "He had come to my father's house for, what do you call it? A celebration of summer—a picnic. Everyone had come from all over the region, and our house was packed to the rafters. It was a glorious afternoon: the meadows were full of wildflowers, with just the slightest breeze to cool us from the mountains. My father had arranged farm carts decorated with flowers to drive us out to the river. The servants had worked for three days to make everything ready for our party." She shook her head as she remembered. "It makes me weak just to remember the food." She took another sip. "Good martini, Grable. Did I ever tell you that we have sixty-two blends of vodka in our province of Poland alone? Where was I? Ah yes, my father had sent cases of champagne and vodka ahead to the picnic ground in baths of ice."

She had another go at the fire, and Grable tossed on two more logs and gently took the poker away from her.

"I will never forget that moment when I walked down into the courtyard: Aleksy rode in through the bell-tower gate and dismounted. He was tall, broad shouldered, and when he took off his hat to bow to my mother, his hair was the color of silver gilt. He looked like a young pagan god standing there in the sunlight." I heard Grable clear her throat, but I had my eyes fixed firmly on her handsome profile as Zofia gazed into the fire.

"'Come, Zofia,' my father called out to me. 'I want you to meet our new neighbor, Count Aleksy Lukasiewicz.' When Aleksy turned to me I thought I was going to faint. His eyes met mine: bright, clear eyes, the color of sea glass. It was as if we had known each other forever." She laughed as she remembered. "Of course, he was extremely correct: his lips barely touched the back of my hand. In that moment it was as if he were the only man in the world—and it has remained that way for me ever since." She bowed her head and Annie leaned forward, her eyes shining. Zofia's reminiscences had the quality of a fairy story.

The countess was no longer sitting in a cramped cottage drinking inferior gin; she was in Poland again. "Our life that summer was—" She nodded into her martini glass. "We rode across meadows bright with the blue of cornflowers and made love in the cool of silver-birch woodlands. In October we were married. I was seventeen and he was twenty-four." She held out her glass to Grable.

"Are you sure?" her friend asked as she shook up her flask.

"Then the Nazis came." Zofia waited until her glass was replenished and took another sip. "The terrible things they did! The cold cruelty of those brute people." She fell silent for a moment. "Aleksy and I, we fled in the November of that year, when we knew all was lost and that any resistance was impossible. It was already snowing heavily when we drove an old farm truck through the country into Romania. 'Wear your furs under your warmest and oldest cloak,' Aleksy told me, 'and pray that the truck can make it.' His plan was to fight the Germans from outside of Poland."

She lifted a clenched fist and held it front of her and said something in Polish as she shook it. Then she looked up at me and translated. "I will return to Poland when those murderous bastards have been wiped from the face of the earth." She made Scarlett O'Hara sound like a child bleating for her mama.

"So, we stayed in Bucharest through the coldest winter in memory. Aleksy was a pilot. He flew in the resistance and when he had time he taught me to fly an old Lublin that was practically falling apart." She shook her head and smiled. "He had to walk around the bloody thing with a spanner before we took off and tighten everything up. Strangely enough, that long winter was the happiest for us. I learned to make *ciorba*: a peasant's soup made from whatever vegetables you can find, and if you are lucky a bit of meat. It's flavored with peppers to keep you warm." We were no longer there with her in the cottage. Maybe, in her mind, Zofia was making pepper soup in a kitchen somewhere in Bucharest. "We made love every night—no need for modesty when the windows are covered in frost and the blankets are so thin you can see firelight through them!"

Grable waved her martini flask at me, and I shook my head.

"We stayed in Bucharest until the rise of the fascist Iron Guard made it unsafe for us Poles there. Again, we fled with the help of friends. This time to France, where Aleksy flew for the French Air Force and I drove an ambulance. We hardly saw each other, but we were doing our best to fight for the freedom of the world." A deep sigh and another sip. "And then of course Belgium, Luxembourg, and the Netherlands were invaded by those bastards in the spring. The Italians marched over the Alps and took France, and that filthy coward Marshal Pétain welcomed the Nazis into Vichy, in the south, leaving de Gaulle to struggle in the north." She shrugged and looked around at our intent faces. "France 'fell' to the Nazis and somehow in the chaos of Dunkirk, Aleksy and I found each other, and once again we were on the run. This time to Britain." She kissed her hand to us. I noticed that her glass was empty.

"We hid out in Brittany until we could find someone to ferry us across the Channel to England. We bribed a fisherman with the last of our money and hid under old sacks in the bottom of a boat that reeked of mackerel. But we were free, free to continue the fight." She looked at Grable and then to Annie and nodded. "Bravest country in the world, England. Bravest country in the world." She waved her empty glass and Grable obediently filled it. How the recipient of her third martini was still upright I have no idea.

"And here we were, in England, in the clothes we stood up in. Aleksy joined the RAF, and a year later I met Basil at a cocktail party, and he persuaded me to join the ATA. I was the first Pole to join." She smiled at me. "And in those days, my dear, all we ATA girls did was ferry those bloody Tiger Moths and Swordfishes all over the place."

"I flew in one, on my first morning here," I said, and Zofia laughed.

"No need for me to tell you, then, that an *open* cockpit means just that, in snow, sleet, or hail. But we Poles are tough: our climate is more frigid than the softness of your lovely island."

Annie interrupted her. "Zofia delivered more Tiger Moths than any other pilot in the winter months of 1940. Please don't tell the rest of your story, darling, if it will distress." Annie's usually severe expression softened. As a mother of two, she was enjoying Zofia's love story just as much as Grable and I.

"It should distress," Zofia answered. She lifted her head and stared at us. If we didn't care to hear the rest, it was too bad. "It should distress us all, for years to come, to know what one deranged man and his pack of cowardly animals did to my country and is trying to do to the world." She drank from her glass. "Death to tyrants," she muttered, and turning to me, she said, "I tell you my story to use as you see fit for your film. The more women who join the ATA, the quicker planes will be delivered to the military, and the quicker we will finish off the Hun.

"Now, where was I? Ah yes, the summer of 1940 and the start of the Battle of Britain. Young men had come from all over the world to fly for the RAF: Australia, Canada, Africa, Belgium, Czechoslovakia, India, and Poland." She rotated her free hand as she peeled off the names of the countries that had joined us in the battle for Britain. "It was an international air force of courage and conviction. And like all brave young warriors, some of them died before their time.

"I saw Aleksy twice after he joined the RAF: once in September and then again in October the night before he was killed." She kept her voice even, almost matter-of-fact, and a cold finger ran up my spine and lifted the hair in my neck.

We English have made ourselves publicly and often privately silent in our grief; perhaps it is the only way we have managed to carry on. But Zofia's proud story of love and courage made me feel deeply honored that she had shared it with us. I glanced at Grable and Annie as they listened. Their solemn faces were rosy in the firelight, like those of little girls being given a lesson on the horror of war—except of course for the martini glasses.

"We won that battle of the air over the Luftwaffe, who had more aircraft than we did. Aleksy had come to Britain to be in that fight. When Poland fell he had made the conquest of Germany his destiny." She got slowly to her feet, as if telling her story had drained her. "I should call it a night before I say something I will regret, eh, Grable?"

Her friend shook her head. "You have taught us to say 'no regrets,' isn't that right, Zofia?"

She nodded and pulled her kimono tightly around her thin body. "I have no appetite for dinner, my dear Annie. I think it is bedtime for me." She turned to me and rested her hand on my shoulder. "Miss Redfern, good night. It was a pleasure to meet you. Please tell the story of Count Aleksy Wladyslaw Lukasiewicz in your film—he was only twenty-seven years old on the day he died. From the day that Poland was invaded, his only desire was to rescue freedom from tyranny."

Holding on to my shoulder, she raised her nearly empty glass. "And here is to another brave pilot." She was slurring ever so slightly. "Here is to my dear friend, the kindest woman in England: to Edwina!"

We joined in her toast.

"Sleep well, Zofia," Annie said, but she walked past us as if we simply weren't there.

We were silent as we listened to her tread the stairs to her room, and I prepared myself for an observation or two from Ilona. *Not quite the victim type I first thought. More like Boadicea riding out on her shaggy pony to vanquish the invading Romans.* A door in the landing above opened and then closed and Grable got to her feet. "No more cocktails until we have had dinner. Is it ready, Annie?"

THE THREE OF US—Grable, Annie, and I—gathered around the kitchen table for generous helpings of bubble and squeak and pork sausages that were sadly a little overcooked.

I closed my eyes and inhaled with blissful appreciation as Annie put a large dark sausage in front of me. "One each—no need to share! I am keeping Zofia's for her breakfast. She'll need it." Her gray eyes were red-rimmed and her mouth drawn in, in its usual tired lines of disapproval.

"How old are your girls?" I asked her.

"Fanny is four, and Linda will be three next month. They live with my mum just outside Winchester." And she shut her mouth in a tight line again.

"Lovely! Winchester is so near, so you see them often?"

She shook her head, and her fine, straight, bay-brown hair flicked over her shoulder and fell back into place. "As often as I can, of course. Now, eat up, before it gets cold." I felt chastised, as if Annie found my prying unacceptable. I hoped that the girls' granny was as warm and as kindhearted as my own.

"You are not too particular about little things like black-market sausages, are you, Poppy?" Grable rushed in with her mouth full.

I would have laughed if I wasn't so busy filling mine.

Grable reached forward and picked up the wine. "The old sweetheart always brings us a bottle of something delicious on a Saturday night, if any of us are at home. Sometimes he drops Vera off with us, but he never intrudes. Must have an endless cellar—I just hope it lasts the war." And even Annie unbent enough to lift her glass and take an appreciative sip. But it was not enough to soften her manner. She was so reserved that it was difficult to draw her out about her life before the war and how she had come to join the ATA. I wanted to hear a bit more about her famous landing in a German airfield.

"You must have been scared stiff when you saw the swastika on the tail fin," I said, hoping that pork sausage and a bottle of Nuits-Saint-Georges had warmed her up for questions.

"We would all be scared if we found ourselves landing in a German airfield," she said. "Flying is one of the joys of my life, but it has truly terrifying moments. It doesn't take much to get lost in the fog. I was lucky." And that was all I could get out of her. It would be hard to count on Annie Trenchard to replace the flamboyant arch-adventuress, Edwina, in our film.

I sighed with relief as Grable took over our dinner conversation. "I'm the one who hasn't had any real adventures," she said as she sipped her wine. "First of all, my father hates it when I fly, and Mummy simply pretends I don't. I think they would be a lot happier if I were nursing or even driving an ambulance."

"When did you learn to fly?" I asked her. "Who taught you?"

She put down her knife and fork. "An uncle: a wicked uncle." She giggled, and I wished I could spend more time with her when our picture and this investigation were over.

She cupped her pointed chin in an elegantly manicured hand. "I was about fourteen." Another sip of wine. "Mm, this is good. My uncle flew during the last war. In fact, he was one of the first of his generation to take to the air, in those far-off days of invention and derring-do. Aircraft were parcels of canvas, wood, and wire with a motor in the middle. Can you imagine anything more terrifying?"

Annie finished a mouthful of sausage. "Edwina said that's all they are still. If you stripped off the thin outer shell of a Spitfire, all there is underneath is that massive Merlin engine that takes up all the nose and petrol tanks. When you are sitting right in the middle of an engine, surrounded by petrol, you don't ask yourself about safety!" The wine, or perhaps my willingness to back down from questions, had made Annie a little less forbidding.

"But all planes are safe now, aren't they?" I asked my drunken question as I thought of Griff taking off in his Mustang. I was ignored.

If wine relaxes some of us, it makes others more assertive. "That's just the sort of thing Edwina would say. And it's simply not true." Grable thumped her wineglass down. "The Spit is incredibly safe. If June were here she would tell you so. Edwina loved to exaggerate everything she did—she lusted for attention. More wine, anyone?" Annie shook her head and took another bite of sausage as Grable splashed wine into her own glass. "Thank God I'm off duty for a couple of days."

"Edwina didn't worry about safety—she was brave." Annie made her statement in a firm voice, and I noticed that her brows were arched as she fixed her eyes on Grable's wineglass.

"What rot: she was reckless. That's what happens when your nerves are shot to pieces. You either cave in or you take bigger and bigger risks. If she were in the RAF they would have grounded her."

"Shot to pieces?" I said to remind them I was still here.

A tut of exasperation from Annie. "Ever since she was attacked by those two Messerschmitts . . ." she said in an impatient and chiding tone. No wonder she found being with her girls exhausting. She twirled a piece of hair with her finger and I felt her kick Grable's leg under the table. "And she was overworking."

A derisive harrumph from Grable. "Annie, what are you saying? She was a wreck long before that. Ever since June . . . when that nutcase sent her the first letter."

Did she mean the month of June, or their fellow pilot?

"Who doesn't overwork these days?" I asked, remembering the hours and miles I had walked every night as the only Air Raid Precautions warden in my village earlier this year.

Annie laughed down her nose. "You hardly overwork, Grable. You are always dashing off when your mum telephones."

"It's true," Grable said with disarming good nature. "True, all true. My parents are very demanding of my time." She shook her head and giggled into her glass of wine.

Annie had stopped frowning now that Edwina's shot nerves were no longer under discussion. "And so are all the glam flyboys at Croydon, Biggin Hill, Northolt, and . . ." Annie waved her arm to indicate countless numbers. "Wherever Grable steps out of her plane and takes off her helmet to shake down that mane of hair, five pilots fall irretrievably in love. And she does her duty, don't you, ducky? She dances the night away all over England."

They were both giggling now, humor restored thanks to the magical combination of sausages, wine, and Grable's willingness not to take herself seriously. I breathed a sigh of relief; there is nothing more intimidating than two strong women in opposition. But I wanted to hear more about the complicated Edwina.

I should have counted to ten. Annie put down her wineglass with the sort of finality that meant she was done with wine and song. "She is our pinup girl, aren't you, Grable? You certainly put poor old Edwina in the shade, didn't you?" The shift in tone made me want to run for the door. What was going on with these two? The mood in the cottage this evening was twisting and turning like a feral creature in a trap: Zofia's story of love and courage had left us softly sentimental, and now this awful falling-out! I pushed away my half-finished glass of superb red wine. I needed a clear head.

They are still coming to terms with Edwina's crash, and they certainly don't know about Letty's death yet. I think we are going to hit what the Attagirls call rough air this evening, darling, so hang on tight. Ilona didn't need to warn me, because I could have cut the tension in the room with a knife.

Grable shrugged. "It isn't my fault that I was born to be tall and blond," she said. "There's something about being a blonde, or a redhead"—she pointed at me—"that makes men behave ridiculously, right, Poppy? Poppy knows what I'm talking about, don't you?" Grable chuckled away like a naughty schoolgirl. "Edwina was the real pinup girl of our group, not me. Until after her Luftwaffe incident."

"You could have been kinder to her when she lost her nerve."

"I *was* kind to her." Grable frowned as she put down her wineglass. "What are you saying? I also stuck up for her, which is more than you ever did. It was me who covered for her with Vera when she went on a bender every bloody night of the week. And it was me who bailed her out when she was so hungover she couldn't fly!" Grable's chin was up with indignation.

"After you got her drunk, which was very irresponsible of you!" Annie's forefinger wagged at Grable: a nanny scolding thoughtless behavior.

"Come off it, Annie, Edwina was soaking it up like a sponge." Grable glared at her friend. "God, you sound just like a Girl Guide—and excuse me for saying so, but you have no idea what you're talking about! You should have seen her. She had been drinking alone all night and she was paralytic when I found her. I had one drink with her before I realized she was a mess and got her out of there before she threw up all over the bar. It's *so* unfair to say I was the one who got her tight, when I was the one who rescued her."

I sat still and silent through this horrifying exchange, barely breathing. But I plucked up enough courage to ask, "What do you think made her drink quite so much?" I wondered if our investigation was a waste of time. If Edwina was a habitual drunk, then "pilot error" was putting it mildly.

They interrupted each other in their haste.

"She was terrified to go up, after the Luftwaffe attack—"

"It was those hateful letters," blurted Grable.

I went for the more informative statement. "Letters from who?"

"No one," Annie said and snapped her mouth shut.

"They were anonymous. You know the sort of spiteful things people who are bonkers send. Usually old ladies, or batty old spinsters," said Grable, avoiding Annie's fierce stare.

Annie sighed. "Old ladies and spinsters who knew about the Luftwaffe incident? Did you hear what you just said, Grable? Until last week, no one but us knew about Edwina's Luftwaffe ambush. Those letters were *not* written by a dotty old lady with nothing better to do. They were written by . . ." She heard herself and folded her arms. "We just shouldn't talk about it."

I wondered how I could get them to talk about it, but I needn't have worried. Grable ignored her friend and leaned toward me. "The letters accused Edwina of making up a story. They said that there was no attack. That she lost her bearings when she was delivering a Spit to Biggin Hill and was late arriving. She got carried away with her excuse and turned it into an act of heroism rather than not paying attention to where she was going." She shrugged as if the truth was anyone's guess.

Annie rolled her eyes. "Some crazy old lady in the village who knew how to spell 'Luftwaffe' and 'Messerschmitt' correctly, who knew there were two of them and that Edwina landed her plane on fumes? It wasn't some old dipsy-doodle who sent those letters, Grable, and you know it. I read one of them. Believe me, there was a point to them. Someone was out to discredit Edwina in the most cowardly way. And it undid her, as it was intended to do."

A spiteful old crackpot, or someone who wanted to undermine Edwina's nerve? "When did she get the first one?" I asked.

"Oh," said Grable. She stared down at her empty plate to concentrate her memory. "They were coming long before Edwina's encounter with the enemy: nasty accusations and lies. It was the Luftwaffe ones that sent her over the top."

Annie looked at Grable with one of those you've-done-it-now expressions. But if either of them said anything, their words were drowned by a fervent pounding on the front door and the rattling of the latch.

"Basil must have inadvertently dropped the snib when he left." I heard the relief in Annie's voice at the interruption.

They both sat quite still, staring straight ahead. I got up, and out of the corner of my eye I saw Grable slide a hand across the table, palm side up, in appeasement, to her friend.

I pulled back the blackout curtain to open the door. June Evesham pushed past me: her hair was disheveled and she was out of breath. The wheels of her thrown-down bicycle were still spinning on the ground behind her on the path.

"Have you heard?" She put her hand up to her forehead as if she could hardly believe what she was about to tell us. "No, of course you haven't, because bloody Vera Abercrombie has only just made her announcement in the mess. Letty crashed her Walrus yesterday morning! And Vera announced it to the whole world, without a whisper to us first. I can't believe it." She paused to catch her breath, and her voice was a lament of anguish. "I can't believe that Letty crashed her plane."

"Good God, is she all right?" Annie got to her feet.

"Didn't you hear what I said? She crashed. She crashed that

bloody Walrus into a bridge—she's dead." June turned away from them as if she could hardly bear to hear them speak.

"Where did she crash?" Grable's patrician voice cut across the heavy atmosphere of the kitchen like a draft of Arctic air.

"Crikey, I don't know!" June turned on her. "Does it bloody well matter where?"

Grable pushed her into a chair and turned to the sideboard. "Here, drink this, June." She put a glass into her hand. "You are in shock, darling. No, I insist, c'mon: one sip at a time." She looked at me over June's bowed head. "She was Letty's closest friend," she explained, as if June's shocked grief needed an explanation.

Annie put her hand between June's shoulders and patted, the circular soothing stroke that mothers and grannies administer to hurt children. "Junie, did Vera say what caused the crash?"

June lifted her head; her face was blotched with the tears that coursed down her face. "You know something?" she said, her accent so thick with pain and Australia it was difficult to understand what she was saying. "The only thing I could get out of the ruddy woman was that it was 'pilot error.' Can you imagine? She was flying a Walrus, for God's sake! She was exhausted and in distress after Edwina's crash and Abercrombie thought it was a good idea for her to fly a stinking Walrus six hundred miles to Scotland, in God knows what weather at this time of year. As if it couldn't have waited another day. Struth!" She pulled a handkerchief out of her pocket and blew her nose. "Sorry," she said as she handed her empty glass to Grable. "Didn't mean to make such an exhibition. It's such a shock, such a terrible shock. At least Vera called me into her office and gave me the news in private, before she made her announcement to the rest of them." She stared grimly down into her replenished glass, breathing deeply, as she struggled to regain control.

Grable stood looking down at her feet. "June, I think she was waiting for you to get back before she told everyone." She put her hand up to her eyes and pinched the bridge of her nose, hard.

"Letty. Whatever happened to you, my friend?" Annie's eyes were wide with shock. I watched her swallow down emotion, her face rigid with the will to impose control over fear.

Grable was busy at the sideboard. She handed me a small glass and I took a cautious sniff. Yes, it was brandy all right. I waved mine in the air. The last thing I needed was to drink it.

"To Letty."

"To a great pilot and an even greater friend," said Annie.

June, knocking back her drink, was practically unintelligible. "She was true blue, all right."

"Perhaps I should be going," I said as I put my glass down on the kitchen table. "I am so terribly sorry . . ." Letty had been my friend for an hour or two. She had been theirs from the ATA's early days. She had helped them make history as the first women who flew for England in wartime, and I was just there to write up a story of that friendship.

I found my coat hanging on a peg by the door. "I am sure you want to be alone, to . . ." I felt I was trespassing on their sorrow.

I pulled aside the heavy blackout curtain that hung closed against the doorway. "Bessie, come," I said and, knowing that she would never leave her bone, walked back to the kitchen table.

Grable came over and stood in front of the door. "You are not going to walk back to the inn tonight, are you?"

Oh yes, I am! I thought. I needed the night's cool air, and its quiet, to try to piece together the odd events of the evening. "Perhaps I can borrow a bike? I can return it to the mess, or here, tomorrow morning."

Grable looked at her watch. "It's half past ten and as black as pitch. Are you sure?"

"I'll be fine," I said. "It's just down the road." I bent down and looked under the table. Bess was asleep with the bone between her paws. "Come on, girlie." She roused herself and returned to her gnawing. "Let's go home," I said, reaching for the bone. She pricked her ears forward and looked at me as if I must be mad.

"It's a good half hour down the road even on a bike. Why don't you doss down on the sofa?"

"No, really, it's all right. I have work to do anyway."

"Here." She dug in the pocket of a trench coat hanging by the door. "Here's my blackout torch. You can take my bike." She slipped ahead of me through the door and I followed, carrying Bess and her foul bone.

With her torch clipped to its handlebars, Grable wheeled the bike out onto the path to the gate. "It's straight on down this lane, past the hangar on the edge of the airfield. After about five minutes the river will be on your right. Keep a sharp lookout at the fork in the road because the turning to the inn is on the right just after the fork. If you continue on you will be on the road to Southampton; go left at the fork and you'll be in the village." I couldn't see her face in the dark, but her shoulders were squared as she stood upright, away from the post of the porch, as if refusing to be defeated by the evening. She reached out and put a hand on my shoulder. "About those letters—you won't talk about them, will you?"

"What letters?" I said blithely, lying in my teeth.

"They were just . . . spite, I expect." She paused. "I don't quite know how to say this, but Edwina was one of those girls who seemed to make enemies wherever she went."

"Not you, though?"

"Me, Edwina's enemy? No, not me." She laughed. "Most of the time I just ignored her silliness. But I admired her skill, her courage. She might have been a pain sometimes, but there was no real malice in her, and in some strange way, I know I'll really miss her. But Letty?" Her voice was deeply sad and still had traces of her earlier despair. "Now, there was one in a million: decent, kind—what June would call a real mate." She bent down and, picking up June's discarded bike, propped it where hers had been against the porch rail. "Both of them were exceptional flyers. So the term 'pilot error' really sticks in my throat." She sighed and then shrugged her shoulders. "Poor old Vera, as if she hasn't got her hands full as it is. All she wants to do is run an exemplary ferry pool, and two of her best pilots go down, one after the other."

"Her hands full?" So far as I could see, Vera's job was shuffling papers and writing up flight schedules: long and tiring work to be sure, but not beyond the average competence of most organized women.

The shock of Letty's death hadn't cleared Grable's head completely, and the brandy had simply added to her loquacity. "She has her hands full with Sir Basil," she explained. "Has a bit of a wandering eye. Nice enough old chap, but it must be hard to be an aging roué—and even harder to be his mistress. On top of that, Vera's senior, the commanding officer at White Waltham, is a real bear."

I tried not to react to this rather revealing remark about Sir Basil, especially as I was having lunch with him tomorrow.

"I'll return your bike tomorrow," I said as she turned away to open the door. She gave a dismissive wave at the bike and stumbled on the threshold. "Second turn on the right. G'night, Poppy."

I put Bess's noxious bone in the front basket of the bike, and with her dancing in front me, backward, we started on our way.

After a few minutes of pedaling I realized that my front wheel was all over the place. *You're drunk!* Ilona was laughing. *What a lightweight: one martini and half a glass of wine. Try eating something when someone offers you a cocktail next time!* I concentrated on keeping my front wheel as straight as I could, and with Bess anxiously trotting alongside, looking up at the basket, we set out for the only inn in Didcote.

FIVE MINUTES OF hard pedaling uphill did the trick. As we came level with the airfield, I felt less thickheaded, and my eyes had adjusted to the dark. I could see the outline of the airfield's largest hangar, the one where Mac Wilson had confronted us, shadowed against the night sky.

Bess stopped, her alert ears pricked forward, and her hackles came up. She growled. "Shush, Bessie. No bark," I said automatically, because for an instant, a fraction of an instant, the flair of a pair of headlights came through the trees in just one brief flash, lighting up the grass track beneath them. They flared once and were instantly doused. They were blackout headlights shielded to aim downward, but in that split second in the dark of the night they were glaringly bright. I stopped, stood astride my bike, and peered down the grass track that led from the lane to the hulk of the hangar.

I heard a voice raised in question. And then silence. Bess trotted forward. "Come," I whispered frantically. "Stay!" To my relief she stopped, sniffed the air, and then came back to me. The last thing in the world I needed was to have a conversation with a man like Mac Wilson.

SIXTEEN

I MUST HAVE BEEN MORE TIRED THAN I THOUGHT BECAUSE IT was half past eleven when I swerved up the short drive from the lane to the inn. To my relief the Alvis was parked outside the door. Griff was back!

I pushed open the door as quietly as I could and fumbled my way into the dense black fug of the inn's hall. Bess, with her enviable doggy night vision, pattered ahead of me as I bumped my hand along the wall to turn the corner from the hall into the lounge. The inn smelled of stale beer, cigarettes, and turnip soup. Not a particularly appealing combination, but it was almost like coming home after my long, cold ride down the endless dark of the lane.

We were welcomed by the light from the still-glowing fire at the end of the room, and the outline of Griff slumped in a chair, legs thrust out in front of him. His head was turned to one side at an uncomfortable angle. I stopped and listened to his even breathing. He was asleep—I reached down to restrain Bess as she lunged forward to say hullo.

There is no pretense in a sleeping face. And in the last of the firelight Griff looked probably much as he had done at eight. His dark straight brows and forehead were smooth, and in repose his mouth, usually so expressive, was slack. I felt like an intruder, standing there watching him in defenseless rest. I stepped back and said his name. "Griff? Griff!" Bess stood up on her hind legs and lovingly started to wash the hand that dangled over the arm of the chair.

"What?" His eyes opened, startlingly bright in his pale face. "Poppy!" He smiled and my heart leapt into my mouth. He reached out his hand for mine and then awoke fully. "Was I sleeping? Must have dropped off. What time is it?" He sat forward in his chair.

"Half eleven." I put a log on the fire and sat down in the chair next to his.

He rubbed the top of his head. "I couldn't decide whether to be worried about you or not. I thought of coming over to the cottage and then decided I might be interrupting something important. That you might think I was interfering. I finally came to the conclusion that if you weren't home by midnight, I would drive over and carry you off to hospital to have your stomach pumped." He was laughing; whether it was with real relief or because he always chooses to make light of things I had no idea.

"When did you get back?"

He looked at his watch. "About half an hour ago. Your uncle Ambrose is a nice old gent underneath all those penetrating questions, by the way."

"And Cadogan?"

He whistled: his expression for amazement or derision. "What a blowhard."

"A what?"

"A talkative know-it-all. What the man doesn't know could be written on the head of a pin."

"Did he know anything about the sort of poison we are interested in?"

He ran his hand through his hair. "Oh yeah, but so much of it, it made my head spin. The biggest problem with academics is that they love to hear themselves talk." Griff lifted a tired face and smiled. "Your uncle explained that I was interested in poison, and Cadogan just took off. I tried to guide him toward giving me useful information, but it was impossible. It was like someone had flipped a switch. He started with cyanide: sodium cyanide, potassium cyanide, hydrogen cyanide. HCN is obtained by acidification of cyanide salts, by the way. And that was just for openers. Then he went on to arsenic."

"Does cyanide have violent symptoms?" I asked.

"Yes, both symptoms and death sound exhausting and probably look awful. Cadogan's endless list of conventional toxins, as he called them, all have two things in common: they act within minutes, and they are rough on the digestive organs. Lots of mess." He shrugged his shoulders, his palms held upward. "From everything he told me, it doesn't appear that either of our Attagirls could have been poisoned. Especially, Cadogan says, by something a layman could get hold of. England has regulated its citizens' ability to get their hands on arsenic and strychnine. Even homemade poisons from plants that grow here along the hedgerows—hemlock, belladonna, and digitalis—have violent effects and act quickly." I could tell he was trying to let me down gently.

"Are there any poisons that are not quite so immediate and . . . milder in their symptoms?"

"Nope, 'fraid not. Cadogan does have a pal who specializes in medicinal herbs that can be used as poisons if given in large doses. He said he'd give him a try for us."

I tried to be gracious about Griff's news. But it was difficult when I remembered June and her friends' devastation at hearing about Letty's death, and the anger that had sprung up between Annie and Grable as they tried to understand what had happened to Edwina before her crash. The misery that Vera Abercrombie went through when one of her "girls" was killed in an accident. I also remembered Zofia, downing martinis and dwelling on happier days before her husband was killed, and her toast to Edwina. I had rushed back to Didcote, determined that Zofia was the murderer's next victim, and discovered that, unlike Edwina, who had been persecuted with vicious poison-pen letters, Zofia was one of life's survivors. A chilling thought occurred: had she pushed her poisoned breakfast toward Letty? Was Zofia capable of murdering two of her friends?

"Perhaps we asked the wrong question. Perhaps we should have asked about poisons that disorient rather than kill," I said helpfully, and then wished I hadn't spoken. He had driven for miles today to have dinner with two old codgers, and if I knew the Travellers, the menu would have been uninspiring at best.

"How was Uncle Ambrose?" I asked out of politeness.

"He interrogated me on my interests. Did I shoot? Oh, too bad. What about hunt? Oh really, never? Not even pheasant? What did I do when I wasn't flying? In the end I told him I played bridge and that seemed to make him happy. He was a huge improvement on Cadogan."

I felt utterly depleted by disappointment that his trip to London hadn't yielded anything other than he had revised his original opinion of Ambrose from arrogant imperialist to an old fuddy-duddy who thought shooting pheasant was good sport.

"Perhaps I should make some coffee?"

"If I drink any more of that stuff I don't think I'll survive. Tell me about your evening. How did you get on with the Attas?"

How best to describe three—no, four—very strong women who were still struggling to accept Edwina's accident and, as I left, had been knocked sideways with the new horror of Letty's death? "They are doing their best to put a brave face on things. You know"— I smiled—"it's how we are." Griff had once referred, obliquely, to our island reticence as cold reserve.

"Did you manage to find out what they thought about Edwina and her death, how they really *feel*?" he asked hopefully. "Anyone have a reason to want her dead?"

"Yes and no," I said, remembering Zofia's passionate recounting of her history. "Zofia has lost so much of her life, and has learned to cope with it on the face of things. But she had three large martinis and was a bit . . . inebriated, so she revealed a lot more than I think she would normally."

"Polish reserve," muttered Griff.

"Not a scrap of reserve about Zofia. But I bet she would be good at keeping secrets if it mattered. I got the feeling that she was pretty cut up about Edwina's death: she raised a glass and toasted her as 'the kindest woman in England,' with the greatest sincerity and re-spect, even if she was three sheets to the wind at the time." I saw the lovely pale face and the large shining eyes. "She would either tell you everything that came into her head," I said as I thought it through, "or you would have to dig really deep and still be left won-dering what else she was concealing."

"Enigmatic?" Griff asked.

"Yes, very enigmatic." I nodded. "But she's also an extrovert—in a reclusive sort of way."

He laughed. "And the other three?"

I thought about the face-to-face falling-out of Annie and Grable. There had been nothing reserved or reticent about my evening with the cottage's inmates.

"Four," I replied. "When I arrived, Sir Basil was hard on my heels with a very expensive bottle of wine, which he left with us. He didn't stay long. But his relationship with them is pretty informal, almost as if he was one of them."

This brought about some raised eyebrows. Griff sat forward in his chair. "How do you mean 'one of them'? He must be more than twice their age."

"Well, Annie, Grable, and Zofia were all in their nightclothes when I got there and didn't turn a hair about Sir Basil marching in with his bottle of wine. I think he is a regular visitor at the cottage." I shrugged. "They were back from working long hours and were just relaxing: washing their hair and making dinner."

He sat up straight, his eyes round as he tried not to laugh. "Nightclothes?" he asked, and then seeing my confused expression: "You mean robes, don't you?"

"Robes?" There had been nothing ceremonial about their appearance.

He snapped his fingers to wake up his memory. "Those heavy plaid things that wrap around you and are tied by cord belt with a tassel, the ones you wear over thick cotton pajamas in unheated English houses in the winter?"

"Yes, dressing gowns, what else could I mean?"

He passed a hand over his eyes and his shoulders shook with inner laughter. "God, I must be really tired. From the way you described it, I thought for a moment that they were all floating around in filmy negligees with those little swansdown thingamabobs on their feet."

It was my turn to stare. "Who on earth wears those?"

"Barbara Stanwyck in *Remember the Night*."

"Oh, a film," I said dismissively, because we all know how true to life they are, and Barbara Stanwyck was hardly the yardstick for English middle-class propriety.

"A *movie*—if Barbara Stanwyck stars in it, it's definitely a movie. So, there they all were, wrapped up in plaid blankets . . . and Sir Basil arrives and gives them a bottle of wine. Did he drink it with you? How long did he stay?"

"No, he didn't drink it with us. He just popped in. Apparently he often drops a bottle of wine off on a Saturday night." I caught his puzzled expression. "It struck me as odd too." I frowned. "It's not the sort of thing a real gentleman would do: arrive unannounced in a houseful of young, attractive women in their dressing gowns with a present of wine. Not even a close uncle or an older male cousin would do that—in my experience, anyway."

He bowed his head to starchy manners. "Anything else that struck you as odd?"

"Yes, since June of this year someone was sending Edwina anonymous letters. Nasty ones. And the last one accused her of making up her Luftwaffe attack story."

A long whistle. "Now, there's something. Were they threatening? 'I will tell everyone you lied about your attack, unless you . . .'" He waved his right hand in a circular motion. "Was she being blackmailed?"

"I didn't get that impression. Grable described them as spiteful, that they were probably written by a lonely village spinster who was not right in the head, but . . ." I saw Annie and Grable at the kitchen table leaning forward angrily as they argued. "Annie disagreed with Grable, quite forcefully. She said they had been written to purposefully undermine Edwina's confidence. The pair of them got pretty hot under the collar about the writer's intentions. But the one thing they both agreed on was that Edwina was drinking heavily, or at least more than she usually did, and she was much worse after she got the letter about making up her Luftwaffe experience . . ."

Griff slapped his thigh with his hand. "There is something wrong here, isn't there? After Cadogan's dissertation on poison, I was all for calling it a day. But someone had it in for Edwina. Someone wanted to knock her off her perch, and they did such a good job, they made her crash. Why the bottom lip?"

"What?"

"I could ledge a quarter on it."

The Edwina I had met had made me feel that I didn't quite measure up: often a tactic of the underconfident. But after I had listened to Grable's account of her drinking and her anxiety, I saw her as a deeply unhappy and overburdened young woman.

"I agree that the anonymous letters were probably a strategy to undermine Edwina's self-confidence, or at the very least to make her jumpy and appear to be unhinged, but she didn't seem anxious after lunch." I saw her again, strolling out to her aircraft to make her demonstration flight, so relaxed I almost expected her to pick daisies on the way. "During lunch that day, she had seemed preoccupied. Perhaps she was bored with having to wait around to do her solo flight, but I would not have said anxious. I think she was looking forward to showing us how good she was. She had a sort of lazy, almost insolent attitude.

"After listening to Grable and Annie arguing about these letters, and why they were written, as well as the effect they had on her . . ." I paused because I wanted to get this bit right. "I think Edwina was dealing with a very complicated situation, but there was nothing about the heavy drinker in her when I met her. How did she seem to you?"

He looked down for a moment, and when he looked up, his eyes met mine with absolute sincerity.

"I thought she was . . ." He hesitated. "At first, I thought she was a bright, outgoing girl, but I have no idea whether she was genuinely confident or not; it was hard to tell. I felt as if . . . she was playing a part. As if she was playing at being . . . a femme fatale. That in her mind she was this sexy, powerful woman who was always in charge: the one with all the answers."

There was a long silence: the fire subsided into a heap of glowing embers, Bessie yawned, and I waited.

"I think you are talking about two different things, Poppy. You are trying to figure out what her state of mind was in the days before the crash, and her relationship with the people she worked and shared her life with. My experience of her when we first arrived was something different. I was a diversion and an opportunity for her to show everyone in the mess that day that she was still a force to be reckoned with. She was playing the part of what we call a 'man-eater' in America, which is neither attractive to most men nor the behavior of a confident woman. I am much more interested in her relationship with her girlfriends. What did June have to say about the anonymous letters?"

I was glad we had cleared up that little point.

"June wasn't there. She arrived after Grable, Annie, and I had eaten dinner and they were arguing about the letters. June had spent the evening at the mess, and it was there that Vera had made the announcement of Letty's death." I described June's desperate arrival at the cottage. "She was devastated. They all were, because . . ." I had to pause to steady my voice. There were few women in the world with Letty's genuinely good heart. "Because Letty was the best of them all: genuine, thoughtful, and kind. I left just after that."

Bess yawned again and I looked at my watch. "It's after midnight," I said and felt the last of my energy and concentration ebb away. "But before we call it a night, I saw something rather odd on my way back to the inn." And I described the brief flare of lights by the hangar, and the very human exclamation that followed it.

I AWOKE WITH a headache. It was still dark. Bess was lying heavily on my stomach and the room was stuffy and airless. I switched on my bedside light; it was half past two. I was desperately thirsty: somewhere in this untidy little room was my tooth mug.

Bess groaned as I sat up and swung my legs out of bed. I found my mug and walked across the corridor to the bathroom. When I returned I switched off the light and, kneeling on the bed, pulled back the blackout curtain and scraped open the warped casement window. My room looked down onto the drive into the inn and the lane that led down to the village. If there was any light at all in the cloudy night sky, I would have been able to see across the drive and the lawn that ran down to the river. I peered out into the dark, waiting for my eyes to adjust to the wall of black in front of them.

A long breath of cool, damp air eased the ache in my head. If I couldn't see the river I could certainly smell it and hear it rushing on its way to the Solent. Its dank odor filled the night and I could make out the gray-white of a heavy mist that had collected under the trees along its banks. This picturesquely dilapidated building would be beautiful in spring and summer, shrouded with trees and a lawn that fell away in a gentle slope down to the fast-flowing river Did. I shivered as the heavy moist air clung to my skin and thought what an unforgivably wretched experience winter would be in this old building.

I called a halt to my breathing exercises and pulled the window to close it, but it wouldn't budge an inch.

"Oh, come on!" I didn't dare to heave too forcefully in case the window latch came off in my hand. I took hold of the top and bottom corners and was about to give the whole thing a brisk tug, praying that the hinges were strong, when I heard the sound of an approaching lorry in the dark night. I concentrated my hearing on the pitch of the engine. Which direction was it taking? I leaned forward and closed my eyes. If it slowed, then it was coming downhill from the village and would stop at the junction of the two roads, but if it accelerated through the bend before the fork, as Griff always did on our way back from Didcote ATA, then it was coming from the airfield.

Bess had wormed her way between my arms and put her forepaws on the sill, her ears pricked forward as the rumble of sound grew as it came toward us. Then the driver changed gears to slow for the bend and accelerated out of it to start the climb of the incline that would take him to the village. I smiled to myself in the dark: it was coming from the airfield and instead of taking the right fork to Southampton was going up into the village. I leaned farther out as it went past the entrance to the inn's drive. A whoosh of displaced air and the thunder of a heavy load. A cloud of dry leaves pattered back onto the surface of the lane in its wake.

My face and hands were wet and cold. I took hold of the window again and heaved. It scraped toward me with an unearthly shriek of wood on wood and rusty hinge. I scrambled back under the thin blankets and spooned Bessie against me for warmth. It must have been a farmer taking vegetables to the food distribution center on the other side of Didcote. I was asleep as I turned onto my side to dream of all the dreadful ways turnips were prepared for the dinner tables of the long-suffering people who didn't own victory gardens.

———

BRIGHT SHAFTS OF sunlight shone through the gap in my blackout curtain and fell warm on my face. Bess was wide awake, fastidiously washing her paws, one by one. I folded my arms behind my head and reviewed the events of last night. I had to admit that Griff's, or rather Cadogan's, toxicology report was a setback. Determined not to let this put a damper on things, and with all the clarity that a good night's sleep can bring, I considered my evening at the cottage. The questions that I pondered coalesced into one question. Zofia: next victim or suspect?

Keep your eye on that one! Ilona is always awake before me.

I next considered my cycle ride back to the inn in the dark, and Griff's reaction to the activity by the hangar. I hopped out of bed and splashed myself awake with ice-cold water. There were two people I wanted to talk to today, June Evesham and Vera Abercrombie, before my cozy lunch with Sir Basil. Griff would surely be up by now and eating his breakfast downstairs.

SEVENTEEN

O H REALLY?" GRIFF SAID AS HE SPREAD MARGARINE ON HIS
toast and bit into a corner. "No, Poppy, I completely understand. You are to interview Vera and June before your solo lunch
with Basil Stowe. Should I go fishing?"

I ignored his sarcasm. Unlike me, Griff is not much of an
up-with-the-lark-to-sing-and-sing type. Fishing: whyever not? I
couldn't possibly invite him along on my sought-out chats with
June and Vera, but he could certainly fish.

"What side of the inn is your room on?" I asked, smiling as I
imagined his reaction to my two-o'clock observations. His eyes
flicked around to see if we were alone and settled on my face.

"My room?" he said.

"Riverside and the drive, or courtyard?"

"Nice view of cobbles, empty beer barrels, the garbage cans."

"My room is over the drive with a view of the river."

"How nice for you."

"Noisy, though, because the lane from the airfield comes up to
the inn on that side just after the fork. If you take the east fork you

come into the village, and the west fork takes you to the road to Southampton." I could see his interest sharpening.

"At about two this morning a heavy truck came along the lane from Didcote Airfield."

He put down his toast and wiped his fingers on his napkin. "What type of truck?"

"I couldn't see it, but I could hear it. It was carrying a heavy load."

"Was it military?"

I shrugged my shoulders. "It was too dark to see. I thought it would go right at the fork and on to Southampton."

"It might if it was military."

"But it went left, past the inn and on into the village." A long, low whistle. "I thought it was probably a farm truck carrying potatoes or cabbages to the food depot."

"No, it wasn't," he said with such finality that the hairs on my arms prickled. "Driving fast?" he asked.

"No, not really, but driving solidly, as if the driver knew he had an open road and wanted to get home."

"I'm sure you already know this . . ." Griff has a habit of using this phrase when he is about to tell me something he thinks I may not know. "After the blitz last year on Southampton and its surrounding aircraft factories, Churchill decided that fuel depots had to be small, many, and hidden." He folded his arms and his face was stern, as if daring me to argue. "So I guess it makes sense for gasoline deliveries to take place on a twenty-four-hour basis now they have farther to travel. What you heard was probably a tanker returning from making a delivery to the airfield."

"Or it might be something else, Griff. You have heard of the black market?"

"At Didcote?" He almost laughed, and then he must have seen my face.

"And here is something else to chew over," I said, embarrassed at the way I had reeled him in with an investigation of his own, while I got on with mine. "I am *sure* the truck was coming from the airfield; I could tell by the way it took the bend that it was going into the village and not going on to Southampton. And if you remember the village high street?" He nodded as if I was confirming something. "It peters out at the bottom by the river, into that little narrow track to the wharf and the fishermen's cottages. This truck was big and heavy. It could not have made it down that track. So, it was not taking a shortcut through the village on to Southampton because it couldn't possibly have made it along that track." I wrinkled my brow as I traced my route from the inn into the village. "There are two left turns on the lane into the village past this inn. One to the old church hall, which was turned into a dormitory for the lesser Attas, and the other one leads off into nowhere."

I sat back and nibbled at cold, leathery toast as he dug in his greatcoat pocket and hauled out a much-folded ordnance survey map of the area. He traced with his finger. "If someone was coming from the Didcote ATA . . ." He tapped his map. "Up into the village . . ." He traced with his finger. "Second turn on the left . . . River Farm, it's a dead end!" He smiled as he folded his map. "It is also a food collection center. How interesting." He continued to study the folded square that was the village of Didcote. "Could be two reasons why a truck would go to River Farm."

I nodded and took another bite of toast. "Yes, I think questions should be discreetly asked."

"Huh," he said, and put his map back into his pocket with a sigh. "Another friendly chat with a local farmer. Hampshire farmers are always a little bit shy when you first meet them. Suspicious that you are going to ask them if they have any ham!" He laughed, and I remembered last night's black-market sausages. He put his map back in his pocket. "Ham or petrol? Petrol or ham? It just amazes me how much trading is going on in rural Hampshire."

And somehow I knew from the moment I had mentioned my bike ride back to the inn last night past ATA Didcote's hangar that Griff had known all along about Hampshire's black market.

JUNE WAS SITTING over an untouched breakfast. "Morning," she said as I walked into a mess noisy with voices. "We're waiting for a green light from our Met Office to fly. Clouds too low right now, and there are fog warnings inland."

I remembered the firm, healthy face of three days ago as I looked into reddened eyes and hollow cheeks. June had first struck me as being one of those straightforward, handsome women who hail from warmer climates where everyone enjoys an overabundance of fresh air. The woman sitting at the table in front of me looked as if one good push would see her over.

"How much time do you spend waiting?" I asked and pulled my pencil out of my pocket.

"About as much time as you spend asking questions."

My eyes must have widened at her brusque tone because she laughed and waved away her awkward words. "Sorry, I'm feeling off today. Vera told me that this was your first film." I nodded. "Poor you; not only does your star die on your first day, but the next day another one of us goes west."

I tilted my head to acknowledge the truth.

"So now you're left with who?" she counted fingers on her right hand. "Me, Annie, Grable, and the lovely Zofia. Four."

I was fed up with nodding along. "Did you know about Edwina's letters?"

She laughed, but there was no humor in it. "The anonymous ones? Yes, of course I knew. Everyone did. At one time we had to stop her reading them out to the entire mess."

"There are two theories. One that it was a local crackpot, or there was a more malicious intent: to put her on edge."

She smiled; it was the saddest smile. She looked at me over the rim of her coffee cup. "You think there are only two reasons? You see, I often wondered if *she* wrote them."

It was quite an accusation and it shocked me. "But what reason could she possibly have?

"Edwina was a complicated woman. The one thing she simply couldn't tolerate was being ignored. She would do anything for attention, perhaps in the end kill herself."

Suicide? Not for one moment had I considered that Edwina was capable of suicide.

"You don't think it was an accident?"

She waved her hand back and forth in a shushing motion. "No, of course she didn't crash her plane on purpose. But she was reckless. Showing off and reckless behavior; that is when mistakes are made."

I returned to the matter of the poisoned-pen letters; at least there was proof they existed. "But to write a letter to herself exposing an attack by the Luftwaffe as a sham, a story that she made up? She must have been . . ."

June nodded: depressed and sad. "Off her head? Who wouldn't be in the world we live in?"

"Does everyone believe that she made the Luftwaffe story up?"

June put down her cup and wiped her mouth with the back of her hand. "It all depends who you talk to." A light flashed off and on over the Met Office door.

"There's the green light. Fog lifted, so I'm off. Will you be around this evening? I only have a couple of short runs; I should be back by afternoon." She zipped up her Sidcot suit and reached for her gloves. "Edwina wasn't a bad sort on the whole. She was a bit crass and a bit obvious, but there was no real harm in her. She had the reputation of being a bit loose, you know?"

I shook my head. "Louche?" I asked, and this time she chuckled.

"Well, I'm just a simple Australian girl; we pronounce it 'loose.' She was a bit of a terror around men. But the most harm she did was to herself." She slung a canvas map bag over her shoulder and muttered, "Map, compass, thermos. Right, I'm all set." She was halfway to the door and then came back to the table. "Edwina's crash was a shock, right? A real shock, especially since we all saw it. But Letty's crash yesterday—" She pressed her lips together and her eyes filled with tears. She shook her head and tried to clear her throat. "Letty's crash was all wrong. For her to have been flying at that height among trees, along a railway line, was the sort of thing an amateur would do. Letty had nearly two thousand flight hours. Edwina might have been the ATA's version of Biggles with her aerial acrobatics, but Letty was a pro. The only reason that Walrus would have crashed had to be engine failure, but she would never have tried to do a forced landing on a railway line." She inhaled her tears, her face so stricken that I reached out my hand to her, but she shook her head and, turning on her heel, left the mess. I watched her walk across to join a dozen or so ATA pilots walking toward their Anson air taxi with their parachutes slung over their shoulders.

The lanky cockney whom I had played darts with reached out an arm and pulled June alongside her. And the strawberry blonde came up on June's other shoulder. They walked her forward between them to the Anson, where Annie Trenchard was waiting, her fine dark hair blowing in the wind.

June, Annie, Grable, and Zofia: they were such a tight-knit group. But did tight-knit groups murder each other in such a merciless way as tampering with their aeroplanes or food?

"Come back safely," I called out as they lined up to get into the Anson, but they were too far away to hear me.

I fed the rest of my breakfast to Bess and looked around the mess. Vera's door was closed, and I had no intention of knocking on it. There was no sign of Zofia. It was time to return Grable's bike to their cottage. Maybe Zofia would offer to make me a cup of coffee.

"COME IN, PLEASE." Zofia was still in the red-and-black silk kimono she had worn last night. "I am making coffee, and then I must dress. I am flying some bigwig from Biggin Hill to the Castle Bromwich factory. But, no, please to come in."

In the early-morning light Zofia's pale face looked older than it had last night. "Grable is still asleep; June and Annie already left," she explained as she filled a kettle and put it on the hob. "I am just cleaning up last night's dinner—such a mess. These girls never know how to clean as they cook."

"I just wanted to return Grable's bike. I borrowed it last night."

"You heard about what happen to Letty? Her Walrus crashed? Yes, of course, you were here when June came back last night." She nodded, not, I hoped, at the inevitability of Letty's crash but acknowledging that I knew about it.

She turned to me, resting the small of her back against the kitchen range, and folded her arms. "There will be a full inquiry by the—whatever they call themselves. The authorities don't like it when valuable planes crash." She reached for the ubiquitous bottle of Camp coffee and shook it before measuring two large spoonfuls into a jug. "Milk?"

"No, thanks, I had breakfast."

"Edwina," she explained to me as if I had asked. "She should not have been flying the other day. Her nerves were broken—broken after the Luftwaffe chased her. I went to Vera and told her: 'Edwina should be given some time off: grounded.' Reluctantly, she agreed with me, but she let her fly anyway." She caught her bottom lip between her teeth. "Sir Basil said that Edwina was a grown woman with nerves of steel!" Her eyes flashed. "Perhaps, I said, but you are not here often enough to know that she is having a rough time." She shrugged off Sir Basil's insensitivity and muttered something under her breath in Polish.

"What do you know about the letters?" I asked, and the look she shot me was triumphant.

"Ah, so you know about those too, do you, Miss Redfern? Yes, I thought you were more than just interested in your film. I said to myself: 'Who is this lovely young woman, who sits and listens to everything so sympathetically and so very closely, and whose eyes don't miss a trick! She is onto something,' I said."

She handed me a tea towel and I dried the cups and saucers that she washed and handed to me.

When everything was put away Zofia turned to me. "For some time now, things have not been right here. You know that? For some time now there has been a lot of stress, a lot of overwork. I know on the surface it is all playful laughter among our little group. But that is just the surface."

She poured coffee, took a sip, and frowned down into her cup. "I hoped if I make it strong it might taste better."

"What do you think was causing this tension, other than overwork?" I dared to ask.

She thought for a moment. "It won't hurt to tell you, since I know you are not a gossip girl. The strain was between Edwina and

Vera. Bad feelings, you know? Because Edwina made a big play for Sir Basil." She paused. "Or was it the other way around? It is sometimes hard to tell with sex." She laughed. "Whenever he came down to Didcote, he would take her for a drive in that ridiculous car. Who drives a Bentley when there is a petrol shortage? We would all be in the mess and look around: no Sir Basil or Edwina. It was naughty of her. I told her to leave him alone. Vera said nothing, but her eyes were sad. Sometimes Edwina could be very selfish; she liked attention, you know, but it was unkind to flirt with Basil Stowe. It hurt Vera and it encouraged a man who needs little encouragement to behave like an old fool."

I remembered Edwina snubbing Sir Basil several times on the evening we had arrived and again when we were filming. "But it ended, didn't it?"

"Their little fling? Well, certainly it has ended. Edwina is no longer around, is she?"

I was so shocked at her outspoken words and the cynical little laugh that accompanied them—words that could incriminate Vera easily in Edwina's accident—that my jaw dropped.

"Oh no, no. Not so fast, my dear. Their little fling ended well over a couple of weeks ago. How, I have no idea. I doubt Vera confronted them; she is too English, too polite. But I imagine Sir Basil got the hint—or maybe Edwina was too much for him."

She looked up at the kitchen clock.

"Nearly nine. I must be running; these senior RAF officers expect me to be in full uniform. No nice warm Sidcot zip-up suit for me today." She walked to the foot of the stairs and then turned as if something had just occurred to her. "If you are interested in those letters, Miss Redfern, you can read them for yourself. It might help you to understand a little more about Edwina's situation. I can tell you are curious." She sorted through the contents of a drawer to a little table and handed me a key with a label. "Address is on the tag. Edwina lived in a little studio down by the river on the wharf. It is attached to a cottage owned by an elderly couple, Mr. and Mrs. Franklin. They liked Edwina staying there because it belonged to their son who was killed at the beginning of the war. It made them feel less lonely. Introduce yourself to them." Her eyes were thoughtfully fixed on my face. "Yes, I would suggest you say hullo to them; they won't mind you taking up their time. And they might make better coffee than I do."

Finally, someone who is not scared of actually saying something relevant. Ilona clearly approved of Zofia; she was her kind of girl.

Zofia turned at the foot of the stairs and looked back at me. Her smile was enigmatic. "Whatever the ATA Accident Committee come up with, it won't help us understand what really happened in the last three days," she said. She paused for a second and then walked back toward me. "May I be completely frank with you, Miss Redfern, or will you shy away and look embarrassed? Such an English response to directness, I have discovered."

"I would be grateful," I said.

"There is no need for gratitude. This is not about Edwina. This is about you and that handsome American pilot who escorted you here."

Oh God, what was she going to tell me about Griff and Edwina? *You need to know,* prompted Ilona. *Pull yourself together.* I took in a deep breath and nodded.

"Well then, first of all the young captain is very attracted to you, but I expect you know that." I started to shake my head. "Forget about Edwina and her determination to always have a man hanging around her, and her rather uncouth approach." Her look was direct, to see if she was wasting her time on me. I returned it equally directly. "Pleadingly" is probably a more apt description.

"Good, very good. Your biggest misunderstanding of your captain is not because he is an American: a man from a progressive culture that is easy and informal in its manners—just like in the movies, yes? Of course, it doesn't help that he looks a bit like a film star, does it?"

I sighed.

"Of course women are attracted to him—he is a novelty. But underneath all that easy American appeal he is no different from any man. He has moments of doubt, he worries that he might have said the wrong thing, he often feels unsure of himself, and he covers all this up with that easy informal charm, and you fall for it and think that he doesn't care about anything. All women do this, because they simply don't understand that men are just as vulnerable as we are. So, forget about Edwina and her big play on the night you arrived. I can assure you that Captain O'Neal is no fool, and he is a gentleman. But more importantly it is you who he wants. It is you who he is interested in—why else would he be here in this wretchedly damp little village, hanging around an airfield on his precious leave? So"—she laughed and tossed her head as if she were an American matinée idol's dream come true—"if you want to be with this very serious American, and I think you do, then *be* with him. It is up to you, *kochanie*. Stop underestimating yourself: you are a smart and very beautiful young woman. Drop the stuffy manners—I think they make him nervous—and be your very lovely and warmhearted self."

And she disappeared up the stairs, leaving me to read the label on the key: 21 Front Street.

EIGHTEEN

BESS MADE IT QUITE CLEAR THAT THE BIKE'S BASKET WAS NOT something she was willing to travel in. I gave up. "Stay with me, Bessie," I warned her. "Otherwise, in you go." She folded her ears back the way she does when she gets her way and trotted on ahead off up the lane toward the village and Front Street.

I thought about what Zofia had told me about Edwina and Sir Basil. How painful it must have been for Vera to have found out that the man she loved was playing around with the best pilot in her command; how humiliating to have to pretend that everything was normal, when it hurt like mad to be made a fool of. Vera's need to be the best woman commanding officer she could be had been compromised by her lover's selfish behavior with one of her pilot officers. If that wasn't motive for murder, I didn't know what was. In her pain and hurt Vera could easily have decided to eliminate the woman who had stolen her lover's affections and either put some kind of poison in her food or sabotaged her plane. I remembered seeing her intense conversation with Mac Wilson outside the hangar when Griff and I had walked over to talk to Mac about Edwina's crash. But that didn't explain why either Letty, or Zofia, had to go the same way, unless they had seen something. I cursed the loss of the piece of film of our picnic.

But I had much more than Zofia's observations on Edwina, Sir Basil, and Vera to be grateful for. How many times had I wished I knew a woman of my age who had lived a full life and who understood the convoluted tangle of doubts that so often exist between men and women? The thrill of attraction and delight in their company, and the fear that they might not feel the same way? I remembered one of my friends, in the village I grew up in, who had found the courage to come out of her lonely shell, and to believe in herself more, and was now living in blissful happiness with a husband who adored her.

"That's it!" I said to Bess. "I am so terrified that he might not like me as much as I like him that I've been really off-putting." I clutched at the brake on the handlebars too quickly and skidded on a patch of mud. *I must have told you a million times just to be yourself,* Ilona scolded. *Stop being so remote, so self-contained, and let him know how you feel. No wonder he is confused!*

But how did I let him know how I felt? By behaving like Edwina?

Dear God, how much instruction do you need? Look him in the eye; don't look away. Stand closer to him, let him know how much you enjoy his company, and stop correcting him when he uses English words he doesn't completely understand!

I pedaled fast and felt the key to Edwina's digs slide forward in my coat pocket. If I got a wiggle on I had time to go to Front Street before my lunch with Didcote's man-about-town, Sir Basil. "Come on, Bessie," I called with more authority than I usually use, and she stopped loitering in a pile of leaves and came running after me.

I felt such an extraordinary sense of freedom and purpose as she ran alongside me that I actually laughed out loud and lifted my feet off the pedals as we sped down the slope of the lane. And then the hangar loomed up on our right, and I pressed the handbrake and trailed the tip of my shoe on the tarmac. My curiosity, stirred by the brief flare of headlights last night, and the rumble of a heavy load into the village much later, brought me to a full stop.

I stood astride the bike. The hangar was well back from the road in the woodland that fringed the airfield. There was a track leading off the lane. I wheeled the bike to the top of the track and looked down toward the hangar a couple of hundred feet away. This was not the building where we had had our one and only conversation with Mac Wilson on the day after Edwina's accident. This one was smaller, with two large sliding metal doors, one of which was partly open. I took a step forward onto the thick carpet of leaves that covered the track, and Bess, convinced that we had arrived at our destination, ran ahead of me.

"Come on, Bessie, this way," I said, wheeling the bike back to the lane. "Bessie, come on, girl."

Usually willing to join me, Bessie occasionally displays a strongly independent streak. Today was one of those days. Nose to the ground, she was following the scent of some woodland creature, her little bobtail wagging in excitement as she coursed forward over the fallen leaves. I laid the bike on its side and walked down the track. "Come on, Bess." I smiled as I remembered what my grandfather always said when she was disobedient: "Don't go after her; make her come to you." And in exasperation: "It's too late; now she thinks *she's* in charge. No wonder she needs to be on a lead."

"Bessie," I implored. She turned her head but was instantly distracted, and on she went. I trotted after her through the trees and into the grassy clearing in front of the hangar, where we both stopped. Bessie because she had lost the scent of the trail she was on, and I because clearly marked in the wet grass were two sets of deep, wide tire tracks. I stopped and bent over them. The exposed ruts in the grass were fresh. They must be the tracks of the lorry I had seen last night on my way back to the inn. My pulse rate picked up, for there, off to the right, were two more pairs of tire marks. I sidled over to them. The distance between right side and left was far narrower, the tires thinner and less aggressive in tread. They were made by a lighter vehicle—the open-top type of vehicle that Americans call "jeeps" sprang to mind.

"Bess, now!" I hissed. "Come here now!"

The last thing in the world I wanted was for Mac Wilson to appear in the doorway of his hangar and ask me what I thought I was doing trespassing on the airfield. As I bent to scoop Bess up in my arms I investigated the marks more thoroughly. I noticed that the deeper tire tracks didn't stop outside the doors to the hangar. The truck had driven inside it and had returned back up the track to the lane.

As I half ran, half walked back to my bike, I was convinced that I was being watched. Why hadn't I left this part of the investigation to Griff? I picked up my bike, tumbled poor Bess into the basket, and, turning my head fractionally to the right, I looked back at the hangar's doors. Someone had been watching us: a gloved hand slid the door closed, and my heart bumped so hard up into my throat that I could hardly breathe.

MY LEGS, FUELED by adrenaline, shot me up the hill and down again into the village in less than ten minutes. I whipped past the ironmongers and was panting for breath when I turned into Front

Street. It is little more than a lane and has a terrace of fishermen's cottages on its left side and the river on the other. It narrows down even further to a stone wharf, once a place where fishermen sold mackerel, and which had been turned into a yacht club in the early thirties. No one could drive a heavy truck, lorry, or petrol tanker down this, I thought as I got off Grable's bike.

The cottages were tiny: two rooms downstairs and two bedrooms upstairs would have housed a family of six at one time. Since the yacht club had been built, most of them had been gentrified: bought by artists and weekenders who enjoyed sailing and who wanted running hot and cold and inside loos. They were pretty, much in the way of all seaside and river weekend cottages: blue front doors, window boxes full of red geraniums in summer, and most of them had names. Number twenty-one had a sky blue front door and a plaque that proclaimed its occupants had "Dunroamin." This was where Mr. and Mrs. Franklin lived. It was at the end of the row, and a one-story stone building with a shed roof and its own front door painted to match its parent had a little sign over it saying "Dunroamin Too." I flinched at the jokey names and immediately reminded myself not to be starchy.

I had barely raised my hand to knock when the door opened. A neatly dressed thin woman, wrapped up in a cheerful pinny, her hands dusted with flour, stood on the narrow threshold, her dark brown eyes curious and expectant. Behind her a stooped, elderly gray-haired man holding the *Daily Telegraph* in his hands looked over his wife's shoulder. His gray brows came down and he took a half step backward as if annoyed at the interruption to his morning.

"Mr. and Mrs. Franklin?" I had the belt of my coat tied around Bess's neck, but I needn't have worried, because she was on her best behavior. Sitting tidily at my feet with her head cocked to one side,

Bess would look completely at home curled up by the fireside of "Dunroamin."

"Yes?" Mrs. Franklin said and wiped her hands on an apron with "A present from Margate," embroidered across its bib.

I had rehearsed my introduction as I pedaled into the village.

"My name is Poppy Redfern. I'm from the Crown Film—"

"Oh yes, please do come in!" His expression no longer irritated, Mr. Franklin stepped aside and waved his newspaper in welcome.

Bess and I crowded into the little hall. It was strongly scented with lavender furniture polish, with a powerful undernote of rising damp.

"Edwina told us all about you, Miss Redfern," Mrs. Franklin confided. "She was so excited about being in your film." She pulled a hankie out from her cardigan sleeve. "She could hardly sleep for excitement the night before you arrived."

This image of an enthusiastic young girl as she tossed sleeplessly in her bed with anticipation of a big day ahead was wildly out of place with everything I had seen and learned of the dead girl. Her husband was nodding as he shuffled along in his carpet slippers into the front parlor. Mrs. Franklin, although probably the same age, hopped forward to the parlor door, a quick little bird; her bright eyes never left my face.

"Well, Mother, are you going to put on the kettle?" he said in a surprisingly thick north-country accent. "Looks like this young lady could do with a cup, and one of your oatmeal biscuits to go with it. Aye, lass?"

"Oh, thank you, yes, please." They were a generation who drank tea with their breakfast, again after lunch, and at four o'clock in the afternoon. "Putting on the kettle" was the first thing you did when someone came to call—an act of simple hospitality. They left the offer of coffee in the morning, sherry before lunch, and a whiskey and soda in the evening to the middle classes. Tea was what helped people like the Franklins through good times and bad.

Mr. Franklin ushered me to a chair upholstered in stiff, scratchy fabric and then lowered himself into an easy chair by the window that looked out onto the street. We could hear Mrs. Franklin clattering about in her kitchen and talking to the "nice little doggy" who had accompanied her there.

Two pale gray eyes regarded me for a moment. "Terrible thing to have happened," Mr. Franklin said in his comfortable voice. "We were hoping someone from the airfield would come by and tell us about it. About how it happened." There was no complaint, no censure that they had been forgotten. His tone was low pitched and his long, slow Yorkshire vowels pleasant and unhurried. "Not that we were expecting . . . a fuss. There is a war on after all."

I wondered how the Franklins heard that their lodger would not be coming home to dinner. Had Mrs. Franklin made shepherd's pie, and had they sat there waiting to hear her footsteps on the lane outside? They must have picked up their knife and fork and reassured each other that she was stuck at some airfield in Norfolk. "Be home tomorrow," they had said.

"We heard all about it in the village," he said in a reasonable voice, as if this was the way news of violent death was brought home. He jerked his head toward the kitchen. "Mother was up at the baker's to get a loaf of Hovis and a tin of something for Edwina in case she was hungry when she got home. And she heard that the girl who flew the Spitfire had crashed." He shook his head. "Terrible shock it was." He lowered his voice. "Her heart's not that strong, you see. Not after our lad"—he lifted a thickly veined mottled hand and pointed to a large photograph, framed in expensive silver, of a young man in his early thirties in uniform that dominated the mantelshelf—"was taken from us." Obediently, I examined the smiling portrait. It was a nice, open face. His slicked-down hair lifted in a cowlick at the crown. His eyes were bright and clear. He looked what he evidently was: a good boy from a kind and sensible family.

I couldn't bear the look on Mr. Franklin's face as he acknowledged his son.

"Edwina was a very skillful pilot," I said.

"Aye, she were that."

"I only met her briefly, but she was so . . . so lively, so much fun. A . . ."

The briefest nod; eyes faded with age and grief flicked to the door as his wife came in with a tea tray. "She were a right live wire was our Edwina, wa'n't she, love?"

Mrs. Franklin smiled. "She certainly brightened up our lives." She set down the tray and took a seat, with Bess sitting as close to her as she could get. Mrs. Franklin fed her an oatmeal biscuit.

"Miss Redford was saying that she didn't know Edwina that well," her husband informed his wife.

"Well, she wouldn't, would she, what with being with the film people and not the ATA. And I believe it is Miss Red*fern*, isn't it?" She lifted the pot. "Milk in your tea, dear?"

"Yes, thank you. I can tell that you were like family to her," I said, determined not to lead anyone into thinking that Edwina and I were best friends.

"And she to us, daughter she was to us was Eddie."

Eddie. There was nothing about Edwina's appearance and manner that made me think of her as an Eddie.

"She was like our daughter, and we were like her parents. She was an orphan, you know."

What?

"She lost her parents at a very early age. A sad story, as you might already know."

I shook my head and took a cup of tea, with a biscuit balanced in its saucer. "No, I didn't know."

Mr. Franklin nodded. "Her mother died when Eddie was a little girl, and not long after that her father—" He looked uncomfortable and glanced across at his wife to finish for him. She merely folded her hands in her lap and tucked her chin down, as if refusing to answer.

Mr. Franklin cleared his throat. "Well, he did away with himself." Mrs. Franklin's eyes slid over to see how I had taken such a shameful act.

"We don't know the details," Mrs. Franklin apologized. "He had been in some sort of business venture after the last war, and his partner stole something from him—patents, wasn't it?" she asked her husband.

"Diddled him right good and proper. Stole the designs of a plane he had invented. Stole them and went on to make a fortune." He shook his head at the evil ways of commerce and those out to make a fortune from the inventiveness of those more deserving and talented.

"And Edwina?" I asked. "How old was she when her mother died?"

"Five, and nearly nine when her dad went. Young enough to understand what had happened she was, poor little lass."

It took me a few minutes to take this in; it was counter to everything I had heard or had been told by Edwina.

The embarrassing and sinful topic of suicide out of the way, Mrs. Franklin became more talkative. "Her auntie took her in. She was a single woman. Strict she was, Edwina told us. A chapel-goer."

I blinked. What about the flying circus where Edwina had been an aerial acrobat? The flying circus that her uncle had owned?

"She mentioned something to me about an uncle who had a flying school?"

Mr. Franklin was quick to shake his head. "No, no uncle. Just a maiden aunt. She ever tell you anything about a flying school?" he asked his wife.

Mrs. Franklin's eyes misted, and she groped for her hankie. "She *worked* at a big flying school just outside of London, in the office. Edwina left home when she was sixteen."

"Her aunt's gone too," Mr. Franklin said before I could ask. "So, you see, when we say she was like a daughter to us, we were like a mother and father to her—her only family."

My tea was stone-cold in my cup. The silence built for a moment.

"Would you like to see her room? It might help you build a picture of her, for your film." Mrs. Franklin's question was tentative, as if she might be presumptive.

I flushed scarlet. These two straightforward old people, who came from a generation who were fond of saying they knew their place, clearly thought that we would continue to feature Edwina in our film.

I stumbled to my feet, hot with shame, as if I were there under false pretenses, and nudged Bess with my foot. She had been blatantly begging for another biscuit.

I followed them through the cramped but immaculate kitchen and out into an orderly victory garden with rows of winter cabbage and stalks of brussels sprouts.

"We came here when my hubby retired from the post office up in Warmington. We are from the north country." Mrs. Franklin ushered me up the crazy paving path. "Our son bought us this little place for our retirement. He lived in Southampton, worked for Supermarine in aviation. He was an engineer." She could not conceal the pride that had crept into her voice. "He lived in the town, of course, but came home every weekend."

She carefully opened the back door of the studio.

"Our son, Malcolm, used this as his studio. He was a painter, you see." Mrs. Franklin waved her hand around at walls crowded with framed paintings. "Seascapes, landscapes, that sort of thing. Watercolor was his métier." I nodded.

I looked around the spacious area Edwina had lived in when she wasn't flying Spitfires.

What had I expected? I asked myself as we stood in a well-lit, attractively furnished room with a divan bed covered in bright cushions. Pinups of American actors on the walls? A dressing table covered in cosmetics?

I stepped forward to admire the paintings. They were mild versions of Turneresque seascapes: misty, ice blue, choppy water raced toward yellow sand beaches. Clouds and sunsets, dawns and rock pools. There were no dark clouds gathering over wind-tormented seas—all was serene. They were soothing in a rather pale way, meticulously painted. There was an easy chair and a small table by the window looking out into the garden. A folded easel in another, and shelves with orderly rows of brushes and paints that were not needed now.

A small bathroom opened to the left: a blue-and-white-check dressing gown hung on a peg at the back of the door; shampoo, Pond's cold cream, a basket of cosmetics, and a tooth mug lined up on the windowsill by the hand basin. I turned back into the room. A small wardrobe stood in one corner, a chest of drawers in another with a vase of paper flowers. The boards were varnished, with a red rug by the divan bed. A clock ticked on a bedside table; a pair of slippers peeped out from under the divan. No photographs, no china ornaments, no books. There was nothing at all here of Edwina, except orderliness—there was, I noticed, far more evidence of its former occupant.

"What a pretty room," I said. Mrs. Franklin nodded. Her husband had remained outside when we had come into the room. He was leaning against the wall and smoking his pipe.

"She was such a lovely girl," she said. "Always willing to lend a hand." She opened the drawer of the bedside table. There was nothing in it except a narrow bundle of envelopes tied with tape. "Sometimes our neighbor would come over and spend the evening. And we would all enjoy a game of cribbage. We would make an evening of it. Nice fish-and-chip supper, and sometimes we'd listen to *It's That Man Again* on the radio. That Tommy Handley is a right laugh, kept us in stitches."

I found it hard to imagine Edwina in this immaculate little cottage, playing crib and giggling over England's favorite radio program.

"Just the four of us." Mrs. Franklin's voice was a whisper. I took the letters from her outstretched hand; the name and address were typed on the face of each envelope: "Miss E. Partridge."

"I think these were from her sweetheart. I am not sure what to do with them. Perhaps one of her friends at the ATA, that Mrs. Lukasiewicz she was always talking about, would know."

"Did you meet Mrs. Lukasiewicz?" I asked, knowing what the answer would be.

"No, dear, they were always so busy." She turned away and opened a wardrobe. "And then there are her clothes."

I couldn't look at them. "I know someone whose daughter died," I said. "She was a pretty girl, like Edwina, and she had some lovely clothes. Her mother donated them. So many young women are going without these days . . . And if Edwina had no family—"

"Yes, yes, of course. That's what my husband suggested. I just wanted to be sure." As if he had sensed her grief, the door opened and her husband shuffled into the room. He put his hand on his wife's shoulder.

"Come on, love. Don't upset yerself. Eddie died doing what she loved the most. Come on, now." He nodded vaguely to me and led his wife from the room.

"Thank you so much for tea," I said as we stood in their hall. "And for letting me see Edwina's room. I will drop you a line when the film is ready, so that you can see it in Southampton." I drew a deep breath. "I'm afraid that there won't be very much of Edwina's flying in it." I decided not to tell them about Letty's death, not just yet. There is only so much shock and grief the elderly can take, and the Franklins had had their full share.

"Never go to Southampton, love," Mr. Franklin said. "Our boy, our Malcolm, was working at the Supermarine factory when they bombed it."

"What a pity they never met," I said. Thinking how nice their Malcolm sounded, and how wonderful it would have been if Edwina had met him, fallen in love with him, and had more stability in her short life. And then I remembered that I was thinking about their Edwina, the one who was helpful around the house, who enjoyed a quiet evening of cribbage with people old enough to be her parents and their next-door neighbor.

She smiled. "Yes, we used to tell her that and she would laugh and say that there was no one for her, she was too independent."

"How sad," I said. Determined that this was not going to be my problem.

"But she did meet someone, didn't she, love? You remember?" Mrs. Franklin jogged her husband's arm

Her husband looked blank for a moment. "Oh yes, he sounded like such a nice chap."

His wife flapped her hand at him as if he hadn't a clue about boyfriends and that sort of stuff. "It was about a year ago; he was a pilot, of course, at one of the big aerodromes."

I tried not to sound too eager. "One of the big south-coast airfields?"

"Yes, one of those." She puckered her forehead. "She must have met him when she was delivering planes. It had a church in its name."

"Hornchurch?" I said, the first name that came into my head.

She shook her head. "It was on the south coast."

"Was she still seeing him?"

"No, dear—he was lost in a raid." She put her handkerchief up to her eyes again.

"August nineteenth, it was." Her husband put his hand on his wife's shoulder and drew her to him. "What a day. The fighting went on from dawn until late in the afternoon. The sky was thick with squadrons of fighter planes. We could hear it all going on from here." I opened their front door and stood for a moment looking out into the peaceful harbor with its bobbing leisure craft. It might be the sort of pretty seaside scene you see on postcards, but I knew only too well how quickly that could change.

I thanked them and put a protesting Bess in the bike's basket. "Someone who shared her interests," I said as I put my foot on the pedal and then took it off again. My head was throbbing with new information: Edwina had had a pilot boyfriend. He was a fighter pilot at one of the big airfields on the south coast! There had been no rich uncle who had owned a flying school, and saddest of all was that Edwina's childhood had been desolate and lonely. Her father had committed suicide when his business partner had cheated him.

She might have been making it all up! Ilona's voice was uncharitable.

Bess tried to scramble out of the basket. I picked her up and set her down on the ground.

If there was no rich uncle with a flying school, where had she learned to fly?

No reason at all why she didn't learn to fly in that school—even if she was an office worker, Ilona pointed out. *It seems that our Edwina was the enterprising type.*

So far as I could see, Edwina was becoming more difficult to puzzle out each day. And why had she not invited her best friend, the Countess Lukasiewicz, back to her digs to enjoy a homey evening with the Franklins? Zofia didn't strike me as being a snob.

Maybe they were not as close as we think they were. Edwina was clearly unpredictable and not much of a girl's girl, and if you don't mind my saying so, I think that countess is a deep one too.

NINETEEN

B ESS COULD HARDLY KEEP PACE WITH ME AS I PEDALED BACK
to the inn. I couldn't wait to share my thoughts with Griff on
what was amounting to Edwina's double life here in Didcote. As I
pedaled up the hill and came to a halt at the inn's side entrance, I
remembered Zofia's words just before I had left her cottage: "It is
you who he wants. It is you who he is interested in—why else would
he be here in this wretchedly damp little village?"

Perhaps Griff and I could stroll down to the pub for lunch and
then take Bess for a lovely long walk along the river, I thought, failing to notice that a strong wind was blowing in from the Solent.

As I came in through the front door of the inn, a tall figure
emerged from the gloom. "Here you are. I've been worried sick
about you. I thought some half-crazed ATA pilot had taken you for
a joyride in her plane and shoved you out without a parachute."

I hung my coat and beret up on a peg. "I have the most
wonderful—"

"Where have you been? Five hours ago, you were going to talk
to the Attas before they left for work, which they must have done at
half past eight!"

His voice had that ominous quality of someone pushed beyond patience into fuming endurance and finally to outrage that could only be expressed in an undertone, because Mr. Evans was polishing glasses five feet away in the bar, and his wife was fussing around with table linen in the dining room. Griff turned and walked down the dark corridor, and, naturally curious to understand why a thunderstorm was brewing, I followed. Together we made a quick circuit of the living room to its farthest corner.

"Edwina was living some sort of double—" I stopped. The light from the French windows illuminated the face of a man who had evidently spent an exasperating and worrying morning: his hair was sticking up in the front, his tie was pulled to the side, and he looked disheveled and tired.

"I drove over to the cottage"—his arm made a wide circle—"and hammered on the door until my knuckles were pulp. No answer. Then I made a tour of both the airfield and then the village." His arm made a wider circle. "I looked everywhere. Everywhere. No one had seen you; no one had spoken to you. And then on top of that, I get back here and Mrs. Evans proudly reminds me you are entertaining that old billy goat to lunch!"

"Billy goat?"

"God give me patience: Sir Basil Stowe. That old dog from the Ministry of I Chase Young Women." His temper had at least cooled now that he could talk above a whisper.

It was true I had breezed off to have a quick word with June and Zofia. And with all the excitement and information that the morning had produced, I had completely forgotten about Sir Basil.

"Griff, I am so sorry." He pulled a postcard from his pocket and flapped it at me. "Really, I am most terribly sorry. Time just seemed to flash by. One moment I was talking to the Franklins, then the next I was pedaling like hell for the inn. I completely forgot about—"

"It's nearly one o'clock!" He strove for reason.

"What?" I looked at my watch and shook my wrist: five minutes past one. "Oh no!" From the dining room I heard the laconic tones of a man who is inquiring after not only his lunch, but his luncheon companion as well.

"I completely forgot about Sir Basil," I said, getting up and wishing I could at least comb through my hair and wash my face and hands.

"I know." His voice and his brow were angry and wrinkled. Bess crawled under a coffee table. "I would rather you didn't—" he said.

"Well, I can't get out of it now; he's already here. Anyway, I know he is a bit of a womanizer—"

He closed his eyes and shook his head like Bessie does with a stick she is trying to kill. "That isn't the half of it."

"I will be fine: Mr. Evans will be in the bar, Mrs. Evans practically sitting in our laps offering us turnip pie with impeccable service. Did you talk to Mac Wilson?"

He was still holding the postcard. "Mac Wilson is a moron," he said. "A complete moron. But this"—he flapped the card at me— "this is important. So, when you have finished eating poison pie with your lunch date, promise, whatever you do, *please* promise that you will stay here and talk to me?"

"What's in the postcard? Can I read it now, just quickly?"

"No, you can't, because here is your pal Sir Basil. I will wait here for you, and when you have finished lunch I will read it to you." He spaced out his words as if I was slow-witted. "Poppy, I'm begging you: no leaving with Sir Basil on some innocuous errand and no taking impromptu flights with ATA pilots. After you have finished your treacle pudding you will come right back here? *Capisce?*"

"Yes, capeesh. All right to leave Bess with you? They don't let dogs in the dining room."

And I left, my head down in contrition and my heart singing. Men who cared evidently tied themselves in knots if you disappeared for five hours in the middle of a murder inquiry.

"CAPTAIN O'NEAL NOT going to join us?" Sir Basil got to his feet as I was conducted to his table by a glowing Mrs. Evans.

"No, he has another appointment."

We were the only people for lunch, which wasn't surprising, because Mrs. Evans, affable, likable soul that she is, may look like the perfect innkeeper—her round, red, happy face greets you to every meal in her dining room—but she and her ally in the kitchen haven't a clue how to create something out of nothing.

When Griff referred to poison pie, it wasn't because of our original suspicion that Letty and Edwina had met their deaths by poison; it was a fact. Everything Mrs. Evans served up in her dining room had a dullish gray patina as if it had waited for you for a long time, gathering bacteria to it like flies to jam. Even her scrambled eggs looked like they had been made for last week's breakfast.

Sir Basil was evidently one of those men who could care less what he ate, but he was admirably and perfectly dressed. From his dazzling white starched shirt collar knotted with an exclusive public school tie to the quiet sheen of his handmade brogues at the bottom of his Savile Row tweed trousers, he exemplified the affluent prewar country gentleman.

"My dear Miss Redfern. I am so glad you can make time for me!" He smiled, and there was just the right touch of Edinburgh in his accent as he scooted me and my chair into place at the table.

"What a busy time we are all having," he said as he smiled across the table. His clear blue eyes crinkled in a smile at the corners. Mrs. Evans blushed as she put down a handwritten menu on the table between us.

"Errfs with pommes frites," she read for us. "Followed by my handmade mutton pie avec pommes de terres, and"—a smile of pure pride—"for afters: a lovely treacle pudding, made fresh yesterday morning." She simpered at Sir Basil, made a little bob that might have been a curtsy, and retired to await our pleasure and gaze at herself in the hall mirror.

Sir Basil wrinkled his nose. "Have you eaten here before, Miss Redfern?"

"Poppy."

"Ah yes, such a delightful name. Poppy. I should have suggested the pub, but Mrs. Evans—" He left it to me to understand that our hostess's feelings would be deeply hurt.

I sipped water and smoothed the way to other topics. "I love the view of the river from here, and you can see Ansons taking off from the airfield."

"Best view in Didcote," said Sir Basil without taking his gaze off my face. "Pie?" He turned to the hovering Mrs. Evans to signal that we were ready.

"We will have the pie," Sir Basil said.

"And to drink?" She batted her eyelashes.

"Why, beer, of course." And to me: "Mr. Evans's ale is extraordinarily good." And with the folderol of ordering over and done with, I launched into the first of my many questions.

"So, you flew with my father, Sir Basil," I reminded him.

There was just the slightest hesitation. "I certainly did. Well, he was transferred to my squadron at the beginning of the war. After the Battle of the Somme, which took tremendous casualties on land, sea, and in the air, he was moved to another squadron with

Bunty Everdean. Great chap, Bunty. Pity he didn't see the war out. Not many of us did."

And not many of them had gone on to such an astounding success. June had told me on my first evening at Didcote that not only had Sir Basil designed and built aircraft of significant importance to the RAF, but from his expensive clothes, his abundant wine cellar, and his beautiful Bentley, which I could see parked outside the dining room window, he had clearly made a packet doing so.

Sir Basil propped his strong, manly chin up on a long-fingered hand. "What I appreciated about your father was that he had a wonderful touch with the common man. He was a real leader: stand them a drink at the end of a long day, that sort of thing." A faint smile. "A bit of carousing rallies the boys when the going gets tough."

Had he got the right name? I wanted to say "Redmayne? Redford? Redwing?" because people rarely get my surname quite right. There are hundreds of names that start with "Red" in Britain. It comes from the Old English "Read," which means red-faced or red-haired.

"He died just before I was born, so I never met him."

"You have his quick wit. He always had a way with words—no one could tell a joke like Clive." Sir Basil's eyes crinkled at the corners again.

That did it; there had to be some sort of mix-up. According to my grandparents, who had enjoyed telling me all about my parents, my father was a reserved and private individual. True, he had a sharp wit, which he shared only with closest friends and family. He wasn't a snob or anything, just a bit of a loner. I knew he had been a war hero, but it certainly wasn't for being one of the boys, for standing a few rounds and getting them all to sing "Pack Up Your Troubles" to take their mind off their raid the next morning. I had rather got the impression from Uncle Ambrose that my father's heroism took the form of simply getting on with it, in his own quiet way, and looking out for the men in his squadron. So much so that he lost his life in the last months of the war.

I decided to test the accuracy of Sir Basil's memory. "My grandad told me that he was very attached to his little Jack Russell, Jock. Took him everywhere," I said, eating a piece of poison pie and washing it down quickly with beer.

Sir Basil smiled into his glass. "So he did. I had almost forgotten Jock. Fearless little chap."

"Used to sit on the airstrip and wait for him," I wickedly lied.

"And loyal. Wouldn't come in for his dinner until his master came home."

I nearly choked on my pie! Sir Basil might have known Clive Redfern briefly during the last war, but my father had left his faithful old Labrador at home when he had joined up. I was done with reminiscing with this ridiculous man. It was part of his charm to yarn away about old fallen comrades. It made him sentimental and likable—more attractive to young women. Well, I didn't like unreliable men.

"So, what is the verdict on Edwina's crash?" I asked him.

"Verdict? Ah yes, I see. The accident committee made their report yesterday evening. They had made a thorough inspection of both planes. Despite the damage done to both, they were able to ascertain that there were no inherent flaws that might have caused either plane to malfunction in flight." He steepled his fingertips together and rested them gently against his well-shaped mouth. "Hmm." He looked across at me and raised one regretful eyebrow. "So, um, yes. I'm afraid it's as we expected: pilot error."

I stared at him in disbelief. Pilot error? "Does that mean that the committee believes that neither Edwina nor Letty knew what they were doing?" I asked. "I mean that they were both flying planes that they were very familiar with, and Vera said that the machines were in top condition. Goodness, even the weather was perfect for October! How on earth could they lose control?"

"Well, now . . . let's not be too hasty. Sadly, we often never know what happened. Look at Amy Johnson—they never even found her—"

I didn't give a hoot about Amy Johnson. "How can they say pilot error when both of them were excellent pilots with thousands of flying hours? Edwina was giving a demonstration she had done hundreds of times."

"Ah yes, Edwina. A delightful young woman." He shook his head. "So full of life, and such a skillful pilot. Nothing I saw her do that morning gave any indication that she wasn't in top form."

"But if she was in tip-top form and the plane she was flying was in tip-top condition, why did she crash?"

"I can see these accidents have distressed you, Miss Redfern. Of course they have." He bent his head as if considering what to say next. "You see"—he lifted his clear blue eyes to mine—"Edwina, well, Edwina had some problems. She was overworked and under stress. Her tangle with the Luftwaffe had left her rather, shall we say, emotionally vulnerable. Women are . . ." He smiled and I gritted my teeth. "Women are more sensitive than men." He nodded at the wisdom of his words and then glanced at me to see how they had been received. "I would never say that out loud, you understand. Our Attagirls are strong, highly intelligent women. All superbly trained; many of them do their job better than their male counterparts." He pushed a piece of pie around on his plate, and I said nothing at all as I concentrated on keeping my breath even. I could bet on it that Letty's accident had been written off as an accident simply because she was a woman. Never mind that she was in her early twenties: fit, alert, and sober. She had flown more hours than most of the RAF top flyboys. *Bosh,* I heard Ilona say, *what complete and utter bosh. I hate it when men say how "sensitive" we are. As if we crumble into tiny little pieces at the drop of a hat. Next thing you know he will be blaming it on the full moon.*

"I see. So, are you saying that Edwina lost her nerve?"

He started to shake his head and then turned it into a reluctant nod. He hadn't mentioned her drinking, her anonymous letters, or the fact that some believed the Luftwaffe story was a fantasy. "I am only saying that she possibly lost her nerve. It happens to the best of us."

Not to you, though, you old crocodile, I thought. You have the coolest nerve.

Bloody piffle, just plain bloody piffle. Ilona was livid.

"Now, Miss Redfern." The old charmer spread his hands wide across the table. "How does the Crown Film Unit plan to proceed with this film you have half made?"

I thought about this for the briefest second. "Most of our focus, and our footage, was on Edwina. And because the Spitfire is a Battle of Britain hero in its own right, an emblem of our superiority in the air, the British people will want to see a Spitfire in the film. Unfortunately, we don't have quite enough footage of it before the crash."

"Which you won't be including."

"This is a film to entice young women to join the ATA, not frighten them off."

A toothy smile. "I have to say, my dear, that most of the great British public wouldn't know a Spitfire from a Hurricane."

"I am afraid you are wrong, Sir Basil," I said. "We are a nation of plane spotters—we know our Spitfires!"

He frowned. Sir Basil, senior official at the Ministry of Aircraft Production, might oversee the Air Transport Auxiliary all over the south coast, but it was Mr. Fanshaw who ran the Crown Film Unit, and we all know that keeping the British public consciously patriotic is Mr. Churchill's top priority.

"We have footage of all the planes the other five pilots flew, but we will probably need to shoot more film of a Spitfire in flight, and then we can call it a day."

He pushed himself back in his chair. "But why? The archives must be full of Spitfire film."

"Apparently not. Anyway, the final decision will be made by Mr. Fanshaw sometime today."

"What about the film Huntley and Keith shot of our lunch? Surely they are going to include that. Surely that will give everyone a sense of what a nice, big, happy family the ATA is?"

I smiled my sweetest smile; I wasn't going to tell this man that that piece of film had been filched. "Yes, it's a nice touch, but basically what the public are thrilled about is the Spitfire. And a Spitfire being flown by a woman."

He frowned down at his plate. "It will be a bit hard to interrupt our work schedule for another round of filming," he demurred.

"Mr. Fanshaw knows that and he will be very respectful of the ATA's schedule," I promised without having a clue what Fanny thought or intended. I made my voice sympathetic. "I know it won't be the same without Edwina. I wish I had known her better." I sighed. "Known about her life a little more. Her family must be devastated. Did she have a large family—brothers and sisters?" The light tattoo of his fingers on the tablecloth as he considered what another day of filming would involve stopped.

He frowned and shook his head. "I'm afraid to say I don't know." He looked rueful. "I knew so little about her."

A snort of derision from Ilona. *Wasn't he sleeping with her? Or involved in a way that upset poor old Vera Abercrombie to no end?*

I said nothing to either of them. The light beat of his fingertips on the tablecloth started up again. "Yes, I suppose we could arrange for another morning of filming," he said graciously.

"Oh good. Who would you suggest fly a Spitfire for us?"

"Not my decision, my dear. That is up to Didcote ATA's commanding officer," he said rather pompously.

"SIR BASIL SAID the ATA Accident Committee inspector thinks both crashes were pilot error!" I found Griff standing on the mossy terrace, smoking a cigarette, as soon as I had said good-bye to Sir Basil.

"Course they did. They are protecting Didcote ATA."

"What?"

"The pilots are dead—there was evidently nothing wrong with the aircraft that they could find, and, well, I guess it's easy to blame the pilot."

How cynical, I thought, how cynical and lazy.

"I know," Griff commiserated. "War is ugly, but bureaucrats and politicians are uglier. But I have some news, and I think you'll say it's 'interesting' news!" He could hardly disguise his triumph.

"Zofia wasn't supposed to fly the day that Letty died." Griff took me by the arm as we watched Sir Basil negotiating the tight turn out of the inn's drive in his Bentley. He steered me away from the drive around to the back of the inn and into the windswept garden that overlooked the river. "Zofia was taken off Didcote's delivery schedule on the morning Letty was killed. Look." He pulled a bent white card from the inside pocket of his coat. "Vera uses these cards to organize the daily delivery schedules from White Waltham's master schedule."

I stared at what appeared to be typed code: "Lukasiewicz, Zofia

(Class III) Thurs. 10/8/42 Ferry p/u Mos Ser. DK134 @ de Hav. Fac. Hat. To Sqd. 398 BHA. 0700." I stared at the card. "I don't understand all these abbreviations, do you?"

"It says: Zofia what's her name, who has a Class Three license, was scheduled to fly on Thursday, October eighth. Picking up a Mosquito, serial number DK134, from the de Havilland factory in Hatfield to deliver it to Bomber Squadron 398 at Biggin Hill Airfield. This was written up at oh seven hundred hours. See the date and time in the corner? But it is crossed through. She was taken off the schedule!"

"But Zofia did fly that day. She flew to Biggin Hill. I was there. I saw her being given one of these cards. Why had she been taken off and then put back on again just over an hour later?" I asked.

He shrugged. "I don't know. You were there. What did you see?"

It had been an awful meal. The five of them silently eating their greasy breakfast like automatons. Zofia, pale-faced and withdrawn, hunched over her coffee, too miserable to eat.

"Zofia was wretched, so wretched she couldn't eat her breakfast, but Letty did—she ate her own breakfast and then Zofia's. Does this prove that Zofia was taken off the schedule because she might have been thought too upset to fly, and was put back on to . . . ?" I couldn't finish my thought because it sounded so incredibly melodramatic.

"To die." His face was as earnest as his words.

Bessie stopped digging out a promising subterranean hole at the edge of the river and ran back to see what was going on.

"How did you find this?" I waved the card at him.

"It's a chit," he said, as if such a thing were public property and available at the local library. His evasive glance meant that he knew I wouldn't approve. "Each pilot is issued with one when her work assignment is made. Some of them have two or three, depending on the number of planes they deliver. The pilot takes her chit with her. When she checks in at the factory, they rubber-stamp it with the date and write the time next to it. It's like her passport to the factory ground crew and riggers to release the plane to her for delivery. Then when the pilot delivers the plane at the destination airfield, they rubber-stamp it again with the squadron code and the date. At smaller airfields they just tear off a corner. When the pilots come back to their ferry pool, they check in with their CO and hand in the cards to be reconciled with the ATA logbook and the pilot's personal flying log. All the returned cards are kept together with the logbook. It's a simple method for tracking who delivered which aircraft where and when."

I looked down at the card in my hand. The abbreviations were quite clear now even if they had two horizontal lines of ink neatly run through them.

"So, where did you find this? Griff, you didn't go through Vera's office, did you?" Regrettably Zofia would have found my tone stuffy—lecturing, even.

"Her wastebin, to be exact." He ran his hand through his hair. "For God's sake, Poppy, it was a wastebin—minutes away from a trash bin!"

I couldn't believe how offhand he was about rooting through the contents of the commanding officer of Didcote ATA's office. Vera's wastepaper basket wasn't the only place he had looked. It was clear that Griff's war duties still blurred from those of pilot to something else entirely. "Did you find any other useful information?"

"I had to make sure that I understood their scheduling method. I went through the logbook for October eighth and compared all the chits with the entries. Sure enough, their system is as I described. But I found another chit, issued for Zofia, the same as the one you are holding. It had two rubber stamps to indicate that she had completed her delivery for that day." He paused; despite his extraordinary discovery, his expression didn't show that he took pleasure in it. "There was no chit for Letty. I'm sure that there is a procedure for unreturned chits."

I held the card in my hands. I was so astonished, all I could do was stare up at him. "I think this proves that Zofia was meant to crash her plane on her flight from Hatfield to Biggin Hill, doesn't it?" I asked Griff.

"Maybe. C'mon, let's walk. My feet are like ice." We paced forward a few yards.

"How far away from us is Hatfield?"

"I can't be sure about immediate flight time from Hatfield to Biggin Hill in a Mosquito because it wouldn't be a straight route. There are so many airfields in the south, both RAF and AAAF, that they all have barrage-balloon protection. Zofia would have those marked on her maps and would have to fly around them. I think it said fifteen hundred hours on the Biggin Hill stamp for her arrival."

I subtracted twelve from fifteen. Three o'clock. "Do you think Vera organized it?"

"She might have. She was in a perfect position to do so, but it doesn't mean she did, does it? Perhaps she decided Zofia was too upset by her friend's death to fly and then Zofia insisted and went. After all, what was Vera's motive to kill Zofia? I don't see that she had one. If Edwina was sleeping with Basil Stowe, I suppose she might take revenge on her in that crazy way. But why would she want Zofia out of the way?"

In my limited experience of what motivates people to kill a second time, it was the fear that their second victim knew something or had seen something that made the murderer a suspect.

I tried to remember everything I had heard and seen in the past forty-eight hours that might give us proof of our suspicions. "I found out this morning, from Edwina's landlords, Mr. and Mrs. Franklin, that their version of Edwina's life was so much more straightforward and . . . well, I suppose I could say acceptable, than the one that involves poison-pen letters and hangovers." And I told him all about my visit to Zofia and then to the Franklins.

To say that someone is all ears is an odd expression, when attention is clearly expressed in the eyes. "The Franklins loved Edwina; they said she was like a daughter to them. Can you imagine Edwina sitting down to play cribbage in the evenings with their next-door neighbor? She sounded so different when they described her." I heard the disbelief in my voice that someone like the Edwina I had met would be happy to sit around playing cards with three elderly people. "And the Franklins told me that Edwina was an orphan. She had no family at all. Her mother died when she was little, and her father committed suicide when he went bankrupt. Did anyone else know about Edwina's family, or her lack of one?"

"Probably not. But it certainly explains her insecurity!"

Insecurity? I was an orphan. Was I insecure? *Oh, for heaven's sake, darling,* said Ilona in her especially patient voice. *Let's admit it. You are dreadfully insecure. Just remember what the countess said and trust yourself more.*

"And there were more revelations from the Franklins. Edwina was in love, really in love, with a pilot who cared for her too. And—" I tried not to gabble the rest. "And he flew out of an airfield on the south coast called something church, or church something. He was killed."

Griff closed his eyes in concentration. "Hornchurch."

"No, not that one."

"Okay let's see: Church Fenton? Eastchurch? C'mon, there are hundreds of airfields outside villages called 'something church.' Were they lovers, were they engaged, was she secretly married? We're talking about Edwina, who apparently liked to play the field."

I started to shake my head. "I had this information from an incredibly respectable old couple in their seventies. People who saw another side of Edwina. Can you imagine I would ask them such intimate questions? They called him her sweetheart."

"Edwina had a sweetheart—why is this woman so hard to figure out?"

We stopped, out of patience with our discoveries, and I crouched to reassure an anxious Bess, who had come running up at our raised voices.

"I feel we are spinning around in circles when Zofia's life is in danger." I was pleased to hear that the panic I felt did not echo in my voice. Soothing Bess made me feel less fearful too.

"Where is she today?"

"Ferrying some brass hat from Castle Bromwich to somewhere."

He laughed. "Safe as houses, then. She'll hardly go down if she's flying an air vice marshal, will she?" I remembered Anthea, Cheryl, and the girl with the strawberry-blond hair making risqué jokes about flying air marshals and giggled.

He reached a hand down to help me to my feet. My pulse started to race, and there was a particularly delicious sensation in the center of me that made me feel that I was made of warm wax.

And then Bessie, sensing that all tension had gone, looked to enliven the afternoon with a bit of stick work. "No, Bess," Griff said firmly. Was he remembering her interruption in the meadow above Elton? He turned toward me with that look I have only ever seen on Robert Taylor's face—on film. I closed my eyes.

"Miss Redfern! Coo-ee! Miss Redfern. You are wanted on the

tele-phone. Trunk call from Lon-don!" Mrs. Evans appeared on her slippery terrace to wave a hefty arm. No use pretending I hadn't seen her.

Griff turned away and picked up a stick. "Trunk call," he said. "It must be from Buckingham Palace."

"THAT WAS HUNTLEY."

"Is that his real name?"

He was waiting for me at the bottom of the stairs, looking particularly well-groomed, not quite as faultless as Sir Basil, but he was wearing a freshly laundered shirt and a new uniform tie.

"Of course it is. Where are you off to anyway?" I asked as he turned to the hall mirror and put his cap on.

"Gotta see a man about a—"

"You always say that when you're being cagey! You can't go yet, because we haven't finished sharing information!"

"Haven't we?"

What was that supposed to mean? "Did you scout about that hangar? Did you find out why a heavily laden lorry was hauling out of there at two in the morning and going into the village and not on to Southampton?"

He took a step closer to me and smiled. "I'm sorry, did I forget to report in?"

I laughed at his poker face. "You haven't said a word about the lorry I might have seen outside the hangar last night."

He laughed his lighthearted laugh, which I sometimes find entrancing and at other times just plain irritating. "What an exhausting woman you are." He held up his hands to ward off more questions and pretended to cringe behind them. "Two things to remember: I offer to help you investigate a possible murder and you send me off to London like an errand boy in your usual command-ing way on a completely fruitless mission, while you have all the fun partying with Sir Basil and the Attagirls."

In my usual commanding way? "I . . ."

"Nope, I said two things. I was the one that found that there was something *definitely* suspicious going on with the schedule when Letty crashed her plane. No word of thanks, by the way." He waved his right hand for silence. "The other is that I have an appointment in Southampton this afternoon—very hush-hush, so please don't ask. And there is a third thing: until I get back, *please* stay away from the hangar and Mac Wilson. And by the way, are we leaving tonight or tomorrow morning?"

He's off doing his secret service thing, said Ilona. *Whatever you do, do not give him the satisfaction of asking him what. He will only shut you up.*

I felt a little shiver of excitement that there might be more reve-lations to come.

"Are you coming back this evening?"

"Yes. Are we leaving for London tonight or tomorrow?"

"That was Huntley on the phone—yes, it is his real name. Hunt-ley and Keith will be returning to film a Spitfire in flight as soon as Vera gives them the go-ahead."

"Really, and who's going to fly it?" His eyes were wide in a ques-tion he knew the answer to.

"Oh, dear God!" I said as truth dawned. "You know perfectly well who's going to fly it!"

TWENTY

T HE LIGHT WAS CLOSING IN ON THE RIVER AS IT WOVE ITS WAY
down to the Solent and then onward into the English Channel
as I took a glass of what Mr. Evans referred to as a light beer into the
empty lounge to sit in its window and ponder. As I sipped I realized
that I had had nothing to eat since the abysmal pie for lunch.

It wasn't long before Mrs. Evans made her way across the
lounge. "Do you mind if I join you?" she asked as she took a seat
next to me, and we both gazed appreciatively at the gleaming river.

"Beautiful sight, isn't it? You should see it in summer; it has to
be one of the most beautiful rivers in England.

"During Operation Dynamo it was a mass of boats. Stem to
stern they were; you could hardly see the water. All those boats
setting off to pick up our boys stranded on the beach in Dunkirk."
She sighed. "Our Percy"—she referred to her son—"is still over in
the African desert with Monty"—she meant Field Marshal Mont-
gomery, the latest of Britain's heroes—"giving those Jerries what
for!" She raised her glass and drank. I cautiously sipped my beer; it
might taste delicious, but it had a kick to it.

A little pause as Mrs. Evans cast about for how to introduce the subject that had brought her over to me. In the end she just came out with it. "Nice man, that Sir Basil. Such a gentleman and so well turned out. Really youthful-looking considering his age. You would never believe he was in his late fifties, would you?"

Aha, said Ilona, *here comes the warning.*

"He's responsible for making sure that all our boys in the RAF have planes to fly. Factories can't turn the wretched things out fast enough." I blinked at this insight into how the war was run. "Oh yes, all the airfields have to count on Sir Basil." She waved a vague arm that encompassed her leaf-strewn garden and the drive. "In and out of here a lot he was at one time, always with one of those pretty girls from the ATA."

I smiled.

"Nice enough man"—she laughed—"but he never seems to be able to stick. You know, with one girl. It must be because he's so 'andsome."

Since she had brought the subject up, there was no harm in asking. "Likes the ladies, does he?" I said in a cheeky voice, flinching at the expression and remembering the other evening at the cottage and Sir Basil's gift of expensive burgundy.

"Bit of a naughty boy." She opened her eyes wide as she nodded. "Stick with that nice American chap, I would." She saw that I completely understood her and decided to give me further advice. "We are hoping that he will settle down with Commander Abercrombie. It doesn't do to be playing the field as you get on in years."

As if on cue, I saw Sir Basil's latest flame put her head around the doorway of the lounge. She saw me and raised her hand in greeting.

With her back to the door Mrs. Evans didn't see her. "Though why Commander Abercrombie would put up with an old boy like Sir Basil I have no idea." She heaved herself to her feet and, half turning, saw Vera Abercrombie walking toward us. "Anything I can do for you, Miss Redfern? Sandwich?"

"Thank you, Mrs. Evans, I'm fine. Lovely lunch."

A deep sigh as she remembered better days. "Used to have a full-time chef here; that was before the war, of course. The yacht club was packed with tall masts, and the weekend trade had us run off our feet. Ah well." Out of habit she produced a damp cloth and gave the table a quick wipe down. "I'll leave you to your little chat. Anything I can get you, Commander?" she said as Vera sat down across from me.

"Nothing, thank you, Mrs. Evans."

Vera waited for Mrs. Evans to painstakingly wipe every table-top throughout her lounge. Her honest doggy-brown eyes were red-rimmed and her skin looked more lined than ever. A tired woman with far too many responsibilities, whose day never ended and whose lover was unfaithful. I decided that the very least I could do was be respectful and wait for her to speak first.

She sighed. It wasn't a sigh of self-pity. It was more of an exhala-tion that she had cleared the last docket, the last chit, and the last bureaucratic infraction from her mind before she concentrated on me.

"Miss Redfern," she began, and her smile was not quite as broad or welcoming as it had been when the Crown Film Unit had first breezed through her door. "I have, today"—I almost expected her to look at her watch to log in the exact time—"received a telephone call from Crown Films."

I kept the respectful look. A little surprise about the eyebrows but nothing more.

"They are coming here tomorrow morning to make more film. Did you know about this?"

Did I know about this? Only since my lunch with Sir Basil when I had blithely informed him of the possibility. "Yes," I said truthfully, "I expect they want—"

"They want more Spitfire *footage*, as they call it."

I cleared my throat and summoned all my tact—and nerve. I wasn't talking to soppy Basil Stowe; I was talking to Didcote ATA's commanding officer: a woman who was in the doghouse for losing two pilots and very expensive equipment. "The footage they took of Edwina's Spitfire is mostly her accident," I explained. "They only have a couple of minutes of usable film."

"You don't have to convince me that we can't use all the film, Miss Redfern. But what you must understand is that we are at war. Our ATA pilots are hard-pressed for time as it is, and soon it will be dark by half past four. Not to mention that autumn and winter weather interfere with the most well-planned schedule and we are always behindhand." Her voice, so matter-of-fact and pleasant on the ear when she greeted our arrival just four days ago, had risen in pitch. The lines of tension around her tight mouth almost quivered with maintaining a stiff upper lip. I wanted to reach out and smooth them away. "Is there any way they can use some other film of Spitfires? Or just cut the Spitfire part out completely?"

It didn't matter what Crown Films could do with archive footage. It didn't matter how inconvenient Griff and I were with our protracted stay. I wanted to finish the investigation I had started because the situation at Didcote ATA was clearly not on the up-and-up.

"Mr. Fanshaw's decision is that we shoot more film." Mr. Fanshaw felt the same way as Vera Abercrombie: he wanted to get the wretched ATA film ticked off his list. Only Huntley's firm insistence that the film would be a "whopper" had convinced Fanny to continue, but if Vera called him and made a stink, then he might agree to use what we had.

Our eyes met across the table and held their gaze. Hers was intense, almost confrontational. I would not let myself look away. "Crown Films want to make a compelling piece about how exciting it is to do this type of work. We cannot possibly have the British public watching the film we have of Edwina's Spitfire. They will go home and tell their daughters, 'Sign up for the St. John's ambulance, Kitty, you are not going up in a plane that looks like it can't stay in the sky.' We *have* to shoot more footage."

And then I gazed pacifically into her frowning eyes and held my breath.

I have to hand it to her; she was a cool one.

"Very well, then," she said, her eyes still fixed on mine. "We will be ready with a Spitfire and a pilot at oh nine hundred hours tomorrow morning for one hour. I hope your film crew can get everything they need in that time."

"We will do our very best not to get in the way," I said in my most compliant voice. "Who will be the pilot?"

I knew her answer before she opened her mouth, and mine went as dry as chalk.

"Zofia Lukasiewicz is the only one of our pilots who is available. I would far prefer not to ask her to fly, but I suppose I have to."

I felt in that awful moment as if it were me who was pushing this ugly situation to the edge of another possible murder. All my fears about what might happen closed in on me in a stifling blanket of guilt. If Griff and I were right, then the number of accidental deaths at Didcote might rise from two to three.

TWENTY-ONE

WHERE WAS GRIFF? I HAVE NEVER FELT SUCH ANXIETY AS I waited through the last hours of the afternoon. Bessie and I paced up and down the drive in front of the inn. My hands were dug deeply into the pockets of my trench coat so I couldn't bite my nails.

Bess heard the Alvis's engine long before I did. Her ears pricked forward, and her bobtail started to agitate. She gazed intently into the dusk with joyful anticipation in her eyes for the arrival of her favorite male.

"For heaven's sake, it's just Griff." I picked her up as the car came into the drive, because she would have thrown herself under his wheels to get to him.

"I CAN SEE you're bursting at the seams with information." He drank half a glass of beer in one long swallow and put it down. "How many varieties of beer do they make in England?" He was looking particularly pleased with himself.

"I don't know. Mr. Evans comes from Kent and makes masses

of the stuff." I did my best to contain my impatience. "Zofia is going to fly a Spitfire tomorrow for Crown Films!" I blurted, desperate to share what I saw as bad news.

"Yes, I thought she might." He held his glass up to the light. "This beer is excellent, by the way."

It was as much as I could do not to take a whack at him. He caught my eye and made a sympathetic face. "Please don't worry," he said.

"It's a worrying thing. If Zofia was intended to have been the murderer's second victim, then here we are requiring a reshoot of a Spitfire in flight, and surprise, surprise, the only pilot available is Zofia. Of course I am worried."

He put his empty glass down. "Then we must do everything we can to prevent Zofia from going up," he said. "What time will the boys start filming?"

"At nine o'clock tomorrow morning."

"We'll have to hold them off. What time are they getting here?"

"I haven't heard—sometime this evening."

"Damn." But he didn't look in the slightest concerned. Not even when Mrs. Evans came into the bar and gave him an envelope.

"Your two chaps from Crown Films will be here later this evening, Miss Redfern. Probably get here at about eleven, she announced. "And this came for you in the second post, sir." I could tell she was fascinated by him; Americans are rare in Didcote. She handed him his letter with reverence bordering on worship; I was surprised she hadn't brought it to him on a silver tray.

Griff frowned. "Thank you, Mrs. Evans," he said, and as she reluctantly left he turned the envelope over in his hands. "Who would write to me here?" he said wonderingly.

"Why don't you open it and read it?" I asked. "Then you'll know."

"You are on edge," he said and opened the letter.

I watched his face as he scanned through the lines on the page. In his other hand was a second page. I squinted so I could see it more clearly. It was written in different handwriting from the first: small and neat, it covered the page from top to bottom in close lines. The page he was reading was written in a hasty scrawl that looped across the page in black ink. Griff looked down at the page in his left hand. "Well, I'll be damned," he said reverently. "It seems that Uncle Ambrose's pal Cadogan has surpassed all expectations!"

Griff started to read the second page and I laced the fingers of both hands together in my lap, knuckles white, and prayed for patience.

"Aha." Griff read on. "Fascinating!" He waved the second page at me. "Absolutely fascinating. Want to know what it says?"

"No," I said. "I want you to be enthralled all by yourself. Please, whatever you do, don't share anything!"

Griff looked over his shoulder. "I think this calls for another beer!" he said and lifted his voice. "Mrs. Evans?"

She appeared like a jack-in-the-box from the kitchen. "Yes, sir?"

"Two more . . . Blondies, is it?"

"Right away, sir."

"No, no," I said. "Really, I've had enough."

"Oh no, no, you haven't!" Griff nodded to Mrs. Evans.

Eyes shining, he lifted the second page to his lips and kissed it. "Our theories, or rather your theory, is correct, Poppy," he said. "There are substances that do not kill, but they do disorient the mind, and many of them if eaten take effect between one to two hours later."

I was almost out of my chair, but the arrival of Mrs. Evans with two glasses in her capable hands made me keep my seat and bite back any exclamations.

She put our Blondies down on the table and said not to mention it as we thanked her.

"What does it say?" I asked, ignoring the beer.

He smiled, took a sip of beer, and leaned back in his chair, thrusting his legs out in front of him and folding his arms behind his head.

"It says we were right."

I felt a little shiver of horror curl the hairs on the nape of my neck. "Please, Griff, no more suspense, just tell me!" I said, and I lifted my glass and waved it in salute.

"Do you need a sandwich or something?" he asked.

"No, I had an enormous lunch with Sir Basil."

"About five hours ago!"

I shook my head. "I'm fine," I said. "Please, just tell me what is in your letter from Cadogan."

He cleared his throat and launched in. "After our dinner at the Travellers Club, Cadogan went off and had a chat with a colleague of his who is writing a thesis on plants that cause hallucinations."

"The Rime of the Ancient Mariner" and Samuel T. Coleridge sprang instantly to mind. "Like laudanum and opium."

He laughed and tilted his chair back on its hind legs. "Yes, exactly that sort of thing."

If you know about Coleridge and opium, why didn't you think of that earlier? Ilona chipped in.

"What does he say in his letter?"

He lifted the page and read: "There are several plant derivatives that produce a state of euphoria, and/or hallucinations, and if taken in larger doses cause heart palpitations and confusion ranging from disorientation to blacking out!"

"And they are slow acting?"

"Not always. Sometimes the body tries to purge them."

I exhaled disappointment. "It wouldn't have been any of those, then."

He picked up the second page and skimmed through it. "No, but there are some plants whose leaves, pods, or roots, when dried and consumed"—he waved the close-written paper at me—"yes, it says here, smoked or eaten, that have a particularly pleasant sensation, or hallucinations which take effect immediately."

Disappointment drenched all my hopes. "But immediately is no good to us and neither is pleasant."

He leaned forward and tapped me on the top of the head with his letter. "Hold your horses, ma'am. But if they are eaten, especially in a large dose, then the unpleasant side effects crop up. Imagine for instance that you are flying a plane, and suddenly you don't know where you are. You don't know which side up you are. Your heart is racing and you see things that are not supposed to be there. The more you panic, the worse it gets."

I drew in a deep breath. Now we were getting somewhere!

"Griff!" I rapped on the table with my knuckles. "Please tell me that none of these plants act instantly."

He closed his eyes and laughed, shaking his head slowly from side to side. "Do you know that sometimes you remind me of a schoolteacher I had in my freshman year? I promise you no one messed around in her geography class."

Starchy, put in Ilona.

I lifted my hands palms upward and made a pleading face. "Please," I begged, "will you stop 'messing around,' whatever that means, and tell me?"

He righted the chair and took a long drink of beer. "My, that's good! Didn't you Brits drink ale for breakfast centuries ago?"

"Griff!"

"Where was I? Ah yes." He scanned the page. "If their roots

were ground to powder and inhaled they act instantly, same as when the leaves and stems are dried and smoked like tobacco. But the effect comes on far more slowly if they are *eaten*. Some seeds and compounds, say, like opium, can take an hour or two to kick in if they are eaten." He looked down at the second page and read for a minute. "But opium tastes really bitter and it doesn't blend well with food."

"What about in something like Camp coffee?"

"But how could you dose a pot of coffee so only one person drinks a cup?"

"We should make a list of different plants and the effect they have."

He smiled as he handed me the page. "We don't need to. It's here. Six mind-altering plants. Six of them, including poppy: *Papaver somniferum*. The opium poppy. Did you know that about your name, by the way, that you were named after a plant that causes beautiful dreams?"

God knows how often I had hoped that Griff had beautiful dreams about me. But my anxiety about Zofia made me desperate for real facts. "After the last war, lots of girls of my age were called Poppy."

He shrugged his shoulders and took another sip of beer. "Let's go through this list. We might find one that could have been used on Edwina and Letty. I think we are really onto something."

TWENTY-TWO

G RIFF DRAGGED HIS CHAIR AROUND TO MY SIDE OF THE table; he was so close to me I could smell the cedar soap he used to shave.

"Salvia," I read obediently, "a species of mint from South America, contains salvinorin, which activates specific nerve-cell receptors. The effects are intense but short-lived and include changes in mood, body sensations, and visions. The leaf, dried and smoked, has a mild effect: a loosening of the inhibitions. Eaten in large quantities it intensifies hallucinations." I looked up from the page straight into his eyes. He nodded encouragement. "Eaten in large quantities, what would that be? Three or four sandwiches or someone else's breakfast as well as your own? Would having hallucinations make you crash a plane?"

"If I was flying a plane it would," he said. He nodded me on, and I bent my head to read.

"This one sounds a bit disgusting to me. Ayahuasca—is that how it's pronounced?—is a South American vine. Culturally important to the Amazonian peoples and used to generate intense spiritual revelations. Studies show significant psychological distress under the influence of the drug: heart palpitations, acute difficulty in breathing, and considerable disorientation. This one sounds perfect! Oh no, it doesn't: ingestion is commonly followed by vomiting or diarrhea, which shamans believe to be the purging of demons. No, not that one." I shuddered.

He finished his beer. "I find the next one interesting." He bent over my shoulder. I could feel his breath on my neck. "Native to the Americas," he read, "the tobacco plant bears distinctive large leaves that are a particularly concentrated source of nicotine. Nicotine is the chief active ingredient in the tobacco used in cigarettes, cigars, and snuff and might be addictive. Interesting, that, don't you think? When ingested by mouth, nicotine is a highly toxic poison that causes vomiting and nausea, headaches, stomach pains, and, in severe cases, convulsions, paralysis, and death. Yes, I know it probably wasn't used to poison Edwina and Letty, but it is interesting that smoking tobacco might be heavily addictive."

I shook my head. "Most people who smoke say it relaxes them. It's probably a different kind of plant. And anyway, there is the business of throwing up again." I remembered Grable saying that Edwina drank to excess so often she was in danger of vomiting in public. Was she being poisoned before we arrived to film her? But that didn't explain Letty's crash.

Griff squinted down at the cramped handwriting.

"His writing is difficult to read. Cocoa? No, coca. It's a tropical shrub native to certain regions of Peru, Bolivia, and Ecuador. Its leaves contain the alkaloid cocaine and have been chewed for centuries by the Indians of Peru and Bolivia for pleasure or in order to withstand strenuous working conditions, hunger, and thirst. When ingested in small amounts, cocaine produces feelings of well-being and euphoria along with decreased appetite, relief from fatigue, and increased mental alertness. With prolonged and repeated use it produces depression, anxiety, irritability, sleep problems, chronic fatigue, mental confusion, and convulsions. Sounds like half the guys in my squadron are on this stuff!"

I remembered a girl at school telling us about her aunt. "After the last war, all the flappers and bright young things used to take cocaine at their parties. I'm sure people still use it. At least we know you can probably get it in this country. The other plants sound so obscure, so out of reach for the average Atta."

"But we are not dealing with the average Atta, are we? These are the greater Attas." Griff tapped his forefinger on the tabletop. "And last but not least is *Datura stramonium*. It grows throughout much of North and South America but is widely used in Africa as a cure-all for asthma and lung problems. It is a weedy annual plant with striking white tubular flowers and spiky seedpods. The leaves and seeds contain potent alkaloids that cause hallucinations. Used ceremonially by several indigenous peoples, datura acts as a deliriant and can produce intense spiritual visions. Users often report terrifying hallucinations and paranoid delusions under its influence and may experience prolonged side effects such as blurred vision after its use. It does not cause the body to purge upon consumption."

"What does the asterisk note?" I asked.

" 'The Royal Horticultural Society has advised British gardeners to dig it up or have it otherwise removed, while wearing gloves.' I guess that means it can be grown in England."

He put his hand on mine briefly and shook it to emphasize what he said next. "And it takes a couple of hours for the effects to come on. What d'you think?"

"That's it—that's the one. It has to be something like that!" But it was a terrible thought. If datura had been used on Edwina and Letty, it would have been a terrifying experience.

He nodded in agreement. "But here's the thing. All we need to know is that it was possible to cause both Edwina and Letty to be so disoriented and confused by a plant like datura that they crashed their planes. What we should really concentrate on, right now, is motive. And that is where you come in, Poppy, because you have spent your entire time here chatting away with all the people who were there the day Edwina was killed, and who were there at Letty's last breakfast. So, spill the beans: who was most likely to want to eliminate Edwina?"

He was wise to start with Edwina as a victim because I'd considered the question thoroughly.

"Edwina was involved at one time with Sir Basil, so that could be a reason why Vera Abercrombie would want her out of the way. But then Sir Basil had a roving eye, so Vera probably would have had to murder all the glamour girls in the ATA. And then, if Sir Basil was embarrassed by Edwina's continued pursuit of him, he might want to get rid of her too."

"So not Vera?"

"Perhaps not. Hard to say. If Sir Basil told her that he was in love with Edwina and that he was leaving her, maybe that would be a good enough reason."

Griff pulled a pen out of his uniform jacket pocket and turned over Cadogan's letter to the blank side. He wrote: "Vera Abercrombie"; a pause, and then: "Don't think of them in order of probability, just say whoever comes into your head who might have a motive," he instructed, his face serious.

"Then if I count everyone except the film crew, you, and I, there are five possible suspects," I said as I considered. "So, the second Attagirl to consider would be Grable—I mean Betty Asquith: the tall natural blonde."

"That's right, the one with the posh accent!"

"During my evening at their cottage, Grable was the most outspoken about Edwina's frailties. She didn't have any problems in listing her faults. She had an argument about Edwina with Annie Trenchard, the quiet one, the one who landed her plane in a German airfield by mistake."

Griff's eyebrows went up. "Wait a minute, Annie who? When did she do that?"

I gave him a brief version of Annie's adventure in a German airfield.

Griff wrote down the two names. He wrote "Grable" as if she didn't really feature, but his handwriting was bolder as he wrote down "Annie Trenchard."

"Grable is one of those girls with lots of boyfriends, who has an exciting social life," I explained. "Perhaps she was jealous of Edwina's popularity as the femme fatale of the group?"

"Jealous enough to murder her competition?" He laughed. "That's crazy behavior. I think this Trenchard woman sounds more suspicious; she would be at the top of my list."

I knew what he was going to say next.

"What does she say happened when she took off from the German airfield?"

"As soon as she realized her mistake, she flew back and landed in France at the first airfield she could see when the fog cleared. She made a forced landing, with barely enough petrol."

"Fumes," Griff said and scrubbed away at his chin with his thumb and forefinger. "Well now, I take it that her story of landing by mistake in an enemy airfield was not corroborated by anyone else?" It was a statement that caused him to think for a moment. "She glides in and lands unhurt, and it's a miracle that she does. And she tells this adventure story to cover the fact that she had actually been to occupied Belgium and landed in an airfield there. There was no fog at the French airfield, but there was in Belgium."

"What?"

Griff wrote a large number one next to Annie's name. "I would have had some very stern questions for Miss Trenchard if I had been her CO"—his voice was grim—"after she came back from her improbable German adventure."

I was staggered. It had never occurred to me that Annie would make up a misadventure to cover the truth. "You think she might be a spy?" I asked him.

"She might easily be. Think of the information she could share. It's colossal. Maps, coordinates of all the major military airfields. Information on the various factories that make aircraft. Masses of intelligence that could end this war right now, with the Germans as victors."

The thought chilled me to the marrow.

"Then why haven't they bombed all the installations already?"

"They did; they brought Southampton to its knees, and the Supermarine factory in Woolton was obliterated. Now Supermarine has dozens of little factories hidden away all over England, just like all our scattered gasoline dumps."

So that's what you were doing in Southampton this afternoon: you were following up on stolen petrol. Was this why he had jumped on Annie as a possible suspect? I glanced up at his face. It was quite composed as he gazed down at Cadogan's information.

I decided to move on with our suspect list.

"June Evesham," I said. Griff was not listening; he was still mulling over the possibilities of Annie Trenchard as German spy. It didn't matter if he was listening or not. June had no apparent motive for getting rid of Edwina, and she was still devastated by the death of her friend Letty. And no wonder; if she was the murderer, she had doctored Zofia's breakfast, which had then been eaten by Letty. June's anguish at killing her closest friend by mistake would be tremendous.

"Griff, write down June Evesham's name," I said.

"Motive?" He was still mulling over Annie Trenchard.

"I can't think of one, but she disliked Edwina intensely. So, there might be a motive there. I have to dig some more."

We contemplated our list. Griff read, "Vera Abercrombie, Betty Grable Asquith, I'm adding Annie Trenchard because if she is a spy and Edwina found out, that would be the perfect motive, and, as you say, Annie might have had to eliminate Zofia because she suspected Annie of Edwina's murder. Next we have June Evesham. What about Zofia?"

"I think she might be the next victim. I think her breakfast was drugged, and then Letty ate it. But Zofia is a very self-contained woman; it's hard to make her out. I don't think she had a motive!"

"Either killer or victim." He put a star next to Zofia's name. "You said six. Who is the last one?"

"That's right, I did—Sir Basil Stowe."

"Oh really?"

"Yes. First of all, he's a liar," I said with complete conviction. "He even lies when he doesn't really need to."

A low whistle from my American friend. "Are you sure about that? Did you catch him in a lie?"

"I did. He said he knew my father really well, but it was quite clear to me that he might have met him once, or that he only knew of his name." Griff's head came up from the list he was making. "My father was a solitary man; he didn't go in for sing-alongs with his fellow pilots," I explained.

He hesitated and then said carefully in the gentlest tone, "But . . . how do you know he didn't sometimes enjoy a pint or two in the company of his squadron?"

I sighed and remembered how I had pestered my grandparents, my uncle Ambrose, and any of my father's old friends for stories about my father. What had he been like when he was a boy? Was he ever naughty at school—a rebel, perhaps, always in a scrape? And how often the answer would be "Clive? Oh no, he was a good pupil. The quiet sort. Never part of a group, always off on his own."

"I set a trap for Sir Basil. I told him about a dog my father never owned, and he remembered it."

"Faulty memory? Perhaps he was thinking of someone like your dad? The first war was decades ago."

"But my father just wasn't a joiner; he liked his own company, and—"

"Bit like you, then." It was a statement, not a question.

"Me?"

"Yes, Poppy, you. You have come out of your shell a bit in the last year, but British reserve didn't begin to describe you . . ." I must have looked stunned because he sprang to reassure me.

"Nothing wrong with being a loner, you know. You are thoughtful. You keep your own counsel. So much more attractive than always braying for attention, or at least I think so."

He thought I was attractive! *Steady on, darling,* Ilona put her oar in. *No need to lose your head.*

Griff wrote down Sir Basil's name. "Perhaps you just don't like him. Why is that do you think?"

"Apart from him being a liar, you mean? He might have wanted Edwina out of the way because things got out of control and Edwina was making things difficult for him."

"Six suspects," Griff said as he ran his pen down the list. "Do you have a favorite? Apart from Sir Basil?" He sighed and looked at his watch. "I'm starving. Apparently, there is a reasonably good restaurant on the way to Southampton. Want to give it a try? Lots of local-caught fish, and of course the usual mutton stew. I think going for a drive would help us think, and no one will be able to overhear what we have to say."

TWENTY-THREE

WE DROVE DOWN LANES LIT BY A FULL MOON AS IT ROSE in a clear night sky to the village of Butterworth, ten miles south of Didcote, and to a black-timbered low building on the side of the road. As we drove we chewed over our list of suspects but were none the wiser by the time we reached Butterworth.

"Not to worry, food and drink will restore our brain cells." Griff jumped out of the Alvis and Bess and I followed. My stomach was roaring.

"Why a *red* lion I wonder?" Griff mused as he looked the painted sign above us as it swung in the wind over the inn's door. Standing on its hind legs, a superb scarlet beast clawed the air and opened its mouth in a full roar. We never pay much attention to our pub signs: we are so used to them swinging above our local inns and public houses, century after century. I looked up at a fantasy creature from the world of Plantagenet kings, knights-errant, and jousting.

"It's heraldic. Most pub names take the coat of arms, the badges of royalty or of the local nobility. The White Hart, the Blue Boar, the Swan, are all popular heraldic names for pubs. They date back through the centuries of our ancient, noble, and not-so-noble families."

"Do all pubs bear the badge of the leading family?"

"Country pubs sometimes have hunting names: the Dog and Duck, the Horse and Hound."

I could tell by the way he had stopped and was still staring at the painted sign over our heads that here was a bit of our history he wanted to know more about. "What about the Lamb and Flag? That's certainly not part of the hunting theme."

"It's a very old and common pub name. The lamb is the symbol of Christ as the Lamb of God, carrying a banner with a cross, and often gashed in the side. It probably goes back to the time of the Crusades. You know, like the Saracen's Head and the Turk's Head. Have you come across those names?"

"Yeah, now you come to mention it. There's a Turk's Head just south of London, in Greenwich. I bet that's where they set sail for the Crusades."

Griff was still thinking up unusual pub names and demanding to know their origins as we were seated in a low-ceilinged, black-beamed dining room. It was crowded with men and women in uniform and there was a celebratory air about the place, as if something exciting was about to happen.

"I had a drink this afternoon in a place called the Cat and Fiddle," Griff said. "What's that about?"

"Easy." I laughed. "It's part of a nursery rhyme: 'Hey, diddle, diddle, the cat and the fiddle, the cow jumped over the moon.'"

"What?"

"I know." I giggled. "It's probably nonsense."

"It's very useful nonsense," a voice from a table on our left hailed us. An RAF pilot with a large and extraordinarily ornate handlebar mustache turned toward us. His girlfriend, a pretty woman in WAAF uniform, rolled her eyes and said, "Don't be a pest, Roger; this isn't a cocktail party!"

"Not being a pest at all," said Roger. "Have you heard the one about the pilot returning from a mission who couldn't locate his aircraft carrier in the fleet below, and in addition failed to establish secure communication? No? Thought not! All right, so I'll tell you: the pilot circled around the formation and radioed: 'Rub-a-dub-dub, where is my tub?' And received: 'Hey, diddle, diddle, right here in the middle!' You see, nursery rhymes do have a useful meaning."

Handlebar mustache twisted his chair around to join us and gave us a smart little salute. "Squadron Leader Roger Brabazon, RAF, and this is my wife, Pamela. Don't pay any attention to her, she's always telling me off for interrupting. Hope you don't mind!"

"Not at all. Captain Griff O'Neal, American Army Air Force, and this is Miss Redfern."

"Stationed near here?"

"No, further north. I'm down here visiting Miss Redfern, who is making a film at ATA Didcote."

Brabazon's head whipped over to me. "Not the Didcote that has been having all those accidents? We heard about Edwina, what a nightmare."

Pamela dug her husband in the ribs with her elbow. "Roger, stop!" she hissed and shook her head in apology to me. "He is a shocking gossip! Can't help himself." She bent down to pat Bess on the head. "Sweet little dog," she said as Bess tried to avoid the caress and crawled underneath my chair.

"Yes, it was a tragedy. Did Edwina ferry planes to your airfield?" I asked.

"RAF Middle Wallop." Brabazon laughed at the scandalized expression on Griff's face as he reached for the most obvious meaning to the name. "I should think she did—Edwina Partridge dated half of my squadron! What a girl—she certainly had a zest for life. War won't be the same without her."

He raised his glass as a salute to good times, and his wife waved a shushing hand at him. "Pipe down, darling. Half of those men are here tonight." She glanced around the restaurant and then at me. "Trouble with Hampshire," she explained, "is that you simply can't get away from the RAF."

I wanted to know more about another facet of Edwina's life. "We were filming her when she crashed her Spitfire," I explained. I knew I was breaking a taboo by mentioning an air crash.

Roger's face became serious. "It was inevitable, in a way," he said. "She lost her nerve after that Luftwaffe business. I mean, can you imagine playing hide-and-seek with two Messerschmitts, with no means of defending yourself? She delivered a Spit to us about a couple of days afterward. It was evident that her nerves were shot. Her CO should have grounded her."

Pamela shrugged off Edwina's nerves with a toss of her head. "Did she have any friends left at Didcote?" And to me: "She was such a trophy hunter!"

I shook my head. I knew what she meant, but I wanted her to tell me. "Trophy hunter?"

"Always poaching on other girls' territory, you know, stealing their boyfriends." She paused, offered me a cigarette, and waited as Roger lit hers, before he returned to discussing fighter planes with Griff. She blew a long, thin plume of smoke across the remains of her apple tart and lifted her hands up on either side of her face in mock horror. "Wanted in three counties by half the WAAF for theft." She giggled and I remembered being told of Vera's agony when Edwina let her fascinating charms loose on Sir Basil. Who else had she hurt in her desire to collect hearts? I wondered.

"Oh, I see," I said, playing the part of the curious but unenlightened. "I had no idea she was like that!"

And Pamela Brabazon was off. "What was the name of that woman whose husband she pilfered? Sorry, I'm so terribly bad at names—she wasn't English." She nudged her husband's shoulder. "Roger what was the name of Edwina's friend, the foreign one . . . the one whose husband she stole? I know she was an ATA pilot at Didcote."

He frowned, "Do you mean the Pole, Countess somebody or other?"

I took a long breath, but Pamela shook her head. "I don't think she was *that* foreign. Anyway, I shouldn't gossip." She turned back to me. "That's the trouble with pilots; they break hearts wherever they go." She ruffled the hair at the back of her husband's neck; it was a possessive gesture. "Not my old man, though, ay, Roger? Come on, ducky, time to go home."

Roger Brabazon got to his feet as the waitress brought his wife's coat. He helped her into a prewar fox fur, which looked incongruous with her WAAF uniform hat.

"All right, old girl, are you fit to go?" He straddled his legs as he stuck out his hand to Griff. "Home time, got to be up early tomorrow." If he smiled, which I am sure he did, it was through a mustache as thick as the collar on his wife's fur coat. "Middle Wallop is only about twenty minutes' drive from Didcote; pop over and have a G and T one evening!" He took his wife's arm and tucked it in his.

"I remember now!" Pamela turned back to me. "The pilot Edwina snitched *was* married, happily married, until Edwina came along. Caused quite a stir, and then the poor chap went west; tragic, really."

"That all happened at Middle Wallop Airfield?" I asked with what I hoped was a disingenuous expression.

"Lord no, one of the big ones. Eastchurch? No, no, it was the other one . . ." She circled her hand as if trying to kick-start her memory.

"Christchurch?" I supplied, astonished at mine.

"That's the one. I know we shouldn't speak ill of the dead, but Edwina really was the giddy limit." She pulled a silk scarf out of her pocket and tied it around her neck. "Lovely to meet you both. Ta-ta!" She gave a jaunty wave and they were gone.

"Phew," said Griff. "Thought they were never going to leave. I'm famished. What's it to be, fish or rabbit?"

But I had lost my appetite.

"Fish looks good. Sole *à la meunière*. Do you think they use real butter?"

I started to laugh. "Real butter? Griff, when will you accept that no one in England ever sees more than two ounces of butter a month—if they are lucky!"

"Well, what the heck are they cooking it with, then?"

"Margarine."

Griff ordered the rabbit, and I noticed that he didn't ask how it was prepared.

"YOU'RE VERY QUIET." We were driving back to Didcote. "No need to worry about blackout tonight; it's as bright as day." Griff turned into the road that led to Didcote.

"A bomber's moon," I said as I remembered my days in London training to be an air-raid warden. How we dreaded a full moon.

"You okay?"

I nodded, and then in the intimate closeness of the motorcar, I told him what Pamela Brabazon had said about Edwina stealing someone's husband. "He was a pilot who flew out of Christchurch Airfield. His wife found out, and then he was killed."

"In the Battle of Britain? Didn't Zofia's husband die during the Battle of Britain?" He sighed. "It sounds from everything we have learned that Edwina liked to collect men."

"She was such a trophy hunter." I heard Pamela's voice. The name given to girls whose need to possess all men was so acute that they made enemies of friends and were referred to in disparaging terms. I had felt that flare of jealous anger myself when Edwina had made a beeline for Griff. The way she had flaunted his interest in her to me had been calculated and cruel. It was not just about the competitive need to collect other girls' men, I realized. It was about hurting other women, taking what was theirs, destroying trust and confidence. It was an act of destruction. Edwina had dropped a bomb on her friend.

"Edwina's sweetheart died in an air raid on August nineteenth of this year. The Battle of Britain was when? Nineteen forty. It went on through the summer, didn't it? But that was before Zofia came to Didcote, before she joined the ATA. And Pamela and Roger thought it wasn't the Polish countess. Pamela said the woman was foreign, but not foreign enough to be Polish."

Griff's head turned, and he stared at me in the moonlight. "Australian?" he said.

I shrugged. "But June is single."

"Are you sure? Evesham could be her married name."

"She never said she was married. No one said she was married."

"But if Edwina stole her husband, and then he was killed, why would anyone mention it? I mean, it would be tactless, wouldn't it?

Can you remember where June was when Edwina was eating lunch? Did she give her anything? Could she have put the drug into her coffee?"

Coffee. A large thermos of coffee had been brought out with the sandwiches, and the tea urn had been replenished. But all the Atta-girls had had their own flasks with them. They had them filled each morning when they left for work.

I made myself go back over that morning. It was impossible to recall Edwina drinking anything. She had wandered back and forth between a solitary spot on the edge of the group and taking sand-wiches from the tray on the picnic table. I had only been conscious that she had eaten at all because she had taken so many of them. But coffee? Had I seen her drinking coffee?

"I can't remember!" I said in panic. "Really, I can't. There was so much going on."

His hand reached out in the dark and closed, warm and firm, around mine.

"It's okay, Poppy. Don't try so hard. You are tired and anxious. Just let it all go, let go of all this business. Relax."

I felt the tension begin to ebb and my jaw unclench. The black-out headlamps of the car lit up the road immediately in front of us, a comforting half circle of light in the dark as the moon slipped behind a thick bank of cloud. I watched the even gray surface surge toward us like a hypnotized hedgerow creature. I felt my eyes close. I wanted to drive like this forever, but his hand slipped away from mine to change gear, and I opened my eyes to watch the road.

TWENTY-FOUR

M Y FEET WERE ICE-COLD WHEN I WENT UPSTAIRS TO MY musty little room at the inn. I folded the blanket in half to double; then I scrambled into my nightie and dressing gown and pulled on a thick pair of socks before I got into bed. I was conscious only of the wind soughing in the trees as I pulled Bess close to me and sank into sleep.

I NEVER SLEEP well when there is a full moon. Were we still driving down the quiet country lanes of Hampshire? Surely the sound I had heard was the Alvis's engine? I was wide awake in an instant. Kneeling on my bed, I pulled the curtain aside and looked out into the night.

I could see nothing in the lane or the drive below me. I strained my eyes to try to make out the outline of Griff's Alvis where he had parked it by the laurel hedge. There was no other car in the drive but his when we had walked into the inn at eleven o'clock.

I groped on my dressing table until my hands closed around my blackout torch. Scrambling back onto the bed, I switched it on and trained its feeble beam down onto the drive and to the right. The light wavered along the hedge from the corner of the inn back toward the lane. Griff's car wasn't there. It *was* the Alvis's engine I had heard.

I pulled the blackout curtain closed and shone the torch on my wristwatch. It was almost three o'clock.

I lay down and pulled the covers up under my chin. Griff was off on a quest of his own. I had no doubt it was something hush-hush to do with petrol. I smiled as I drifted back into sleep.

I HALF OPENED heavy eyelids as dawn broke and lay, still and warm, in the drowsing state between sleep and wakefulness when the mind is reluctant to leave dreams and still too lazy to try to make sense of them.

I saw aircraft swooping through a tunnel of trees or turning lazily in a sky lit by a bomber's moon. "Your coffee is cold." I turned on my side and drifted back into sleep.

"Your coffee is cold." Someone was inviting me to share her coffee. It was delicious, she told me: prewar. Freshly ground from perfectly roasted beans. The water hot but not scalding. There is nothing as unpleasant as burned coffee.

I spooned a luxurious spoonful of crystal white sugar into my cup and stirred as I inhaled its aroma, the scent of perfectly brewed coffee. I turned on my side and took a long, deep breath: warm dog smelling slightly of ditchwater; damp air filtering through the warped window frame; and an undernote of mildew that was the inn. I sat up in bed, sniffing the air like a questing hound for coffee. *All a dream,* Ilona informed me. *You were having a prewar dream, sweetie.*

There would be no crisply fried bacon either. Nor would there be delicate triangles of ham sandwiches and buttery shortbread for tea. All were gone!

I sat up, swung my legs out of bed, and scuffed my feet into slippers. The linoleum floor was ice-cold. With my coat around my shoulders over my dressing gown, I shuffled to the bathroom and hoped that at least the water would be hot enough to bathe in.

GRIFF WAS HALFWAY through his breakfast when I arrived in the dining room, and so were Huntley and Keith. They half rose in their chairs to say good morning.

"You look like you slept well." Griff resumed his seat.

"I wish I could say the same for you!" I teased, to let him know that I knew he had been up and about at three in the morning.

Huntley turned to Keith and rapidly started to outline how we could manage to shoot the film we wanted and get back to London. And Griff cleared his throat and grinned at me across the table.

"Fanny's upset because we have gone over schedule," Huntley grumbled.

"Hardly our bloomin' fault if the star goes for a Burton in the middle of the sodding pitcher." Keith may be wearing his cap back to front, the way cameramen do in Hollywood, but his vowels and missing consonants were emphatically from the Mile End Road. Griff, who often tries to imitate a cockney accent, hung on his every word.

He picked up the pot, "Coffee?" he said. He poured an inch into my cup. "Uh-oh, there is not much left and it's probably cold anyway. I'll get you some more." He leaned back in his chair and caught Mrs. Evans's eye. "Another pot of coffee, please, Mrs. Evans."

It had been in the coffee! I put my hand over my mouth to stop myself from blurting out what I knew. The drug had been in Edwina's thermos of coffee, and someone had wandered over to share a cup with her! We had been eating our lunch on the edge of the airstrip, enjoying the sun and one another's company, and trying to pretend our sandwiches were made with ham and not Spam.

I saw it now, as clear as day. Zofia had taken a sip of coffee from her thermos and poured it out on the grass, her nose wrinkled in disgust. "It's cold." She got up from the grass and walked over to where Edwina was sitting. She crouched down, gesturing to Edwina to pour her some from her thermos. Without looking up, Edwina had poured coffee into Zofia's tin mug. Zofia nodded her thanks as she stood up and lifted the cup to her lips.

"Zofia." Vera's voice had been sharp, and she had turned in surprise to her commanding officer. "You don't have time for—" Vera's voice had been drowned out in a shout of laughter from Grable, Letty, and Annie. But she had covered the distance to Edwina in three strides and *taken the tin cup out of Zofia's hand.*

Then Huntley had turned to me and asked me what plane Zofia was flying, and conscious only of being a newly minted expert on aircraft, I had turned to him and forgotten the incident as if it had never happened. Until this morning, until my dream.

I looked across the breakfast table at Griff. He was reading the *Times*, shaking his head at the patriotic headlines. "Everyone wants to be a Churchill," he murmured and, looking up, caught the expression on my face.

"Everything okay, Poppy? You look like you've seen a ghost."

"I have!" I said. "And everything is more than okay; it's perfectly brilliant."

Had I actually watched Zofia about to drink Edwina's drugged coffee when Vera had prevented her? Loudly and with determination? Had Zofia been startled by Vera's intrusion, her taking the tin mug away from her and directing her to get ready? As she had taken off in her Hurricane, had Zofia mulled over the incident? And not realizing that she was putting herself in terrible danger, had she said something later to Vera? The Attagirls were respectful to their commanding officer and "ma'amed" her when there were outsiders around, but surely Zofia had said something to someone who had treated her like a child late for school.

I didn't have time to speculate. I had to talk to Griff before we got to the airfield. My coffee came and I nudged Griff under the table.

TWENTY-FIVE

—————

WE WALKED OUT INTO THE AUTUMN MIST.

"It's a ruddy pea-souper!" Keith laughed.

Huntley cursed and pulled the collar of his coat up around his ears—he had been irritable since I had joined them at breakfast. "I sometimes think this damn film will never be finished, and I am doomed to spend the rest of my life in blasted Didcote!"

I glanced at Griff and he lifted his eyes to heaven. "He's a bit tense, isn't he?" he muttered.

"It will all be gone by ten, mate, and we only need half an hour. We'll be done in time to be back in the smoke by early afternoon, just you wait and see." Keith's cheerful optimism did little to set things to rights, and the pair of them fell into an argument about light and filming aircraft against cloud.

"We might as well have used archive footage," Huntley fumed.

"Are you okay?" Griff was at my elbow. "You keep disappearing into your own world. Anything you want to tell me?"

"It was in the coffee," I said with complete certainty. "The drug was in Edwina's thermos of coffee."

I could have kissed him for his immediate understanding. "Do you know who put it there?"

If Keith still had the film he shot of our picnic lunch on the airfield, I would have all the proof I needed. "I know it sounds potty, but I think it was Vera." I waited for him to ask me if I was crazy. But he stood quite still and frowned at the ground as he added things up in his mind.

"Yeah," he said, as if something had been confirmed. "Yeah, that makes sense. But where would someone like Vera get her hands on datura seeds?"

"It grows in England!"

"Yes, of course, but how would she *know* about it?"

I noticed that he didn't ask about motive, his favorite question over the last few days.

KEITH AND HUNTLEY were still in animated argument as we assembled on the wet grass of the airfield. "I can barely see ten blasted feet in front of me!" Huntley's frustrated voice was thrown back at him by a wall of fog. We stood, huddled together in the damp cold, with mist clinging to our clothes, and waited.

"Just sea fog. I talked to the Met Office; it will be cleared by ten." Her voice reached us first as Vera tramped across the field. "Supermarine have just telephoned. Their pilot will bring in a Spitfire as soon as they are cleared for takeoff. You might as well come back to the mess and have something hot to drink."

Keith and Huntley stumped back toward the mess like dutiful schoolboys, Huntley with his hands in his pockets and his collar still up, hiding the irritation on his face, Keith shambling along with his tripod and camera over his shoulder, whistling through his teeth, determined not to let the rest of us spoil the fun of a morning's shooting.

Griff pulled me back by my arm as we approached the door of the mess.

"Are you going to tell me everything you are thinking, or do I have to guess the rest?" he asked.

"I will if you will," I answered.

"Oh no," he said, "here we go again. You know I *can't*. Why didn't that annoying Mrs. Evans put you up on the other side of the inn?"

"It's not my fault if you drive a car that sounds like it has a bad cold every time you start the engine. At three o'clock you went off in your Alvis and were clearly gone for the rest of the night. It is quite evident that you have been off investigating. An authorized investigation, because your leave ends today. So, now you are official." I smiled. Of course I would share, but he had to go first.

A long sigh. "Look, you know what I do, but why do I have to spell it all out for you? Isn't just knowing enough?"

I called Bess over to us and found myself saying, "No, I suppose it isn't. You see, it's infuriating, and I'm sick of it. Are you here to keep me company on my first film assignment, or are you here for some other reason that you won't tell me about, or are you running both together? At any rate *we* are in the investigation of Edwina's and Letty's pilot-error accidents together. Trust me with what you know. If it contributes to our investigation, then you are obligated to share." I paused to catch my breath; it's really hard to shout at someone in a whisper. "It would be the polite thing to do." He started to laugh. Quietly at first, muffled by the thick folds of the scarf around his neck, then a full-throated roar.

"Polite?" he managed to get out. "You think what I do is polite?"

There was silence. I could practically hear the wheels turning in his head. *Well done, darling,* said Ilona. *God, I thought you'd never ask the blighter!*

"Yes, I am onto something. I thought you understood without me having to explain, because I can't do that. And certainly not *now*. Believe me—it is for you own good that I don't tell you now." I can't stand it when people put spaces between their words, as if the person they are talking to is either daft or deaf. "But if you can rein in the wild horses for a moment, all will come clear, hopefully by the time we are ready to pack up and leave this frustrating place with all its viciousness, greed, and what you English call carrying-on. Do you trust me on that?"

He was standing very close to me, so close I could see the sheen of mist clinging damply to his cheeks.

"Here is something I can tell you." He raised his eyebrows as he smiled at me. "I checked out Mrs. Annie Trenchard. Her adventure at an airfield in German-occupied Belgium happened."

"In what way? Are you telling me she is a spy?"

He puffed his lips together and huffed. "No, it was, after all, an honest-to-goodness mistake on her part . . . What?"

"That's *no* information, Griff. I told *you* about her adventure. You thought it sounded suspicious and now you are telling me you were wrong?" I shook my head in frustration. "I don't care about Annie Trenchard's stupid landing in a German airfield. I only have one question. Do you think I am right about"—I mouthed the word—"Vera?"

His nod was emphatic, his eyes wide with sincerity.

You're caving! Ilona pointed out.

"Now all I have to do is find out where she got datura from."

I heard a long sigh of relief. "We *are* running two investigations, but they coincide," he said. "Do *you* know where she got it from? You do, don't you? Come on, you have to tell—we are sharing!"

I laughed and flapped my arms at my sides in mock exasperation.

And then I caved. "There is only one person here who could possibly have known about a drug like datura, but I am not sure about her motive."

"Who? Come on, give me names." He was laughing now.

"Someone so heartbroken by her husband's infidelity with a woman she admired and trusted that all she wanted to do was wipe her off the face of the world."

"Zofia?"

When he said her name, I wondered briefly if I was wrong. If when she had gone over to ask Edwina for a cup of coffee Zofia had slipped something into the thermos. I hadn't been close enough to see. I shook my head. "I'm not sure . . . yet. But I am so close I can feel it."

"Okay, let's think about Letty's death for a moment. Did Zofia murder her because she saw something? Did she drug her breakfast and push it toward Letty?"

I closed my eyes to concentrate. "Come with me. I want you to read these anonymous letters that were sent to Edwina over the past weeks. Maybe they will help to convince us that Edwina and Letty's murderer had completely lost all sense of reason. Maybe there is some sort of indication of motive."

"Have you got them with you?"

"Yes, I do." I patted my coat pocket. "There aren't that many of them, five, maybe, at the most. But we can't read them here."

"Have you read them?"

I shook my head as we set out up the drive to the Alvis. "No, I couldn't quite bring myself to. They were given to me by the Franklins, to give to Zofia. They thought they were love letters from Edwina's boyfriend, but they are far from that."

By the time we reached the car, I was shivering with cold.

"Come on, hop in." Griff opened the door for me, and I scrambled in. He switched on the engine and the heater. "This should warm us up," he said, revving the engine. He took off the brake and put his foot on the clutch. "Come on, let's drive out from under these trees and find an open space so I can read these things. Why didn't you tell me you had these letters before?"

I shrugged in despair over my proper upbringing. No one reads someone else's letters—it just wasn't done. But if that was the case, why had I accepted them from Mrs. Franklin?

We drove down the lane and out into the field where Edwina's Spitfire lay stranded, waiting to be towed away.

"Perfect spot for reading poison-pen letters," said Griff as he put on the brake. "Warmer now?" I nodded. "Good, then hand them over. I'll read them first and then I'll pass them over to you. Okay?"

I handed over the packet and he slid a sheet of paper out of the first envelope.

"Usual sort of thing," he said, and I wondered how he knew what was usual about anonymous letters. "Made up of letters and words cut from newspaper headlines and pasted on cheap paper from Woolworths. See this one, and this?" He pointed to different letters. "This looks a bit like the *Daily Telegraph* newsprint, whereas the others are of lesser quality: thinner paper and a bit smudgy, probably the local *Didcote Herald*." He read the first one. "Nasty stuff, but nothing you can't handle." He handed it over.

**HOW DOES IT FEEL TO BE HATED BECAUSE
YOU ARE A WHORE A LIAR & A CHEAT?**

Griff read on, sliding pages out of envelopes, reading them in silence, and then handing them over to me.

They were all pretty much the same.

**DO YOUR FRIENDS KNOW WHAT A FILTHY
SLAG YOU ARE?**

I thought that one was the most unpleasant until I read the last one.

**EVERYONE KNOWS YOU MADE UP A STORY
ABOUT YOUR LUFTWAFFE ATTACK TO COVER
YOUR WHORING. ARE YOU READY TO DIE?**

My skin crawled as I read it. Small wonder, I thought, that Edwina was on edge.

Griff slid the letters back in their envelopes. "The last one was sent two weeks before she crashed," was all he said as he shuffled the envelopes into postal date order and tied the packet up with its string. "The intention of the last is clear. It was a death threat." I swallowed and reached out to turn off the car's heater. Through the condensation streaming down the windows I looked out at the lopsided Spitfire.

"Whoever made these was insane. It must have taken hours to cut out letters and words and carefully paste them on a piece of paper with the sole purpose of threatening someone anonymously," I said, with enough disgust to cover my fear of what could happen next.

He nodded and cracked the window. "Yes, that's what cowards do. They make their ugly opinions public without owning them."

I thought of Pamela Brabazon's eyes gleaming with the pleasure she had gained from passing on gossip. "Edwina's reputation was ruined by gossip."

He tapped the edge of the stack of envelopes against his thumb as he thought. "Gossip feeds on itself and grows. Innocent people can be destroyed by malicious gossip. But if any of it is true, then it implicates two women at Didcote with a motive for murder."

"What if June was married? Is that reason enough for her to kill Edwina? Annie Trenchard is married, and she has never once talked about her husband. She talks about her mother, and she talks about her girls—we don't even know her husband's name, what he does, and if he is living or dead."

He smiled. "So not Zofia, then?"

"No, because Zofia's husband flew out of Biggin Hill and was killed during the Battle of Britain long before she met Edwina. And the husband that Edwina stole flew out of Christchurch."

He nodded. "Maybe Zofia came to Didcote because she was connected to Edwina through her husband?"

I shook my head as I remembered Zofia's story. No, no, no.

"Not Trenchard," he said with finality. "Her husband is alive and well . . . I know all about him. So, June's married name is Evesham, or something else? As soon as we have the name of her husband—if she was married—we can contact Christchurch Airfield and find out if a pilot of that name was killed in the raid. But that is only motive for murder, Poppy, not proof."

I sighed and wiped away the condensation on the window with my glove. We watched in silence as the fog outside started to thin and then lift up through the trees, leaving traces of itself among the bare branches.

"How could Edwina have had an affair with someone's husband?" I asked the world outside the car.

"Sexual attraction is a funny thing, and war makes men and

women do strange things. Maybe all Edwina, or the men she slept with, wanted was a release from tension and fear. Maybe he was only interested in the physical side of what happened between them. Maybe Edwina had no idea he was married.

"So, Vera is off the hook, then. How does datura fit in with June?" he asked, and I told him.

He watched me closely as I laid out my reasons, and then he said, "Okay, but does that incriminate her?" He shrugged his shoulders. "You are an intuitive woman and you have a robust imagination, so let's make a plan."

TWENTY-SIX

"ARE YOUR PEOPLE READY?" VERA ABERCROMBIE WALKED across to Huntley. "Because . . ." She focused her attention on the plane that had just landed. "What on earth is that?" she asked the young woman pilot who proffered her chit. "I sent you to get a Spitfire and you bring me this thing? It has two cockpits."

The pilot was one of the ordinary everyday Attagirls. She didn't get anonymous letters posted through her letter box, and she was rarely, if ever, asked out to the pictures by a glamorous flyboy from RAF Biggin Hill. She took off her helmet and ran her hand through springy fair hair, her expression sympathetic. "It's brand-new," she explained. "Supermarine are making two-seaters for training schools. Anyway, there must be a flap on somewhere, because this is the only Spitfire they have available. If we want a single-seater, we'll just have to wait until next Thursday. At least that's what I was told."

Vera, busy with the paperwork on her clipboard, merely sighed in exasperation. "Want to stay and watch them film?" she asked.

"No, thank you. I want some breakfast and then a nice hot bath. How long do I have?"

"Couple of hours, that should do it. How did she fly?"

"As if she were a single-seater, but the cockpits are tiny; can't imagine how they would fit a great big lug of a bloke in either of them." And she strolled off to the mess.

"Right then, everyone, whenever you are ready. Ah yes, here's Zofia." She waved her hand as Zofia came out of the mess, stopped to have a few words with the pilot who had brought in the Spitfire, and then continued on toward us.

After my planning session with Griff, I was too nervous to catch Zofia's eye, but I caught Griff's and he reached out his hand and gave my shoulder a pat. "Keep alert and don't look surprised; we have to look like simple bystanders."

As Zofia came striding toward us I thought how different she looked. Her shining black hair was plaited in two braids and wound around her head. Her large dark eyes were clear and snapping with purpose, and her mouth was crimson with perfectly applied lipstick.

"She's wearing the Polish flag as a scarf," Griff said under his breath. "See?"

Tied around Zofia's neck was a silk scarf with two horizontal stripes of equal width, the upper one white and the lower one red. The tail of one half fluttered in the wind. There was something celebratory, or even triumphant, about the dashing figure she made.

She said something to Vera, continued on toward us, and came to a halt in front of Huntley.

"Good morning," she said. "I am Zofia Lukasiewicz, the Spitfire pilot for your film." She extended her hand as if she had never seen either of them before. Huntley shook it, and I saw him gulp.

"Good morning, Countess," he said.

"Zofia."

"Zofia." She nodded as if they had set something straight between them. "And what would you like me to do?" It was the politest question, but I felt myself tense.

Griff felt my tension and whispered, "Don't worry about Zofia flying under the influence, Poppy. I have a feeling she is a very smart woman, and no one's fool. She looks fully in control."

Until she turns her plane upside down and falls to earth, I thought.

As Huntley, Keith, and Zofia got into a huddle of instructions, the mess door banged closed, and across the grass, bundled up in mufti, came June Evesham. She waved good morning to us but joined Vera, and the pair of them fell into a discussion about the two-seater Spitfire as they walked toward the plane and climbed up on the wing.

"All right, then." Huntley broke up his conference with Zofia and Keith. "Are you ready, Poppy?" He turned and looked at me. "Zofia's going to do it the way . . ." He hesitated. ". . . it was done before."

Zofia bent down and lifted a small thermos from the grass. "Do you mind, June, or is it yours, Vera?" she called out, waving the flask. Before either of them could answer her, she poured a little coffee into the lid cup, raised it in salute, and tossed it back. I felt Griff stir next to me as I caught my breath. And then we both watched in complete silence as Zofia walked toward the Spitfire and the two ground crewmen who were waiting for her. She got up into the cockpit and started putting on her leather helmet. One of the crewmen climbed up and closed the Perspex canopy. I was so tense I could hardly breathe.

"Chin up," Griff said, but out of the tail of my eye I saw him lick his lips.

The ground crew removed the chocks from under the plane's

wheels as the propeller started to rotate. I glanced at Huntley; he was holding a stopwatch. Keith was already bent over his camera. Vera and June had stopped talking and were shading their eyes with their hands. And just as I wondered about Sir Basil Stowe and where he was on this fine morning, his car drew up beside the Alvis and out he got.

He was almost with us when Zofia's plane started to roll toward the airstrip. She increased power and the plane raced along the turf to the marker for takeoff.

"And she's up," said Huntley to Keith as he clicked his watch and turned to me with a thumbs-up. Good nature restored, Huntley was getting the film he needed to finish our project.

Up and up the plane climbed, and then, just as Edwina had done before her, Zofia zoomed back over us nice and low and waggled her wings.

"Yes, perfect," shouted Huntley, as if Zofia could hear him. "Can't even tell it's a two-seater."

A vertical climb and Zofia brought the plane around to circle the airfield, banking right to climb into our midview; then up she climbed. We watched a series of victory rolls. I looked at Griff. He had his hands on his hips as he watched with a smile on his face. For the next ten minutes Zofia performed with style, showing us what grace and speed the plane had in the air. Would she do the Immelmann turn? I asked, and felt my stomach clench as she climbed to gain height. I think I closed my eyes because I heard a round of applause.

"Well done," said Griff. "Well done."

I opened my eyes. The plane was coming round in a great circle to land on the airfield. Down she came and with perfect precision bumped down onto the grass.

As Zofia walked toward us taking off her helmet, the red and white of her scarf flew straight out behind her. Sir Basil stepped forward. "Nicely done, Zofia," he said. She nodded and continued on toward June, and the two women hugged. June slapped Zofia on the back.

"She's down safe," I said and realized that I had held my breath until she had jumped out of the cockpit.

"And not the next victim after all." Griff smiled.

"It's a wrap!" cried Huntley.

"Congratulations," said Sir Basil.

"Oh my God." Keith smacked the palm of his right hand to his forehead. "I forgot to put film in the camera."

"You did bloody what?" Huntley turned on him like a viper, and Vera was already halfway across to him with her clipboard to the fore.

"Just kidding." Keith ducked. "Blimey, can't you take a bleedin' joke?" he yelled at Huntley. "Have you completely lost your sense of humor, mate?"

"Does this call for a drink?" Sir Basil was laughing.

I turned to Griff.

"What happens now?" I asked him.

"I'll keep them all talking while you check out their library for one of June's books, and if you find what you think you'll find, then duck out the back and I'll meet you by the dustbins, okay?"

"Yes, but we have to be quick. I don't want Huntley and Keith to leave while we are out there."

"Just stick to the plan," Griff said. "I won't let Huntley and Keith leave."

We were the last up the steps to the mess, where we found Sir Basil, looking frightfully pleased with himself, holding a bottle of chilled vintage champagne and glasses. "Come on, gather round. Now, in a couple of weeks' time, we'll all go down to the Gaumont in Southampton and watch our film together." He looked around. "Hold on a minute, where's Vera?"

"Phone call," Vera's voice came from her office. "With you in a sec."

"And be quick about it, please—we're thirsty!" He grinned around at all of us.

"Beautiful bit of flying," said Griff to Zofia. She lowered her eyes and tilted her head on one side. "Who taught you to fly?"

Her large dark eyes gave him an appraising stare. "My husband," she said simply. "He flew against the Germans in Romania, then France and here in England."

"Ah," said Griff, nodding, his face serious. "Battle of Britain?"

"Yes, he died in that fight."

"I'm sorry to hear that," said Griff, but Zofia didn't acknowledge his condolences. Vera's office door slammed closed as she came back into the mess, her brown eyes crinkled at the corners as if she were squinting into the sun. "That was White Waltham Accident Committee's Captain Amherst." She turned to Sir Basil, her eyes concerned. "They have completed their findings on both accidents; the report is finally formal, so I can share it with you. Edwina . . ." She paused, bit her lip, and looked down. I held my breath. "They could find no fault with the plane at all, and they have reached the conclusion that Edwina's accident was caused by pilot error." There was a sigh. But I had been watching the expressions on Zofia's face, and on June's too. Zofia didn't bat an eyelash. She looked straight at Vera and said, "Did you tell them about her nerves?"

Vera nodded; then she looked up at June.

"And Letty?" June asked her. Griff's shoulder nudged gently

into mine. "Go on," he breathed, and I edged away from the group and walked back toward the dartboard and the bar. If anyone saw me walk away they would assume I was going to the loo.

"There was nothing wrong with the Walrus. But there was with Letty," I heard Vera say as I reached the tall wooden bookshelves at the room's far wall. I could hear them quite well, but they couldn't see me.

"Since there was no evidence that Letty had been killed in the crash itself, they did an autopsy. She died, probably in flight, from a brain aneurism." I froze as I heard gasps and exclamations from the front of the mess, but loudest of all from June.

For God's sake, concentrate—you don't have long, Ilona instructed.

I reached up and ran my finger along a line of book spines and the last names of their authors. "*C, D, E.*" I caught my breath. There was no Evesham. I searched the *D*s and the *G*s just in case someone had misplaced the books when they returned them.

"What's an aneurism?" asked Keith.

"Shush," I heard Huntley reply.

Think girl, think! I told myself in a panic. What was June supposed to have written about, anyway?

Stop panicking, you ninny. She was a travel writer, Ilona instructed. *Look for books about travel.*

I obediently skimmed on, running my finger along countless titles, and then there they were, three of them: *Travels in Tunisia and Morocco*; *River Travels: The Amazon*; and *River Travels: The Nile*. I glanced at the author's name J. S. Holmes.

I heard Sir Basil say, presumably to Vera, as I opened *Travels in Tunisia and Morocco* to search for information on the author, "Poor little Letty. Who would have thought she was ill? It has been such a strain on you, Vera, I know. But it's all over now."

"What is a brain aneurism?" Keith was not going to be ignored this time. There was moment of a silence, and then Vera's voice, still husky with emotion, said, "I believe it is caused by a rupture of a vessel that bleeds into the brain. Which is why the man who saw the crash described the Walrus as flying erratically. They believe Letty died just before the plane crashed."

I was just about to turn to the back of the book, but Vera's last words froze me on the spot. That wasn't right! That wasn't what Mr. Mackenzie had said at all! He had said that he thought Letty was "trying to do something" when he had driven alongside her plane when it crashed. And when he had gone into the Walrus's cockpit he had said that it looked as if she had been trying to put on her parachute, when she should have been trying to pull up the plane's nose. I could remember the despair in his voice. "Why wasn't she trying to get the damn thing's nose up?"

I stood there with my mouth open at Vera's evident lie. And then to my horror Huntley must have said something about saying good-bye, because I heard Keith say, "Where's Poppy?"

I looked down at the book I was holding and saw a black-and-white photograph of a younger version of June. "Born in the out-back of Australia, June Holmes was an engineer and pilot before she turned to . . ." Got you! I almost said out loud.

Then I heard June's voice. "But would Letty have known?" she asked. "Would she have been in pain?"

"No, June," Vera's voice answered. "She was not in pain. Her end would have been instant: one moment she would have been flying; the next she would have gone."

The room was silent, and then I heard June say, "That's such a relief," but Griff was talking over her to Huntley: "—hang on for a second or two. I think Poppy was planning on driving back with me. But we should ask—"

There was no time at all to ask myself why Vera was sharing this new information about Letty's death with June. I had to be quick. I looked down at the book in my lap. I skipped through a brief foreword written by June about her love of the people of North Africa, acknowledging the diversity of the food region by region and the different local cultures. The table of contents listed chapters by the different regions. I flipped to the back of the book and the index, aware only of a babble of shocked discussion about brain aneurisms and train timetables from my friends gathered at the other end of the room.

I lifted my head briefly, at the sound of Griff's voice, as I ran my finger down the index to *D*. Nothing for datura. I turned to *M*. Medicines? Nothing at all. What else could it be listed under? What had Cadogan's friend said datura was classified as? A plant? A herb? Herbal cures. I fanned the pages back to *H*. "Herbal remedies: datura, uses of . . . p. 59."

There was a confusion of voices as Vera and Sir Basil called out good-bye and presumably left the mess.

"It's always been something I've wanted to do," I heard Griff say as I frantically thumbed through pages. "I think all American fighter pilots have a secret hankering to fly a Spitfire."

I turned to page 59. There was a short paragraph that dealt with the various herbal medicines used by nomadic desert people for eye infections and lung problems. Datura was mentioned several times—it was called Alghita by the Moroccan people. And then right at the beginning of the next page, it said, "Unlike the indigenous people of South America, the desert tribes do not use the seeds of the Alghita plant as an aid in spiritual ritual, as Islam forbids the use of alcohol or hallucinogenic drugs." I caught my breath. June Evesham née Holmes was quite clear in her travelogue about datura seeds and what they should or should not be used for. I dog-eared the precious pages 59 and 60. And closed the book.

I hadn't a moment to think, as I heard Zofia say, "We don't have much time. The Spit has to go back to Supermarine—" I tucked the book under my arm and dodged behind the bar. I could still hear Griff and Huntley arguing about departure times as I opened the bar door into the kitchen, ran across its greasy floor, wrenched open the back door, and found myself in the smelly outside world of dustbins.

TWENTY-SEVEN

S TRUTH, WHAT A PONG." KEITH, HUNTLEY, AND GRIFF CAME
through the wooden gate to join me in the walled-in area behind the mess kitchen. "Blimey, don't they empty these things?"

"I really hope they haven't, at least not since last week," I said.

I felt a hand slide the book out from underneath my arm and a
voice say, close to my ear, "This it?" I nodded.

"What exactly are we here for, Poppy?" Huntley sounded irritated again.

"The piece of film that was taken from the back of your van," I
said. I took the lid off the first bin, and Huntley stepped back and
put his hand over his nose.

"We don't need it this badly."

"But we do," I said. "Because it contains something so useful
that it could mean the difference between Edwina being written off
as a drunk and an incompetent pilot and her being . . . murdered."

Huntley took the lid from me and put it back on the bin. "Are
you crackers? We all saw her plane—" He stopped himself and
said, "Was she drunk when she flew that Spitfire? Well, that explains
everything!" He turned away in disgust. "Come on, everyone.

Let's go back to the inn for a pint and some of Mrs. Evans's terrible food."

"Wait a minute." Keith put out his hand. "I didn't lose that bit of film, Hunt, it was nicked. Pure and simple." He turned to me. "What do you think was on it, anyway?" He held his hand up to Huntley. "No, mate, listen to her. Come on, Poppy, come clean and tell us what's been going on in this hellhole."

I looked at Griff and he nodded his agreement.

"We think that Edwina was given a drug. Something that she ate or drank before she flew had been doctored with a hallucinogenic." I heard myself and stopped. It sounded like the worst sort of thriller. "We suspect we know who, but if we find that piece of film it might be useful evidence as to their identity."

Keith lifted the dustbin lid. "It was in a can, a film can. But if someone nicked it they might have thrown them away separately." He lifted out a parcel of oily newspapers. "Crikey, this is full of fish bones and heads."

"What a waste," Griff fumed. "They could have been used to make a very tasty fish stock. Too late now."

Huntley lifted another lid. "This one's full of wood ash. Give me that broom handle." He stirred. "No, ash all the way down."

My dustbin yielded nothing but potato peelings, cabbage stalks, and at the bottom a mess of fried flour that had once been part of an attempt to make batter. There were two more bins left. One was full of torn-up documents. Old buff envelopes used so often that the sides had split. Shorthand notebooks covered in the lines and dots used by Pitman shorthand writers. Carbon paper worn transparent with use and two empty ink bottles. Gaily decorating this mess were pencil shavings by the bucketload. I turned to a smaller bin and lifted the lid.

The combined smell of fish scraps, rotting bones, and a tub that obviously contained stale lard used for deep-frying was so over-powering that we all fell back.

"Aw, come on, you lot," Keith said as he stripped off his jacket and rolled up his sleeves. "In for a penny, in for a quid." And he carefully lifted the foul-smelling articles one by one and put them carefully on the ground. Underneath were more oily newspaper parcels. We lifted out each one and spread its layers open. At the bottom of the last one, nestled among the grease, was an envelope.

"Bloody bingo!" said Huntley as Keith lifted it out. "Look." He opened the envelope, peeked inside, and, laughing, tipped its contents out onto Keith's jacket. A slither of shiny brown thirty-five-millimeter film showered down onto its inner lining.

"Damn it all to hell," said Griff in disgust as we looked at a pile of film neatly cut into six-inch lengths. "It's been exposed."

"Nah, mate." It was almost a sigh of pleasure as Keith reverently gathered up two strips and held them up to the daylight. "We develop all our film after shooting so we can check it. That's why we call them dailies."

"But it's all cut up!" I said, devastated with disappointment.

"An hour in the editing room will have this little lot sorted in no time. Look." He lifted his arm and we all peered upward at what appeared to be a group of people.

"That's it, all right enough: the ruddy missing film. Not only nicked, but someone tried to ruin it," said Keith. "So, Captain, wotcher going to do now, ay?"

"I'm going to fly a Spitfire!" Griff said. His voice almost squeaked with pleasure. "The countess is going to take me up for a joyride in that beautiful plane."

"No, Griff." I was so horrified I picked up a bundle of fish-oily newspapers without even noticing the thick grease on my hands.

"Oh yes, Griff," he said with his eyes shining, "Yes, yes, and yes."

———

"THIS WASN'T IN the plan," I said as we walked back to the Alvis to store the book and the envelope of film.

"I know, I know, but it is a perfect way to flush out our murderer. And you agreed to keep a cool head and go along with whatever happened, didn't you?"

Had I used those words when Griff and I had planned to search for one of June's books and the missing film before the dustmen arrived to empty the mess kitchen and office bins? I turned to Keith and Huntley, who had decided that the last thing they would do was leave Didcote now that something worthwhile was finally on offer.

They were standing by the main door to the mess, smoking cigarettes, when Zofia swept by them. Her head was held high and her eyes were glittering with excitement.

"Ah, Captain. I see you are waiting to fly the Spitfire. I have cleared everything with Commander Abercrombie." She gestured up the drive. "As you can see, everyone is turning out to watch an American Mustang pilot take up Britain's most revered fighter plane." Grable and Annie were walking up the drive, looking like two schoolgirls let out of math class early for a spree.

I wasn't too sure that I liked Zofia's tone and the challenging look in her eye. There was a slight wildness to the countess's personality this morning, as if unpredictability simmered beneath the surface of her outward composure, and at any moment she would act on an inner whim that could be anyone's downfall.

I gazed down at my feet and held my breath as I heard Griff say, "Well, I would love to, er . . . Countess. How very kind of you! Are you quite sure that Commander Abercrombie has given us the all clear?"

"You can ask her yourself." Zofia jutted her chin in the direction of Vera's house on the other side of the mess. Coming toward us were Vera and Sir Basil, and in an informal mood too: Vera was without her clipboard, and Sir Basil had loosened his tie.

"I'll go and check with the Met Office, just to make sure this beautiful weather will continue for us." Zofia swaggered into the mess, the tails of her Polish flag dancing behind her in the breeze.

Griff ran his hand through his hair.

"Of course I didn't really expect that Vera would give us permission . . ." he said ruefully. "But I am sorely tempted."

I bet you are, I said to myself. We drew together so no one could hear us. "How easy is it for a Mustang pilot to fly a Spitfire first time around?" I asked.

The face that turned to me was surprised by my question. "Easy, really easy," he said. I held my breath while he rattled off some pilot jargon about throttles, maximum boost, and I don't know what else.

"What are you going to do up there, exactly? You have the controls, right? Is that how it works with trainer planes? You have the controls, but if something unfortunate happens the other pilot can take over?"

"No, not always; depends on the plane. Depends how far Supermarine have gone with their prototype."

"Well, you will be at the controls, though, won't you? I mean, that is the point of this joyride?"

"Yes."

"And if Zofia goes bonkers, you will still have full control of the plane, right?"

"I should damn well hope so."

I nodded. I didn't like this one little bit. Supposing I had it all wrong? Another moment of agony.

"All right, I'll go along with it. What do I do?"

"Poppy." He put his hand on my arm, and I felt my knees weaken. "This is your show; tell me what you want me to do."

I had to clear my throat, but when I spoke my voice was firm with the decision I had made. "When you are comfortable up there at the controls, can you do what they all seem to do, fly overhead and waggle your wings?"

He drew closer and took my hand. "Do you remember that movie we saw together, *Mrs. Miniver*?" I would never forget it.

"Do you remember what Vin did?" I nodded, too stricken to speak. "When he returned from aerial combat he would fly over his parents' house and 'blip' his engine briefly, to signal that he was safe?"

My eyes filled with tears and I blinked them away, embarrassed at my show of weakness. It was Griff's life that might be in danger, not mine.

"Do you remember?"

"Yes."

"Good, then that will be my signal that all is well. Don't muff it, okay?"

TWENTY-EIGHT

W ELL, CAPTAIN, SO YOU FINALLY GET TO FLY ONE OF BRITain's greatest achievements in aviation!" Sir Basil came toward us like a sleek ocean liner breasting through the water, with its attendant tugboat nosing at his heels. He inclined his immaculate silver head toward Vera. "The commander has given her permission, haven't you, Vera?"

Vera smiled as she nodded her acquiescence. "Whyever not? Today is a holiday before the real work begins again tomorrow!"

Sir Basil was already striding out toward the Spitfire. "I'll be your groundman," he called over his shoulder to Zofia. "Miss Redfern, put your dog on a lead, please."

"I have control, then?" Griff asked Zofia, and she smiled her most dazzling smile.

"Yes, of course. You will be flying solo. I will just be there because the ATA is responsible for this plane. She's all yours, Captain!"

Griff bent his head and grazed my ear with his lips. "When I blip the engine, that's your cue! Okay?"

Vera beamed at Zofia; she looked ten years younger. The ATA Accident Committee had found in Didcote's favor: death by pilot error for Edwina and death due to illness for Letty. I watched her glance at June and smile, and the Australian travel writer beamed back. Harmony, or something like it, had been restored to the team.

June came over to me. "The only thing he is going to find really different is how fast she is. Mustangs are fast, but in comparison the Spitfire is like lightning and probably far more responsive. She's dead easy to fly, though. And it will only take him a minute to adjust. Then he's going to love every moment." We watched wind ruffle Sir Basil's silver hair. "Chocks away!" she said merrily as Sir Basil started to run back toward us.

"Giving her a bit of a warm-up," she explained as the Spitfire's props spun into a blur.

The Spitfire started to move forward toward the head of the airstrip.

"Have you ever seen him fly before?" Grable asked as she and Annie arrived to join us.

"No, I haven't." I dug my hands deep into my pockets so no one would see them shaking.

"Perfect afternoon for Griff's first flight in a *real* fighter," said Annie, and gently pinched my arm, her stern expression gone in the delight of an afternoon free from duty.

I couldn't take my eyes off the plane, but it was astonishing how quickly everything happened: one moment they were on the ground and the next they were circling above the airfield. "Nice smooth takeoff!" said Huntley as Keith took off his cap and waved it in the air.

"Huntley has become an expert." Annie smiled at him, all criticism of disrespect toward women pilots forgiven.

"No, I'm the bloomin' expert," Keith said, looking at me to see if he could work out what Griff and I were up to. "I've looked down my lens at more planes than I can count in the last few days."

I wanted to tell them all to shut up. Until I got the okay from Griff, I was a bundle of nerves. But despite my fear that something terrible would go wrong, I felt a silly thrill of pride as I watched the Spitfire circle the airfield and bank elegantly to the right to stay within our sight. Griff climbed, leveled off, banked left, and climbed again. And then down he flew toward us, as Edwina had done just days before, and Zofia this morning. As he flew over us he gave two short blips of his engine.

Grable cheered and waved both her hands above her head. And Annie turned to me with a kind smile and said, "We open and close the throttle to make that signal," as if I were one of her little girls on visiting day.

I cleared my throat and lifted my voice—it was time. "Anybody know anything about datura?" I asked loudly as the Spitfire disappeared in a wider circuit.

"Sorry, what did you say?" Vera asked me.

"What sort of plane is that?" Huntley asked, and was shushed by Keith, who had been watching me closely ever since Griff and Zofia took off.

"Datura," I repeated. "I think it's a sort of plant: a herbal cure, apparently."

"Dat . . . what?" Grable's aristocratic voice was loud in the silence now that Griff's plane was a speck in the sky.

I felt June stiffen next to me; her hand was shading her eyes. "I hope he doesn't go too far . . . there's a limit how far out to sea we may go. I'm sorry, what did you say?"

Keep calm, don't scare them. I took a breath.

"Griff was given some sort of herbal remedy the other evening by a pilot from South Africa. He said it was good for coughs and asthma."

"Surely he doesn't have asthma?" Vera asked. "He looks so fit!"

"No, but in this damp weather he coughs at lot, especially at night. He's not used to our seasonal mists and fog." I glanced at June and Grable; their faces were set. Grable stared fixedly at the sky.

"It's just that Griff tends to overdo things—you know, if one is good, two is better, and I thought I heard this pilot say that if you took too much of the stuff it made you see things!" I laughed. It was a terribly forced laugh. Annie looked at me as if I were potty.

"What are you talking about?" June asked, and Annie's head whipped round at her tone.

The Spitfire hove into view and did several victory rolls.

"Showing off already!" Grable said. "Men!"

"Excuse me, American men," replied Annie and then shot a glance at me. "Are you sure he should be flying?"

I shrugged. It was meant to be a careless shrug, but my shoulders were rigid with tension. Sir Basil had his hands on his hips and shook his head. "Zofia will tell him to rein it in, in a minute," he said as Griff showed off some more.

I glanced at Vera. She still had her hand shading her eyes.

I felt a strong, hard hand on my shoulder. And a voice close in my ear. "I asked you what you were talking about!" Fingers like iron dug into my shoulder. I turned to face June. We were so close I could feel her breath in my face. I raised my voice, half turning my head. "I am talking about datura. If it is taken in excess, it causes strong hallucinations, doesn't it?" I asked her. Her hand dropped from my shoulder. I stepped back and turned to look June in the face. Her jaw was clenched, and there was a little muscle jumping in her cheek.

"Hallucinations," cried out Vera, as Griff threw the Spitfire across the sky and then went into a dive. "He's flying a plane that costs thousands of pounds-—and Zofia is on board!"

"Christ." Sir Basil was staring at the Spitfire. "Has he been drinking?"

"No," I said as their horrified faces watched the Spitfire plummet. "He was given a hallucinatory drug. You know all about datura, don't you, June? You know, from your travels in North Africa. Of course, there it's used for—"

I got no further; June stepped forward, brought back her right hand, and hit me squarely on the jaw. She didn't knock me off my feet, but I staggered backward. I completely understand what people mean when they say they saw stars. My little dog, dozing in a patch of sunlight a second or two before, was on her feet, her teeth bared.

"June, what on earth are you doing?" Vera threw herself between us, her face horrified, as Grable scrabbled for Bess's leash and pulled her away from June. I am glad to say Bess got in one good nip before some sort of order was restored.

"That bloody dog bit me!"

I felt Annie's arm around my waist. Her face was white. "Stop that at once, June," she shouted. "Have you gone completely mad?" But this was no nursery tiff.

"What the merry hell is going on?" Sir Basil, oblivious to the violence on the ground, pointed up at the sky.

I heard Annie cry out, "Pull up, for God's sake, pull up," as Griff put the Spitfire into a steep nosedive.

"Jesus Christ." Sir Basil's complexion was dark with his rising blood pressure. He gazed around at us all, his eyes bulging, as the Spitfire screamed toward us. "I think the bugger's going to crash!"

"What are you talking about, Poppy?" It was Grable, the only one of my witnesses who had kept her head. "What is happening here? What did you say someone gave him . . . some sort of drug?" I could have kissed her for having the presence of mind to keep the conversation fixed where it needed to be. If you could call what we were having a conversation. Grable put a deeply ruffled and still growling Bess into my arms and I felt her warm tongue curl around my swelling jaw.

Vera was hanging on to June's arm, sobbing. "You didn't, June? Please say you didn't?"

Sir Basil, still unsure where his attention should be directed, demanded to know what the hell was going on, his face was almost purple. The shriek of the Spitfire's Merlin engine was deafening now.

With a supreme effort I lifted my voice. "Yes, she did, Vera—now, how will you explain the death of two more pilots to White Waltham?" I could barely get the words out: my lower lip was beginning to swell, and the sound of the Spitfire's shrieking engine set off a thrum of pain in my jaw.

"June!" Vera cried.

June stopped staring at the Spitfire and turned on her. "Shut up, Vera. Don't say a thing. You'll wreck everything."

Sir Basil's fury was exceeded only by his confusion. "Wreck what, for God's sake? Vera, what the hell is going on?" The Spitfire banked and roared up into the sky.

I took in a breath, taking care to stand well out of June's range. "June put a hallucinogenic drug in Edwina's thermos of coffee before she flew on the day she crashed the Spitfire, didn't she, Vera?" The commanding officer of Didcote ATA started to shake her head. "And you knew about it. You saw Zofia ask Edwina for some of her coffee. You stopped her from drinking it because you knew what was in it." I drew in a deep breath through my nose and swallowed down the pain. It didn't hurt too much if I spoke without moving my lips. I glanced up at the sky. The Spitfire was doing a lazy circuit above us. "You don't have to say anything, either of you. Keith has it all on film, don't you, Keith?"

"Gordon Bennett," said Keith.

"Yes, he does." Huntley was smiling. "God I wish we had *this* on film," he said to Keith. "We'd make a bloody fortune."

"It's a trap. Vera, don't say anything." June took Vera by the arm and shook her, hard.

"We don't you know what you mean." Vera gasped, righting herself with difficulty and reaching for June's arm to steady herself.

"You both worked together to get rid of Edwina," I said.

"No, no . . ." Vera whispered, clinging like a child to June's arm. "No, we did nothing."

June growled something unprintable and Bess started to struggle in my arms, her lips drawn back in a snarl.

Grable, God bless her, stepped forward. "So that was it," she said. "That was what happened. You"—she stared at June—"you gave Edwina some sort of poison, and she crashed her plane, just because she stole your stupid husband? Just because of *that*?"

June shook off Vera. "Edwina knew what she was doing—she did it to hurt . . . like everything else she did."

"The letters, the anonymous letters," said Annie, her eyes beseeching us for the truth. "June, did you write those terrible things?"

I heard the Spitfire give two blips as it flew overhead. I thought my knees were going to give out, I was so relieved. "June wrote them. She did it to unnerve Edwina," I said. "That's why Edwina was drinking so heavily, and when she crashed her plane everyone was convinced that . . . she was probably drunk, or that her nerve had gone," I said to Grable, who was staring at me.

"How do you know all of this?" she asked me.

"I probably wouldn't if Griff hadn't been so surprised by the way Edwina flew that plane before she crashed. And then when Letty died the next day when she was flying the Walrus . . . I decided to look into things." I put my hand up to my face. After the first shock, the pain was beginning to ease. I opened and closed my mouth gently.

"Look into things?" Vera looked as if she was going to be sick. Her voice took on a begging note. "But we didn't, we didn't." She turned her head. "You don't believe her . . . June?"

Sir Basil had finally managed to bite back the only thing he had uttered in the last five minutes. "Vera." He put his hands on his hips and glared at the woman he sometimes slept with when he was at Didcote. "You said Letty died of a brain seizure!"

"She did, she did." All Vera's self-possession had gone. "At least that's what the ATA Accident Committee reported. Brain aneurisms run in Letty's—"

She got no further. "You gave her datura," shrieked June. "You crazy bitch. You told me you'd changed your mind, that Zofia had no idea about Edwina's coffee. That you had taken the film."

"Actually," I said rather recklessly, "Vera put ground datura in Zofia's breakfast because she couldn't be sure whether she had guessed about Edwina's coffee or not. And then Letty ate it. I was there; I saw it happen."

"You see, June, Letty's death was a mistake!" Vera was so distraught she put her hands over her eyes.

"And what about Edwina? What in God's name did you both do to Edwina?" Sir Basil's blood pressure was rising again as he tried to keep abreast of events.

"Please try and concentrate, Sir Basil," I said as I watched the Spitfire bump gently along the airstrip toward us. "June and Vera doctored Edwina's coffee before she flew the Spitfire. It caused her to hallucinate so strongly that she lost control of the Spitfire."

Sir Basil's head weaved back and forth between June and Vera, his mouth open.

"You killed her?" he asked, as if he could hardly believe what he was saying. "You killed Edwina. But I told you there was nothing between us . . . nothing at all. Have you all gone mad?" He blazed at us. "This will mean the end of everything, Vera. Everything you have worked for! I have worked for!"

Vera had stopped crying. She tried to lick her dry lips. "But I did it for you, Basil," she whispered. "I did it for you . . ." The tears started again. "I did it to stop her—"

"Blackmailing you." Griff came up behind us. His face was glowing with health and the sheer joy of flight.

"Blackmail?" June finally understood. I stepped back behind Griff with my growling dog. "Vera, you told me you wanted Edwina out of the way because he was sleeping with her." Her voice, hoarse from shouting, had been reduced to a croak. "Edwina was out of control. If she saw a man, she couldn't get him into bed fast enough. She was a wrecker!"

"Blackmail?" Sir Basil finally found his voice. "Blackmailing me?"

A discreet cough from my American friend. "Yes, sir, blackmail. Edwina had found out about the thousands of gallons of gasoline, I mean petrol, siphoned off from not only this airfield but the others in the area: Middle Wallop, Nether Wallop, and all the other smaller airfields in Hampshire. I expect she found out from Mac Wilson."

Zofia, who had been silently taking in what amounted to the last of a public confession, asked her first question. "She was sleeping with Mac too?" Her voice held a note of—well, I have to say it: admiration.

"Struth," said Keith to Huntley. "This is like one of those French what's-a-names."

"Farce," said Huntley, his eyes gleaming with delight behind his spectacles.

"You don't know what you're talking about," Sir Basil roared at Griff. "We have petrol dumps all over the county, hidden away, so the ruddy Luftwaffe don't bomb our supplies. It was simply a straightforward deployment of resources."

"No, sir." Griff produced two typewritten pages from the inside pocket of his flying jacket. "You were dealing in black-market petrol stolen from fifteen Hampshire airfields and petrol dumps. I have lists here detailing how much petrol you and Mac Wilson stole, how often, and the names of your contacts. The ministry are aware of your operation, watching you for the past few weeks. Thousands of gallons. You must have made a fortune."

He turned to me and the smile disappeared. "She hit you?" I nodded, too tired to speak. He lifted his fingertips to my face and I winced. "You were right about the black market, Poppy. Edwina found out about it, didn't she? And she was blackmailing Sir Basil."

I closed my eyes as he took Bess out of my arms and put her on the ground. His hand returned to my face. He stroked my cheek and smoothed the hair out of my eyes.

"Edwina was blackmailing Sir Basil?" Annie asked, and Grable pounced on her friend. "Yes, Annie, wake up. It's been staring us in the face for weeks. "That's why Vera killed Edwina—not because she was sleeping with him."

"He had nothing to do with Edwina's death." Vera pulled herself together. "He is innocent of any real crime!"

Grable laughed. "Real crime? Seems like stealing petrol is close to murder, when our planes can't defend our country because there is a fuel shortage."

I don't know whether it was because I had been socked on the jaw, but I heard a click as if someone had put something down on the surface of a wooden table. Still looking up into Griff's face, I opened my mouth far enough to say, "I think Edwina had more on you than just stealing petrol, Sir Basil. She found out that you were in partnership with her father and his brother, just after the last war. A little matter of crooked dealing and stealing nonpatented aircraft designs, wasn't it? She confronted you recently, didn't she?" Griff was right; it is amazing that if you don't think about a thing too hard and try to jam all the pieces in together how everything just floats into place by itself.

I closed my eyes, the better to enjoy Griff's hand carefully stroking back wisps of hair from my forehead. I saw again Sir Basil's jovial attempts at conversation with Edwina as she waited on the airfield that morning to fly, and her cold snub in return. A shaft of complete surety and understanding. "It was more than just stealing petrol, wasn't it? You stole her father's livelihood, and he killed himself in despair. Edwina's childhood was a nightmare because of you."

Sir Basil's face was ashen now. He opened his mouth a couple of times, but nothing came out. Vera put her head down and I saw tears streaming down her thin cheeks. "Oh, Basil," she said. "Dear God, then it was true."

HEADS TURNED AS two army vehicles bumped across the field, followed by a civilian police car.

Griff stepped forward and had a short conversation with a businesslike sergeant who was already walking forward before the truck came to a stop.

"What the hell?" Sir Basil drew himself up in a last moment of bluster. "I know absolutely nothing whatsoever about petrol." He pointed a finger at Vera, June, and then Griff. "These women have given this American some sort of hallucinatory drug. This is all poppycock." He shrugged his shoulders and put his tie in order. "Absolutely no need for all of this." He waved at the second truck and words seemed to fail him as he saw the china blue eyes of Mac Wilson staring out of the back at him.

"It would be better all round if you cooperated, because you will be getting in that Land Rover," Griff said to Sir Basil as the brawny sergeant and his subordinate rattled up with several pairs of handcuffs.

From out of the police car stepped what was clearly a detective in scruffy plain clothes and a young police constable in uniform. They looked at Griff, who waved at June and Vera.

All my earlier energy and determination evaporated in that minute. The side of my face throbbed and my legs were shaking. The vision in my right eye was obscured by my fatly swelling cheek and jaw.

"Grable," Griff said, ignoring the policemen. "You know what happened—you talk to them. Poppy . . ." He put his hand under my chin. "Oh Lor'," he said as he examined my face in the last rays of the sunset. "Teeth okay?" I nodded. "Going to be a bit of a bruise there." He gently felt along the side of my jaw and then pulled me close to him.

"Damn," he said as he lay my good cheek against his shirt and swayed slowly from side to side with his arms tight about me. "I would have given anything to have been down here when you first spilled the beans, anything." I felt his warm breath and then his lips on the top of my head, as he planted kisses.

I buried my nose in the warmth of his jacket and his arms closed more tightly around me. "And miss out on throwing that Spitfire around?" I said and listened to his heartbeat quicken a fraction.

A deep sigh. "Well, it was wonderful, of course; maybe just a tad bit faster than my old Mustang."

A voice at my elbow whispered, "You would think, my dear Poppy, that he was born to fly. Just like my Aleksy."

And right on cue I heard Ilona's light laugh. *Watch out, darling. Keep your sweetheart away from that woman, whatever you do.* And I buried my nose more deeply in Griff's shoulder.

HISTORICAL NOTE ON DIDCOTE AIRFIELD AND THE AIR TRANSPORT AUXILIARY

Didcote Airfield is based on the real-life No. 15 Air Transport Auxiliary Airfield at Hamble, near Southampton in Hampshire. Hamble was one of the first all-women ferry pools and the original eight civilian pilots mentioned in *Poppy Redfern and the Fatal Flyers* were loosely based on those women who joined the Air Transport Auxiliary (ATA) in 1940.

The original eight Attagirls were recruited because they had already been trained to fly small aircraft, often taught by fathers or uncles who had flown in the Great War. There was a huge craze for civilian flying in the 1930s, but it was an expensive hobby, so early ATA recruits were from well-to-do families. With the need for more pilots a government flying school was opened and woman pilots trained to become part of the ATA.

ATA pilots worked long, hard hours ferrying new, repaired, and damaged military aircraft between factories, assembly plants, transatlantic delivery points, maintenance units, scrap yards, and active service squadrons and airfields. They also flew service personnel on urgent duty from one place to another and performed some air ambulance work. Notably the women pilots of the ATA received the same pay as their male counterparts from 1943 until the end of the war, an astonishing first for the British government.

Overall during World War II there were 166 women pilots, one in eight of all ATA pilots, and they volunteered from Britain, Canada, Australia, New Zealand, South Africa, the United States, the Netherlands, and Poland. Women pilots flew close to one hundred different types of aircraft during the war years and many of them had far broader flying experience than most RAF pilots. Unfortunately at the end of the war it was made clear by the RAF that it would still not accept women pilots into the service. It wasn't until 1991 that Flight Lieutenant Julie Ann Gibson became the first full-time female pilot for the Royal Air Force. Neither did the world of commercial aviation leap to hire these superbly experienced and skillful pilots.

THE SUPERMARINE SPITFIRE

During the war years the Supermarine Spitfire became an emblem of Britain's air superiority. More than twenty thousand single-seat Spitfires were built, with only a few dozen remaining airworthy today. Supermarine did come up with the concept of a two-seater training version of the Spitfire, but none were ever ordered and only one was built. It is this prototype that I used for Griff and Zofia's flight together, so that he could experience the supreme speed of one of the most responsive fighter aircraft of its day.

BLACK MARKET PETROL AND AIRFIELDS

Precious petrol was heavily rationed to civilians during World War II. After the Luftwaffe bombed the Supermarine factory in south Hampshire and its petrol supply dumps, Churchill decided that it was safer to have hundreds of small petrol dumps hidden all over England. After the Battle of Britain, he arranged for small military airfields to be built, some of them tucked away in heavily wooded country, all over England, but with the greatest concentration along the south coast. Phony airfields were also built, with painted wooden planes as decoys. My father told me that sometimes the Luftwaffe would fly over a decoy airfield and drop a wooden bomb on it.

ACKNOWLEDGMENTS

Without the massive amount of available information available at the ATA museum and the archive of the Maidenhead Heritage Centre, in the UK, the historical background of *Poppy Redfern and the Fatal Flyers* would have been sketchy to say the least.

Aviation historians have described the ATA collection as a "gold mine." Historians, students, journalists, novelists, filmmakers, and family historians have access to the archive at Maidenhead, so my greatest thanks go to this wonderful organization.

I owe thanks to so many who have encouraged and supported me in writing this book. And my first thank-you goes to my agent, Kevan Lyon, whose professional support and positive encouragement have been unfailing in the last seven years.

At Berkley my many thanks go to my editor, Michelle Vega, both for her great insights—and for making the process so much fun. Also at Berkley, thank you to Brittanie Black, Elisha Katz, Stacy Edwards, and Jenn Snyder and of course to Robert Rodriguez for the design of yet another perfect cover—gray and yellow have always been a favorite color combination of mine!

ACKNOWLEDGMENTS

As always, I am in debt to my family and friends for their patience and encouragement, but most of all my heartfelt thanks go to my amazing husband and partner in life who has so much fun dreaming up titles and lets me know when it is time to press Save, close up my PC, and have a glass of wine.

TESSA ARLEN was born in Singapore, the daughter of a British diplomat; she has lived in Egypt, Germany, the Persian Gulf, China, and India. An Englishwoman married to an American, Tessa lives on the West Coast with her family and two corgis.

CONNECT ONLINE

TessaArlen.com
🐦 TessaArlen
🅕 TessaArlen

Ready to find
your next great read?

Let us help.

Visit prh.com/nextread

Penguin
Random
House